I0761555

THE TAVERN AT THE END OF HISTORY

—*a novel*—

MORRIS COLLINS

2580 Craig Rd.
Ann Arbor, MI 48103
www.dzancbooks.org

First edition: February 2026
Interior design by Michelle Dotter
Cover design by Matthew Revert
ISBN 9781938603525

Printed in India

10 9 8 7 6 5 4 3 2 1

To Jessica

In those days, in the war's last months, we did not think of the future.

We must have been children, or that is what you would call us, if you who are alive and reading this, and therefore were not there, had seen us—then you would call us children. You would call us children, though all the adults who had ever known our names were dead and we—who had words for the maggots that we ate and for the hunger boils that formed on our shins and for the gray larval smell of our own pus and for the gift of fish that glowed in the full moon and the sound of rats as they coughed and snuffled through the loose soil after days of feasting in the ditches filled with the town's dead—we didn't speak of ourselves at all. But we must have been children, and we lived for that last winter in a bombed-out mill above the black river. And though we were careful not to make fires during the day so that no one would see our smoke, and thought hard about whether to kill lone German deserters who sometimes passed on the road or whether to follow them back to where they might have a camp with others from whom we could steal, we did not think of the future.

Still, we knew the war would end.

The war would end, and who would remain living? I admit, it was the only question I asked at first. Who among us would live? And then, soon, when everyone was gone, it became: how would I live? Nothing mattered. I was a wicked scrabbling thing, the human world flamed out and fell like a leaf from the birches on the other side of the river—it seemed that ornamental and unnecessary and frail, and I was huddled in the long bare winter of my survival, and then the war was over.

The war was over and we were alive, living skeletons moving west with everyone else fleeing the Russians. We were alive and in German towns. In German homes. Touching ourselves, feeling our flesh, moving in daylight through a kitchen that was not ours, standing sometimes before mirrors discovered in a Hausfrau's closet, terrible and bright as a knife's bare blade.

In those moments, seeing what had become of ourselves, we found the next question:

The war was over, we were the living—now what would the living do?

—Alex Baruch, *Let Us Reach an Understanding: A Survivor's Account*

BOOK I: THE KNOCK

IN THE MOMENT BEFORE the old man grabbed him, Jacob was thinking: history must include the dreamlife.

The night before there had been a fire in the building across the street that he watched and then a phone call that he answered, that he always answered when his wife was not home, no matter how much he didn't want to, and his sister, on the other line, said, "She's with him now. They've lit candles, a bunch of candles, maybe ten candles, in these little red glass candle things."

"Votive holders," Jacob said. His room whirled with the fire across the street. It caught in the glass. The flames lapped on the walls like water.

"She's kneeling in front of him," his sister rasped, almost breathless. "He's holding her hair out of her face and she just stopped to tie it back. It makes it easier to see."

When Jacob hung up, the fire was almost out and it had begun to rain and in the morning, when he left the apartment and headed over to inspect the abandoned Kabbalah school, the air smelled less like ash than something rank, the rotten center of a tree split by lightning. He bought brown bread and pickled herring, a weird breakfast, except that it would go with the aquavit chilled to a near-syrup in his freezer. Now that it was summer, he had nowhere to be and, as he did most mornings on his way back from the school, he walked, among people, through the park. The people were of two types: the vigorously healthy and the clearly demented. Increasingly, Jacob saw the world divided this way. And where did he fit? He imagined he trembled on a special threshold for men buying pickled herring for breakfast and then wondering what happened to their marriages. Well, he wasn't the only one. If he answered the phone it was because someone else was calling. History must include the dreamlife.

"Come with me," the old man on the park bench said.

For a step, Jacob kept walking. The man's voice was that quiet. Almost a whisper and Jacob thought he was just another codger sitting on a bench talking to himself, or to the air, or to the dead. But he said it again, and Jacob stopped, and when he did the man grabbed his wrist, said "Come with me," and then let go as if he were surprised by what he had just done.

Jacob stepped back. Two women jogged by, glanced over, moved farther to the outside of the path and kept going.

"Are you okay, sir?" Jacob asked.

"Come with me," the man said, and said it louder and his voice was accented, the *W* more of a *V* and Jacob recognized him as he should have immediately, as any Jew, as any person at all with their eyes open in this neighborhood would, as Hasidic: the beard the color of dust, the bad shoes and baggy pants, the long black polyester jacket—a rekel—in the rarer, single-breasted Breslover fashion. But the rekel was frayed and torn at one arm, rubbed white at the collar, and his hair was matted to his scalp. Here was what was wrong with this picture: he had no hat and his head was uncovered.

"Come with me," he said.

"Where?"

The Hasid nodded over his shoulder, at the frog pond or the dogwood tree or the street beyond.

"What do you need?" Jacob asked.

The man held up his hands. His eyes were wet. He was shaking. Overnight the park had ruptured into the heavy damp obscenity of late summer. The frog pond steamed with mud and floral air.

"Please come with me."

In the Hasid's dark apartment, with the lights off and the radio on, Jacob felt like a fool. He should have realized the situation in the park. It was Saturday, the Sabbath, and the timer controlling the lights and radio was broken. Jacob was a Jew and beyond that he was, at least by the most cursory or ridiculous of definitions, a scholar of Jewish philosophy, and yet his Jewish upbringing had consisted mostly of his father snarling over candles, kicked between rage and terror, saying *Remember your grandfather*, or his mother, before she left them and returned to Israel, scoffing that the new Jew needed no shul and also Jacob did not need to remember a man he had never known and neither did his father for that matter, which may have been good advice, but not for a six-year-old.

But still.

Even in the unlit gloom he could tell the apartment was tiny, squalid, with its one window facing the backside of another, higher building so that though the day was lovely, only an ashy gray light squeezed in, but the Hasid was not allowed to turn the lamp on, or to turn the radio off. And he was not allowed to ask anyone to do it for him, as this would be, in another way, a violation of the same general law. Of course, some rabbis would say even the timer violates the law, while others would argue it's fine to have a timer, but not to adjust it if it breaks. And really, if someone was going to adjust it, that person shouldn't be a Jew. Still others, of a definite minority, would maintain that adjusting the timer was okay, and Jacob's presence here was unnecessary.

On the other hand, almost all would agree the radio—making noise as it did now—was not allowed.

Jacob found it all ridiculous. And yet he appreciated an ethical system that did not try to hide what he knew: the world is almost impossible to live in.

He reset the timer. The radio turned off and a few lamps buzzed on. The apartment was worse than he had realized. The narrow foyer, cluttered with old shoes, opened into a kitchen where the cabinets were ajar and empty and the one counter was stacked with plates that were either dirty or broken or both. A three-year-old JCC calendar hung on the fridge. Under the grimy yellow bulb light, the rest of the apartment looked like something sickened. It shambled before him out of a haze of fever.

On the coffee table stood two empty candlesticks. The Hasid must have lit them last night for Shabbat. Below them were magazines splattered in wax, a full ashtray, and a roll of toilet paper. The bad smell he had noticed in the park was thicker: urine, cigarette smoke, kitty litter. In one corner was a sack of dry cat food, torn open on the floor; in the other squatted an enormous, matted orange cat. "Meh," it said when the light came on.

The old man stood in the hall and stared at Jacob.

"Sir," Jacob said, "do you need anything?"

The man shook his head. "I'm sorry," he said. He was still trembling, and his head was still uncovered. "I'm sorry," he said again. "I've recently had a shock."

Like in a dream when the world alters—you are not in the deli ordering a sandwich, but your childhood home sitting down to supper—for a moment, less even, a wheeling nanosecond, Jacob thought that the man was not Hasidic. He had no hat or kippah, he had no forelocks. The clothes he wore were simply scavenged.

The feeling passed. As usual, it had been a deflection. He had imagined the moment to be other than it was because that's what he wanted. Now, simply: the abjection of shame. The man had lost or forgotten his hat. The apartment was beyond his upkeep. Jacob did not know where to look. On the wall was an avocado-colored rotary phone, filmed in grease. Beside it hung a tiny, ancient framed photograph of a family. Parents, three children, and a baby held by one of the kids. All standing against the studio drapes. The unmistakable Hasidic garb and solemnity. The baby with its eyes wide open. In the bottom left was the studio seal, and name, and the date—1937.

"The Shabbat timer," the old man said to Jacob, "is it broken?"

"It's set for now. But I'm not sure it will work next time."

"You can't fix it?"

Jacob picked up the timer. Clearly, it didn't work. He could say that about a lot of things, and to the question *Can you fix it?* his answer would be the same. He shook his head.

"Is there anything I can do?" he asked.

The old man waved his hand, *no,* and shuffled over the cat. It stood wobbily and bumped against his leg.

"I don't live far from here," Jacob said. "If you need anything—" He fumbled in his pocket and came up with a pen. He wrote his name and number on the JCC calendar, and the man lifted himself from where he was bending to rub the cat and looked at him with his mouth hanging open. Then he nodded again and turned back to the cat.

Jacob left the herring and brown bread on the counter and went out the door. The world was an impossible place to live in, but that's all you could do there. Some knew this better than others. In the sunlight, through his tears, he looked down at his feet. When it came to the big questions, philosophy was as useless as anything else. The mysteries remained mysteries. This is what made them mysteries. It was the rest that required the soul's struggle.

As in, if you want aquavit, you need no excuse.

Jacob stood in the street looking up at his apartment, his window, the window he had watched the fire from last night. Maddie was probably home. How quickly, even when he did nothing, life changed. The building, like the statue of a building. And Maddie waiting inside it, similarly remote, unaddressable, desirous, silent.

Like a figure made strange in nightmare.

The ways he lied to himself. Maddie was easy to address, at one point even desperate to be addressed, but she wanted to know what had happened to their lives, to his job, to their future—and where was he supposed to start?

Again: history must include the dreamlife.

He might have said: if, as Spinoza claims, we cannot control our actions in dreams, then we cannot control our actions in real life. Of course, Spinoza didn't actually claim this, but outside of the classroom Jacob did not believe that he needed to stick to the exact parameters of a given theory, and now his life was entirely outside the classroom.

Back when she cared to argue, or to criticize, back when her goal was to reveal Jacob to himself as if that would lead to improvement rather than horror, Maddie would say, *Life isn't a proof. It isn't an if/then proposition. You feel things because you're human. To feel something doesn't produce an escalation of moral consequence.*

This was their refrain. Some things were simple. They required faith or love, or faith in love. He should, she thought, stop pretending to be so confused, or, better still, stop being so confused. But what he wanted to explain was that it wasn't the *if* he was concerned by, but the *then*. *Then* is what said *This is where you are*. Which was what everybody wanted. To arrive at their life's crisis and have the good fortune to know it.

He was at it and he knew it and it didn't feel like fortune. Or maybe it was already behind him. What had he needed? An angel to appear with a heavenly bugle and a flaming sword? A voice out the whirlwind? To require signs you didn't believe in was just another kind of denial. He had lost his job; his wife was planning on leaving him, and in the meantime she was having an affair.

And yet, when they still fought, they fought about his desire to intellectualize everything, to qualify and equivocate. If he were honest with himself, he knew Maddie didn't really care about the way he scrutinized things—he didn't even really scrutinize things that much, not things that mattered—but it was safer to fight about the way they fought rather than about the real issues, because Maddie, essentially, remained kind. Why bother telling him how much he had disappointed her when it was clear how vastly he'd disappointed himself?

Early in their marriage, Maddie had become pregnant, and then, in the fourth month, lost the child. They talked about everything, but did not say much about this. They treated it with care, tended it between them, almost silently, and had assumed they would try again—even if they hadn't been trying the first time—when they were more prepared.

But how do you prepare? Maddie had greeted the first pregnancy with such reckless pleasure that Jacob felt he had let her down by not being adequately afraid. The next time he would be ready: uncompulsive and sane, well published, well employed, loving and well loved. And while Maddie waited, he began, almost with intention, to demolish the life they had agreed on. He stopped doing his scholarship, he stopped requesting additional grant funding—funding they needed—he stopped teaching in the summer, he floundered, bided his time and watched as he began less and less to resemble the person he had wanted to be.

And then a student had become upset by a reading in class, by the world, by a guest speaker Jacob invited—and Jacob, first trying to intervene and then trying to extricate himself from the consequences of his intervention, made things worse. There had been a complaint. The dean had been involved. Then the student had attempted suicide.

Jacob lost his job and did nothing—what could he do? He did not explain himself, he took walks and drank aquavit, he did not move out and Maddie didn't ask him to. Their apartment was small and hers. It was her inheritance from her father and their only asset. Without a job, he couldn't afford rent, and there was nothing to divide that, once divided, either could keep.

In the last of their fights, before this new indeterminate period of silence, she had said, "So what are you going to do? What do you even *want* to do?"

And he had said, "How should I know? I'm a Jewish philosopher."

"Is your point that you should definitely know better? Or that you'll never learn?"

At first he laughed. Maddie was always clever. But her eyes had filled with expectation, she'd flung open her hands as if scattering ashes, letting go of something she could no longer hold, and he realized, silently and too late, that they had in that moment transcended squabbles or banter and that she really needed the answer, that maybe their whole lives together hung on it, but of course such stakes changed the question, it no longer meant what it meant, and he didn't know what to tell her.

Maddie was home. Her shoes lay discarded by the door. The left one to the right of the right one, and pointing backward. He fixed them. Left to the left, right to the right. This was an old habit. In the empty shoes he saw the ghost of the person, so that an impossible alignment summoned a mangled body: twisted legs, a crippling accident, dismemberment. He had spent so much of their marriage doing this, trying to arrange the usual objects of daily life into whatever order it took to keep her safe. At night before bed he wandered around the apartment fixing her shoes, straightening envelopes on tables, making sure no water glasses left on the chessboard-tiled counter were placed between tiles of different colors, holding their world together while she looked on with affection that gave way over the years to bemusement and then to whatever it was that made her shout from their room, when they still shared it, "Leave the fucking shoes and come to bed." And he did. After he finished checking the stove and the doors and the windows.

Now, Maddie was home and he fixed her shoes and realized, as he did it, that he didn't have to. Whatever relationship his action had with her safety was gone. Again the world was whatever the world was. When he bartered with the universe, he could no longer speak for her. He did it now out of tenderness. He aligned her shoes, heel to heel, as a dancer might stand before the music starts.

Sometimes he'd forget. He'd be thinking about something or talking on the telephone and step into a room where she was sitting, and for the briefest second, with the memory of the body, expect her to smile and hold out her hand to him, expect to feel the comfort he used to feel of turning a corner to someone who loved him—a surprise he would never recover from. Instead, she would be there, silent, angry, sitting in the present. Other times maybe she'd sense the expectation he didn't mean to feel, and then—and this was almost worse—she just looked sad.

And sometimes she was the one who forgot. It would be the same: he'd turn the corner and she'd be reading, or lost in thought, or she'd be asleep on the couch with her laptop murmuring British murder mysteries and as he broke her reverie, if he did it smoothly, without startling her into full consciousness, she'd look up and smile at him, she'd open her mouth and widen her eyes like she really wanted to tell him something, or she would say, "Hi Jakes" in a voice bright with love and he'd feel his chest rip open, from his sternum through his throat, in the second before she remembered and he had to watch her recoil from her instinct, swim into disappointment, and realize that she didn't love him anymore.

That night, after he came home from doing nothing, from meeting the old man in the park and doing nothing, she went out and when the phone rang his sister said, "They've closed the curtains this time. I can't see a thing. Sometimes the curtain moves a little. The one closer to the bed. It could be from gasps. Or cries. Did you know humans are the only animals that make sounds during intercourse?"

"I don't think that's true," Jacob said.

"I'm not counting male animals," she said. "Or grunting. I mean sounds of pleasure."

"Please stop."

"I'm practicing. It's not illegal."

"I think it is."

"No one makes you answer the phone."

The next morning Jacob bought bagels and cream cheese, some lox, a tomato, a red onion. Then he stopped at the hardware store, picked up a new Shabbat timer, and strolled into the park. Joggers swept through the morning swift and silent as ships. Frogs burped from the little pond. He was a man with nowhere to go walking among flowering trees, bushes, shrubs. Flowering flowers. Everywhere, birds. Once when he was in high school he took a bus to Montreal to visit a girlfriend. He switched Greyhounds in Albany and fell asleep while it was still in the dock. He awoke at the border, in Vermont, where immigration asked everyone to get off. To fall asleep in a bus station under sour light and ceilings of vaulted concrete and awake to mountains humped against the dusking sky, woodsmoke, the sound of a creek shattering with snowmelt beside the road, a girl speaking French waiting for him on the other side of the rouged horizon. He had thought, *Finally! My life!* and lunged into the moment that was, it seemed now, the exact opposite of this one in the park under lurid trees where he felt like a man sent to clean a room where others have been sick.

Pigeons slept in the lobby of the old man's building. There was trash in the stairwell. When the man answered his door, Jacob held up the bag with the food and the timer in it and said, "Good morning, sir. Just checking to make sure the lights were working properly."

"The lights are fine. It's the clock that's broken."

"Of course," Jacob said. "Well, I was just checking."

"Yesterday you left your fish. I thought that was why you had come back."

"I figured with all the commotion, you might not have remembered to get food."

"The problem was with the clock. I can buy my own food."

Jacob held out his hand and smiled. Behind the man, the herring jar was on the counter, empty.

"Me too," he said. "In fact, I just bought bagels but forgot that my wife isn't home this weekend. Have you had breakfast?"

Inside, the radio was on, a repeat of a weekday baseball show that Jacob sometimes listened to. Even with the lights on the room seemed dark, hazy with smoke, bad light through bland plastic blinds. He placed the bag on the kitchen floor and took out the food. Today the counter was clear. The room had been tidied, which is to say things had been stacked or thrown away and the garbage can was overflowing onto the floor. The plates, even the broken ones, were drying on the rack, but Jacob saw, as he selected two, that they were still far from clean. Flecks of food stuck to the edges. The man had paper towels but no sponge, or dish soap, or sink stopper.

"I've been rude," Jacob said. "I don't know your name."

"What?" the man said. "Oh." He glanced first to the picture on the wall and then to his feet. "Baer."

"Do you like lox, Baer?"

"Everybody likes lox."

"Not my wife."

Jacob made the sandwiches. Baer was shifting his weight from foot to foot and holding his hands together by his chest.

"Sometimes to wash up," he said and paused a second. His hands were clenched in front of his heart. "It's hard. I can't see well at night."

Jacob had assumed the man would be unaware of how bad the apartment was. He must have been embarrassed yesterday to have him there. And now, with his unrequested visit, Jacob was embarrassing him further. He reached into the bag for any diversion and held up the Shabbat timer.

"If you haven't fixed the other one, I picked this up."

Baer put his hand to his mouth and turned away, suddenly, as if he were quelling an urge to spit, and for another errant second Jacob thought he was angry. But then he heard the cough that was not a cough, Baer swallowing his sob, and he just stood there, waiting with the plates in his hand. When Baer turned back around there were still tears in his eyes.

"These are expensive," he said. "I don't know what I would have done."

"It's nothing," Jacob said. "The store was right next to the deli."

"You didn't have to do that."

"Please, sir," Jacob said. "I'm a philosopher."

"It's the job of philosophers to buy clocks for geezers?"

"If I'm any indication, there's no job for philosophers." Jacob tried to laugh. "But it means that though I can diagnose the nature of the problem—the timer is broken—I have no idea how to fix it. I'm afraid it's like this with everything."

"Ah," Baer said. "I know just what you mean."

They sat at the coffee table and ate. "A little crunchy," Baer said, taking a piece of bagel out of his mouth that he couldn't chew. "But delicious." He ate quickly, rounded his shoulders over his food, lifted the bagel and didn't put it down until he was done, a few bites later. The massive cat wobbled out from the closet to lean against Baer's leg. Occasionally Baer would tear off a tiny piece of salmon, balance it on the tip of his finger, and let the cat lap it off.

"He likes smoked salmon," Jacob said. "Pretty fancy cat."

"You have no idea," said Baer. "He's a little czar. When I sit on the chair to read he won't sit on my lap, we have to squish side by side. He takes up two-thirds, and I? I'm lucky if I am allowed to slide into the corner. It's the same way in bed. It's a good thing I'm alone."

"He's sharing the lox anyway."

"It's because I don't eat very much," said Baer. "He's territorial in this way. If I were a glutton for lox, he would be too."

He reached down to rub the cat's head, and the cat, sensing the motion, raised its head to his hand.

"What his name?" Jacob asked.

Baer removed his hand. "It's better not to name him. I don't want him to be confused when I die and someone else takes him."

They sat a while in silence.

"Did you see the fire the other night?" Jacob said.

"That was Benny Diamond's place. Sam was supposed to take it over. After Sam died, Benny decided to sell it. Even then he said, 'For all it's worth, I should burn this place down.'"

"Sam was his son?"

"Now Sam, Sam could cut lox. From the belly, thin as paper. Not like this. This is delicious. A treat. But Sam Diamond could cut it so that it would melt in your mouth. It's a lost art. Now they just chop."

Jacob's father had been the same way. Obsessed with the slicing of belly lox, pastrami, whatever. And not just him. The neighbors would come over for a holiday, a birthday, a party, and suddenly you had fifteen adults brandishing slices of meat and smoked fish in their fingers, shouting, *Look how thin!* Jacob had once asked, *What difference does it make how thin the slice is? Why is that better?* His father had appeared confused, as if his idiot son were the first Jew in a thousand years to ask this question. *It's a skill*, he had said.

"Sam died of a heart attack. He wasn't even forty."

"When was this?" As far as Jacob knew, the grocery had been owned by Koreans as long as he had lived in the city. Ten years next spring.

"1977," Baer said. "Back then, if you can believe it, there were three delis on this block."

Jacob whistled. "Now at least, if you're going to eat all that pastrami, you have to work it off a little bit."

"It's no surprise they're gone," Baer said. "Who needed so many? You would have thought that in the Old World all we did was make sandwiches, though I didn't see a deli until 1948."

"What did you do before you came here?"

"Me? I did nothing. I was a boy. I went to school. At first I thought I wanted to be a rabbi, if you can believe it. And then an artist. I even knew a famous painter who said he would be my tutor in Paris when I was old enough. But the war came before I could go."

"And after?"

He held up his fist and opened it as if he were releasing a firefly. He stared at it a moment, the emptiness there, seventy years in a gesture, and then he waved it away.

"Nothing as well," he said. "You had doctors becoming deli clerks. Great wise men, tzaddikim, opening groceries. After liberation I met a professor, a notable man, in the camp for displaced persons. He was a historian who studied the Ottoman Empire. Somehow, he had survived with his daughter. I was friendly with her, and we corresponded for a few years. They went to Canada, where not a single university would allow this great man, this scholar of the Turks who spoke five languages, a position. He became the assistant to the cobbler in a small town in Ontario where no one wore anything but boots. So you see, if there was nothing for these people, there was less for me."

The cat moved away and sauntered over to the corner where the bag of food still lay on the floor, split open with kibble spilling across the carpet. Baer watched him, glanced to the corner and the window there, and in its weak light his face stilled like the surface of a pond where the wind has suddenly dropped.

"I know this wasn't the case for everyone. I know there were some who came over and thrived." He reached down to hand the cat, who wasn't there, a piece of salmon. "But not me."

"I can't imagine," Jacob said, though he wanted to say something different. Jacob, who had never felt settled in the world, not at home or in school, not when he tried to be a professor or scholar, not in love or in the bedroom, Jacob who saw in two millennia of diaspora a reflection of his own soul which meant, he knew, that essentially, deep down, he didn't understand what he studied, wanted to say to the old man, *I know what you mean*. Which of course proved—beyond pity, beyond fear of the man's poverty, his aloneness and loneliness—that he didn't.

"Most of my life I worked at a sporting goods store. Ableman's.

When Ableman got old, he sold it to me. I kept it a while before it closed."

"My father was also in sporting goods," Jacob said. "And outerwear. It's impossible for independent stores these days."

"Maybe," said Baer. "But my store never made any money. For Ableman, sure. But not for me. I didn't have the knack for it. I couldn't imagine the future. The Dunlop man would come. He would say, 'Do you want to buy some handballs?' I would say, 'Sure.' 'How many?' he would ask. It's a reasonable question. How many cans of handballs do you want? I would stall, I would pretend to look in my ledger. 'They come in cans of two?' I'd ask. 'Of course.' 'Okay. Give me twenty cans.' I just made it up. It was a guess based on nothing. How was I supposed to know how many handballs a person would want? I couldn't imagine. Of course, I knew that when I bought the store. It was just a thing to do. Speaking of which, why aren't you at work?"

"It's Sunday," Jacob said.

Baer clapped his hands together, again, in front of his heart. "That's right," he said. "I forgot."

"And, anyway I have the summer off." It was true, even if it wasn't honest.

"Still you must have better things to do." Baer seemed suddenly anxious.

"I don't."

"Not with your wife? On a day like this?"

"She's busy."

Baer pointed at him. "You said your wife doesn't like lox?"

"She doesn't."

"Then why did you buy it? Was it for me? I can shop. There's an organization that's supposed to help with things like this. I'm on the waiting list."

"I'm sure you can," Jacob said. "It's not that. We're getting divorced."

"Divorced? Why?"

Jacob shrugged. "Marriage is hard."

As soon as he said it, he knew he shouldn't have. His fake shrug—he was not a shrugger—his fake nonchalance—he was not nonchalant. And now Baer was clearly upset.

"It's hard? Marriage is hard? What, you want to be like me when you're my age?"

"No," Jacob said. And then, to cover, or to explain: "It wasn't my idea."

Outside, in the street, a truck began backing up. Beeping in reverse, stopping, beeping again. And then cars, everywhere, on a Sunday, honking. Baer was looking at the ground. It was time to go. Jacob would plug in the timer, set it up, and then he would leave.

"All right," he said. "I've interrupted your morning."

Baer looked up, wild. He put his hand on Jacob's knee.

"I'm sorry," he said. "Your wife is not my business. You forget this when you get old. You need things from everybody. You can't hide anything. So you forget that others might not be this way."

Jacob did not know what to say. He had always longed to be open. When intimacy appeared, he wanted to welcome it. Surely, this is what it was to be a person. And yet. There were many things he wasn't and one of them was a cynic. "It's nothing," he said. "We're neighbors. Let me know if you ever need anything. Even just someone to walk you to shul."

Baer withdrew his hand. "You're very kind. But I don't belong to any shul anymore."

"No? I figured with the clock. And the jacket."

"I do that for my parents." He let the sentence hang. Jacob couldn't tell if that was the whole thought, or just the beginning. It was like in his arguments with Maddie. Take the statement *We are in love.* All you had to do to subordinate it into terror, into the unfinished, was add the word *if* to the beginning. "And anyway," Baer said, "we won't be neighbors much longer. They're selling this building and I have to go in October."

"Where are you moving?"

"I've lived here twenty years."

How terrible, Jacob thought. To live in this shithole for twenty years. To be forced to leave.

"I don't know where I can afford."

"Yesterday, when we got here, you mentioned a shock. Is that what you meant?"

"No," Baer said. "That is not it."

"What then?" It was not his business. But this man had found him, had reached out into his own lonely morning and asked for help. The hot room smelled of cat piss and cat food. Baer's head was still uncovered.

"Yesterday," Baer said, "when I saw you, you were at the Kabbalah school."

"Just looking around."

"It's closed, I thought?"

The Kabbalah Center had been the flagship school of Alex Baruch, a famous humanitarian and popular theologian, a public intellectual whose intermingling of Kabbalah and psychotherapy had for a while been a fad feeding the world's hunger for mysticism and mental health (as if mystics were sane) and whose memoir—first of his upbringing in a sanatorium on the Aegean, where his German father was the chief physician, and then of the Holocaust, where he escaped a transport train to Auschwitz and lived alone in the Polish forests—had been a touchstone of public education before it was debunked. Apparently there had been no such German Jew as Alex Baruch. Since his disgrace, he had fled the public scene, the school was closed, and he was living in what was, by what few accounts there were, a sanitarium he had opened near the Canadian border, where he and his remaining patients or followers or students continued to study his methods.

Early in Jacob's academic career, he had known Baruch; in those days Baruch was a giant and the great man had supported his work and now, out of nowhere, out of the blue, he had reached out to Jacob—*a fresh, young face,* he wrote—to help him reopen his New York school. He had invited Jacob to come to Maine, to Nod, which is what he called his sanitarium, to discuss it. Jacob did not know what the truth was about Baruch. That he was not who he said he was seemed certain, but no one had discovered an alternate identity, and his work on the Kabbalah was still fascinating, insightful, essential even. But he had reached out to Jacob to be the face of his enterprise, and to Jacob, this, more than anything, revealed how far he'd fallen.

"I might be reopening it," Jacob said. "I don't know."

"You are a follower of Baruch?"

"I would just be the manager. Are you interested in Kabbalah?"

"What do I know? My education ended before it began. I did my bar mitzvah over here at twenty."

A bar mitzvah alone in a new country. Jacob stared at his empty plate. "You said you've had a shock," he said again.

"There's a woman. A cousin of a cousin. She's your age. She works for the Museum of Jewish Art. She has her doctorate. I don't know what she does, though."

"Is she a curator?"

"No. She answers questions."

"A docent, then."

"No," Baer said. "I know curators. I know docents. She sits in a room and answers phones all day. She's the one who found out about the sketch by Lurio. She told me about it on Friday."

"Alexander Lurio?"

Beyond a collection of Lladro figurines, Jacob's family had not been interested much in art, but every older woman in the neighborhood had a Lurio print on the wall. Wild angular depictions of shtetl dreamscapes. Rabbis tilting over Torahs, men dancing through the blue Polish night, women on their way to the baths, their skirts rippled by wind, the faces of curious yeshiva students peering from impossible angles at the margins. There was also his earlier work, the work he did in Paris. Naked women reclining in lush red boudoirs. As common as the Hasidic wonderland works were with the grandmothers, in graduate school Jacob's professors favored these Paris portraits. They displayed them in their offices, atop their bookshelves, stretching nudely into office hours.

"He stayed in our house when I was a boy," Baer said.

"Lurio did?"

"Yes. He was the artist who said he'd find me a tutor. Even then he was famous, but not like he is now. He was commissioned to illustrate a Torah, and they offered to send him to the Holy Land, but he grew up in our town and wanted to set it there. He stayed with us for six months. Before he left, he gave me the sketch for his painting of Job."

Jacob knew the work, if only for its weirdness. Job dancing in something like ecstasy as his dead family and livestock are gathered up into the blue air behind him, pulled limp into the whirlwind.

"We took it with us when we fled. We were heading to Kyiv. From there we were supposed to go to—" He looked away from Jacob. "Instead, the ghetto. The militia confiscated it with everything else."

"And it's turned up?

"In an antique store in Maine. She called and told me. It's going on auction. And Baruch is the one hosting the auction."

"Wait," Jacob said. "That's the piece?"

"You know it?"

"I've been invited to the auction. I didn't realize it was a Lurio."

"My cousin says it is."

"Is that why you were sitting by the school?"

"I was looking for Alex Baruch."

Jacob stacked their plates. Next time he would bring a sponge.

"Did you report the theft after the war?"

"I was a little boy. I was missing more than a sketch. And how would I have proved it was ever ours?"

"It wasn't insured?"

"We didn't have it for long. And then the Nazis invaded and began confiscating property. You didn't want them to know what you had."

"Did he tell anyone he gave it to you?"

"I don't know. He was always writing letters."

"Have you checked?"

"The letters he wrote were to Jews."

For a moment Jacob didn't understand what he meant, and then felt foolish. This story was terrible, but it was probably not unusual. Still he found himself saying, "There must be something someone can do."

"You said you are going up there. You have an arrangement with this man?"

"I barely know him. He invited me to go up and discuss a business partnership."

"Then you can help."

Doesn't he realize, Jacob thought, that when I met him, I believed he was nuts? I drink aquavit for breakfast. I couldn't even fix the timer. Instead, he demurred. He tried to explain that he didn't know Baruch well, that he didn't think he'd have credibility, that he didn't even think the sketch belonged to Baruch, and Baer, who wasn't listening or hearing, who had his plan already made, said, "Take Rachel with you to Maine." Jacob didn't know who Rachel was. "The art scholar. She'll know if it's real, and she'll know what to do."

Jacob wasn't sure how knowing what was real had ever helped.

"You'll see the piece," said Baer, still excited. "You'll maybe touch it. You'll be able to do whatever it is you need to do next."

THE AFTERNOON THAT JACOB CALLED, the Yitzhak Bloom Senior Curator of Modernist Paintings came down to Rachel's office in the basement of the Museum of Jewish Art and asked her, as he sometimes did, if she wanted to go to lunch.

Rachel worked alone, in a room with a desk and a phone. It was a setup out of East Berlin, the interrogation chamber from every spy movie: bare floor, neon light tubes affixed to the ceiling, a metal desk in which all the drawers were locked, and two chairs, one she sat in and one she faced, though that one was always empty, and she was never sure whether she should feel like the prisoner or the interrogator. Beyond this, she had only a map of the galleries and a chart providing each painting on display with a numeric code. At first there had been a Monet print on the wall, as well as a framed Ansel Adams photograph leaning in the corner, so that the room felt less like an interrogation chamber than a high school guidance counselor's office, but they both disappeared during her first week, and the room reaccrued its essential character. Several times she had moved the empty chair into the closet down the hall where the coffee machine was kept —if everything else could vanish, so could a chair—but it was always returned by the next day, sitting across from her, bare, somehow recriminatory, vaguely expectant.

So having another person in her space was always a little surprising, even if the curator, gazing at her with his usual mix of mild reproach and gauzy concern, seemed not abundantly different from the empty chair. Also, he would not cross into the room. He hesitated on the threshold as he asked her to lunch, brisk, polite, a little genteel and a little sweaty, dressed totally in seersucker.

For lunch they got sushi. "Who could eat anything hot in this weather?" the curator said, every time, no matter the season. Perhaps she was supposed to derive something meaningful from this. She did not like sushi that much, but enjoyed how long it took the curator to eat it. He was a precise man and he separated the chopsticks with a single clean snap, rubbed them together, locked them between his fingers and never once put them down or had to readjust them during the meal. He was dexterous and blond, fortyish, his face changed colors as he spoke, went from sallow to florid, his name was Simon, and because he had to avoid getting soy sauce on his seersucker suit, he took forever to eat.

He liked to ask her questions about her aspirations. "Would you want to work back upstairs?" "Did you ever intend to go into academia?" "Have you considered digital platforms?" Between questions he dipped his fish in soy sauce, raised it vertically, and then at the very last moment, in ridiculous slow motion, leaned in with his mouth already open like an ancient tortoise and closed his teeth around it. He didn't much listen to her answers, but in her experience with curators, it was rare enough that he even asked the questions. After Trump's election he had started coming by more often, ostensibly to check that she was doing all right, that this had not been the final blow. "You know," he said. "The straw. The camel. After the year you've had."

He'd hired her originally—she supposed—because they hit it off talking about Cubism in her interview, and she'd long ago noticed that his syntax matched his interests. He was a Cubist conversationalist. All fragment and implication. She liked it. The tenuous logic, the straight-on side-eye of a simple sentence. The way he referenced her grief only in euphemisms. She could pretend not to know what he meant.

This time, Rachel ordered miso soup and udon noodles. He looked concerned. "Deviation is the heart of progress," she said and smiled and slurped soup and wiped her chin and then watched his eyes. Beneath Simon's precision lurked, she felt sure, a simmering prissiness.

"Are you looking forward to our Lurio exhibit?" he asked.

Rachel had managed to ensnare a noodle with her chopsticks, but it was a very long noodle, and caught between sucking it slowly into her mouth while he watched or biting it, she chose to bite it. The severed half plopped limply back into her bowl. She smiled. Lurio was her specialty. A chapter from her dissertation on his depiction of desire, what she had called "subject-object intimacy," in his early Paris portraits had been well published. Their standing collection and the coming show and all the opportunities for study and scholarship were originally why she had wanted to work at the museum. But since she'd been hired, over a year ago, no one had mentioned it, and it was only two years out. Did he imagine she'd stay in the basement for all that time, content and unconsulted?

"Of course," she said. "I haven't seen *Juliet Goldman* or *Jewess on the Eve* since I was a grad student." These were both on almost permanent display at the Prado, where, as a student, she'd been given a three-month summer fellowship. She never knew just how much of her CV to remind him of in these conversations where the power dynamics remained inscrutable.

"Oh, those," he said. "We'll have them. Bit of concern where to put them. Wallwise. I don't think we'll go chronologically, but they'll need some different backing. Early and all. Very red."

"What are you thinking for themes?" Rachel had been curating the exhibit in her head for months now. Simon would insist, of course, on a thematic organization of his own devising, but for Lurio a chronological display would actually make sense: his fin de siècle affectations, followed by the period of silence and then, almost overnight, his sudden passionate adoption of what he'd been hiding ever since he changed his name from Lurtz: his eastern European Judaism. They could end with the last few works done in Canada after the war. The sequence of Enoch among the heavenly hosts, violent, shattering with Blakeian geometry and color. If these were, as most scholars claimed, the mournful eulogy to a lost world, she didn't see it. In all of them Enoch, witness to the divine machine, seems struck not by wonder, but rage. Yes, she always thought of Blake; whatever hand or eye dreamed up the world must be monstrous. Enoch confronts the celestial hosts, all wearing capes of swastika red under an oppressive horizon of jutting lightning and glaring orange mountains. It's supposed to be heaven, but if he believed in it, she couldn't imagine how else Lurio would fashion hell.

"What are you thinking for themes?" she asked again. For the previous ten seconds, a huge green piece of a caterpillar roll had required the curator's entire attention.

"Oh, right. Well, it's early days you know. But probably going with Devotion and Temperament. Inner Storm, Outer Order. The Artist's Journey. That kind of thing."

Lurio had been into absinthe and hashish while in Paris, though he quit when it began hurting his health and slowing his output. Still, it was what everyone focused on. The Bohemian excess, the booze, the drugs, the naked muses.

Rachel put down her chopsticks. Here was something she had learned when she started volunteering at NextSteps, a support group for young people trying to leave their ultra-Orthodox communities: Give someone a beautiful particular, and they saw only the ugly generality. She had tried the particular, the peculiar, she had taken Samuel's hand and led him out of his father's house. She had tried love. But she had not tried it gently enough. She had believed that the storm of Samuel's leaving his community, the passion of exodus would protect them in the world. She had not warned him how fast the world could change. One day you could be one of the Haredim, ultra-Orthodox, speaking Yiddish, living in a Brooklyn anachronism of fanatical rigidity, and the next you could have a reform wife in Manhattan, you could be severed from three hundred years of tradition, you could abandon your family, you could shave your beard, you could laugh at the Law, you could be eating a cheeseburger, you could, as he was, be dead. Or you could be Rachel. One day you could save the man you love, with your heart usher him into freedom and stand by and watch as he so badly misunderstands what that means, you could be married, you could be a widow, you could be grieving and then past grief and into what—what is on the other side of grief? Just the silly inanity of daily life: a tasteless curator, a slave to cliché, a man who, where he deviated from cliché, was even worse. For Rachel, there was never an escape from the particular: what kind of Jew wears seersucker?

She asked a question of her own. "Aren't you afraid of mercury poisoning?"

He was like a sea creature himself. A cuttlefish sweeping along the reef. His face seemed to flash through colors, his cheeks rouged, then went pink, then yellow. There goes his liver, Rachel thought.

He pointed a chopstick at her. "Did you know Lurio's name was originally Lurtz?"

Later, walking back to work, she mentioned the Lurio sketch found in Maine.

"Actually, I'm the one who authenticated it," he said.

"You never told me."

"Went all the way up to Maine. To this estate on an island."

"They're holding an auction next weekend, right?"

"In Maine," he said and then whistled the way children do, by sucking in. "How does anything get there?"

Even in the wake of Sam's death, she could not totally escape the routines of her old life in the city (drinks, brunches, the occasional coffee), and in these situations—although people rarely ask questions of the grief-stricken—she told people that she worked at the Museum of Jewish Art, which she did, but the museum was more than its galleries, and if you have a PhD in Art History and a Masters in Museum Studies, people expect that when you say you work at an art museum that you work with, or near, or in some way in view of, the art.

But Rachel worked in the basement. Beside each painting in the gallery was a small placard with the code that corresponded to her chart and with the number to the phone in her office. If anyone had a question about the work before them, they could call it, and Rachel, sitting in a room three to five floors below them, alone, a little cold, immune by now to the smell of mildew, would answer. Previously the museum had educators on site, in the galleries, available for questions, but no one ever asked them anything except whether they were allowed to take photos of the paintings, to which the educators only had to point to the sign saying NO FLASH ALLOWED. To the museum board, this seemed like a poor allocation of resources; certainly the guards or docents could instruct people on flash usage. Gesturing wordlessly to a sign did not require a staff with PhDs. But when, after culling their ranks and muddying their titles, they moved the "adjunct education and curation staff" down to the basement and made their expertise both invisible and a service you could access with your phone, people began to take advantage. To be fair, after the first hectic weeks of an exhibit's opening, not many did, but enough to keep Rachel her job, especially since, by the time she was hired, all the others had quit.

So when the phone rang and Jacob asked for her by name, she was surprised, both because he was asking for her personally and because he was asking anything at all. For the most part, men didn't call the "question line," and the ones who did didn't ask questions. Sometimes they were on dates and were having a disagreement about the work with their girlfriends. These phone calls began, "Isn't it true…" As in "Isn't it true Diane Arbus was the Anne Sexton of the photography world?" Usually, though, if a man called, it was, by the sound of his voice, an older gentleman who wanted to tell her about the painting. These calls would start with a quiz: "Do you know how many children Lucien Freud fathered?" or "Can you tell me in which massacre Anna Klein was executed?" If she paused, she usually got a chuckle, then a hint. "I'll give you a clue. It was in Lithuania!" Because the museum monitored call volume and length, Rachel stayed on the line. At first she tried to show that yes, she knew the answers, or address the premise of the statement specifically, or suggest that perhaps this trivia was not quite verifiably correct. But any of this—her knowledge or disagreement—did not go over well, so she just took to playing her own game, acting surprised and mispronouncing as many names as she could, either with syllable emphasis or vowel sound, until the caller became confused or uncertain of the pronunciation himself and stopped talking. Then she said, "Thank you!" more brightly than they expected and hung up.

Women called more often. Usually mildly insane, pill-addled art students who were looking to theorize, to share their revelations, to describe to her something they saw in the painting and, always—and this is what made their theorizing different from the men's—to ask her if she saw it too. They were all in some kind of pain and they were all a little afraid. They believed she was perched in a security booth and was watching them through the cameras. When they asked, "Can you see me?" she learned to say yes, to tell them they were beautiful, to agree, through her own tears, that, "Yes, yes, looking at the painting this way does make it feel better." As best she could, she cleared her mind in these conversations. She had no idea how to take care of another's pain; her track record here was perfectly miserable. Pain was not an emotion. If they were feeling pain, she could not tell them otherwise. She had tried that at first with Sam's sister, Rivkah; afterward, with Samuel, she had been more careful. Both strategies had been wrong. The best thing was to show these people that the rest of the world was not so bad, the rest of the world was beautiful, well composed, full of light, full of love. She knew she was lying, but only about herself. It was the least she could do.

When Jacob called, she answered the basement phone, and the ringing continued. This was a dream she had now, trying to answer a phone that wouldn't stop ringing. But it was her cell phone that was ringing, and she answered it this time, as she always did now, even though she didn't recognize the number. He told her why he was calling, how he'd met Baer and what Baer had asked him to do. He was polite, but not apologetic. When she agreed immediately, without him needing to convince her or spell his last name, he sounded surprised. She also said she'd drive.

"Great," he said. "I'll bring CDs." It was only a slightly stupid thing to say.

After he hung up, she called Baer. She thanked him for finding Jacob. She said, "Can you do dinner tonight?" Silence, static, a fault on the line: he was on his cordless phone, shaking his head. "Uncle?" she said. He was her cousin, but she called him *uncle*.

He barely muttered, "No. Nights are not good," he said.

She waited for more. Nothing. "I can bring something over? I can get takeout?"

Again he said, "Nights are not good."

"Tomorrow then? How about lunch?"

"At the cafeteria?" He sounded almost hopeful. There would be other old ghosts there. He despised them all. But he could, as he usually did, pretend that she was his granddaughter.

"Tomorrow," Rachel said. "Tomorrow, the cafeteria, noon."

Baer assented and the line went dead. She checked her watch. Two in the afternoon. Above her, she could almost feel the museum's emptiness. The tread of the guards sweeping through the galleries, the hum of the central air, the golden light falling unwitnessed through the great glass windows in the lobby. She had the sensation, strange, but not for the first time, that the silence originated in this room, with her. It wasn't the slumberous silence of above, but sudden and dull, like in an airplane, the muffled quiet of altitude. There was something to be heard, but she couldn't hear it. Her dreams of late had all been like this, trying to pack without a bag or leave the house without her keys, trying to read without her contacts. Clearly, her absurd office dredged its barrenness from her. It would be good to get away this weekend. To see the Lurio sketch. To try to force an accounting. Against a wider perspective, it was a simple enough thing to make right, and once she did it, her life would begin to change.

In the meantime, she could scream. She could accumulate clothes with colored feathers attached; she was thirty-two, in the first months of Trump, and grieving—hysteria was expected, but she felt terribly sane. Which might be a problem this weekend, where they were going. She would need to practice at neurosis. Tomorrow perhaps, she could ask the curator out for a drink and then spill wine on his suit. She would stare at the stain and say, *I've touched the back of the page where Lurio's pencil scratched.* She'd say, *Nothing goes unmarked.* She could say, *By now your thighs are damp*. She would slap his soft and sallow, stupid face and sneer, *What kind of name is Simon*?

As usual, Baer was at the cafeteria before she was. In the past she had tried getting there early, fifteen, twenty, thirty minutes, but he was always already there. She saw him too rarely, she knew that, but he would not allow her to visit his apartment, and she had the feeling that to meet her out, to make a noon appointment, was a cause of significant anxiety for him. He would arrive hours early, just to make sure that he could arrive at all.

She saw him through the glass of the front window, and then through the glass of the door; he was facing the street, staring out over his coffee. His eyes were unblinking and vacant. He looked old, he looked slack, he looked like someone failing to recover from a shock, he looked like everyone else in the cafeteria.

There used to be many similar places on the Upper East Side where, just after the war, the Jewish refugees and immigrants, the lucky ones who survived by coming over before the catastrophe and the unlucky ones who did not and survived anyway, would meet to chat, to eat stewed prunes, or chicken soup, to read the Yiddish papers. This one was the last of its kind. It smelled of grease and soap. The food was heavy, generally tasteless, mostly gray. Everything was available with a side of jarred horseradish.

She stepped inside, the bell on the door chimed, a few people turned to watch her enter—she was about sixty years too young. They squinted and stared. The sheer human devastation witnessed by the half-dozen people pretending to eat their lunch in here could nullify any legitimate emotional experience within twenty city blocks. She felt, as she always did, the sickening throb of self-disgust: against theirs, her sorrow was nothing, her guilt was nothing, her grief was a joke. She could not even relate to their world with the communal righteousness of a fellow Jew; her parents did not practice and she had come to her religion intentionally in college. Intellectually she knew that grief masqueraded as unwarranted anger, but she still felt the shame of her resentment. You people don't own loss, she thought, looking around. And it's true, they didn't. Loss owned them, and in this she felt another permutation of her grossness—she still coveted her wound, she clung to it as to Samuel himself.

When they first met at NextSteps, when she first saw him looking up from the handout she had made on dating in the secular world, when she saw his smile run aground as he raised his hand to ask a question in an impossible Yiddish accent, she had known the world would not accommodate someone who entered it so uncertainly and she had reached out to ease his passage, yes, but also to feel the vicarious tremor of his awe. She had opened her heart even as she thought, *Here is heartbreak.* You only had to spend a single afternoon with Samuel, with his sister Rivkah, with any of the Haredim looking to break free of their communities to know that their pain would never wholly disappear. At the time it seemed perfectly melancholy, letting her life be defined by another's sorrow, but now, confronted by her own loss and then seeing it dwarfed by the cataclysm of incurable grief in this room, she could only think of Lurio's Enoch apprehending the cosmic revelation with his perfect human disgust.

Baer saw her and he smiled and waved. She swept into the room and took his hands and kissed his cheeks—one, two—as they did in her family. She sat and tried to exchange pleasantries. He wasn't really interested. He was looking over her shoulder and fidgeting with the handle of his coffee mug. She got up and ordered them some soup. It was both easy to eat and not too hot.

"Uncle," she said, "tell me the truth. How are things?"

"I'm fine," he said. "I'm always fine."

"I've talked to the people at HUD and at Yad Vashem. I've got some apartments for you to look at."

"Can I afford them?"

"I don't know. Did the social worker call you back?"

He shrugged. The soup was ready. They called her name and she went up and got it. Baer cupped his hands around the bowl, pulled it close to his chest, and hunched forward as he ate.

"Do you need any groceries?" Rachel asked.

"I can get groceries."

"It's not a problem," she said. "We can go after lunch. I'll have time."

He didn't look up from his soup. "That boy, Jacob, he left me herring. And then brought bagels. Apparently I am that pathetic. To see me is to know."

"I'm sure he was just being kind. He was probably just worried about you. We all are."

"Listen to her," Baer shouted into his soup. "She's a widow. Her husband was a suicide. And she's worried about me?" He dropped his spoon and covered his mouth. "I'm sorry," he said in a whisper. "You know my moods." He pointed at an old woman sitting in the corner reading the paper. "Sophie also has to move. And she can hardly walk. She needs a new wheelchair. She came over here with no one, she still has no one. She has had no one since she was six years old."

Rachel looked down at her soup and then up at Baer, at Sophie. She watched the woman slowly begin to fold the paper.

"My point is that there are people who deserve help more than me," Baer said.

"Uncle, when you say 'deserve,' what could you possibly mean?"

"Nothing," Baer said. "Gornisht."

They sat in silence for a few minutes. Baer called over to Sophie, "Come meet my granddaughter!" but she just waved.

"Are you ready for the weekend in Maine?" he said to Rachel.

"Not really," she said. "Is Alex Baruch as much of a charlatan as everybody claims?"

"How should I know? Who cares?"

"How can you say that?"

He reached down into his lap for his napkin and dabbed his chin. "Maine," he said. "I've never been."

"Rednecks with boats."

"Stop," he said. "Some sea air will be good for you."

"An abandoned sanitarium on the coast? Sounds creepy."

"Stop."

"Who even still has a sanitarium? Will there be lepers?"

"Lepers do not go to sanitariums."

"Of course not," she said. "Because there are no more lepers. Just like there are no more sanitaria."

Baer grabbed the arms of his chair and began to stand. "Come on, granddaughter," he said. "Let's go bother Sophie."

Before she went home, Rachel went to the cemetery.

She waited until after six. At five, the cemetery was still congested like everywhere else: crowds on their way home, stopping to do their grieving. People stood as if they were waiting for the subway, or sat chatting by graves, bags of groceries at their feet, cell phones out and playing music as if they were at home in the kitchen with their loved ones. Sometimes this community, its blunt everydayness, made her feel better, and other times it was crushing. A lie they were all telling themselves, sitting in grass, mumbling to nothing.

It was almost seven when she arrived. Dusk, and with it a wind out of the east and the smell of the river, rich, domestic, a smell from childhood: the wet, mulched yard after a thunderstorm. They'd be closing the gates soon to keep teenagers out. Already, on her way in, she saw four of them leave, heads down, hoods up despite the heat, backpacks on badly, only one strap in use and upside down. It was desperate, and she felt, as she always did, a pang of tenderness for the desperate. They bristled with anger and masculinity—their shoulder-rolling walk, their hands in pockets, the one who, seeing her, turned aside to spit—and yet they couldn't even carry a backpack. She had smiled and said, "Hi" as they passed, and they didn't respond but they slowed, as if surprised, as if on the verge of speech, like they might actually have something to tell her, before hustling out of the graves and into the summer street.

The cemetery was divided in two by a windbreak of giant elms. Passing through them on the path, she always felt like she was back at college, walking down the quad from the library to her dorm. In those days, late at night when the elms' leaves silvered under light from the globes of lamps, when the whole quad, the grass and leaves and bushes shimmered as if with frost, she had believed, had known even, that she was finally entering the life she had always imagined, approaching its threshold, walking a line that with one more step would reveal full-formed the sensual world, the sensual life, her own future body and soul in total clarity. Here in the cemetery, the elms triggered a shiver of this old pleasure, though in feeling it she was in fact experiencing its opposite. These trees, this graveyard, her walk among them mocked that memory. Her beautiful life, her possibility and longing, the things she had to say to the world and the love she had to give, had come to this. Which was what she was thinking when she broke through the windbreak and stepped into the back half of the cemetery and thought for a moment that she was lost, that she'd taken a wrong turn and entered a construction zone or an area of intentional refurbishment.

At her feet: broken stones, flowers torn apart, everywhere slurs sprayed in candy pink paint. Her hand was over her mouth. She was off the path and scrambling among the graves, among the petals, the mourners' stones kicked into the grass, where she also was on her knees, rubbing at random at names—GREEN, HERSCH, KOPPLEMAN—trying to rub the paint off them, the KIKE and JUDEN and YID and the swastikas and iron crosses and slogans of ADOLPH LIVES and ZYKLON-B, all in neon pink balloon letters. Like a joke. Like the scribbled notes of teenage girls in the margins of a notebook. She was laughing. And swearing. She was a crazy person in the park. And then she was on her feet again. There must be somebody to alert. Or more importantly: somebody to protect. She looked over her shoulder. The teenagers were gone, but there might be a mourner. Some poor soul wandering in after work to say a Kaddish. Someone who should not stumble into this, who should not have to see the grave of her loved one defaced. She turned, wildly, again. Because of how Samuel died, the rabbi said she should not rend her clothes. She was rending them now. She slipped and stood again and her skirt caught on the row of tended rosebushes lining the path. She saw someone on the other side, near the gate. She could stop them from looking. She took off her shoes. She ran toward her.

THE FIRST TIME THE PHONE RANG with the blocked number, Jacob answered it because Maddie was out and you never knew who could be calling—the police, the hospital, Maddie on the side of the road after a wreck, on a stranger's phone.

"Jakey!" his sister cried. He hadn't spoken to her in over five years, since before his wedding—which she didn't come to—but she was the only person who called him this, *Jakey*, and he had never known whether to take it as an acceptance or mockery of his new name.

"Maya," he said. "Hey. Is everything okay?" The line clicked. He heard a car horn and a flare of music on her end. She was somewhere outside, in the street. "Are you all right?" he asked again.

"One hundred percent, Jakey. Better than ever. But I've got some news."

"What's up?"

"Mom's dead."

"Really?"

"Definitely not. Or not as far as I know. But why else would I be calling?"

"Fuck, Maya."

"Close," she said. Then she told him that his wife was having an affair.

"The man has a beard," Maya said. "A nice one. Did you know that?"

"The man she's sleeping with has a beard?"

"A little too nice. It ends at the bottom of his chin. Below his chin it's like a baby's ass. He must have one of those, what are they called?"

"Trimmers?"

"Trimmers. Sure. Sometimes I forget words. Trimmers. He probably uses it on his balls. Good. Men always expect you to lick their balls. This is the least they can do."

Jacob was holding the phone in front of his face, staring at it.

"Waxing would be going too far," his sister continued. "Don't get me wrong, a ball should still resemble a ball. There's something vaguely masculine about balls. Do you know what I mean? I don't like the way his beard looks like it's glued on. Maybe it's fake?"

Jacob had just lost his job. He had told Maddie a week earlier and she didn't seem surprised. But this? Like a gift, like waking from a nightmare, he realized that Maya might just be nuts.

"What's she wearing?" he said.

"What isn't she wearing? A leather jacket, a T-shirt, an orange scarf. Long pendant earrings, gold bracelets. Some kind of amber necklace. I wouldn't put amber with orange. It clashes, but still, Jakey, she looks good. Did you tell her she looks good?"

"Why are you doing this?"

"I'm becoming a private investigator," Maya said. "I'm getting licensed and everything. It's easier than you'd expect, if you don't mind the sitting still and staying quiet. Some animals would be very good at it. Cats, for instance, you could train."

Somehow, despite moving to Israel at twelve, she still had the New Jersey accent that Jacob never let himself acquire.

He was just back from sitting outside the Kabbalah school for an hour. It was dusk, he was in the apartment, standing at the window with Coltrane's *Lush Life* on the turntable. The leaves of the dogwood were glowing and he felt ready for the alchemical moment when the elements of this new catastrophe would produce a transformation. He didn't believe in it, but that didn't matter. A prior history of belief was never necessary. The Kabbalists claimed that revelation could erupt at any time out of the present. He was poised and expectant. As if Maya might say something that explained all this.

"Do you remember the time we went to New York?" she said.

Jacob did. He knew she knew he did. He waited.

"Remember Dad with those plants?"

"Of course."

"You can't treat your wife like a plant," she said. "But maybe you should treat her a little bit more like a plant."

When Jacob was a boy, he was not named Jacob, and when he was a boy not named Jacob his father could not ride the subway. They had come to the city and were staying in the apartment of a friend of Jacob's mother—all their friends were his mother's—who had gone to Florida for several weeks, and they had intended it as a kind of holiday: they could stay rent free as long as they fed the cats and watered the plants.

From the start it didn't go well. They arrived and there was a doorman in a gray uniform and he asked Jacob's father their names. "We are guests of Mrs. Herschel," his father kept saying. "Why do you need our names?" He held out the key. "We have the key! We are allowed! We are expected! This is the key!" He was talking too fast, motormouthing, as Jacob's mother called it, not angrily—Jacob never once saw his father angry outside the house—just in a slur of panic until suddenly he stopped, blinked, smiled, and gave the man their names.

That evening, when it was time to go out for dinner, his father could not take the subway. They paid their fare and stood on the platform, but when the train came, in the crush of the evening commute, he could not board.

"Oh, for fuck's sake," his mother said, took his sister by the wrist, and got on. "We'll be waiting at the bar," she said as the door closed. At the time Jacob was glad she didn't try to get him to go with her. It would have been cruel to leave his father alone, trembling under the air vents, and would have been cruel, also, to make Jacob choose whether to go or stay, and yet looking back at the moment he wonders if this wasn't so much his mother's kindness as her condemnation, or if not a condemnation—as far as he could tell, his mother had liked him—a simple case of recognition: she already saw in Jacob a mirror of his father.

As they walked the twenty blocks together, holding hands, even though, at ten years old, Jacob was too old for that, his father told him about the cattle cars. Thousands of Jews crushed together for days, forced to squat and shit in the sloshing mire of the back corner of the car, grandmothers slipping in the filth and not being able to stand again, all of them without food or water, cramped with heat and exhaustion, with old parents dying standing up, leaning against their children and young children dying slumped against their parents' knees, and then, with no place to put the bodies, watching them bloat and rot before you. For twenty blocks he explained this, talked about the long stops, the rare splashes of tepid water hosed at the windows and the howling scramble toward them that followed, the fear, the boredom, the click of the tracks switching, curling into the Polish wastes, the terror of what awaited at the journey's end and the constant, throbbing desire for the journey to be over, to be out of these cars even though they knew, and still could not know, or knew but could not realize they knew, what would happen at the end of the line. His father told him of the tricks the Nazis used in Salonika and Austria, giving them receipts for their luggage, discussing the factories where they would work, or even, in some cases, the countries that would welcome them. The elaborate sham adding to the humiliation of what was to come. You were not only degraded and murdered—by trusting them, by going with them, by answering the calls, the roundups, by giving your name, you were made complicit in that degradation and death. "Which is why we should walk instead of take the subway," he said and squeezed Jacob's hand as they neared the lit restaurant.

There was a time, a few months after Maddie lost the baby, when she began to want to make love in the mornings. Under bright light, immediately upon waking, she'd come back to bed from the bathroom and cling to him before consciousness could gather between them. But these were also the days, in that first aftermath, where Jacob began to dream, or dream again, of his father, and it was in this season that Jacob went down to Alex Baruch's newly opened Kabbalah Center in Manhattan.

The Center was across from the park. In its polarized windows the trees changed color as he approached the glass, silver to purple. Inside it was glossy as a spa: red couches in the lobby, wooden floors painted white, an electric fountain fluting water over stones, smooth and blue where the water darkened them, like the breast of a dove. In each conference room was a framed poster of the ten sefirot, the entangled emanations through which God's will is revealed, linked in gilded calligraphy of transliterated Hebrew. On other posters, on other walls, even in the bathroom were framed translations of each of the sefirah: BEAUTY, WISDOM, KINDNESS, GLORY, and so on. People arrived carrying water bottles, dressed as if for yoga.

But there was also a basement where Baruch held Second Generation meetings for the children and grandchildren of Holocaust survivors. A man had stopped Jacob in the street with a pamphlet. His face looked heavy, like waterlogged wood. *Take it*, he said.

In the mornings Maddie came out of the bathroom, her hair covering her eyes, the windows open, the world as threatening as a river. Jacob found himself arranging her shoes, knocking on the walls, checking the oven, the stove, the front door. In the pamphlet the man had given him, Alex Baruch had written, *Aren't all dreams memories?* The pamphlet was designed to mimic the *Zohar*, the foundational work of Jewish mysticism, and it was disguised as a conversation between two Kabbalists. *Aren't all dreams memories?* says Rabbi Ben Eliezer, to his mentor, Rabbi Isaac.

Yes, says Rabbi Isaac. *But of what?*

It was Maya who explained, finally, ten years into Jacob's life and a few months after they'd come back from New York, that these were their grandfather's experiences, not their father's. Much of what Jacob's father expressed as memory he had learned from research, which he did alone at night, in what he called his study, which was just a room with a chair and a lamp and books on the Holocaust piled neatly on the floor.

Jacob's father used to say, "There's no sin worse than cynicism." But he did not believe in authenticity. Instead, he wanted to remain hidden, to maintain a secret life, to dissemble. This was practical, not cynical. The antidote to cynicism, he claimed, was faith.

But faith in what? Here his father never provided an answer. Assumably in the God of Israel. But for God his father could never feel anything but accusation, and about Israel he was silent since that was acknowledged as a topic on which only Jacob's mother, who was an Israeli, could speak and Jacob's mother wanted no God, certainly not the God of exiles, the God of the European dead, the Ashkenazi lambs padding dumbly toward slaughter.

Beyond this, Jacob's father did not have ritual or tradition or a history of religious practice to lean on or transmit. Instead, he had a picture of his own father, hung above the kitchen table. To any question or complaint, argument or doubt, he referred to the photograph, he'd glance at it or point at it where it overlooked them, blurry, dated 1906, the face of authority in the family, the face of judgment and obligation and guilt, the one against whose suffering they must always prepare, prostrate themselves, match their faith and sorrow and hardship against this blank, slightly bored portrait of an eight-year-old boy.

Jacob could not sleep. This was nothing new, but it was getting worse. He could not sleep, he could not even get into bed.

At first, early in the relationship, Maddie would say, "Come to bed," but she was always asleep before he got there because before he got into bed he had to make sure that bed was a safe place to be. He tapped the door three times, the wall three times, the dresser three, the window three. Then, into bed. Unless he missed one, or if one tap sounded different than the others, or if he touched the surface that he was trying to touch with anything except the middle knuckle of his middle finger of his right hand, or if when he did, his knuckle landed on anything except smooth, bare wood. The doorframe had ridges, the windowsill had molding, and it's possible that Maddie, not realizing that their lives hung in the balance, left a penny on the edge of the dresser, and if his knuckle touched that, a stray penny or hairpin, he had to start again. The door three times, the wall, the dresser, the window. Three, three, three. Then he got into bed and thought, *Have I checked the oven?*

When he did sleep he dreamt of his father; when he was awake, which was most of the time, he began to resemble him. He was distant, irritable, quiet, frightened, ashamed. His life was beautiful. The apartment was full of light, Maddie grew herbs in gray pots along the windows. She worked two jobs—as a grant writer for an arts nonprofit and as a freelance copy editor—to support them while he was in school and then when he was looking for secure teaching work. She made tea and burned sage, she touched his face. "Jacob," she said, "when will we try again?"

In the reoccurring dream his father is naked, in the attic, reading the baseball scores.

But first, always, Jacob finds the ladder, the hole in the ceiling where the panel he had never noticed has been pulled away—and climbs. In the new darkness he moves toward the smoky blur of a skylight, round as a porthole, under which his father, huddled and naked, squints at the sports page. He looks up and says, *They didn't bunt.* No matter how many times Jacob's had the dream, it's not until this moment that he realizes that his father is terrified. Terror pours out of him. Even though it should be morning, the room is leaden, the pull-string bulb is unlit, and his father's voice, repeating *They didn't bunt,* becomes a whisper, something important he must reveal even though they are in hiding. Early in their relationship, Maddie used to like to ask him what he dreamt, as if this was some clue to who he was, as if, he suspected, she thought he was a rock she could turn over, see the centipede scrambling for cover and say, *there you are*. But because when they first met this dream was already old, and there's not much you can take from *they didn't bunt,* he shared it with her. Not long before they decided to separate he started having it again, and he told her, hoping to give her at least this, to be available in this way, or to show her some shadowy version of himself that hadn't already been defined by its failures—a reversal of her original query: she used to ask him his dreams so she could know who he was, now he was telling them to her so she might think she didn't know him after all—and she said, "Jacob, that's not a dream, it's a memory."

"IS THIS THE WORLD?" Rivkah had said six months before she died. She gestured a little drunkenly around the bar. Before them was a tray of limes cut days ago, scrunched and desiccated as shrunken heads. The hanging lamp over their stools was broken or off and the only light came from the yellow jukebox in the far corner. They were in the Upper East Side near where Rachel worked. The bar was out of place in the neighborhood, and they were out of place in it, and they felt giddy and safe. Simon would never come in here, and neither would the spies who followed Rivkah through Brooklyn.

"This is the world," Rachel said.

"They tell you it's not there. That it's an illusion."

"Nonsense." Rachel pointed behind the bar where one of those animatronic talking trout was mounted. "This is as real as it gets."

Rivkah laughed. "Turned off like that, with his mouth open—that fish looks just like my husband."

For a moment they said nothing. Someone came through the door and a murky crescent of day toppled into the room, and then slid out like a wave as the heavy door closed.

Rivkah's head was uncovered and her hair was cut short to accommodate the wig she still usually wore. Here, she was in jeans and a T-shirt. She kept running her fingers along the inside of her bare arms. "I don't want to live in the future," she said. "I don't want to live in the world to come." She reached out and put her hand over Rachel's. "But I would like another whiskey."

"Me too," whispered Rachel.

Rachel had never quite solved the problem of friends. How is it that some people discover themselves in another? Or even discover an Other at all? She had always, actually, felt likeable and liked. But this, maybe, was the opposite of friendship, where instead of being liked, she imagined that she would be known. Once during her freshman year in college she had called home, crying. It was a Thursday night, she had chosen not to go out with her roommate, and she was wearing sky blue pajamas patterned with clouds. "I swear," her mother said, "when you speak I don't know what you're saying." "Sweetie," she said when Rachel kept crying, "you're on the track team."

And yet this seemed to be the central question for the Haredim at NextSteps meetings: how do you find community in the secular world? How do you find friends? Love? For their whole lives the ritual of *us* had veiled them from the world's infection. They felt isolated because they were, they felt that the basic elements of living in the world had been withheld from them because they had, and now they wondered, What does everyone else know? It was her job to answer these questions. What is the secret of an intimacy born of choice? How do you discover a life with others in it? She lied, she guessed. What she wanted to say was, *I don't know either. That's why I'm here.*

In college, at a loss, she had gone to a Hillel Shabbat service. After all, she was a Jew, she had been bat mitzvahed at the reform synagogue where Cantor Ken played the guitar. At the Hillel dinner following services, she sat next to a girl named Sarah who quickly revealed that she was a member of about ten Jewish organizations on campus and president of three—Jews for Two States, Jews for Social Justice, Talmud Study. "How would you describe your Judaism?" Sarah asked.

"More than culinary," Rachel said. Sarah laughed and repeated the comment to the guy sitting next to her.

"That's good," he said and reached out his hand to shake. "But don't tell your grandmother."

Alexander Lurio once wrote, *I try to meet the world as if I myself am the empty canvas.* For most of graduate school, Rachel had this taped above her desk and she repeated it once, maybe more, in NextSteps where it seemed uniquely applicable. These were days where she felt both empty and expectant, brand new, ready to be touched by the world and then burst open in some expression she wasn't quite sure of. She hadn't planned or prepared for a career outside of the academy, but when the life she hoped for didn't emerge, she had to discover a new shape to hang her longing over. If she felt any guilt at seeing the Haredim as empty, as blank canvases for her instruction, it was tempered by the way she was hoping to redefine herself in the process. "I try to meet the world as if I myself am the empty canvas." She spoke it with passion, she felt the skin on her arms pimple under its charge. Rivkah scowled and raised her hand. This was the first time she'd spoken unprompted in a meeting. "And the world," she asked, "does it meet you too?"

"This," Rachel said, "is the world."

They were at the Museum of Jewish Art, and tipsy, standing in front of a wall of Modigliani nudes.

Rivkah was flushed and lovely. She leaned too close to the paintings and then shuffled all the way to the far wall, and came back. "He was a Jew? Really?

"They both were."

"The woman too?"

Rachel nodded.

"No!" Rivkah covered her mouth.

When she lets herself remember Rivkah, this is the moment she plummets back to: Rivkah happily aghast before a Modi. Discovering in the painting, in her very ability to view the painting, the possibility for a life no one ever told her she could have. She talked about it for days afterward, how she'd been stunned not so much at the work's erotic point of view but that the sexual gaze seemed to flow both ways—out as well as in. "Look at her," she said. "She's so..." She waited, she covered her mouth again, a trait both she and Sam had learned and made sweet, and then carefully dropped her hand from her bare mouth and finished her sentence: "Satisfied." Rachel leaned against her, they both smelled like whiskey, and then she pulled away slowly, even if in memory she wishes she didn't, to back up and look at her. The waist on Rivkah's jeans was too high and they were a chalky blue acid wash, like jeans from the eighties, which is what they probably were since Rivkah had picked them out for herself at a Goodwill. It was the era of low-slung skinny jeans, but she'd loved them immediately, and a few months later, after she'd escaped for good, when she had a date with a woman she'd met in rehab, she asked Rachel if they were okay to wear and Rachel said, *Yes, of course, they're perfect* and then felt guilty. Later, the style came back, both the cut and the color, and Rachel wanted to tell her this, to celebrate this small and fickle fortune with her, but by then Rivkah was dead.

At that time, though, Rachel turned away and went downstairs to find some poems by Anna Akhmatova that she had originally hoped they would display alongside Modigliani's sketches of her. Simon had rejected the idea. "Curation is as much about what you leave out as what you put in."

"I just thought maybe it would be good to put in the woman's words as well as her body," Rachel replied, but five minutes later and like a question and he had smiled, not quite sure what she was referring to, and then suggested they carry some Akhmatova in the gift shop.

Near the end of her life, Akhmatova had written directly about meeting Modi, *We both did not understand one important thing: everything that happened was for both of us a prehistory of our future lives: his very short one, my very long one. The breathing of art still had not charred or transformed the two existences; this must have been the light, radiant hour before dawn.*

Rachel decided that she wanted to read this passage to Rivkah, but when she came back from her office with it, Rivkah was gone.

She found her in the next gallery, standing just inches from Arbus's "A Jewish giant at home with his parents, in the Bronx, N.Y., 1970." In the photograph Eddie Carmel, the son of Orthodox Jews who immigrated from Palestine to the Bronx, towers awkwardly over his parents in their apartment. He is a giant, not just tall but huge, proportionally enormous and muscular, and shockingly fragile too, stooped under the ceilings, perched on a cane and staring down at his parents with his mouth open. His father, Israel, wearing a suit, glares at his son with obvious resentment while his mother gapes up at him with a sort of tender surprise. He is clearly hers, of her, they look so alike, Eddie and his mother, except that his features are an exploded version of hers, his lips are the size of her chin, his head is as wide as her wide torso, no wonder she's startled: he looks like a dream she is having.

"This is me," Rivkah said.

"No," Rachel said. "You're beautiful."

"So is he. But that father. That room." She sounded almost angry. The ceiling pressed on his head, the lampshades were wrapped in plastic, a dark fabric cover protected his father's chair. "That room is killing him."

Rachel touched her bare arm. "You need to leave."

"I have kids. My brother Schmuley has a kid."

"You're not leaving your children," Rachel said.

Rivkah reached up and touched Rachel's chin. When she pulled her hand back there was force in the gesture, it turned Rachel's face like a slap.

BEFORE JACOB LOST HIS JOB, he came to the conclusion that others were also coming to: the students were in distress. It had never been rare to have the odd kid with emotional problems. But now it was general, it was the rule, it was a reaction to Trump but it preceded Trump too, it transcended politics despite what people in politics said, it was like a weather event, large-scale, moving, a barometric hum or the appearance of a miracle, a seraphic download, it infected them en masse, it was in the air or in the electromagnetism sizzling off their phones, or in the corn syrup, or Ritalin, or internet porn, in the glacial melt or the silence left by the absence of bees, it was a message the world was sending and they were receiving, and maybe they were on to something, maybe it was reasonable, certainly it was reasonable, but one way or the other, the students were all in distress. And into their sorrow and fear, into their doubt and rage, Jacob debuted his class on Jewish Theology after the Holocaust. He should have known better; after all, he was in distress too.

But it had seemed perfect at the time: theology was a bulwark to fear, an attempt to wrangle chaos into the geometry of logic. The Talmudists, Kabbalists, the Rabbis, the medieval philosophers had excelled at this—you take an ancient story, a myth, a plague, bad luck or bad weather, a burning temple, exile, diaspora, and like a watch, you pop off the back and find the perfect, unceasing, hidden movement, the rightness of the world still at work. And yet, against the Shoah, while the impulse to make sense remained, the machinery broke down. The theologians were left with either disbelief, heresy, or desperate rationalization. Against the Shoah, theology failed, reason failed, the human talent to comprehend, make excuse, or give comfort to itself collapsed. There remained only faith and faith made for bad theology; there remained only faith and against the Shoah faith looked like delusion.

He should have known better.

That's what they said—the dean, his chair, Maddie. And yet, Jacob thought, how couldn't it help to see great minds failing to comprehend catastrophe? The point of his class wasn't to create faith, or reinforce it, it wasn't to produce an ethical system that could accommodate, let alone make sense of, genocide. It was to show how necessary it was, despite incomprehension, to try to understand, to expose how we crave meaning, how we build these palaces of philosophy against the chaos and how still ultimately, at its core, at its most essential—and what was the Holocaust if not something essential—the world, the universe, the things our own hearts will do and allow, remain mysteries.

This had been his life's story. Jacob's father's parents had met and conceived him, Isaac, in Bergen-Belsen after the war when it was a camp for Displaced Persons, and lived there for several years until his mother died and his father moved to America with him. He grew up in New Jersey, went by Izzy, learned to play handball and watch baseball, bought his sporting goods store, took bets on the side. Jacob's mother had been drawn to the flash his father showed in the world, his disarming shrapnel smile, which at first she took for ease, but was, as Jacob later learned, actually its opposite, a fragment of his damage breaking through.

On their trip to New York, because it was his responsibility to feed the cats in the apartment they were staying in, Jacob's father refused to leave until he saw the cats eat—though the cats, being cats and only slightly less crazy than he was, didn't want to eat in front of him. So he waited, hulking over their bowls in the kitchenette. Whistling at them, snapping his fingers, shaking their food, taking breaks only to get up, once every hour or so, and water the plants.

"Let's go, Izzy," his mother said. She waited at the door, she was holding her purse in the crook of her arm, her sunglasses were already on and Maya was at her side, looking at her feet.

"The cats haven't eaten yet," his father said. "They just hide." He watered the plants again. "Make one mistake and who knows what these people might do to you?"

"What people?" his mother screamed. "The Herschels?" But he just shrugged, watered the plants, and went back to the sink to refill the can.

If she wanted to live in an asylum, she said, she could have stayed in Israel, where all the old European ghosts acted like this, plodding about, wailing in the night, haunting their new Israeli families with their own Ashkenazi dead. "It's not even our lives," she shouted. "It didn't happen to us."

She was weeping on her knees. "Please get up," his father said. "Please, please." He was begging, he was standing there in his undershirt and dopey white briefs holding a cat's food bowl. Finally, she rose. The plants were swollen and already rotting from overwatering. Outside the city was alive and noisy. The apartment was on the fifteenth floor, they could see light reflecting on the river. She put her wet hand on his cheek, he hadn't shaved since they'd been there.

"What was the point," she said, "of any of them living?"

For a while, after she left, she sent blank postcards from Israel. Just landscapes—the Ramon Crater in the Negev, a bare beach in Eilat, the port in Acre, a weird empty ski slope in the Golan Heights. And then, nothing. A couple of years later, she somehow got in touch with his sister and his sister, like that, just as simply, went to be with her. Jacob was twelve and he was alone with his father.

All of this he'd told Maddie early in their relationship. It made sense, it was a basic coherent trauma, it was like the beginning of a story you could understand. But, though he can guess at psychology, can use it to explain his low-grade OCD, can imagine or infer anger he never remembered feeling, he could never make it explain the part he never told Maddie, which is what he, a boy not yet named Jacob, actually did.

When it was time to leave home, he moved to Israel. Not to be with his mother and sister. They weren't there anymore anyway. They were living in France, from where his sister sometimes sent him emails boiling with what he read as self-hatred—*Israel is like Bushwick, it would be great without all the Jews*—though it was the indiscriminate slogan of her disgust that repelled him—the self itself seemed a perfectly valid thing to hate—and by then he was doing his own writing. His articles began as screeds in chat rooms frequented by disaffected Israeli youth before getting picked up by a zine in Tel Aviv and then quickly a paper in Jerusalem, in which he argued for a New Israel and new Jewish experience that forgot the Shoah, that abandoned history, that consciously, willingly, intentionally severed itself from the traditions of the European diaspora, the Ashkenazi, the exiles, the "Golah ghosts" as he called them.

Basically, he claimed that all of contemporary Jewish practice and identity was a response to the Fall of the Second Temple in 70 CE. Until that point Jewishness was fundamentally linked to the sacred practice within the Temple. But after the Romans destroyed it and took Jerusalem, a new question arose: how to be a Jew without a Temple, how to be a Jew outside of Jerusalem? And every major development in Judaism since—prayer instead of sacrifice, the Talmud, Kabbalah, Hasidism—all were profane compensations, a response to this, and even worse, to subsequent trauma—the Yizkor (the Crusades), Lurianic Kabbalism (the Spanish Expulsion), Hasidism (the Cossack Pogroms). It was a tradition based on the memory of fear, a refugee's tradition—and one cannot be a refugee in their homeland.

Jacob was not right wing, but Rabin had only been dead for a few years. The Labor party was weakening. In Israel's march to the right, in the way they responded to bombings in cafés or on buses, he saw a people fighting an older war. Everything was a response to the Shoah, but to keep responding to trauma, to replace the tattooed numbers with the slogans *Never forget* and *Never again*, to interpret the present and to build a future based on one moment in the past, was the legislation of trauma, a roadmap to insanity and ruin. Israel was beginning to make it perfectly clear: if you are a survivor constantly in a fight for your life, you have the right—perhaps you are even obliged—to do anything to protect yourself. Everything is allowed. For Jacob at eighteen, it all seemed simple enough: the past annihilates the present, and a world without a present is a world in a moral vacuum. The only way toward a moral life is to forget.

And then one day the smoke cleared. It was sudden as birdsong. He was in the street in Tel Aviv, leaving a café and then, in the first few steps out of the café and into the ravishing morning, where the wind off the port poured down the avenue of white concrete heavy with light and lemons, the wooden slats of his life twisted open and he felt everything, alive and glad and assailed and lonely in the fragrant street and then he was weeping as people walked around him, gave him wide berth, let him lean against a wall where an old man found him and patted his back and his shoulder and reached up and touched his face and Jacob, who was still not called Jacob then, kept his eyes closed so that he didn't see the man's bare arm. Then the man took his hand, as if he were a little boy, helped him cross the street back to his apartment for tea with mint and honey and Jacob understood, somewhere between the cobbles and the curb, how wicked his articles were. Even if they were right. Even if he believed them. They were a betrayal he had crossed the world to commit and nothing he did could redeem him.

On the first day of class Jacob said, "the problem with the Deuteronomic system is that most lives do not get better." It was, maybe, a bad way to start.

"In Deuteronomy, the fifth book of the Torah," he said, "God further clarifies the terms of His contract with His people. Be righteous and you will flourish in this life. Follow the Lord's law and the Lord's word, be obedient and kind, and you will prosper. Sounds good, right?"

They knew it was a trick, they knew to distrust any relationship with authority, but they also wanted to have the right answers and knew to nod when professors asked them to—so they nodded anyway. Then he said, "But the Jews were exiled from the Holy Land, the Temple was destroyed and rebuilt and destroyed again and they were cast into the world in diaspora. So clearly the Lord wasn't upholding His end of the bargain."

He could have left it there. His point was made. Even this close to Long Island he didn't need to tell them that to be a Jew in history was to be an exile. But he wanted them to feel the significance of the issue. So he said, "The problem with the Deuteronomic system is that most lives do not get better." They stared; he sensed, if anything, the first embarrassed tremble of pity. He clarified. "Over time, I mean." They nodded again; maybe they were thinking of their grandparents. "I'm talking about your lives." A girl in the back began to suck through her straw at the ice in her empty plastic tub of coffee. It sounded like logs being fed to a woodchipper.

Jacob was sensitive to stimuli. When he knocked on the wall before bed he knew how the knock should sound. But what kind of knowing was this? Let alone what kind of knowledge? Either way against his dizzy nausea he had to get the sound of the knock just right and in class sometimes, while talking, while trying to connect the fundamental problems of human experience with the lives the students led, he would be derailed by a sudden discordance of pen clicks and computer taps, zipper snarls and the one student who always, for whatever reason, believed that halfway through lecture was the appropriate time to try, and not quite manage, to open a bag of chips. And then Jacob would find himself about to become his father, standing before the doorman in New York, gesturing in angry panic—*We are allowed, here is the key!* But today was the beginning of a new semester; he did not want to be irritable or crazy.

"That's the problem with mortality," he said. "Actually," he said, and it was only after he said it that he realized he was, at the very least, irritable, "you're probably living your best years right now. From here on out—statistically—life will be an accumulation of losses."

This was the first day of class. Usually reserved for liturgical recitation of the syllabus and then a quick dismissal. But Jacob had ignored the syllabus and gone right in with Time and Loss and the mortal human predicament and now morale was not good. A student raised his hand. He raised it from the top of his head where it has been resting as if holding in place the briar of curly black hair under which lay a face as bland and wobbly as a scoop of ice cream. His name was Joshua, and he had already asked two faintly querulous questions. Jacob called on him again. Joshua said he didn't see the point? What did Deuteronomy have to do with the Holocaust?

Nothing, Jacob wanted to say. Nothing at all. Nothing has to do with the Holocaust. You see that kid playing baseball? The one you're watching with your father as he shouts at Little Leaguers he's never met? You see those plants rotting on the sill? The subway, the steam sullying the cold air—Nothing. The Shoah is a black hole from which no image can return. I'm showing you the vast failure of representation and understanding at the heart of the century. I'm showing you why every theological response will fail.

Instead, he said, "The Deuteronomic system lays the groundwork for an essential point. To understand the theological response to the Holocaust we have to understand the way Judaism responds to human experience in general."

He decided to write this on the board: what he wrote on the board, they would write in their notes. In such ways knowledge is communicated, though maybe not preserved. He imagined that, in years to come when they looked back over their notes, they would be baffled by the collage they found: ABRAHAM—FEAR & LOATHING—SEX BTWN THE ELDERLY=ANGELIC LAUGHTER? But now, he had promised something essential, so he said, "Jewish salvation is supposed to come"—and now he began to write as he spoke—"*in history.*"

They waited. They blinked. They were bored as fish. "What is history?" he asked.

Maddie will say, "What happened?"

After class, that first class when the other students had left: Joshua, waiting feet crossed, hands clasping, unclasping, talking to himself.

Joshua in the seminars that followed: raising his hand to answer every question and questioning every answer. Talkative, curious, confused, elated. Afterward, as if the previous fifty minutes had been a personal training session, he would shake Jacob's hand and thank him and tell him how much he had learned.

Or, on other days, he would go silent. Stare at his open notebook, write nothing, refuse to look up, then rush off—pushing past the students still in chairs—when class was over. Usually, on these occasions, he would be waiting outside Jacob's office, where he'd sit: sweating, playing with his hair, scratching behind his neck, and then stopping, stilling, staring.

These were his moods: obsequious and ingratiating, angry and sullen, diffident and revealing. In these ways he was like the other students, but around more.

The second week of class: Jacob assigned an essay by the Talmudic scholar, Joseph B. Soloveitchik called "The Voice of My Beloved Knocks," where Soloveitchik aligns God's apparent absence during the Holocaust with traditional Jewish belief. He accuses Jews—in trying to understand why God might allow their genocide—of missing the miracle of their continued existence in the state of Israel. To do this, he relies on biblical precedent and recalls the moment in the *Song of Songs* where the Shulamite maiden living in Solomon's court, despite spending days yearning for her lover, fails to open the tent when he knocks. For Soloveitchik the unanswered knock represents the way we often fail to recognize the divine miracle when it happens.

"I don't want to have anything to do with Israel," Joshua said.

Soloveitchik wrote: "It is good for a Jew not to be able to hide from his Jewishness, but to be compelled to keep answering the question 'Who art thou…'" He accuses assimilated Jews of cowardice, self-hatred, confusion. He is almost raving by the end of the essay.

"I don't hate myself," Joshua said.

The essay is, Jacob feels, beautifully written, elusive, insane, totally enraging; viscerally, in his bones, he rejects everything it is trying to say. He had hoped it would trigger a passionate response.

Joshua stood before class was over, slammed his book and slammed the door and Jacob found him, as usual, waiting for him, hopeful, accusing, in distress.

One morning in bed, not long after they were married, Sam said, "Did you love my sister?"

It was morning, but the moon was out and the sun wasn't up yet. Their early days were like that, confused, dream-paced and disorienting. They had barely begun dating, they were engaged before his wife even granted his *get*, they were married. The moon was out, she was asleep, and the alarm was going off.

"Of course I did," Rachel said.

"I mean like a lesbian."

His back was to her, a blue shadow humped against the blue glass and the blue moon.

"You're a child, Sam."

"Why? I think she was like that. That's what her husband said when she left."

She had asked Rivkah once: *Does he know?* They were looking at Lurio's eight-panel depiction of the *Song of Songs*. Rachel had opened to her favorites, the two paintings depicting the poem's third chapter: the maiden alone in bed with her desire.

"Schmuley?" Rivkah had said. "Get real."

Get real. Her expressions were off like that, old like that, aslant as morning darkness. Rivkah would laugh when Rachel teased her. That day in the bar, she held up her bare arms glowing in jukebox light, ran her hand across her exposed scalp. *I don't need words to speak.*

Sam had told Rachel many times that there was no one in the world he was closer to than his sister, and he didn't even know her. Everyone talked about mystery, but love was supposed to be more than a mystery, more than a yearning to understand and be understood. More than desire. At the other side of desire was consummation, satisfaction not in completion, but expansion. Consummation as it was phrased in the Bible, to *know.*

"You shouldn't talk to Moishe," Rachel said. "After what he did to your sister."

Rachel slept with her phone silenced and in most seasons gauged the morning by how the light opened out of the trees directly beyond her apartment. Sam's alarm went off again. He'd meet the sound each time with a shout of disbelief, but it was long past when he should have been up. He had an interview for a job he would not get, and Rachel would have to help him with his tie.

"Who am I supposed to talk to, then?" he said.

For a while after she started dating Sam, men would watch her apartment. This was before they were married and there was still a chance of Sam returning to his wife. She'd look out the window and see them: across the road, standing under the streetlight outside the laundromat, smoking cigarettes. Two Haredi men, staring up at her.

"They're Shosha's brothers," Rivkah said.

"They don't want their sister to get divorced," she said the next night. "I had the same bullshit with my husband's family. Always lurking."

And they were: across the street, gazing up at the apartment, from the same place, standing slotted in the green shimmer of the mercury lamp like Martians beaming down in a rectangle of space light, or Elijah ascending.

Finally, after about a week, Rivkah opened Rachel's window and began shouting obscenities. She shouted for ten minutes straight, without pausing, called them cockfaces and pussybrains and shiteaters and little yellow grasshoppers. She said that God covered his nose when they were born, called them donkeys and little shit dicks. She said, *When fish fart it's better than you.* Instead of shouting at her to shut up, or calling the police, people stepped out on their stoops or opened their windows to hear more. Neighbors whooped and laughed. Pigeons flushed and could not settle. She was sweating and incandescent. She said, *You are flabby and soft and your dicks are as bad as herring.* Then she closed the window.

"Ignore them," she said.

Sometimes this is what Rachel wanted: to see everything as if for the first time. With the pleasure that follows surprise. To come to the world unsullied by expectation or the ten thousand old ideas she was supposed to conjure hers out of. To be not-yet-touched, and then touched.

Other times she wanted mastery. To look at a painting and see every bit of it. To consume it with her gaze, sure, that was the old trope, the constant conversation, but she wanted more than that. She wanted it not to exist until she saw it, for it to be invisible until she saw it, inscrutable before she saw it, for her seeing and understanding to make it. Lurio, Modigliani, Kitaj, Bloom, they were her muses, unborn until she made them naked with her sight.

Rivkah had asked, "Why are these your favorites?"

Open on the table before them: Lurio's *"Song of Songs,* Chapter Three: The Shulamite Maiden Welcomes Her Beloved."

Earlier that night Rachel had led an informal NextSteps meeting to discuss "Women's Issues," or, as some of the women called it, "OTD and DTF." OTD stood for *Off the Derech;* it meant *off the path* and was an expression their families spat at them like a slur and, after years of feeling like abominations, they took it, or some of them did, and reappropriated their apostasy as rebirth—*OTD and I'm free.* Now Rachel was back in her apartment with Rivkah drinking wine and giggling over how awkward the meeting had been.

"Look at it," Rachel had said. "I love all that blue. Also," she lowered her voice huskily to reference the euphemism that had dominated the talk earlier that night. "It's so *intimate*."

In the *Song of Songs*, the third chapter opens: *Upon my couch at night/I sought the one I love.* Lurio had lightly inked these lines onto some of the studies that preceded the finished painting.

"But she's alone?" Rivkah asked—and then got it and blushed. This was the quality Rachel would think she loved in Sam—the brashness, the confidence and then, sudden as a laugh, the whole vulnerable world appearing.

They were eating tiny perfect cubes of cheese that Rachel had stolen from a function at the museum where she had run into an old boyfriend from graduate school. He worked as a curator for a Digital Arts gallery now in Williamsburg. "You would be surprised how much of it is on VHS," he said.

"Would I?"

They were hanging out, as they had in graduate school, near the food. The cheese was a problem. Such shapely cubes, golden, exact, cut surely by some perfect machine in Wisconsin—but so small. She wasn't entirely not high.

"What's protocol here?" she said and pointed to the cheese. That is, she asked, could you flip your toothpick around to spear a second cube, or was it one cheese, one toothpick?

"The second one."

"With a K then," she said. "Protokoll. Very strict."

Her plan for the function had started out as a dinner plan: eat as many cubes of free cheese as she could. But then, between the cheese and the grapes, she bumped into him and now was telling jokes requiring a German accent. Was this flirting? He had, she remembered, liked to choke her, lightly, in bed.

"So, this must be, like, a dream job," he said.

The choking, actually, had been too light. More like a caress, except that he looked angry when he was doing it. "It's a *symbolic* choking," he had said when she asked him if maybe a little more force was in order. Now she found that she had speared five cubes of cheese on her fresh toothpick and arranged them there, in a row, like a kabob. Her ex-boyfriend was frowning, but what could he be worried about? He was wearing unmatching Chuck Taylors, he worked in VHS and she remembered an argument they had once after she had come back from a bad meeting with her dissertation advisor. She had been a little drunk, a little indignant. She was looking for commiseration. "Sometimes I don't care what the artist is thinking. I just care what I'm thinking. What's wrong with that?"

"Sounds like you want to be the artist not the critic," he had said.

"You can be both," she said. "Donald Judd, Marsden Hartley, Some Woman of the Future."

He was playing a video game where people cooked dinner, got dressed, drove red cars down neon streets. "I guess," he said. "But you don't make art."

Rachel wrote several chapters of her dissertation on differing views of intimacy in Alexander Lurio's work. She disagreed with the common readings: Lurio wasn't a devotional artist and he wasn't the ethnographer of a vanishing culture, he wasn't interested in what was disappearing or invisible. For Lurio, a painting occurred at the intersection of different gazes, or as Rachel framed them, *converging intimacies.* The tensions, the energy, the sensuality of a work caught like a message on an electric wire, between who was seeing whom and how—a recognition or desire to see or be seen that was sensual not just in the early Paris portraits, but all through his career, even when the Other, the one seeing or being seen, became increasingly spectral, in doubt, off-canvas.

"You give the viewer too much power," her advisor had said. Her chapter was stacked neatly on his desk, and he was poking it with bottom of his pen, as if to check if it were really dead. "I care less what one sees than what Lurio intends them to see. Does that make sense?" His voice was patient, kindly, he was talking maybe a little slower than usual. "After all, Lurio is the one making them look."

"But they might not look," Rachel said. "They might *choose* not to look."

"To not look at a painting is not a form of knowing what it means."

The same professor in class had once described Rothko's work as a seduction. "He's forcing us to stare at him, to interpret him, to invest his forms with meaning."

But Rachel thought: that's not how seduction works. Seduction is not a performance, but a gaze. You seduce by seeing. By letting another realize that you see them and letting them see themselves through your wonder. An artist does not seduce, but begs to be seduced.

Her advisor poked the pages again. "What's important," he said, "is what Lurio sees."

He was probably right. And yet, Lurio's figures were always gazing at one another or spying or staring into the heavens demanding the Lord's awakeness and awareness. But did they receive it? She was not God, she was maybe not even very good at looking, but did that mean she should cover her eyes? She nodded, she took notes; she changed her dissertation.

Later Sam would write, *You wanted to invent me but you didn't.* What she had done was bring him back to her apartment that first night. She excused herself into the bathroom and then stepped out of it without her clothes. In between she had lit some candles. He wasn't prepared. He was sitting on her bed in the dark, still too nervous to turn on a lamp after sundown on Friday. Then the open door, the light slipping into the room like a spoon. He put his hand over his mouth. She knew how she looked.

For a while she had been thinking, let's say every theory is right: we are born wanting. We fill and hollow. We yearn. She was always being instructed in yearning. The paintings were about yearning, the criticism was about yearning, her experience in graduate school was a ritual where everyone imagined the exact same future and fought over who wanted it the most.

But the only real desire did not have to be the unsatisfied kind. This was another lie, Lurio's lie even, the insistence on the inadequacy of the Other, the sense that only the self was real. All his lonely subjects—portraits of people looking into corners—not at the painter, not at the viewer, not at us—or his surreal shtetl hookups where the dancing couple or trysting lovers corkscrew their necks in spinal distress to peer away into their own darkness. Lurio was wrong. Under the color and windy line her grandmother loved so much, her mother loved so much, she—Rachel—loved, was his secret thesis that the world was broken, unsatisfying, empty of comfort, without succor.

She crossed the room and took Sam's hands, she pulled him to his feet and then knelt before him. He wasn't speaking. He wasn't the guys from grad school. He understood the importance of shutting the fuck up. In the gutter of candlelight, with his thighs trembling against her face and her hands trying to do something significant with his balls, she was supposed to feel this as false? He was? Everything was real. Let the experts assemble and bear witness. The mystics and painters and professors. Her mother and *Bubbe*. Her thesis advisor. Let them gather and watch. Make room for the sixty warriors surrounding Solomon's couch in the *Song of Songs* with its frankincense and myrrh and acid-trip similes. Everything was real. Her hair was like goats, her mouth was a flock of ewes. And her eyes were doves, wings wide in flight, above the world, seeing everything.

ONE NIGHT, MIDWAY THROUGH THE SEMESTER, Jacob held a dinner party. After drinks, but before anyone had taken more than a few bites he asked, "Does the Holocaust bestow Israel with meaning?" Maddie looked up from her brussel sprouts at him, incredulous.

The dinner did not go well. The party was for Morton Becker, Jacob's graduate school advisor, whom he had invited to the school to give a talk. Becker was a significant theologian, and the department had been excited to get him for what was, because of Jacob's relationship with him, a slightly diminished rate. Even so, the honorarium had cost them most of their budget for the semester, and Jacob's chair suggested that instead of going out to a restaurant before the talk, Jacob host a dinner. Of course, the menu was a problem: some of the guests didn't eat meat but did eat fish, others would only eat meat but not "marine proteins," two were vegans, three had gluten intolerances, one could not digest "anything green." In total there were only five guests.

Jacob and Maddie decided on an array of tapas. The idea was to set a Bohemian tone: crudité and tartines and dips and hors d'oeuvres and charcuterie munched amid candles, music, art on the walls, ideas bandied over drinks, essentially an evening both stimulating and casual—like at a Parisian salon where nobody ate anything they were allergic to. Jacob was a lecturer, a semi-permanent fixture in the department, but not on the tenure track and therefore, unlike the rest of the faculty, it was important that people liked him. So they spent two days in advance cooking, and borrowing extra plates and servingware and a few more chairs from friends.

After cocktails they sat down to the tapas, which wasn't what Maddie had imagined. The silverware was unnecessary. All the academics at the table used their fingers. Immediately Jacob asked his question. "Does the Holocaust bestow Israel with meaning?" He tried to clarify: "What's the difference between history and memory?"

"I've always felt," said his chair, "that it's important to remember our history." His chair, who primarily studied comic books, hadn't understood the question.

"I meant, does the creation of the State of Israel reveal the divine purpose of the Holocaust in history?" Jacob said, holding a smoked salmon tartine.

Baruch had written, *If the end does not begin, then no sequence predicts it. From any moment the end could explode—shimmering, vivid. A bird that dies in mid-flight.*

Here, then, thought Jacob, the end showing its shadow: Becker bored and annoyed looking up from his goulash.

"Of course it does," Becker said, as everyone who knew Becker knew he would. This had been the cause of their falling-out. Jacob, who had once suggested that it was Israel's obligation to forget, didn't know how to remember. If it is sinful to forget the Shoah, then we must remember it. But what are we remembering? And what does it mean to remember something you didn't experience? And if you do remember, what purpose does memory serve? For Becker the answer to all these questions was Israel, but for Becker, Israel had also been the question.

Before dinner, Jacob tried to explain the falling-out to Maddie. "If we remember something we didn't experience," he said, "then we are not remembering it. We're just telling a story about that experience based on what we want it to represent."

"God," Maddie said. "That's basically the definition of *to commemorate*."

"But commemoration is like glue," Jacob had said. "It fixes what you're remembering in place. It determines meaning, and by deciding on the meaning of the past we decide on the meaning of the present. But the Shoah was insane. It didn't mean anything, did it? And if it did, if somehow this perfect expression of moral insanity prepared the world for Israel, isn't that even worse?"

Maddie was watching him. His hands were everywhere. He was knocking on the counter as he spoke. He was ranting, sweating, drinking aquavit from the bottle, eating herring from the jar.

"Jacob," she said, "how did I find myself in a Dostoevsky novel?"

What Jacob wanted to ask was: when I remember my father who am I remembering? That is, if the person I knew as my father was just my grandfather's shadow, and I am my father's shadow—because I am certainly not a whole person, or who I am *as Jacob* is a response to who I was as my father's son—then am I my father's ghost or my grandfather's? Or, if I am a ghost, who am I haunting?

Instead, he had said, "What the difference between *ritual* and *haunting*?"

"Ritual represents the hidden, haunting represses it," Maddie said. This was one of her great gifts. There wasn't a question she couldn't distill into an answer. She handed him a can of chickpeas. "Open this."

For their wedding, Maddie's cousin had given them a fancy can opener with a tiny blade and hidden teeth and he was never sure how to use it, but Wittgenstein had written, *The world is everything that is the case* and Jacob approached the problem of the can opener and the canned chickpeas with optimism unsupported by history. He handed the mangled can back to Maddie.

"This is a dinner party, Jacob. For an asshole who was never very nice to you. Pour wine and don't bring up Israel."

"Any other advice?"

"Be easier on yourself. Commemoration, memory, ritual? These aren't real questions," Maddie said.

"Of course they are," Jacob had said. "You can tell because I'm asking them."

Maddie took the jar of herring away from him. "Let me try again," she said. "These aren't questions real people have."

"So," Becker said to Jacob in front of his colleagues, "still dragging your feet in Alex Baruch?"

Several around the table chuckled. They were never all supposed to be sitting together. But there was nothing Bohemian about goulash.

"I'm not kidding," Becker said. His pettiness was as magnificent as a bird of paradise: a shocking, unnecessary adornment, florid with anxiety and competition. Maybe this is what it took to be a great scholar. "You should have seen him, back from some conference in Berlin, all excited that he had met the Great Baruch."

It had been the beginning of the end of Jacob's role as protégé. Baruch rejected what was fundamental to Becker: that Zionism fulfilled the progress of Jewish history. And Jacob's question tonight about Israel and the Holocaust had reminded Becker of it.

"I was like a father to him," Becker laughed and held out his arms across the table to Jacob, "and he betrayed me to follow that fraud."

"I'm not working on Alex Baruch," Jacob said.

"So what then?"

"Dinner," Jacob said. He gestured with a spatula at some spanakopita. "That puff pastry didn't roll itself."

To watch Jacob try to reach over his glass of wine and dip his chip in the hummus was enough to know that he did not roll the puff pastry.

"Ah, the life domestic," Becker said. "It must be nice." Which was code for: he's chosen his wife over his career.

"I wish," Maddie said, rushing to the rescue. "He's always working."

When he was still Becker's student, he had sat in Becker's office and expressed his doubts about the direction of his study. "I wasn't in the camps. I wasn't born in Bergen-Belsen. I didn't want to live my life as if I was. And now I feel like the Wicked Son."

In the parable of the Wicked Son, the Wicked Son asks his father a question about the Exodus from Egypt. "*What does this story mean to you*?" This was the question that made him Wicked. By saying *you* and not *us,* by suggesting that he did not experience the suffering in Egypt and could not remember what he did not experience, by severing himself from traumatic memory, he separated himself from his community. It was Becker's favorite parable. "I should spank you," he had said.

"I thought you were taking a break," said Jacob's chair.

"From what?" Jacob said.

"Otherwise," Jacob's chair said, "why didn't you apply for your summer teaching or research funding?" Shrimp tails were scattered across his plate like dead birds.

"Wait," Maddie said, looking across the table at Jacob. "You didn't apply for any summer funding?"

What are the customs of dinner? Jacob sat at the head of the table, his plate covered with finger foods—all in different shades of brown—as if he'd made a mistake at a buffet. Everyone was waiting for Jacob to answer. But what answer could he give? Maddie was working two jobs—she had three grants to write that week and was freelance copy-editing a manuscript at night, and had still gone to extraordinary effort to put this dinner together—and he hadn't applied for funding they needed and then picked a fight with his advisor. There was a line in the Talmud: a mistake you make twice is no longer a mistake.

"We only have the future to imagine," Becker said. "History and memory? Liturgy and exegesis? Those European Jews make too much of all that. What's the point? In Hebrew the word for repentance is teshuva. It means 'to return.' But where are they going to return to? Lvov?"

BECKER'S TALK DIDN'T GO WELL. There were ways in which this was Jacob's fault. He was the one who had introduced his students to Becker's work, who had troubled their minds with outrage, who had brought Becker, and let them make their choice about how to respond.

He had imagined a debate, the moral clarity of the young, Becker's frustration with how simple they made it all sound. Perhaps the moment was impure. There was the element of authority—he had required that they attend, which they did, his students, with signs, and a megaphone, with balloons filled with paint.

"The thing is," the dean said the following week in Jacob's chair's office, "one of your students has made a complaint."

The chair's office was full of comic books, hundreds, maybe thousands of comic books in dusty plastic, stacked face down on the shelves and piled on the floor so that the office smelled of some mix of green tea and Mylar. And in the corner, sitting in a rolling chair among the gray prophylactic sheaths: the dean wearing a lilac sweater vest.

"Don't be alarmed," he said. Before he became dean he was a professor of sociology. As if to remind everybody of this, he sported Birkenstock dress sandals throughout the year. He must have kept them in his office to change into after his commute because they were spotless, unstained by salt, and although this wasn't what Arendt had meant when she coined "the banality of evil," Jacob was, in fact, alarmed by a powerful man who was fussy about his sandals.

"A complaint?" Jacob asked.

"A serious one. From one of your students."

"Joshua," Jacob said.

"A complaint was made," his chair said. "I can't say who made it."

"It was Joshua," Jacob said.

"Okay, okay, it was Joshua," said the dean.

"What could Joshua have to complain about?" Jacob said.

The dean smiling with his lips together, like some kind of frog. "If Joshua doesn't have anything to complain about, how did you know it was Joshua?"

For the last several weeks, Joshua in class: with a black eye, with a split lip, with band-aids applied poorly to his knuckles. He lifted his pen to take notes and a band-aid, which he had put on horizontally, peeled off. Jacob thought: this is attention-seeking behavior, this is a flagrant display of minor issues, this is a total red flag. He took his cue from the other students and pretended not to notice.

During the last class, he pointed to the day's reading and said, "Do you agree with Eliezer Berkovits that *the experience of God's absence is not new*?"

They looked down at their reading. Though they had never considered that God might be present in their lives, until this moment they had not experienced this as an absence. Did this count as agreement? Also, Berkovits had meant as an agent in History, not as a feeling in your heart. But most of them had grown up around here, they were toddlers when the towers fell and the idea of God-in-History sounded as psychotic to them as it should have. Also, they hadn't done the reading. Joshua sighed, removed an entire box of tissues from his backpack and began blotting a speck of blood from his lip.

Jacob asked, "Is it radical to believe that the Holocaust proves God's absence? Berkovits writes that in response to His silence during the Shoah, the Lord *had no choice but to grant us a measure of national redemption* in Israel."

Joshua slammed his book and gathered his sunglasses and packed his tissues and stood and tried to put on his backpack, but there wasn't room because everyone else was still sitting. So he dragged it behind him, as he clambered—finally the others were starting to half-stand in their seats as you might in a movie theatre—out of the classroom.

After class, in office hours, he showed up with his sunglasses on.

"You can lose the glasses," Jacob said. "We've all seen your black eye."

Joshua did. Beyond the bruise, the skin was a yolky custard color.

Jacob reminded himself: be a person. But what was it to be a person? To be open, to be hospitable to the damage of others. Like a house during the Passover Seder, with the door ajar to welcome a stranger. Here was the problem: how do you protect yourself from the craziness of others? As inheritance or infection. How do you be a good son, a good husband, a good father if you ever got to be a father?

"What's going on?" Jacob said.

"I've been fighting."

"With whom?"

He told Jacob he'd started going to protests. The first was just after the semester began, a march to protest the president's Muslim ban. There had been some guys there, Joshua said, white supremacists from Coney Island, at the margins, shouting things.

"Do you mean Staten Island?"

"I don't know. They were white supremacists. Or firefighters. They had jackets."

"Like a club?"

"No, they were just..." Joshua put his left hand on top of his right hand on top of his head. "Shouting things."

Jacob had been at the same march with Maddie and hadn't noticed anything, really, beyond Maddie. Her outrage felt different from his. Quieter, troubled by confusion. She was not chanting as he was chanting, not waving the sign she had made. Before they'd left the apartment, he had prepared by sitting on the radiator in the kitchen and drinking aquavit. She hadn't said anything and then she had said, "A little early?"

"Registries," he'd said. "Muslim bans. What's next," he said, "apartheid?"

She took the bottle from him and slid it back into the freezer. "Of all the words you might choose," Maddie said, "why do you think you chose apartheid?"

Outside, the winter sky looked fresh and raw as a maple branch with the bark peeled back. "The world is full of horrors," Jacob said. "Even here, in this very kitchenette. I don't know how anyone can even imagine raising a child in this world," he said.

Joshua told Jacob, "That was my first fight. I lost," he said. "Bad," he said. After that he couldn't stop. He attended more marches, more meetings, even those for the campus Young Republicans.

"They're all from Long Island," Joshua said. "Most of them are Italians. But some are Jews. Can you imagine?"

Jacob didn't know exactly what he was being asked to imagine. "You shouldn't fight on campus," he said.

"I don't. I follow them to bars afterwards."

Jacob thought: say something sane. "We all want to punch Nazis."

"Then why do you assign them?"

"I don't assign Nazis," Jacob said.

"Becker, Berkovits, Soloveitchik. Israeli fascists."

"Don't be stupid, Joshua," Jacob said.

"When I think of theology," said the dean, "I think of uplift. Was there uplift?"

"In my class?"

The dean nodded.

In smoke, Jacob thought. In fire, in ash.

"I'm not sure what you mean."

"What's the class called again?"

The chair squinted at his computer screen: "*From the Garden to Job, From Diaspora to Anne Frank: Jewish Theology of Exile and Holocaust.*"

"Kind of a long title for a class," said the dean.

Given character limits, on the registration page it had read: *Garden to Holocaust*. Some of the students had seemed confused. Perhaps student confusion was to be expected. But was it to be prevented? If confusion was the subject, why could it not also be the result?

"I hear," the dean said, "that class has not been going well."

In class he had tried to let them confront Berkovits's conception that "*whatever God created, he also created its opposite,*" and got nowhere.

If a thing was defined by its limits, what was a Nazi defining? What was Auschwitz defining? Getting nowhere here was fine; it was almost the point. The impossibility of finding the perfect opposite to Auschwitz proved the flaw in Berkovits's logic. Which is why Berkovits wrote that throughout history there have been "innumerable Aushwitzes." Anyone could tell this was wrong. And here's how the theology worked: in order to make the Shoah align with historical precedent or religious practice, they couldn't look at the Shoah. "But we have an obligation to look, don't we?" Jacob said.

They weren't sure. What good does looking do? Doesn't it just make you angry and scared?

"Maybe," Jacob said.

"And then what?" Joshua asked.

"And then nothing. We have an obligation to look and see. We have an obligation to be terrified. We don't have an obligation to be consoled."

He understood the danger of this logic, the problem it presented them with. Those who do not know the past, repeat it. Those who are traumatized by it do the exact same thing. It was the black hole against whose pull civilization crumpled.

"It would make you sick," Joshua said.

No, Jacob thought, *it would make you Israel.*

Security chased his students out of the auditorium and Jacob had followed, behind them, down the corridor, into the street. They were his students after all. He called out to them. No one turned and security did not pursue them beyond the curb. Later, he went back to his office. Going home was impossible; Maddie was not answering the phone. Around midnight, there was a knock. The building was dark, abandoned, locked. "Who is it?" Jacob called. As in a story, another knock: Joshua in the exit light neon, bleeding from his forehead.

"What should I have done?" Jacob asked his dean.

"What did you do?"

Jacob let him in and sat him down and raised his hair off his brow so that he could see the gash in his forehead—a wide and shallow crescent, like the hull of a ship, and studded with black grit, asphalt—and then unlocked his desk drawer where he stowed a half pint of aquavit and used it, and the tissues every professor kept for when students began to cry, to clean the cut.

"How did you get in?" he asked when he was done.

"I broke a window."

"Did he ask you to clean his cut?" the dean said.

"He didn't really say anything."

His chair was taking notes, typing something on his computer between the comic books and a row of several large figurines, bigger than action figures, specialty models maybe. He stopped and waited for the question that was coming.

"And that night," said the dean, getting to it, "that night, what did you say to him?"

After the meeting with the dean, he went back to his office and found

Joshua there, sitting in the hallway with his back against the door.

"I want to talk about the other night."

"That would have been nice," Jacob said. "A good idea, even. But you've made that impossible."

Joshua stood, still in front of the door. "It's just that, I don't think you have a right to make me feel bad."

That night Joshua had told him the source of his troubles, why he was so upset—and it was a small thing, really, a little self-righteous betrayal of his own values, and Jacob had misread the moment, had not realized that he was looking for absolution, and had not tried to give it to him, he had tried to teach him, to put Joshua's little fuck-up in historical perspective, theological perspective. And when that hadn't worked, when Joshua was still upset at one in the morning, crying, bleeding, smelling of caraway, Jacob, the Wicked Son who had done so much worse, tried to meet him in his shame.

And now Joshua before him, clasping his hands, looking at his feet, obsequious and apologetic.

"Oh, Joshua, just fuck off already," Jacob said. Which Joshua did, right before he went to the liquor store and bought a handle of vodka.

ONCE, WHEN HE WAS STILL ALIVE and her husband, she had come home and found Sam at prayer. He was davening. She knew the motion but had never seen him do it. His back to her, bobbing slightly in their bedroom, deaf to her entrance, lost to an awe she thought he didn't want. She felt betrayed. This was the life he had renounced, a ritual from his days before her, bending to the Law, living as a supplicant. These were *his* critiques of Haredi life. She hadn't asked him to abandon religious practice; in his Jewishness she felt like she was finally discovering her own. But now, catching him at prayer was like finally seeing the coyote whose call you heard at dusk, she was seeing something real, his true self, a Hasid in the wild; after all, Haredi meant *those who tremble before God*, and in this furtive orthodoxy she recognized dissatisfaction with his new life, their life, that he must find lacking in adequate ecstasy.

And then she saw the computer open before him, the breasts bouncing, the neon acrobatics playing for some reason without sound—and realized that he was masturbating.

They hadn't yet solved sex, but still sex was better than she'd thought it would be. On one of their first nights together, his mouth was everywhere, like a boy's, roving her torso with an indiscriminate and goofy ebullience, which was also a little annoying, and she was relieved when she felt the hesitation of new focus, as his mouth, now stranded someplace below her armpit, started shifting lower, and then, frustratingly, paused. In high school, boyfriends facing similar hesitation had just put their hands on the top of her head and pushed. Her own rule was that to instill desire one should display it: she arched her hips and made what she hoped was a series of illuminating gasps. Also, she found her palms on his shoulders, pressing down.

"As far as I can tell there are four kinds of secular rapture," Rivkah had said once, a little drunk, in better times, and Rachel was giggling as Sam eventually rose to meet her with tears in his eyes. A dawning buzzkill. She woke from her body. "What is it, honey?" Eventually, he explained: He had not known he could bring pleasure to another. That his body could be a source of pleasure. She was struck by what he had already told her: How lonely his sex life had been, how he and his wife had been strangers, had gone to bed with the terror of children. So when she found him in the apartment now, she invaded his loneliness, closed the computer and pulled him into bed, where she'd sometimes have to slap him into the moment, out of the stale, dull place his marriage had forced him to fuck from, she'd slap him, she'd grab the sides of his face, *Be with me, Sam, look at me,* shake him into presence, which never quite happened this time, where he remained alone, his eyes glazed, not seeing her where she lay numb and quiet as a video on mute, until he shouted and shifted, pulled out, and came on her face.

After the sputtering aftermath and towel demands: "Fuck, Sam."

He explained, "I just thought. In the secular world."

"You have to ask."

"Ask? What do I ask?"

"May I come on your face? May I please come on your fucking face?"

"I couldn't say that, Rachel."

"All the better."

Later he was shy, apologetic, glum as her childhood golden retriever when they stepped inside from a cookout and found he'd eaten all the cold cuts on the counter.

"Life isn't like pornography," she said. She saw him try to hide his disappointment. "It can be. But we have to decide together." She coined an aphorism. "Sex is something you do. Pornography is something you watch. Do you know what I mean?"

"So it's wrong to watch?"

"Of course not. That not what I meant."

He nodded. They were still in bed, but mostly dressed, sitting cross-legged facing each other.

"It's okay to want things," she said. "I want you to want things." Why was she talking this way? She felt like she was on the Sesame Street episode about facials. "But we should talk about what we want."

"What do you want?" Sam said.

Perhaps life did not need to be lived in ecstasy. The ecstatic was fleeting, a transition, but a transition to what? She knew—because she was told—she was supposed to curate her life, her body, her diet, her experiences until she thrummed with the available miraculous. She was supposed to seek out epiphany. Or not even seek it out, create it. She was supposed to be a living expression of bounty, renewal, her life, even professionally, in art or academia, a visible flourishing.

Cy Twombly had claimed that a painting was the product of "an ecstatic impulse." She had read this in graduate school and never doubted him. The angel appears, and the brush begins to move, one long dripping current of passionate motion like an oar touching water, or the loop of the first starling, the one whose desire stirs the flock to murmuration. And yet she felt unprepared for the revelatory moment. *One ecstatic impulse.* Clearly, the language of epiphany was the language of ejaculation. But then the flaw was in the language. The numinous glow of a Twombly was in no way related to anything Sam might do to her face.

One night, not long after they first met, Rivkah leapt off her stool at the bar and ran into the back room. The lights were low, the ceilings were low, the pool tables were too close together and directly in front of the dart boards. Butt ends of pool cues made dents in the walls, elbows easily swung back into kidneys, to raise a cue above the table was to risk sticking it in someone's eye. Misthrown darts hung from the ceiling like wasps, quivering when the music was loud.

"I'm looking for some real men!" Rivkah shouted. She extended her arms and formed her hands into pincers.

The room's peril did not induce the attitude she was seeking. The guys playing pool had to perch sidesaddle on the top rail—one foot dangling, one hip over the felt—or stand on their tiptoes to take a shot. They did not like it when Rivkah clasped their biceps in her fingers and made a shrill, loud robotic buzz as if they had given the wrong answer on a game show.

"We need to find a better bar," Rivkah said.

Back in her apartment, Rachel unpacked some old pajamas, black ones with white cats on them, that a boyfriend had given her. Because cat pajamas were a weird gift to give someone early in a relationship and she couldn't figure out his motivation, whether the pajamas were a joke or a threat, she had never worn them. She helped Rivkah take off the makeup she had helped her put on. They washed their faces at the same small sink and got into bed.

"I wanted some men to kidnap my children for me," Rivkah said. "Is it too much to ask?"

"No," Rachel said. "That's what men are good for."

"Am I wearing cats? I don't like cats."

"I know, sweetie."

"I'm so lonely," Rivkah said, and in the next moment Rachel made one of her many mistakes, or what felt like mistakes in the months that followed when Rivkah and then Sam turned their gazes, naked and ferocious, on her and she quoted for Rivkah some of the last lines from the *Song of Songs*, lines that Lurio had inked into his final panel: *O you who linger in the garden, a lover is waiting.*

She had meant it as a promise. Confronted by their desire for the world, she pretended she was the world. But she had forgotten what the world was. She had, she later came to feel, misunderstood the poem's tone in a way that a real Jew never would. The moment in the garden has passed, it passes in dream, the lover knocks but you have already chosen not to open the door. Her education should have prepared her for this. All art is about the longing of exiles. You believe, remembering the fragments of some older summer day—ripe fruit, cut flowers in a vase by the window, the sound of children's voices in the park—that this is something you can offer as your own. And yet, what is bounty but a consequence of reaping? It was always already too late. The new trees are stunted, sun-bleached. The angel is behind you with his flaming sword. The garden was the one place you could not linger.

JACOB'S FATHER USED TO SAY, "If you are lucky, even your ox will calve."

Jacob's luck, and Joshua's as well, was that although Joshua drank lots of the vodka he bought after leaving Jacob's office and took lots of pills, the pills were Benadryl and before he took them he texted his RA, his parents, and most of his friends in his dorm. So he recovered, and after he recovered things moved swiftly and Jacob was informed that his contract would not be renewed.

He did not tell Maddie why. He said only that a student had been upset by class and had attempted suicide.

"Can they fire you for that?" She didn't sound convinced. They were taking an evening walk, one of the early summer habits they had not deserted, and from the basketball court around the corner there was music, men's shouts, the squeak of sneakers reeling on the blacktop, the wide thud of the balls blurring into echo. Someone was having a cookout, the streets were full of blossoming trees.

"Do you blame me?" he asked.

"For what?" She stopped walking. She looked at him. Her expression was as vague as a traffic jam. He watched her decide to say where she was stuck. "So what are you going to do now?"

It was a question about his future that did not include her. The next week, Maya's phone calls began.

Two months later, a few days before the fire and the morning in the park, he came home and found her in the kitchen drinking wine and slicing tomatoes. He tried to gauge by the number of tomatoes whether she was making dinner for both of them, as she still sometimes did. How many tomatoes would one person eat? Another mystery. He put down his bag, poured himself a glass of wine and then wondered if he should have asked.

She smiled, handed him a sliver of fresh mozzarella. "How was your day?"

The results were unequivocal: getting fucked improved her mood.

"Good news," he said. "I'll be able to move out sooner than we expected. Alex Baruch has offered me a job."

She turned away from him and washed her knife in the sink. The water ran over the blade, but she didn't reach for a sponge or soap. "What does that man want?"

"He's reopening his Kabbalah school down the street and thinks I should run it."

"You don't know Kabbalah and you're not a therapist."

"I know more about Kabbalah than most people."

"So does Madonna."

Jacob laughed. He tried to make eye contact with Maddie. Two nights ago, when he picked up the phone he said, *Why are you doing this to me?* He poured more wine.

"I won't be teaching or doing therapy. I'll be managing it. Helping shape curriculum. A public face. And a partial owner."

He watched her expression change. It was like the brief moments when he caught her unawares and she forgot she was leaving him, pleasure followed by disappointment. "So he wants an investment."

Jacob nodded.

"Oh, Jake."

"It's not like that."

"It isn't?"

"He's rich. He doesn't need money."

"Jacob, he's a liar and con man. If he didn't need money, why would he ask you for it?"

"Are you saying I'm a mark?"

She was holding a bunch of basil. She brought it to her nose to smell and hid behind it. "Why do you trust him?"

"He trusts me," Jacob said. He was almost shouting. "He believes in me."

"Why?" Maddie dropped the basil on the counter, she moved toward him, she reached for his arm but he pulled away. Her eyes were bright. "You don't even know the man."

It was true, Jacob had only formally met Alex Baruch once. At a conference in Berlin when he was still a graduate student. Jacob had just given a paper about the way early, secular Zionists misrepresented Enlightenment philosophy. The paper did not go over well and it didn't deserve to. He had known when he wrote it that it wasn't very good, it was reductive, shaped by outrage, smug. That he believed what he wrote didn't matter. Standing there at the lectern, a little dazed by the light of the projector, wincing as no one else had seemed to wince at the illumination, he felt himself revealed as a fraud.

Afterward he had immediately left the conference center and begun drinking, wandering from bar to bar through Berlin, whose streets were wide and busy, then narrow, contoured amid its hundred architectures, the slow glint of the river Spree and the electric streetcars stopped at intersections, filled with light.

At some point every bar he went into had live music playing, and he didn't want to hear live music; he was back in the street, on cobbles now, and lost. It was very late. The few people who passed him barged by in groups, laughing or shouting, unaddressable, eating kebabs, curtained with smoke—which was when he ran into Alex Baruch.

He had seen him earlier in the day, moving through the hotel lobby. There had been a murmur in the room, a change of atmosphere, the crowd compressed and then released and then there he was, Alex Baruch, radiating energy like a storm—such was his gravitas at that time, the great man whose words had passed sentence on the century. He was walking slowly, alone, out of a conference room and toward the lobby bar, his unnecessary nametag hanging from the lanyard around his neck, its laminated cheapness jarring against his beautiful clothes, the cornflower blue shirt and tan linen blazer he wore even though it was winter. A woman in a dress like a flight attendant's—stiff, sleeveless, emerald, the hotel uniform—approached him. She whispered something in his ear and he nodded and touched her hand and she swished away into the soft shadows of the far bar near the piano where the lights were lower, her dress paling like absinthe as water is added. It was the first time Jacob had seen Baruch since he attended the two Second Generation meetings, almost a year earlier, after Maddie lost the baby, where neither of them—Baruch in the back standing against the wall, or Jacob in the nervous circle—had spoken. But now they were together, alone in the street, and Baruch looked him directly in the eye and took his hand and shook it and told him that he had liked his paper, that he agreed with his conclusions, even if the premises were all wrong.

"In which case I'm honored," Jacob said.

"For what?"

"To be wrong in your presence."

Baruch waved it away—but how could he? He was a legend, likely to be a Nobel laureate. An intellectual whose capacity for forgiveness, for compassion, transformed the very acts of writing, of speaking, of thinking into humanitarian gestures. When it came to the Shoah and the life of the soul after it, there was no voice more hopeful or popular. He had counselled Rabin, sat with Arafat in Ramallah. He was impossibly good, definitively wise, an angel, a tzadik, a *lamed vav*. He was presenting the keynote.

Even though it was February, Baruch was not wearing a coat over his linen blazer. His hands were gloveless. He reached into his jacket and removed a flask, which he pointed at Jacob. "I've seen you before."

He must have been referring to the Second Generation meetings.

"I can't believe you remember me."

"Remembering is the easy part. Knowing what to do with memory, well there…" Baruch frowned, he sipped from his flask, lights in the building across the street went out. "But you never came back."

Jacob did not know what to say. He didn't want to be a second generation or a third generation, he wanted no part in the lineage of someone else's suffering. But saying that, insisting upon it, as he had in Israel, felt only like a betrayal of that suffering. People loved Baruch's work because in the jugular spurt of apocalyptic violence he had found meaning and forgiveness. Apparently the world could learn something from Alex Baruch. But *what*? Baruch could understand or forgive or forsake or forget because it had all happened to him. For Jacob, there was no history that could explain anything. It was just dreams all the way down.

"Did you know this city is full of boars?" Baruch asked.

Was this a joke about Germans? "I'm sorry," Jacob said. "But I can't tell if you're speaking literally."

"Wild pigs," Baruch said. "Thousands roam the streets in winter. They come out of the forests and live in the sewers. Or so I'm told." He handed Jacob his flask. "Have a drink. To give a talk is a big thing. Especially so early in one's career."

Although he had been drinking all night, Jacob could still tell that whatever Baruch had offered him was significantly above his paygrade. He felt a flood of gratitude toward the world: he had given a paper that nobody liked and suddenly he was alone in a European capital with a genius, drinking cognac. This was how life might go from here.

Baruch slapped him on the back and then took his elbow. "Come on. Let's go find the pigs," he said.

Sometime before dawn, in an empty street, a family of boars appeared, trotting out of the wide horizontal rectangle of white light—the entrance to a subway station—at the base of an otherwise dark building. Cars hadn't passed for a while and no windows were lit but the vapor lamps were still on and the boars snuffled orange steam and

Jacob could hear the furnace chugging away in the building that he leaned against with Baruch. He was tapping, as quietly as he could, on the bricks. There was something wrong with the night, with him being here in Berlin, enjoying himself in Berlin, with an old man he admired in Berlin, among these people, in this terrible country, watching monsters eat trash.

"The first one I killed was a baby," Baruch said.

"Excuse me?"

"The first boar. Its mother had been shot by partisans in the woods. I was hiding in a log and I was starving and all I could smell was them cooking this boar. I was sick with hunger. I chewed my own hand, I chewed the inside of the log, I chewed on insects, as they cooked the boar and ate it. Certainly I was delirious, dreaming, sweating, stuffing rags into my mouth to keep myself quiet. Had it happened another time, a few days earlier, or later, it would have been worse. I might have wandered out into the forest and approached the group. Either way, by some luck, I passed out and when I awoke it was dawn and the partisans had left and a baby was crying. That's what I thought. The soldiers had left a baby. I remember, even now, lying there crammed in a hollow, half-rotten log thinking: *They have left a baby*. And then I believed I was the baby and that I was the one who was crying. And who knows? Perhaps I was. And later, as the cries continued, my perception shifted and I dreamed that the baby was with a woman, a Russian peasant, though we weren't in Russian territory, and the woman was his mother, who was then—as easy as that—my mother and she was calling to me, telling me to come out, which terrified me even more because my mother had been dead for two years and once a parent is dead, even when you dream about them, even when they are alive in your dreams and touching you, or chatting about the weather, or reminding you of a chore, you always know that they are dead, this is not knowledge that you can forget, and then, when I said that to myself, my mother has been dead for two years, when I said that, the sound shifted, like a charm, and I heard the cry for what it was—the baby boar wailing for its mother."

He passed Jacob the flask again. The building before them was like a head tilted back, opening in a gaping symmetrical scream.

"In any case," Baruch said, "when I found it, it was surrounded by several other baby boars, but they were already dead. Certainly, an animal would come to eat it soon. An eagle or a wolf, or another boar. Or, this is what I tell myself now. At the time, I was weeping with gratitude as I ate it."

Jacob was impressed by how easily he told the story. Or how, in telling it, he made it seem like a story, not a revelation of trauma requiring Jacob's empathy or understanding. And yet again he was struck by his own inability to relate to the way Baruch bore his history. What for Jacob was terrifying in its groundless unreality, nightmare or myth, the genesis of the adult world, was for Baruch a simple fable. In the past, interviewers had noted the same thing—the way Baruch owned what his story meant—which was why when he opened his school of Kabbalistic Therapy for the Healing of Trauma and Self-Actualization, replete with what scholars would otherwise scoff off as a mix of Jewish mysticism and Jungian mumbo-jumbo, Baruch's famous ease with his own trauma was taken as a sign of the validity of his therapeutic model.

And it would still be, for several more years after that moment in Berlin, when Baruch turned and placed his hand on Jacob's shoulder and said, "I liked your talk very much. And I liked how uncomfortable you were giving it. How else should a person be?"

Jacob did not see him again. That morning, after returning to his hotel, he came down with a stomach bug and he did not make it to the keynote lecture. Back in New York, Baruch invited him to talks and functions at the Kabbalah school, but in those days he could not bear to return there, to sit again as in perpetual shiva among those people, in that community that included him, and he never visited the Kabbalah school even after he got his doctorate and his new job and was, by that time, living just blocks from its door. And yet, they kept in touch occasionally via polite postcard or email, and it was a small and lovely thing in Jacob's life, this correspondence with a great man, and when Baruch was revealed as a fraud and chose to flee the city, it felt almost right to Jacob, or if not right, then inevitable, and he knew then what he had never known before: why Baruch had approached him in the first place.

For years, as his career as a scholar and academic floundered, he had used that night in Berlin to assuage his doubts and bolster his sense of his own possibility, but now he realized that, as if by some alchemy of unstable elements, Baruch had been drawn to a similar soul or mind—that of a grifter—and Jacob felt found out; his relationship with the renowned scholar, the respect they seemed to share, was just another lie he was telling. So, though a surprise, it felt only right when, late that spring, he received a letter from Baruch saying, *I hear you are in need of a job?*

A WEEK AFTER HE FIRST LEFT his community and moved in with Rachel, Samuel's parents showed up at her door.

They stood there, side by side, darkly bedecked, wild-eyed. They seemed tired, surprised, as if she was the one who had appeared unannounced. They would not cross the threshold, but his mother peered in, past Rachel, saw the mezuzah on the door frame and frowned.

"Jewish at least," she said.

"How can you tell?" his father muttered. "What kind of Jew… what kind of woman…" He held out his hand, it was trembling, he could not speak. Rivkah had told her about his rages. His hand was still extended, he opened and closed his mouth and both women waited for him to finish his thought. He was used to this, he took his time, he trembled, he stammered, he struggled for just the right word. "A whore," he said finally and spat on her doorstep.

Samuel was in the bathroom, in the tub with the shower curtain closed, hiding.

"I'd like you to go," Rachel said.

"So he won't come out? He won't even face his family?"

"He's not here."

"He's here," his mother said.

For all Rachel knew, the building was still being watched. Samuel's mother said something in Yiddish.

"What?"

"You know he has a wife already? And a child?"

"He also has a sister," Rachel said. Rivkah had left her family a year earlier, and her parents had never mentioned her or gone looking for her. They disowned her and let her husband's family harass her and steal her children. Once she had seen them in the street. It was a month after she'd been hit by a car and she was in a cast. She had grabbed her father's arm and begged him to intercede for her. "They're going to kill me," she said. He had slapped her face, spit at her feet, and said, "To me you are already dead." Since then, she had been hospitalized twice for overdoses, and each time, when Samuel called to tell them, they hung up the phone. Now they stood at Rachel's door, daring to accuse her of anything. She said it again, "He has a sister too."

"No," their father said, "he does not."

His words were prophetic. A week later Rivkah threw herself off the Brooklyn Bridge. That night, after they got the call, after they found out that his parents refused to identify the body, that her husband had told the police he didn't know her, after Samuel, finally, had gone to the morgue with Rachel, after drinks in some bleary bar, Rachel stood in the street under the awning of a Korean supermarket, with a pretzel in one hand and a Dr. Pepper spiked with gin in the other, and started to cry. She had been the one who invited Rivkah out for coffee after a NextSteps meeting, who befriended her and told her—the World-to-Come notwithstanding—this was her life, right now, this very moment, and she should start living it. She had encouraged her to leave and then not known how to help her once she did; she had not been able to find her a good job or afford rehab and now was asking for comfort when she was the one who should be giving it. She reached her full hands around him, tried not to spill, put her head on his chest and sobbed. Later, once he was also dead and it was too late, she would think back on that moment and realize it was the one time in their relationship where she acted like he had something he could give her, where she needed something from him.

He took her wet cheeks in his hands; he stepped back so he could see into her eyes; under the grocery's neon window lights his face was blue and smooth, shadowless, handsome—he dropped to his knees and asked her to marry him. His wife had not yet granted his divorce, his sister was in the morgue, he was wild with pain, he was not free—she said yes. She had never been one to consider omens, so she did not imagine this a bad way to start a marriage. And she also did not consider psychology, why he might be asking her, why she might be agreeing. Isn't this what the world wanted? For her to doubt everything, for her to think everything needed examining, for her to read her every desire as a symptom? To insist she was nothing but a tangle of hungry emotions, of want, of need, to make her distrust every impulse, to make her scorn impulse entirely, as if any choice she made based on something she wanted must be wrong. Well, fine, she thought in the days following his proposal. She would use her expertise. It was a question of composition: the moment was fraught and beautiful, its danger made it real, his sorrow made them both alive, and what was marriage if not a celebration of life? When the angels appeared before Sarah and told her she was going to be a mother at ninety, she laughed—she laughed at the angels, she laughed at God—not because she doubted fortune or grace, but because when those gifts appeared, they always appeared impossible.

His parents did not turn up again after his death, not at her apartment or his funeral. But for a while men stood in the street watching her windows, taped notes to her mailbox, and at night sometimes the phone would ring and she'd answer it to silence, not heavy breathing, not a threat, just the palpable throb of recrimination and longing—her job had trained her in the nuances of phone silence—so that at first she imagined it was Samuel calling her, that these were calls from the dead, and she was hopeful and terrified both by the possibility of speaking with him again and by the fact that she was even thinking this way—and then she realized one night with certainty that it was his mother who was calling.

"Eliana," she said into the quiet.

"I'm sorry for your loss," she said after a while. "For both of them. I can't imagine." Saying this made her angry, even if it was true. They were her losses as well. Rivkah was her friend, Samuel her husband, and no one who knew them was comforting her. Still, into the silence she whispered each time, "If you ever want to talk…"

The day before Rachel was supposed to head up to Maine, Eliana finally appeared at her door. They stood together in the living room where she had lived with Samuel. Eliana held her handbag in front of her body. She didn't know what to do. It occurred to Rachel that she hadn't known why she was coming, she just wanted to see something of her son's. Rachel offered her a drink and she declined, she offered her a seat and she took it.

"So, it's true," she said finally. "From you even he divorced as well?"

Rachel nodded.

"Twice divorced." Eliana whistled, and looked up at the ceiling. "There was even another woman, I heard? Is this the son I raised?"

"I don't know."

"It breaks my heart."

"He also threw himself in front of a train," Rachel said.

Eliana covered her mouth like she was going to cough. "They never told me how," she whispered.

Rachel went into the kitchen and got her a glass of water. When she returned she said, "I'm sorry. I shouldn't have said it like that."

"No." Eliana took the water and started to stand and then sat again. "No. Thank you. A mother should know."

She sighed. Her face softened. She was much younger than Rachel had at first thought, not even fifty. Standing next to Samuel's father, Rachel had barely glanced at her, she was focused on the older, angry man calling her a whore on her doorstep while his son hid in the tub. But she had just told Eliana how violently her son had died; she was obliged to look her in the eye—and her skin was unlined, her eyes were dark and bright and her hair, well Rachel didn't know what color her real hair was or how old she must have been when she conceived Sam and it occurred to her that these were things she had never asked Samuel and now every part of his life, even this trivia, the ugliness and futility of sitting with his mother in their apartment, made her miss him. Maybe Eliana was thinking the same thing. There must be a thousand things she had hoped to say or ask or discover about her son as well.

"When he left we assumed you must be big and blonde with the broisten out to here," Eliana said, waving into space. "We thought it was the strangeness of another woman he was looking for. But you. It's not an insult, but you look like a Jew."

"I am."

Eliana looked down: she didn't agree, or didn't care, or it wasn't her point. "What I realized when I saw you is that he wasn't leaving for a woman. It wasn't for love. It wasn't for pleasure. He was just running away from us."

There was so much Rachel wanted to say. But what good had saying anything ever done. Tomorrow she'd drive with a stranger to the sanitarium by the sea. Again, she felt like the lover from the *Song of Songs*. It was as if she were asleep but her heart was wakeful, just listening for the right knock.

"Why did you come here tonight?"

"I don't have any pictures of Samuel. My husband never approved of them and he destroyed them when Sam went off the derech."

Rachel only had one non-digital picture: a polaroid taken at a house party in Queens. Sam with his beard shaved and his Mets cap on backwards, toasting the camera with a Pepsi spiked with schnapps. He looked drunk and young and happy.

Eliana's eyes widened when she saw it. "Oy, Sammy."

"I know," Rachel said. "But he's smiling."

The sun was down. Huge moths, moths the size of birds, banged at the windows. Eliana nodded, brought the picture to her lips, and then put it in her bag.

BOOK II: NOD

Why Does Jacob Limp?

The Talmud tells that every person has a secret name and for every name there is an angel who knows it.

The secret name is given to us at birth by our parents, or just whispered by them to themselves in the dark, or passed between their mouths during conception, or dreamed and never spoken, and it contains in its syllables the entirety of our character. It is to this that our angel, the angel that knows our name, bears witness and it is this that the angel, when the time comes, proclaims before the Lord.

Our angels represent our secret self—they know it, they reflect it, from the soul's shadows they arise and testify to its contours. And yet, and here is the contradiction: they cannot be known.

Genesis 32: The patriarch Jacob, son of Isaac, fighting through the night with his angel demands to know the angel's name. The angel: "You must not ask me my name."

What is the nature of the encounter? A wrestling match, an accusation. The angel approached Jacob after he sent his family away, and they fought through the night. They could not see each other's faces. The striving was done, as it always is, in darkness.

To say that something is done in darkness, what does it mean? Not that it cannot be experienced. But that it cannot be fully apprehended. Or, what we apprehend, we resist. And yet when the angels bear witness to our lives, it is this life they will be reflecting. For although the secret self is always unknown to us, it is also all we know.

And so we must make our account, our defense and prosecution both, to our angels.

This is what Jacob was doing in Genesis when he fought with the angel at the ford of Jabbok. The angel wrenched his hip from its socket, but Jacob kept wrestling. The angel cried, finally, "Let me go for dawn is breaking."

And when Jacob would not, the angel relented and opened his mouth and in his mouth, suspended like the webbing of an adder's fangs, was a silver mirror where Jacob perceived the shape of his own new syllables.

(The voices of angels like our faces in a mirror).

To encounter our angel is to be transformed.

Jacob's name forever after: Israel. A man who walked with a limp.

But why a limp? The injuries our battles with our angels reveal are the ones we already carry. Jacob who was Esau and then Jacob again and then Israel walked with his old name in his pocket like a stone. It was small—at any moment he might even toss it away—but it was heavy, it held him down and back, and his leg dragged when he tried to place it on the road ahead.

—Alex Baruch, "Why Does Jacob Limp?" from *Dreams from the Talmud: Ancient Lessons for Personal Acceptance and Spiritual Healing*

THEY DROVE NORTH in Rachel's orange MG with the top down, the wind in their faces, and sounds of the highway, the open road letting them slide out of conversation when they needed to. They were taking the long route through the center of New Hampshire, they had a map open between them, they had all day and more: it was Tuesday morning, Jacob was not expected until dinner time, and the auction was not until Friday.

She hadn't driven in over six months, and not this car since before Samuel died, since before they were married, even, when she took him on a road trip in early summer with the top down, raced up through the Connecticut Berkshires into the Western Massachusetts hill towns. It had been a surprise: she had packed a bag of clothes she had bought for him and he was surprised—he had stared at the old convertible and kept saying, "I didn't know that you were rich." She told herself this was the wonder she was expecting, but it was more childish, more startled, than delighted. When they passed farms he covered his nose. She gave him a baseball cap and he insisted on wearing it backward. Now she was driving in the open air, in high summer, with Jacob, and he looked properly appreciative, relaxed, leaning back, taking it in.

In his lap he held a pile of CDs. She had not been sure she would take the MG, and so when he offered to bring music she hadn't told him the car didn't have a CD player. He had also brought a map and seemed self-conscious about it. "I like to keep my phone off," he said.

"I know you wanted to take the scenic route," he said, "but the scenic route isn't a good place for lost Jews."

The map thrashed in the open air. He held it out, away from his face, like a baby that wasn't his. "You can never put the map back in the bottle," he said.

Bordering the road on both sides was a dark screen of forest. The clearings were cluttered with trailers, broken furniture, a sign selling deer tags, another selling silt.

Before that morning Rachel hadn't known if she would be able to generate the enthusiasm the sports car demanded. She liked to tell people it was a gift from her grandfather, a hand-me-down, when in reality she had bought it herself, crazily, after passing her exams, with her last four thousand dollars. "Your *last* four thousand dollars!" the few friends she told the truth to had said, gaping at her from the hardscrabble awe of their own bookish debt. But the fellowship at the Prado had netted her a good deal of freelance work, and at the time the work, academia, the future had all seemed like gifts that the present would keep giving. She imagined herself arriving at her first job at a liberal arts college somewhere in the country, the young professor sweeping into town in her orange MG, a soft calfskin leather satchel on the seat beside her, boots the same color as the satchel, glasses the same color as her hair and a small collection, eccentrically curated amid the golden fields—but that life, all the lives she had imagined, failed to materialize. Now Rachel kept the MG at her parents' house. Her mother drove it sometimes, on weekends with her friends, to keep it, she claimed, from rusting.

At first, after Jacob's call, she'd been eager, and then doubtful—*who was this person her uncle had found?* —and then annoyed, but Baer was right: Jacob was Baruch's guest and potential business partner, he had access to Baruch, to the Lurio, and besides, he said he'd pay for gas. When she'd picked him up he was standing on the curb looking slightly confused, peering each way, not sure from which direction her car would come. He smiled when she pulled up before him, he waved like a child might at a passing fire engine, he had only one small bag and wasn't wearing seersucker.

"What kind of tree do you think that is?" he said now pointing at some especially tall evergreen.

It looked like a spruce, but she wasn't sure. She knew Van Gogh's cypress, Monet's willows and poplars. She had thought that in learning them she was learning what she'd need. It shocked her sometimes how unprepared she was for the life she actually led.

"I don't know," she said

"It's a spruce. I think it's a blue spruce."

If he knew, why was he asking her? And yet his expression was as guileless as a puddle. On the highway, with the CDs in his lap and the map clutched to his chest, fluttering around his chin, he had looked slapped and baffled by speed; on backroads, now, he was more relaxed, affable and chatty, not very nervous.

"It's not blue," Rachel said.

Often people would call Rachel's museum line to ask questions about colors she couldn't see, to say, "Why is the sky green in this painting?" or "What does the purple in his skin symbolize?" These were the words they used, as if the art was a code and Rachel possessed the cipher and yet she'd look at the painting, stare hard at what they were staring hard at, and she'd have no possible idea what they were talking about. She thought most likely they did not actually want her to explain any hidden symbolism but to confirm the interpretation that they already believed. Maybe perception is relative—after all, the spruce *was* bluish—but she was surrounded by buffoons and lunatics.

She mentioned this to Jacob. She said, "I'm surrounded by buffoons and lunatics," and then when he didn't respond she explained what she meant and did not care if he thought she was being uncharitable.

"You don't think I'm being uncharitable?" she said.

"Maimonides claimed that the worst form of charity was the kind given out of pity. But I should warn you in advance that I have never accurately applied philosophy to life."

They passed a billboard for a fertility clinic. The babies looked like enormous pink tadpoles listing toward the road with drunken human smiles. Or maybe it wasn't a fertility clinic? She glanced again in her rearview mirror: pigeons roosted on the struts and crossbeams on the back side of the billboard.

She said, "Ultimately, I wonder if it's my job to tell them that what they see isn't there, or to ask them to better explain what they see."

"It's like the difference between a good therapist and bad one," said Jacob.

She laughed. "Exactly."

A river flowed alongside the road. They were on the other side of town now, surrounded by shops for skis and water sports and hiking gear and beers, and she was suddenly hungry or sick of driving or in need of a drink. She pulled over and parked by the village green with its small memorial for some war dead and a flaking white gazebo where a few homeless men slept.

"Wait," she said. "Which one is the good therapist and which the bad?"

"I have no idea," he said. "It's probably something I should ask Alex Baruch."

They ate lunch suspended above the river in a refurbished mill that now served as a brewpub. Rachel ordered some kind of stout. "May I ask you a personal question?" she said.

He waved his hands in an expression of beneficence, as if he were offering her all the beers.

"How can you trust Baruch?"

"Trust in what way?"

"He's a fraud."

"On the other side of fraudulence, there's what?"

"My uncle." She turned away from him to stare at the draft list on the chalkboard.

Their food appeared from behind the bar like a bad trick and her salad was mostly bacon and potatoes. They sat and ate quietly. On the open road, as she drove, they had entered these pockets of comfort, and though she didn't know Jacob she felt a sense of ease, she felt visible and real. And now, suddenly, the moment swiveled back to reality: visible to whom? Understood by whom? The conditions of her satisfaction required that another be there to witness her. She looked up from her ludicrous salad and watched Jacob swish and smell his beer like wine, drink it, stare at his phone—which was off—and she was filled with a fresh incomprehension.

"Why are you going up there?" she asked.

"Alex Baruch invited me."

"But to do what?"

"I don't know. To have dinner, to discuss his methods, to meet some of his patients and attend the auction."

"That's the itinerary. But why are you going?"

"To sit by the ocean? To read without the sound of traffic? To see a moose?"

She became, briefly, her mother: she arched her eyebrows, lowered her chin and stared at him, hard, down her nose, over the rim of her beer.

"If I'm going to invest, I need to know what I'm investing in," he said.

She wanted him to explain something essential. He went out of his way for her uncle, a poor lost-looking old man who accosted him in the park. He had a moral compass that not only allowed him to feel, but to act. And yet she could not square that with this sham.

"Baruch's reputation is built on a lie. Won't you feel sullied?"

"Even if he's not who he says he is," Jacob said, "he's still a great scholar."

"If you respect scholarship so much, why not stay in academia?

Jacob finished his beer. He looked wildly down for a moment at the empty glass as if: now what?

"Teaching is no longer an option."

Baer had told her Jacob was getting divorced. He had said it like somehow this would make the weekend more enticing for her, like people who were entangled in failing relationships made for good company. She put her hand to her mouth. "You didn't…" she said. "Not with a student?"

"No," he said. "God no. Nothing like that." And then he began to laugh.

She didn't pry. How could she judge the endpoint of an academic career from her empty basement with its lone black phone? She waited for him to stop laughing. It was like when someone has a sneezing fit in public, it shouldn't be embarrassing, but it is—you get the sense of something out of control, something hidden now escaping, like a rat that gives birth in the walls.

When they left the bar, both sides of the street were empty and bright and under the river breeze the shadows of store awnings ruffled across the brick sidewalk. The homeless men were gone from the gazebo. Something scrabbled in a black iron trashcan. The sun was in her face and she felt the beer. She placed her hand on the hot hood of the MG.

"At the inn, don't tell Baruch who I am," she said. She reached back to put up her hair, but she had not taken it down. "Tell him I'm your wife."

"He knows about my marriage," Jacob said. "He knows I'm getting a divorce."

"In that case, we won't have to fake much intimacy."

"Is that what you're supposed to do with intimacy?" Jacob said. "If only I'd known."

She had to look: he was smiling and game, and she was relieved.

"What kind of name is Nod? It's like a cult there, isn't it?" she asked.

"It's a retreat."

"Is it?"

"I don't know," he said.

Afterward, driving again, north and out of town, into the mountains, the air was suddenly bright with the smell of freshwater and pine. Cooled by pockets of damp green mountain shadow, the sun felt wonderful on her face. She wanted to take her hair down, but the wind would wreck it. In flashes, summer would always give her the feeling that she was twenty again.

"Are you going to try to steal the Lurio?" Jacob asked her finally.

In the Jewish graveyard, she had felt the limits of her knowledge. She had said a Mourner's Kaddish, but was that even the right thing to do? She had gathered mourners' stones from the grass, but on which graves was she supposed to put them? An old man in a light blue suit, carrying flowers, stood at a plot not far from her and began to bay like a calf. The world was a mess of pain she could not remedy. She knelt and reached down into the dirt. To feel the earth on her hands. To find a little rock and lift it. To put one pebble on the right stone would be a start.

"I don't know what I'm going to do," she said.

THEY ARRIVED AFTER SEVEN. It had been a long drive: for hours they had driven north, and then for hours they had driven east. Jacob had never been up here; the continent seemed to keep rambling away from itself, spilling into the Atlantic, and though it was late, though they drove away from the sun, its rays were so low—tangling in the bare pine branches, caught in the spray at the water's edge—that the sense he had was not of heading into darkness or even dusk, but into increasing light. The reversal was a gift, a small enchantment. He felt like a person stepping into a lit and heated pool at midnight in the country.

Not far from Nod, a man with a wild red beard and a walking stick stood by the side of the road, in front of an abandoned gas station, with his arm extended. He looked like a prophet: the thicket of hair, the staff and the outstretched hand.

"Look," Jacob had said. "Moses."

"Who still hitchhikes?"

Jacob had seen the hand, but missed the thumb. As with Baer in the park, all the signs were there—he had seen them and still failed to recognize what they meant, and then the man was behind them as they crossed the causeway and hit the dirt road following a valley of granite-strewn grass down toward the cliffs, land's end, and Nod. Now what was he missing? Across the wide glacial plain, little bonfires seemed to flare. As the car moved, the angle changed: they were not fires but tall clusters of metal sculptures, catching sun.

"This, by the way, is what I meant by cult," Rachel said.

The road wound along the hill, dropped into the pines, and then opened again into a clearing for the final approach to the manor. Rachel drove slowly. Her mouth was tight, her sunglasses were still on, flashing, and Jacob felt as if he should say something to her, welcome her to this place he had never been, but aside from being presumptuous, he knew that to welcome her here would put him, with Baruch and his patients, on the other side of their secret.

The manor, directly before them now, was as he had imagined it: columned, porched, hunkered in brick and stone. Long slabs of razored slate scaled the roof. The windows shimmered with leaded panes, too many and too small: the house seemed to be squinting. It was a place out of season. You would want to approach it in winter, in the snow and the dark where the only light was its own.

They passed through the open iron gate, turned into the rotunda, and like a trick, another glimmer of enchantment, Baruch was there, waiting for them. Of course, from his vantage Rachel's little orange car must have announced itself like a flame sweeping down the long wick of the road.

They parked and stepped out onto the gravel; Baruch danced toward them with wide open arms.

"Jacob! At last!" He pulled him into a hug. He smelled of sunscreen and cloves, his forehead bumped Jacob's chest, he was shorter than Jacob remembered, he must have shrunk, and the physical contact, its simple intimacy was surprising, but when he stepped back, still smiling, he was as Jacob expected: decorous, genteel, only slightly stooped, wearing immaculate white linen pants and a long sleeve pink polo shirt buttoned to the top. He was standing before a wild bush of sea roses, and his skin, deeply tanned, glowed like clover honey—against it, his white mustache looked whiter. Leaning on the bench where he must have been sitting and waiting was a Malacca cane.

Jacob gestured to Rachel. "This is my wife." He waved between them like a mime indicating a table. "Rachel, this is Alex Baruch."

Baruch bowed. "How lovely to meet you, Rachel. And what a surprise. Living so close for so many years, it's somehow funny that we meet here."

"It's an honor," Rachel said, but she had not stepped fully around the MG, her arms were crossed in front of her body, and her shoulders had rounded like she was trying to close a set of wings. "Where should we put the car?"

He brushed the question away. You did not ask the master of the house about the car. "Let's get you settled first. To here, it's a long drive. From anywhere. You must be tired."

If he was annoyed, Jacob could not hear it. Baruch lifted his cane and held out his hand in welcome. He was graceful and undiminished. Rachel approached him in a burst, the way a cat finally decides to enter a room, and he took her arm, and Jacob stood there looking around and, because he was supposed to be her husband, lifted her bags from the boot and followed them into the manor.

Inside, the foyer was dark and cramped. A plaster ceiling with black wood crossbeams hung low and unevenly above their heads, the walls were close and stone. It was a cold hall out of a gothic novel, Rachel thought. Before her was the count striding with his cane, behind them—she turned once to see him—Jacob hustled along, a bag in each hand like a porter or the mad doctor's assistant, someone complicit in this world.

They turned the corner into a wide shock of gilded rooms.

"This is the lobby," Baruch said, waving his cane like a wand. A teak desk with a banker's lamp was positioned against the wall, unmanned. Beyond it, the room opened into settees and armchairs, coffee tables and bookshelves all arranged around a great stone fireplace in purple and green, rich, wintery hues echoed in the frayed array of Persian rugs placed over the golden pine floors so that the room recalled a Swiss chalet except that the whole far side of the building gave way to enormous French doors, propped open onto patios, courtyards, the electric green of the lawn, heading down to the cliff, the shore, and the moving summer shimmer of the sea.

"I hope you're not too hungry," Baruch said. "We don't eat until nine. A nod to how my father would do things."

In Berlin? Or the sanatorium that didn't exist? Rachel wanted to ask. But the moment passed. Baruch was now explaining that he had recently installed a windmill to power the island. He gestured toward the sky, the direction the wind came from. What kind of man points at wind?

"And now a brief tour," Baruch said.

All the rooms—the drawing room, the dining room—lay open to the sea and were connected to each other by wide unclosed doors, so that Rachel felt less like she was passing through individual chambers and more that, as in dream, the space was simply shifting around her. The white tablecloths, the plants, the pages of books all fluttered in the breeze that moved through the corridors. It was as if the house were breathing.

"Where is everybody?" she asked.

Baruch ushered them out onto the lawn. Empty Adirondack chairs faced the sunset, the crushed shell path among the stone planters gleamed like glass. The air had turned lilac.

Most of the house was still unknown. When they entered the main room again, there was a young man standing in the corner behind an armchair like a butler, staring at them.

"Daniel," Baruch said. "Perfect timing. Can you show Jacob and—" he paused and smiled and touched his mustache—"Rachel to their room?"

The young man, Daniel, nodded, but did not move. He was beautiful. He had a face like a Russian ballet star's: violet crescents bruised the hollows beneath his eyes. His lips were full, sensuous, and burgundy. He sneered when he tried to smile, or perhaps he was trying to sneer.

"Of course," he said. When he moved his mouth, his beauty wriggled away like a colorful insect. He crept around the chair. His chest sagged like a collapsed accordion. He took the skeleton key from Baruch and his hand dropped to his side from the weight of it. He looked tubercular, like he had been consigned to the country for his health, like at dawn he would be aired on the shore covered in fur blankets, like sometimes Nursey was cruel to him. For all Rachel knew, this was absolutely the case.

In the room, their room, a bridal suite with a canopied bed, a settee and a claw foot tub in the bathroom designed, she was sure, for two, they unpacked in silence. They were on the third floor, and the view was stunning. Dusk and the dark lawn, the bushes of wild roses hedging the cliffs, and then the wide darkening sea below the wide darkening sky.

She opened the window and the smell of the ocean filled the room. She could imagine married couples coming here after dinner, watching the other undress for the first time in years. The sound of earrings placed on the marble sink, the luffing curtains. They would open a bottle of champagne and both laugh at the sudden pop, their shyness would feel like a reprieve. She could not imagine being here with Samuel.

Daniel was crossing the grass. He stopped and faced their lit window. He stared at her, they made eye contact across the distance, and then he twisted away and headed back to the shore. She also turned from the view; soon it would be too dark to see. Jacob pulled a bottle of aquavit from his bag. On a little marble table by the window were crystal tumblers and champagne flutes. Oddly, he chose the flutes. "It's not cold anymore," he said. "Want some?"

No one had ever wanted warm aquavit and, anyway, who wanted aquavit, warm or cold, in the height of the summer? In such a simple gesture she was sure she saw the wreckage of his marriage. It was a little pitiful and a little endearing.

He handed her a flute and then clinked her glass. "I've left the top two drawers empty for you."

The MG was not meant for packing for manor life. Most of her clothes, unrolled now out of her weekender bag, hung on the windowsill, doused in wrinkle releaser, swaying in the wind.

Jacob poured himself another drink. "I'll sleep on the sofa," he said.

"That's a settee, not a sofa."

"I'll sleep on the settee then."

When the phone would ring in the basement, she'd smile and say *hello* three times, each time warmer and brighter, before she answered it. She didn't know how she ended up sounding but often the person on the other end thought they had called the wrong number. She smiled and breathed and sipped her drink. "I meant you can't possibly sleep there. No one can sleep on that. And the bed is enormous."

They both looked at the bed: vastly white, ruffled, frilled, like a wedding cake.

"Unless you're uncomfortable," she said. "Because you're married."

He poured more aquavit. His face was flushed. His phone was vibrating on the nightstand. "I told you my marriage is over," he said.

"Then who is calling you?"

He reached down like he was slapping a fly and silenced the phone. "Jehovah's Witnesses."

"Really?"

"Or Mormons."

"I shouldn't have asked."

"God, actually. He wanted me to go to Nineveh and preach destruction." Jacob pointed his empty glass at the water. "But I made a wrong turn and ended up in Maine."

It was time to check on her clothes. Framed at the open window, in this room, against this horizon, they didn't look like hers. In the wind they moved like people dancing with their backs to her. She held a thin blue sweater up to the light. What would Jacob's wife wear? And would it be different from how Sam's widow would appear? Even thinking about herself as Sam's widow felt like a lie. Like the night before, when she said to Eliana that she was indeed a Jew and watched the woman's face try to hide her doubt.

Her head hurt from keeping her hair up all day. She put the back of her wrist to her forehead: greasy. The warm aquavit had made her nauseous. Why had she accepted it? An absurd drink in an absurd room with a man she didn't know. The clothes swayed sleepily against one another. She stepped into the bathroom and opened the window. Through the smaller aperture, she saw only the edge of a stone balcony and the open ocean. "I'm going to take a bath," she said, and closed the door.

Jacob came downstairs before nine to let Rachel change in private.

He had expected when he reached the landing to be in the foyer, but instead he was in a long hallway uncarpeted and bare except for a painting on the wall, about waist height, of a goat. He turned right and walked down the hall until it ended at a small square window overlooking the dark patio and lawn. The wrong direction then. The house was silent and the doors on the hallway were closed. He turned the other way, walked as quietly as he could in his dress shoes, and reached what looked like a study—dusty binoculars propped on a leather-topped desk, a few bookshelves, and an armchair where an old man sat cupping a brandy snifter to his face with both hands.

"Oh," said Jacob. "I seem to have lost the lobby."

The man didn't look up. "Did you come down the stairs?"

"Yes. Our room is upstairs."

"So is mine."

Jacob was sure that this section of the house had not been on the tour. Perhaps he was not supposed to be here. He explained that this was his first night, that he had just arrived from New York, that his name was Jacob.

The man stared up at him. His mouth hung open like an unclosed attic door, he wore a bright red pocket square in his jacket, he was at least eighty years old and his hair was dyed a vibrant, oily black. "Boris," he said.

"Are you"—Jacob didn't know whether to say a guest or a patient—"staying here?"

Boris waited to see, it seemed, if that was actually what Jacob was going to ask him. He took a heavy breath. "Sort of," he said, and raised his snifter to his mouth.

"Well I better go find the lobby," Jacob said. Perhaps if he were going the wrong way, Boris would tell him.

Down another hall, there was another little window, this one a thin rectangle that he had to angle his body to look out. He could not recognize anything: he seemed to be staring directly at a hedge, leafy, heavy, agleam at the very edges with what might be light from the moon or a security lantern. At the end of this hall he came to a new door. He turned the handle and found himself on a screened porch among stacks of all-weather furniture, buoys, and an inflatable dinghy. Here at least there was a door to the outside. He had imagined that the house was rectangular, but although he had wandered what felt like a ninety-degree angle, he still found himself, now, standing in the dark grass behind the house.

The sense of confusion felt about right. Baruch had paused dramatically over Rachel's name; he must know she wasn't his wife, that his wife was named Maddie—certainly Jacob had told him that before, over the years or maybe even recently, in email. Or he was just annoyed that Jacob brought anyone at all. Or he was what everyone said: old, dotty, a crank.

Jacob walked around the perimeter to the front door. It was almost nine. Rachel might be down by now. Windchimes tinkled from the shadows on the other side of the gravel road, where there were no buildings. He looked up into the wide sky but the clouds had come in with the dark and covered the stars. Above and behind him he sensed the rising plain of empty fields leading to forest, the forest, even darker than the sky, opening away into the night like a cave in a rock face. He decided to call Maddie.

Amazingly, she answered. She sounded surprised, but not upset, to hear from him.

"We've arrived," he said.

"We?"

"How did you think I got here? I didn't take the car. I left it for you. Didn't you notice?"

She was just out of the shower, or at a public pool, or Russian bath, water and echo on the line. He couldn't understand what she was saying, he asked his question again.

"No," she said and the signal cut out.

Back inside, in the main room, just past the lobby, Rachel was talking to Boris.

"I see you met Boris," he said.

"Yes she met Boris," said Boris. In direct light his hair was blue, iridescent, like the feathers of a bird.

"Where were you?" Rachel asked.

"I got lost."

"You got lost where?"

"I must have taken the wrong stairs."

A woman padded silently into the room and stood beside them. She clasped her hands under her chin and smiled without opening her mouth. Jacob smiled back at her. "Good evening."

"It's my turn to give witness tonight," she said.

"Give witness?"

"After dinner," the woman said. She had some kind of accent. "Tonight is my night."

In the park, Jacob had seen Baer and thought: a lunatic. Homeless, confused. When he answered the phone, his sister described a Maddie to him he could not remember. Perhaps now he should reach out, past Rachel, past Boris, and take this woman by the face and scream, *What are you talking about?*

"By the way," he said instead. "Where is dinner?"

She stopped smiling. Her white hair was cut into a bob, with a hard line of ruled bangs hanging down like a wall. Now she seemed severe, suspicious, angry. "I don't think he's moved it tonight. Has he, Boris?"

"It's our first night here, and everything is still a bit of a mystery," Rachel explained.

"I'm dead," Boris said. "And there are no mysteries."

Baruch appeared. Bouncing in from around the corner with a linen blazer over his pink polo shirt. "Come in, come in," he said. His face was bright, wide-eyed, he was not looking at anybody. "Dinner is served!"

In the dining room, the French doors to the sea were now closed but the curtains were not and the glass, bordered by the night, was like a mirror reflecting the immaculate table: a pink lace cloth, crystal glasses, good silver recently polished, bone china plates, and decanters of wine at both ends linked by a row of lit tapers. Several silver covered trays were arranged on a sideboard against the left wall, directly across from the French doors where Baruch stood. His jacket was too big; it draped around him like sagging skin. Gone was the dapper elegance from that night in Berlin. He seemed old and small and giddy.

"Jacob, Rachel," Baruch said. "We have no staff, alas. So we serve ourselves."

Immediately, as at a cafeteria, there was a line. A man standing behind Jacob tapped him on the shoulder. "I'm a sexologist," he said. He was about sixty and wearing a younger man's clothes: a dark blue suit with charcoal pinstripes, a matching waistcoat and a pink tie with little yellow designs on it. He looked like a banker, not a sexologist—whatever a sexologist might look like—except that he was wearing sneakers.

"What kind of sexologist are you?" It was all Jacob could think of to say.

"Intergenerational."

"What is an intergenerational sexologist?" Rachel asked.

The man had not noticed Rachel or imagined that she might join the conversation and he took a step backward into a woman who must have been his wife, because he didn't respond when she said, "Fuck, Mel." He blushed and then smiled and then wiped his hand on his jacket and held it out to Rachel. "I'm Mel," he said. "I've been coming here since this place opened. Also the one in New York."

Jacob lifted the lid to the first tureen: some kind of chicken. "New York," he said. "You mean before it closed?"

"Vultures," Mel said. "The way they turned on Baruch. What do documents prove?"

"The Nazis documented everything," Rachel said.

"What does it mean to say *documented?* They kept lists," Mel said. "What are lists? What are numbers? Is a man's soul a number?"

Mel's wife spoke. "A man's soul is the same as an animal's." She held up both her hands in fists as if there were a penny, or a Quaalude, in one of them, and she was asking them all to guess which—and then opened them both to emptiness.

Jacob dropped a piece of chicken on his plate. His phone was buzzing in his pocket. Once Maddie smashed a wine glass on the floor and screamed, "What kind of philosopher can't ask a question?"

"Anyway," Mel was saying to Rachel, "the New York school is going to reopen after the auction. Baruch's bringing in some young hotshot scholar to run it."

Are these people patients or guests? Jacob still can't tell. Luckily there is a lot of wine and it is excellent. At the table with all of them sitting, Baruch holds up his hands, palms out as if to bless the meal. "How do we welcome guests? There is no question in the Torah more essential. Especially for a people in diaspora. Imagine a closed door. On each side you might have strangers, but when it opens?" Rachel and Jacob are the strangers, that is clear. The others ignore each other with the ease of long acquaintance. Baruch begins to introduce them. First there is Boris. "You might have heard of him," Baruch says. "Boris Nevsky, the Yiddish poet." Of course Jacob has heard of him. He was a little famous with the older people in Israel; loved by the old, reviled by the younger Hebrew literati. In secret, Jacob had admired his poems which were all about shtetl life, or country life, anyway—they were lyrical, nostalgic but timeless—pastorals portraying a world untouched by war. But the ones he'd read were from the seventies, and by the subject matter, by the absence of the Shoah, he'd assumed their author was long dead. And then the woman from before, Anna, a classicist from Cambridge. And the other two: Mel, a therapist. His wife Sophie, a medical doctor. "A researcher," Sophie says. "I don't practice." "A poet, a professor, a therapist, and a doctor who doesn't practice," Rachel says. "It's like a Jewish joke where no one's mother is happy." She's holding the glass of wine with both hands. Her smile wilts under the static of a weird silence. She's more awkward than Jacob expected, after the day's drive. "If there's one thing we hate around here, it's Jewish jokes," Sophie says.

"Like any community," Baruch says, "we have our ceremonies and our taboos, which I think you will come to understand. Still"—he raises his glass to Rachel—"this is Rachel, who I have not had the chance to meet, who though I know of, I do not know. Yet, she graces us like any surprise. Welcome, Rachel." He seems impatient, he has explained nothing, he does not say who Rachel is other than someone he does not know, and he's talking again before anyone except Mel, who is waving across the table, can welcome Rachel. "And finally, Jacob," Baruch says, "is a great young scholar whose career I've followed for years now and who I'm proud to say will be joining me, will be joining us, as my partner in New York." He raises his glass again. "To Jacob," he says. Jacob puts up his hand. "No, please," he says. The spine of candles separates him from Baruch's gaze. As in Berlin, at the lectern, he tilts and squints. He has not agreed to anything. He has absolutely not agreed to anything. Everyone drinks.

"I can't believe it," Mel says to Sophie. "I was just talking to him in line."

The table is set for eight but the eighth chair remains empty. Anna points at it with her spoon. "Where's our chef tonight?"

Baruch shrugs in his big coat. "You know how he is," he says. "Perhaps he will join us soon."

"Maybe he got lost," Rachel says. "Jacob did on the way to dinner." Everyone stares. The food is delicious: the lemony chicken fricasseed with garlic and green olives, Spanish rice, grilled figs glazed in a balsamic reduction. Baruch looks bored and sleepy, his eyes are lidded; he pokes his chicken with his fork but does not lift it to his mouth. It's an expression and manner Jacob recognizes from his childhood. Like every dinner growing up. Sophie says, "Fricassee is a North African dish." "Sephardic," says Mel. General agreement. Sophie pours more wine. Baruch is suddenly lively. "When it comes to Jewish cuisine, the Ashkenazi have nothing on the Sephardi. Of this, even the Baal Shem Tov would agree." The first year after Jacob's mother disappeared, his father tried to make Passover dinner. Jacob remembers him standing in the kitchen, in his bathrobe and slippers, brandishing a matzah ball in his fingers shouting, *Look at this! A canonball! A canonball! Like lead!* "Wait," Rachel says, "fricassee is a French dish." She provides etymology. A combination of the French word to fry, *frire*, and to break into pieces, *casser*. It first appeared in a medieval French cookbook in the year 1300. A moment's silence swamps the table like a wave. The candles flicker. Baruch is smiling and Jacob wants to ask her how she knows the history of their dinner but figures this is the sort of thing he would already know about his wife even though, in reality, Maddie is a mystery to him, and he is a mystery to himself and he reaches for his empty wine glass and says, "It's hard to know," which Sophie and

Mel, in sudden sympathy of belief, take as either challenge or agreement, and insist that, no, fricassee is a classic of Sephardic cuisine. Rachel is flustered. For some reason she has decided to argue with these people, who in the year 2017 are patients at a sanitarium. In Maine. She repeats the etymology. “What does language prove?” says Mel. “We are a people of diaspora!” “Exile,” Anna says and puts a wheel of lemon in her mouth. Rachel snorts. “First you said numbers don’t mean anything. And now words too?” “It’s a good question,” Baruch murmurs. “Where does authority reside?” “In an olive,” Mel says and picks one off his plate. “There is no authority,” says Sophie. “What do you think, Boris?” Jacob shouts, wanting to take the heat off Rachel, but Boris is asleep.

Baruch asks Jacob: “Have you gone inside the Kabbalah Center yet?” He knows Jacob has. He sent him a key, unless he’s forgotten.

“When are you going to reopen?” Mel asks.

“I thought we were waiting for the auction first,” Jacob says. “To see how much it raises.”

“The auction is on Friday,” Sophie says.

Jacob makes some kind of noise. Everyone is looking at him. He shouldn’t have said *we*. “I haven’t actually agreed yet.”

“I would love to ask you some questions about your methods, Doctor,” Anna says.

Jacob, who means to say *I have no methods*, says, “I think my role would primarily be administrative.”

“Modesty is refreshing in the young,” Baruch says. “Trust me, Jacob is a great scholar. I attended a talk he gave in Berlin.”

“Speaking of Sephardic cuisine,” Rachel says, “do you know why Ashkenazi avoid rice and beans on Passover, while the Sephardi do not?”

“Latin temperament,” says Mel. “Always made me jealous. It’s no sacrifice if you can have rice and beans. I could *live* on rice and beans.”

Baruch sits up in his chair. The motion is abrupt as a gust of wind. "Kitniyot," he says.

"That's right. Fleeing Egypt, the Israelites didn't have time to make bread that rose, so the Passover prohibition is against grain that rises. Rice and beans are not a grain, they are a legume, kitniyot, so there's no actual reason not to eat them, except that the medieval rabbis in France thought that they looked similar enough to grains to be confusing."

"It shows you how much bread the rabbis made. They should have asked their wives if they were confused," Anna says.

"The point is," Rachel says, "*kitniyot* look like one thing when in fact they are something else altogether. The French rabbis recognized the danger of a mistake."

The room has gone quiet. There is nothing left to eat.

"What danger is that?" Sophie says.

"If a forgery resembles the real thing, do we stop caring about authenticity?"

"Well," Baruch says, "during Passover, I always eat kitniyot."

In grad school, Jacob and his friends had played a drinking game called The Wisdom of Solomon. The goal was to take a common issue and produce an extreme solution. As in, solving a maternity dispute by chopping a baby in half. The secret to the game was identifying "the object of authenticity"—the life of the baby, rather than possession of its body, say—by which the essential stakes could be revealed. It wasn't so much a game about functional solutions—the solution only worked because it was inadequate—as it was about useful questions. Where does the real encounter the fraudulent? Maddie for instance seemed to have solved the problem of her emotional life by asking, in the face of diminishment, why not add someone else? Baruch was offering Jacob a future, which was, as far as Jacob could see, something that he didn't have, but in its fraudulence it looked very much like Jacob's past, in which, of course, there was no one named Jacob.

"I'd love to read some of your work," Anna says.

At last, the wine takes the room. The tide is slow and constant and the sea shuffles over the rocks. The tapers stoop in the candlesticks like old men. Long shadows on the sleepy table. "Well," Baruch says, "I think it's time to try again." The others know what he means by this and stand immediately.

"What's going on?" Rachel says.

"Now we go down to Jonah's," Baruch says.

"Jonah's?"

"It's a tavern."

"It's my turn tonight," Anna says, and Sophie reaches out, across the table, over the low candles, and squeezes her hand.

"Don't worry," Baruch says, "we walk there."

Rachel is the only one still sitting. She's wearing her dismay like a feather boa. "I'm sorry," she says, "it's been a long day. I need to sleep."

"Going to Jonah's is just like sleeping," Baruch says.

RACHEL STOOD BY THE WINDOW and watched Jacob's shadow move through the border of light beneath the bathroom door. They had left the window open and the room sighed with water: the ocean outside dragged itself over the rocks, the faucet gurgled on, then off, then on, Jacob's hands interrupted the flow, water splashed across the standing marble basin, then he turned the tap off again. He was brushing his teeth, she could hear him, he was conscientious of water use, he washed his hands, his face, he was a diligent tooth brusher, the toilet did not flush, at one point he sighed. It was a body sigh from deep in his chest: he must have been looking in the mirror.

She put her hand to her mouth and bit her finger. This was a kind of intimacy—unintentional, unrequested, and unearned. She felt like an imposter, an accidental surrogate, she did not know him, the closet was closed and she could not see any of her things: the bed, the windows, the settee and drawers, everything was recognizable but she did not recognize anything. At the next moment someone might walk through the door and expect her to do something impossible. Jacob sighed again, softer. In the sigh, she felt the electric connection of his pain catch in her chest; it was not for her.

How many nights had she lain in bed, just feet from the bathroom, listening to Samuel, his humming while he dried himself, the sloppy vigor of his toothbrushing, the occasional odd and furious scrubbing, the ritual washing he sometimes performed after sex? At these times she had felt like a new believer groping for the dumb ablution to allow her access to his real, untouchable—or no, not untouchable, not untouchable but untouched—self. But it never happened. He withheld it. In sleep, in the glow of a bottle of wine at the dinner table, or even when he was inside of her, crying out in

Yiddish. Between them remained an unbridged distance. He didn't want to be known or understood and he didn't want, as she had first thought, to know her or join his life to hers. He wanted to vanish. *You can't just disappear*, she had told him once, finally, after he'd left her, and had been, as with so many other things, wrong.

Jacob came out of the bathroom. Rachel looked at her feet; she had painted her toenails for this trip. She couldn't help feeling that she was dishonoring something by pretending to be Jacob's wife. But what? She had given Samuel the divorce easily; she told herself that by providing him this freedom she was giving him what she always wanted to give him. But if that wasn't a parody of what she had hoped for, this night in this suite with this man certainly was. Baruch had known she was a fake; Jacob had not even tried to sell it. A loon called on the water and was not answered.

Jacob was standing by the bed in fresh clothes—a pair of jeans and a shirt as wrinkled as the last one. "I thought it would look strange if I didn't come up with you," he said. "But I'm going to go meet them there." He saw that she was crying. He was shifting his weight from foot to foot. "I brushed my teeth already," he said. "When I get back, I'll sleep on the floor."

She held up her hand. She could not negotiate one more thing. Against this sudden simplicity, nothing seemed to matter: She missed Samuel. She reached over and turned out the light.

ONCE HE HAS FOUND HIS WAY out of the house, Jacob follows the crushed shell path into the forest. All he can see in the dark is a pale glimmer where the tavern must be. The shells glow under his flashlight and the forest is too dense to wander off the path and the trail ends, as he expected, at the tavern, which is also where the land ends.

It sits on the cliff, rundown, sagging, beleaguered like it came there with the intention of tossing itself off but died before it quite made it to the edge. The roof slopes to the right, toward the water, the windows are cracked or busted out, the screen door hangs on one hinge and the other door is half open so that he feels like he is looking into a dead mouth where a dumb tongue lolls fatly. Somehow, the sign—Jonah's—still perches over the misty awning. From within pulses a smoky blue light.

Inside, Jonah's is not a bar. There is a bar, in the far corner under a tinted, glass-shaded light fixture, but there are no barstools, or bar patrons, or bartender, or bar bottles. There might be a bar mirror, but a canvas drop cloth shrouds it, and the rest of the place, which is loosely nautical—three buoys and a rusted harpoon lean against the wall by the door—is in shambles. The smashed and lightless jukebox, the overturned tables and booths with their stuffing torn out all haunt the room under the spectral blue phantom of a pale spotlight pointed at an empty wall and Jacob stands in the doorway, blinking like someone just awake, staring hard at what doesn't seem so much a tavern at all, but a sailor's cabaret, dreamborn and bereft.

Arranged in a semi-circle, about ten hightop tables face the glowing point where a bare patch of wooden floor intersects a bare patch of wall and, because this is where the light shines, Jacob realizes that this space, salt-stained wood glowing over salt-stained wood, is intended as a stage. Here Anna is going to do whatever Anna is going to do, but right now Anna, like Boris and Mel and Sophie, is sitting at a hightop in the shadows staring at the blue circle on the empty wall. Surrounding them, propped at the other tables, are a series of large wooden statues.

Of what? Men maybe, but bigger, carved from chunks of sea-bleached driftwood. Like this whole bar, they seem weathered, wind-bent and wind-scoured, as bright as bone, their sharp carved faces, solemn and long, extend on rigid necks away from the wings, folded, but arcing above their shoulders, so that for a moment Jacob thinks he knows what they are, and it makes sense, almost, in a bar like this, to have a collection of figureheads scavenged from the prows of old ships.

Jacob steps into the room and closes the door and the statues turn, all of them, to look at him. When they do, their wings raise and unfold slightly, shudder and drop again. The motion is almost like that of half-sleeping owls ruffled by wind, except the sound they make is not feathery at all, but a high skeletal rattle.

Baruch, out of some corner, puts one hand on Jacob's arm, and with the other points as if at the zoo. "Angels."

Jacob can see that and he looks away, to Baruch, an old man with brandy on his breath, and then back. The angels are still there, sitting at hightops, facing the stage, where one of them now stands.

"They've lost their memory," Baruch whispers. "They know some things, but it's more like instinct. The rest they've forgotten." He nudges Jacob, he is giddy. "You see now why I wanted you to visit."

The angel on stage is speaking. It says, So a man I know, a friend of mine, has been married for forty years and he trips on some ice.

The angel says, And now his wife has to do everything for him. When I tell my wife this she says, *At least.*

Baruch shakes his head. "I don't know how long they've been

here. One day, when I was considering buying the estate, I was walking the property line and here they were."

The angel's voice: hoarse, slow, garbled. Stones tumbling over stones on the tide.

It says, So my son said to me.

It says, Did you know I had three boys and my wife still wasn't happy. One was a doctor, one was a lawyer, and the third.

"Can I ask a question?" Jacob says. "Are they telling jokes?"

Baruch nods. "They're trying. It seems to be all they can remember."

The angel: When the mohel shows up my wife points at me and.

In public, out in the world where he rarely went, Jacob's father liked to tell jokes. Later he would tell the story of the matzah balls—*like lead!*—he'd pantomime freaking out over the stove—*like lead!*—and this time he'd smile and everyone would smile with him, then grin, then laugh, and he'd laugh too with his mouth open wide and the bottoms of all his teeth as black as if he'd been chewing soot.

Baruch has a flask that he passes to Jacob. The angel on stage still has not blinked. Its eyes are stones, but its head begins to bob a little and its wings rise and fall with strain. Baruch takes back the flask. "Sometimes I think I should burn this place down," Baruch says.

The angel asks a question, Why don't Jewish mothers drink?

Silence. Under the blue light his carved feathers look sharp, razored, like something adorning an iron fence. Sophie reaches out and pinches Mel. "Why?" he shouts.

The angel bows and shuffles off stage.

It is Anna's turn.

"You wanted to know what we do here," Baruch says. "We tell the angels what they cannot remember."

In the blue light Anna looks younger, smaller. She's wearing white velcro sneakers with her dress. She says, "Tonight I will sing a lullaby my mother used to sing to me." The accent Jacob had noticed earlier is now clearly British, her voice is deep, she stands with her feet together and her hands clasped, palms upward, down by her belly, and the act of doing that, clasping her hands in front of her body as, Jacob imagines, she was taught to do for drawing room recitals in her youth, rounds her shoulders and pulls the drooping neckline of her dress away from her chest. The dress is silk, frilled, faded, pink. She begins to sing and her accent changes. There is wind in the room; it must have come through one of the shatttered windows; it flings old napkins into the air. "Oh!" someone cries. Jacob turns again but the wind has dropped with the cry and in that instant he recognizes the song; it is Yiddish, "Raisins and Almonds," he knows it from childhood.

Slumped at a hightop, Boris lights his pipe. Anna's voice isn't right, it's too deep for the song. The fog from the beach is in the windless room. The song is beautiful, keening, for some reason he can't follow the Yiddish, the fog is not fog but pipesmoke, Mel reaches out and takes his wife's hand. The whole room seems to be gripping itself, condensing, charging, gathering like a sob. Again, the wind. The spot swivels and now Anna is at its limit, in its weakest halo, and under the low light her face looks blotched and dented, he cannot see her eyes but she must be crying because, shining, in a diamond of light, one of her cheeks is wet. She's singing the same verse over and over again.

Baruch rustles up against Jacob and whispers, "At six years old, she was allotted space on a Kindertransport." Mel lets go of his wife's hand and covers his face. The angels perch in their chairs like enormous, inquisitive parrots. The song is about a goat. The Yiddish clears for Jacob. *Under the baby's cradle stands a goat. He'll bring you raisins and almonds, so sleep, little one, sleep, little one.* She's repeating this. And then she stops and no one claps. The angels nod, look at each other, and nod again.

"My mother used to sing that to me. It's what I most remember about her," Anna says. Her British accent has not returned. "Before the boat my mother gave me her book of recipes. Everything else disappeared. I don't have any pictures of my parents or my sisters or my aunts or uncles or grandparents. I have no photographs and I have none of their things and I don't remember my mother making honey cake, but she wrote a note to me in the margin that it was my favorite, and that I should make it on the New Year to celebrate life's sweetness."

Outside, in the sleeping reaches of forest, the dark whirring as the windmill gathers wind.

Anna says, "For years, if anyone asked me about my life before the war, my life in Danzig, my lost life, which they usually didn't, in the years following the war the last thing anyone in Britain wanted to talk about was the war, but if they did, if they asked about my life before the war, I would tell them about my mother's honey cake. How she made it on Rosh Hashanah just for me. How it was my favorite."

She begins to speak faster. Now that her song is finished and the angels are still, or just, Jacob thinks, statues, still as statues. Their confusion insults her. The rapt impossibility of their silence. Her voice: an urgent, low blur of accents. The truth was, she explains, that she remembered almost nothing. And what she did remember only evoked what she couldn't. Her mother wrapping the recipe book in a blanket, stuffing it into her hands. The faint cursive in the margin, *This is your favorite.* How was it that she couldn't remember what she was supposed to have loved? The question accrued weight when her mother herself grew elusive and unreachable, a voice she listened for and couldn't hear, a voice she knew, but couldn't remember until it would wake her shouting her name, out of sleep. She remembered the song and its melody and her mother singing it to her, but could not remember how that sounded. Her memory of her mother's voice joining her mother like a shadow dragged from a room by a closing door.

During her childhood, Anna says, the idea of honey cake—as a real and practical object—correlated with the idea of honey cake as an overdetermined emotional symbol. She stops and looks at the angels, she checks, Jacob thinks, to see if they've registered this sentence. Instead: pipesmoke, loon cries, wind. No one says anything. In those early years honey was dear, eggs were dear, sugar was dear, flour was dear, an orange to juice or zest was impossible. To make a honey cake would be a ridiculous extravagance. In idea and actuality, the honey cake was impossible, the forgotten past, the improbable present. Her mother in the moving panic of a crowd, stuffing the book into her hands. *This was your favorite.*

When she was nineteen, at university studying classics, she got news that her father was alive, and living in Tel Aviv, and wanted to see her. She went to him. He helped buy her tickets and a local evangelical organization celebrating English Christian philanthropy during the war, the East Midlands Ministry, paid for her adoptive parents to go with her. They wanted, at the appropriate time, to meet the man whose daughter had become theirs.

But the first evening she went to him alone. She asked the driver to drop her off a few blocks before his apartment. She stepped out and walked, at dusk, among Jews. "I knew I was Jewish but had no feeling of being Jewish. In England I had not known any Jews. All I had of Danzig was a song in a language my parents didn't even speak and a recipe. And yet, being Jewish was the most significant thing about me. I was not my name or the marks I got in school or the boy who had kissed me, or the lies I told, or the candy I stole once, or the way my adopted brothers taught me how to catch and cook hedgehog during the war shortages. No, the thing that was real about me, why I almost died and what I was saved for, what was essential, what made me worthy of murder, was that I was a Jew. But it felt like a lie." So she walked, at dusk, in Tel Aviv. She said to herself, these are my people, but, she says, now to the angels, "I didn't look like my people or speak their language." So she tried again. She walked. Though it was clear overhead, the bank of clouds behind the white houses was the color of smoke. Against them, the buildings seemed like a stage set, painted façades propped on emptiness. The sky was a bowl holding light. She walked, she tried again, she told herself: I am going to my father.

When he opened his door, he said, *yes?* She knew him immediately—the downturned corners of his eyes, the red lobes of his ears, the long oval crease of his brow arcing in some tender sorrow she had forgotten and was immediately comforted by, he was hers, she knew him—he opened the door and said, *yes*? He was looking over her shoulder. She turned, too, and looked. It had begun to rain and pockets of steam rose out of the gold dust beneath the date palms. The street was empty. *Yes?* he said, again. Then in Hebrew, she realized later, *Ma*? What? He was angling his body around hers, away from hers, so that he would see his daughter when she arrived. She had been prepared for him to be unrecognizable, damaged, strange and a stranger; she had not been prepared to be a stranger to him.

Later, in his small kitchen, drinking first orange juice and then a little brandy, trying to recover from the moment that had followed. The way she had clutched her hands to her chest and said, *It's me.* She didn't use her name or explain herself, there was no self to explain, her world compressed to her father, this man like a trick mirror refusing to reflect her, even as she repeated again and again *It's me, it's me,* until—and it was only a second, two—his eyes cleared and he tried to speak her name.

And still, at the table, something was wrong. He could not settle. The anxiety she had recognized, when he was looking over her shoulder for his daughter, had not abated. He sat and stood and then sat again. He covered his face with his palms and then removed them and looked at her. He said her name, but he did not say *daughter*, he asked her questions, but as soon as she told him anything about her life, he interrupted her to ask about her childhood in Danzig with him. *Do you remember*, he kept saying, *do you remember when*...and he'd refer to an incident in some murky shorthand, like a hint, tracing its edge with his prompt and then expecting her to fill the rest of it in, *Do you remember the time you got mud on your lace slippers*? This wasn't what she wanted. She had hoped he would explain himself, where he'd been all these years, why it took so long to make contact, but in the absence of that—of reason or justification—she had hoped at least, if he wouldn't explain himself, that he might explain her. She had hoped for her father to hear and understand the events of her new life, her whole life, really, and in hearing them, in understanding them and recognizing her in them, to see her, his daughter still, and to unify one life with the other. Isn't this what parents did? Provide history, psychology, class, values? Was it too much to hope at least for her confusion to be coherent? Still, at first she understood: he who had lost everything—parents, siblings, wife—whose life was elegy, whose arm was tattooed and whose past was wreckage, was clinging to what he remembered of the possible world; but soon it felt different—this was a quiz, not nostalgia. He still did not recognize her and he was looking for proof. That's why his questions, in English only, began to come faster and faster. He was groping for her. She had an idea.

Anna stops speaking. She wipes her face with the back of her wrist. "What do you think I did?" she says to the angels, and the angels nod. "What do you think I did?" she says again, louder, and in response one of them calls out like a loon.

The next day she came with her parents. This time her father was prepared and less manic. He was polite and quiet, he made them tea into which he squeezed some kind of citrus she had never seen. He thanked her parents, each, formally, for what they had done. He took her father's hand, he kissed her mother's, and then they all sat, the three of them, facing him, in his little sitting room. With her parents he made careful small talk about the travel to Israel, the road closures due to security measures, the way when it rained here, the rain fell through the sunshine. This was a kind of conversation her English parents could engage in: discussion of roads and weather and even a cursory joke—*In Leicester,* her English father said, *sometimes a little drizzle peeks through the rain.* The room faced west and, on this evening, with no storm, the low sun fit through his narrow, barred windows in rectangles of tangerine light. He did not talk to her. It was as if she were not what joined them all, but instead just an uninteresting member of this English family who had plopped, for some reason, into his sitting room. Here she was, in his new bright and bare life of sun and citrus tea and the faint smell of mildew, a life he had been living for however many years now, and she felt lumpy and gray, a clot of cobwebs tangled out of somebody else's past.

Without saying anything she stood and lifted the bag of supplies she had brought, slipped into his kitchen, and began to make her mother's honey cake. He never asked her what she was doing, but at a certain point, when the smell from the oven reached them, he looked over at her with an open mouth. When she served it, his eyes filled with tears. *Is it right?* she asked, and he nodded, wordless, crying, holding the plate under his chin and staring at her, for the first time, as if she were real, moving his mouth around some word that it took her a moment to conjure from its shape—*Ruth*—her mother, the woman he was remembering now as he stared at the girl who had just barged like an imposter into her own life and made his wife's cake.

Anna stops. Mel rushes from the bar, through the broken doors, into the dark. "Honey cake," she says. "It was my favorite." And very carefully, from memory, Anna begins to recite her mother's recipe. Without anything to hold it open, the unclosed door flaps on its hinges, into the empty night like a wing. "First, the honey," says Anna to the angels.

RACHEL WOKE IN THE NIGHT. She slept, she woke, she slept again. She was a corpse bride accosting Samuel on his way to his wedding. She stood on the banks of a river, at the lip of her own grave, begging her husband to marry her, but he turned away, in disgust and terror. He hid under the canopy and the river sloshed with waves. She was holding a can of soda to remind herself to keep her hand closed since the ring he gave her kept slipping off her dead finger. I can't let him see, she thought and woke and didn't know where she was and then did and felt for the difference another body makes in the bed but Jacob was not there. She realized, after a while, that he would not return to the room. She was grateful. She said to Sam, I'm still your wife, but he said no, no, no, my wife is alive. Her teeth, loose and then falling, filled her mouth as she said, I baked you a honey cake. I used your sister's recipe. Then morning. Boat motors and birds on the water. She found her glasses on the bedside table. She stood and pulled back the drapes: the sea rocking under the sun, rising and falling like the chest of the world.

Downstairs the drawing room was empty and full of light. Gone was the wintery opulence she had sensed when they arrived. The doors to the lawn were propped open with old, salt-bleached lobster traps and the sun, still low, hung in visible rays over the furniture. The green couch had faded into a comfortable minty shabbiness, the red armchairs looked pink, like berries not yet ripe. As she crossed the room, shimmering dust motes rose and twirled from the threadbare rugs.

The adjacent bar, bedecked for buffet breakfast was even brighter: on the wall behind the food the reflection of the sea rocked in boiling patterns of marbled light. The forks and butter knives and silly little egg spoons glinted as if sharp. The chamber was as placid and sun-drenched as a still life. Curtains drooped white and limp, sketched their own shadows on the floor. She was alone and the whole house was silent and drowsy and abandoned, but somewhere a violin sighed faintly.

The left side of the buffet table was laid out with several tureens of eggs and trays of fruit and yogurt and steaming silver samovars of coffee. Who made all this? She had seen no staff. No voices echoed from the kitchens. She didn't usually eat much breakfast. She took a few handfuls of blueberries and a mug of coffee, and then stepped out the open French doors onto the lawn.

Near the cliff edge, Sophic and Mel were sitting in Adirondack chairs, watching the morning. She did not greet them and they did not turn around. Carrying her mug, she followed the crushed shell path that wound around the house, and as soon as she turned the corner, she stepped into an image out of Lurio: there was Boris standing in a huppah, a raised wooden marriage canopy, in a jacket and tie and red slippers, playing a violin while the sea rocked behind him.

"Good morning, Boris," she said. "That's beautiful."

"If it is, it is," he said and kept playing..

The shell path wound around the northern side of the estate, and for several yards fell into shadow as it passed below the high stone walls of one of the house's mysterious wings. But then she was beyond the walls, in sun again, and rows of sea roses bordered the path like English hedges. Some of the roses were white, but most were a light, powdery pink with a felty butter yellow center. She leaned down to smell them. Bees droned around her; she straightened, the air was still sweet, buzzing, she sipped from her coffee, it was very strong. On this side of the island, above the low tangle of scraggly pines, wind swept off the water. She smelled mud and seaweed and then a wave-crash far below freed a fresher scent—salt—as if the sea were clearing its throat. She finished her coffee. There was sun in her face. She felt suddenly happy.

Once she was beyond the estate and its gardens, the path ended and she had to choose: the road or the meadow. She began to climb through the grass, up the hill they'd driven along last night. Soon the house was below her, with its empty balconies and patios, its strange columns, its little blinking windows. At the top of the hill the headland wind came stronger, the cliffs were charcoal smudges, the tide must be out, there were rock shoals shimmering in the open water, snatches of Boris's violin reached her on the right gusts. At this height she could see the other side of the hill, invisible from the house, tumbling down to the forest. There, just before the pines, stood another larger cluster of sculptures and statues like the ones they'd seen driving in last night. They were in shadow, but were arranged geometrically, like standing stones, like ruins. She headed toward them.

Jacob thought: what is that noise, what is that light? Late, in the dark, moving through the middle of the house, he had come up the stairs to a landing. At the end of the hall there was an unlocked door; on the other side: a bed, a desk, a radio. Even if he could find it, he couldn't go back into the bridal suite where he left Rachel crying. He slept where he was.

Now in the room, cramped as a ship's cabin, assailed. White noise and waves, static, waves, a man counting in French. He sat up. The radio was on and the tide was coming in. The round dial opaque and green as frosted sea glass pooled on the table. He turned off the radio that he hadn't turned on. He stood at the window.

For a while after she lost the pregnancy, Maddie ran every morning, before dawn. "It's not safe," he said to her the first time, as she dressed. She did not like to be told what to do. She wanted him to speak but not speak constantly, she did not like repetition. Unfortunately, there was no possible human way to sever repetition from safety. "It's not safe to run in in the dark," he said. But her earbuds were in, she was already closing the door. From the window, he watched her cross the street under the lamplight into the park. Her new sneakers, pink as coral.

Confronted by fear, some people would pray. At the end of the Second Generation meeting, the group leader stood and said, "We will now say Yizkor for our lost." Jacob was not intending to speak and he was certainly not intending to pray and if he had prayed, if you had told him they would ask him to join in prayer, he would not have expected the Yizkor. For one thing, the Yizkor, the Jewish prayer of memorial, was usually only said four times a year, and the prayers for specific family members were not said out loud as they were doing here; and for another, it was a prayer of precise machinery.

The words *yizkor Elohim, may God remember*, insisted on divine attention and understanding. As Jacob had written in Tel Aviv, the prayer arose in the Middle Ages as a way to memorialize victims of crusader violence. That it evolved over the years away from the simple recitation for the martyred to a prayer for the dead in general did nothing in his mind to disentangle everyday Jewish life from the memory of slaughter. In college, in his first days of his new name, a professor lecturing on Hume had written on the board, *The past does not determine the future*, and Jacob cleaved hungrily to the idea—he had etched it into his notebook, underlined it, circled it, written nothing else, heard nothing else, and did not believe it. What does the memory of slaughter do except prepare us for slaughter?

When finally Maddie asked him, *Did you secretly not want the baby?* Jacob didn't know what to say. But with her, silence was impossible. She believed that anything could be articulated and so, because he needed to somehow explain the anxiety he knew she'd discover at the heart of any of his aspirations, he said, *My father thought that since the world would not spare children from its malice, why should parents?* This was unfair, a tiny act of aggression on his part, assigning some hard-knocks philosophy to his father who, actually, never considered sparing children because he didn't realize that there was a world in which children were spared. His father, in fact, was always loving and always kind but he had not had a childhood of his own and did not recognize it as a developmental or psychological stage requiring any specific tenderness. Children, in his estimation and experience, were just smallish people who needed lots of instruction.

Which wasn't what Maddie had asked.

But this is what Jacob knew: Not being understood, not being able to transact a simple human conversation did not make his father angry, but frightened. The law of the Shoah: to not understand or be understood was to not survive. But what was there to understand? In the Shoah's intentional incoherence, let alone in its long resonant throb. And then what? As a kid, what did Jacob learn from this other than that the world was full of menace? That in any basic interaction, even between an adult and child, there must be threat—and Jacob did not want to be a threat to a child.

Again, he felt unfair. Despite what his mother liked to say, his father wasn't crazy and he wasn't cruel. He knew a person needed to feel loved and safe—so he thrust upon Jacob his own refugee methods of safety, developed in the DP camp and then in Palestine and then in New Jersey. For him safety was not the absence of possible harm, but a series of routines to ward off surprise when the inevitable violence occurred.

At Nod, at the window, he watched Rachel walking the grounds. He felt none of the old fear, as when he'd stand waiting for Maddie to return, waiting at the window for half an hour, forty-five minutes, afraid to break his vigil against the punishment he knew he deserved, until she appeared again at the edge of the park, and he'd hurry away into some other room so she wouldn't see him when she'd burst back through the door—sweating, bright, music still blaring—and toss her shoes in the corner, askew again as broken feet.

Rachel stood at the bottom of the hill, before the statues. They were figurative, bronze-painted, characters out of folktales it seemed: an old woman with a rolling pin, a child with a basket, a wild-eyed demon, prancing and priapic.

There was a sound; she looked: someone moved at the far end of the installation. She did not want to be snuck up on. She walked toward them, past what looked like a bronze rabbi, hunkered and glimmering, twelve feet high in a prayer shawl, with eyes broken open like eggs, and there he was on the other side, Daniel.

"Oh, it's you," Rachel said. "You scared me."

He was wearing purple corduroy pants and a tight black T-shirt. His hair fell over his brow. Twice, self-consciously, he swept it out of his face.

"I'm not what's scary here," he said.

"They're wild," Rachel said, nodding her head back at the statues. "Kind of totemic."

"Like if Gaugin were Hasidic."

Rachel looked at him with surprise. "Yes! That's it."

"And horny."

"Gaugin was very horny."

"And yet Alex isn't, I don't think? But it's his way, I guess," he said. "A little bit of this, a little bit of that."

"He made these?"

Daniel looked up at the demon with the huge erection and shrugged. "There's nothing that the great man can't do."

Again when he spoke he seemed to sneer. Or maybe it wasn't a sneer. It didn't really register in his eyes. Like he didn't want to be saying what he was saying. Underneath his aloof and easy beauty he was angry.

"You know Baruch well, then?"

"Since I was a boy."

"What are you doing out here?" she asked.

"At Nod? I'm convalescing."

"From what?"

"The fall of old Europe, the Great War, the appearance of trains, of photographs, of shell shock, of industry, of desire and syphilis, of magnetic interference, a creeping terror of automata. Of, to be comprehensive, what my father called 'The Wounds of the Age.'"

"You're quoting Baruch, right? His memoir."

"Of course."

"So you don't really have syphilis?"

"Unlikely."

"And you're not afraid of automata."

"Actually," he said, "I'm afraid of everything."

He turned away from her and headed over to another statue. He walked with his toes turned in just a little. The motion should have seemed fastidious and weak, like his mouth, but he was nimble and slow, his arms swayed when he walked, there was sun in his black hair and then the forest, where the clearing ended, began to sigh. The grass leaned on their ankles and she looked toward the treeline, but the gust, wherever it came from, was down and the trees were quiet and still, and, all at once, full of birds, bursting out in a stream, twirling and chittering overhead, and diving back in.

Last night, in her dream, she waited in a graveyard staring beyond the rows of graves to a field where a marriage ceremony was about to take place. In the middle of the field, surrounded by wildflowers, was a huppah. They had thrown the white silk cloth over the wooden canopy and it hung down like a veil so that she could not see who was beneath it, but somehow she knew that it was Samuel standing on the platform, waiting for his bride. Rachel approached and called his name. She heard him shuffling, crouching, hiding from her. She took the fabric in her fleshless hands and drew it back.

Daniel was staring at a statue of a woman surrounded by children, or dwarves—they were tiny, stooped, and faceless. She held a rolling pin above her head like a club.

"You didn't answer me," she said.

"About?"

"What are you doing here?"

"I told you. I'm convalescing."

"Oh," Rachel felt like a hammer. All she did was say the wrong things to people in pain. But it's not like anyone ever said the right things to her. It felt like the whole fucking world was convalescing and no one was getting any better. "I didn't mean to be rude. I thought you were kidding. I thought you worked here."

"I'm a patient and a guest and I work here. Alex does not believe in definitional boundaries."

Like truth and lies, she thought. Like a sword swallower and a dying child with a bayonet through its throat bleeding in a snowy ravine outside of Minsk.

The birds were gone but she could still hear them. In the first spasms of her grief she had determined to be proactive and made an appointment with a grief counselor. The woman had suggested yoga and a vacation. *You have to fall in love with the world again*, she said. Life would be better if you were able to worship surprise. A certain kind of person could always be full of awe. She stared at the statues. Dumbfounded rabbis, big-dicked demons, pregnant women. Were they meant as decoration, or did they have some kind of significance? And what mode of thought, what religion or philosophy or ethics with these images at its center, would have anything useful to share with the world?

"Why do you like these?" she asked.

"I don't. I'm just gathering courage to go into the forest."

"You're afraid of the forest?"

"Alex told me never to go into it. He said it's dangerous."

The forest was old and unlogged, a mix of tall conifers whose names she didn't know; it looked tangled and dark and lovely. Rachel reached out her hand and took his. He was shy, a boy. He didn't know what to do.

"Shall we?" she said, and pulled him in.

Jacob found Baruch crouched on a mossy terrace on the estate's west side, clipping mint from terracotta planters and putting the leaves in a small yellow bowl.

"I used to do this at my father' sanatorium," he said.

"Garden?"

"Gather the mint for the guests' drinks in the afternoon."

When it came out, the exposé had been clear about two things: Baruch was not the child of any Berlin doctor. And although there was at least one sanatorium for TB patients in Greece, it was grim and inhumane, rundown, in ruins even while it was operational, and the staff—none of whom were German—did not live there.

"When was this?" Jacob asked.

Baruch braced his hands on his knees and stood without his cane, which was leaning against the far wall. "You're up early. Do you have trouble sleeping?"

"I saw Boris outside. Mel and Sophie are on the lawn. Everyone is up."

"Everyone around here has trouble sleeping," said Baruch. "How did Rachel sleep?"

The sea was invisible from the terrace, but you could sense it by the smell, the density of the air, the dim, inconstant movement in the small windows. It was the same way, Jacob felt, with people's critical judgement.

"You don't actually know anything about me," Jacob said.

"Where did you sleep last night?"

"I mean I'm not a cynic. I want to live my life honestly."

"Here's a problem the medieval rabbis had with your biblical namesake," Baruch said. "How is it possible that Isaac blesses Jacob instead of Esau? What kind of blessing could that be? What is bequeathed?"

Jacob had known what it meant to name himself Jacob. Isaac was blind and, with his mother's help, Jacob disguised himself as his brother, Esau, and deceived his father. But for Isaac's blessing to be a blessing it needed the Lord's power, and would the Lord provide a blessing for the wrong son?

"The consensus in the Midrash," Baruch said, "is that God condoned the blessing. I don't agree. Or, I guess I have another question. What does Isaac, of whom we know almost nothing beyond his ordeal, the moment his father almost sacrificed him at Moriah, have to offer a son? Terror and the memory of his terror, his father's obedience to a gruesome command, being trussed and bound and prepared for slaughter? And what kind of life does Jacob make from this birthright? He leaves his father confused and angry, calling out for his son. He has nightmares, he fights with an angel, he wanders, he lives in fear, he ends his days alone."

"I get it," Jacob said. "I may not have many prospects. But I also don't have much money."

Baruch batted the words away, as he would a fly. "An investment is important because it's important to be invested. As you said, you are not a cynic. We'll have the auction, the auction will bring cash, but also attention. With attention come investors. Of this, I have knowledge. Most of your cut can come from that. How does that sound?"

Jacob did not know how to spot deceit. Even if he was without belief, he was willing to believe anything. He was not a cynic. He trusted everyone but himself. He was the charlatan, he was sure of nothing, understood nothing, was afraid of everything, he lived in a panic of discovery that had no model. For both his parents the world was fixed, the idea of revelation of any kind was absurd: his father knew that all was spoiled, that snow was ash, the subway a death train, the factory on the other side of the river a crematorium spilling human smoke, and his mother was equally certain that the past was a ghost the world needed to exorcize, that the future was the only real thing, fully defined, already tended, the fertile homestead for those whose righteousness had no memory.

"Where did you get the Lurio?" Jacob said.

"I have a neighbor,"

"In New York?"

"Here," Baruch said, "on the other side of this island."

"I thought you owned this island."

"As I was saying last night, we power it primarily by a windmill. There's a backup supply of diesel for the generator, and solar panels. But wind is the only method that really works."

He pointed to his ear, looked down, closed his eyes, lifted his hand like a conductor suspending a note: the windmill thunking the air.

But his neighbor, he said, was stealing diesel from the backup generator. He went to his home to confront him. Maybe not wise. "I went to his home," Baruch said. "I stepped over a lot of dogs. I saw it on the mantle."

"The Lurio?"

His neighbor didn't know what it was. At first he claimed he found it at an antique store, but Baruch—faced with the backwoods shamble of so much shit, the pictures of naked women cut out of magazines, the detritus of lobster traps and old buoys—was dubious about how much antiquing his neighbor might do.

"The obsessions of others are always mysterious," Jacob said.

The obsessions of others were always mysterious, Baruch acknowledged, but a house without antiques might not indicate an interest in antiquing, and if you did not go antiquing would you buy a sketch at an antique store? He inquired again. The man sensed his interest and insisted on its personal worth: he found the sketch in his father's trunk after his father died. The neighbor wasn't quite sure where his father had gotten it, though his father was a Canadian, apparently, and had many nice things, of which Baruch saw none, but then he did not hold the idea of being a Canadian in the same reverence as his neighbor, who struck a hard bargain: five hundred dollars and Baruch drop the matter of the diesel, five hundred dollars and Baruch pay to hook his house up to the wind power so he could better produce his podcast.

"His podcast?" Jacob said.

"It's some kind of radio show," Baruch said. "Who cares? He thought that he was crafty, and I was an effete old Jew, moved by sentiment, willing to be suckered."

"Canadian podcasters with precious art. There are worse neighbors to have."

"No," Baruch said. "Neighbors like these are the worst kind."

At the forest's edge, a barrier of small, knotted conifers leaned against the open meadow. To cross the threshold, they had to break through a lattice of branches and Rachel let go of Daniel's hand and put her head down. For a moment she thought she'd made a mistake: maybe Baruch was right, this was a border she shouldn't cross, unwelcoming, and anyway, impassable, but that thought, the idea of the wild life being withheld from her, only made her want to cross it more and then, like that, they were through the thicket and into the open wood. The birds began to sing again, and in the openings between trees the sun fell in slashes and pooled on golden swards of needles banked, generations deep, over swollen roots.

For a while they walked in silence. Daniel loped behind her. Whenever she changed her speed, he'd start to hang back, staring at his feet or looking up into the trees. Either way she figured he'd fall down soon. Maybe he'd impale himself on a low branch. She imagined the explanation: death by diffidence. Like a heroine in a gothic novel.

Her grief therapist had said, *Check in on yourself from time to time. Make sure you're not just going full steam ahead. See how you're feeling.* She was kindly and older, beige and a little bored—she wore a beige cravat and a beige scarf. Rachel suspected that they were custom-made. Could you trust your emotions to such choices? *I always know how I'm feeling*, Rachel had complained. *That's the problem*. Her therapist nodded. *After you check in, then check out.*

Rachel found herself searching now for the sudden happiness she had felt drinking coffee on the cliff, to see if it had stayed with her. It had not. But for the first time in months, she wasn't angry. They were heading downhill into a valley where the trees grew denser, and from far below she could hear, and then smell, the cool floral billow of fresh water.

She stopped walking and turned to look behind her at Daniel, but he, like a shadow, stopped too and turned also to see what she was looking at. When he faced her again his expression was mismatched, his mouth round and pilled like a pulled thread and his eyes still wide, looking for whatever they had stopped to see.

"You skipped dinner last night," Rachel said.

"Alex doesn't make me go."

"But you have to eat?"

"I eat while I cook."

"You're the chef?"

He took a step toward her, his hair was almost violet, he could not meet her eyes.

"I cook the meals."

"I'm glad. I was beginning to think Baruch was also a gourmet chef."

"Alex couldn't care less about food. None of them could." There again: his hands in fists, his child's pout. "All they do is tell me about the food they ate as kids. The food their mother made. Or the uncle that brought them bonbons."

The low sun didn't reach into the valley. The forest went gray and leafless: muddy, mossy, dark.

"Apple trees in their yard," Daniel said. "Beehives. Honey. Or chicken soup. The dreams they had of chocolate."

He stopped. Suddenly he was looking at her.

"You must think I'm a monster," he said. "You don't understand." She waited for him to continue. It would be nice to know what she didn't understand. Increasingly she had begun to believe that nobody could put anything into words. "I was raised by my grandparents," he said.

Without the wind, the valley was hot and airless. She reached up and covered her mouth and he did the same thing. They stood there for a moment covering their mouths. The birds in the pines were listening to them.

When she began to walk again, she heard him follow.

"I learned to cook in boarding school," he said.

"Where was that?"

"I don't remember."

What do you say to anyone? In their little kitchenette with all the Prado magnets on the fridge, Rachel had tried to cook for Sam, and had tried to teach Sam to cook. There was no room to move, it was always hot, she had thought, mistakenly, it would be a kind of sex.

"I love to cook," she said. "And I've got nothing to do here. Maybe I can help you?"

They followed the creek out of the valley. Leaves again, lichen on boulders, ferns and rotting logs, the smell of rain. She was back for a moment in her dream, standing in the field by the hot river. Now they were coming to the forest's end. Another tree barrier, but thinner, and a screen of light, a clearing, on the other side.

"Last night," Daniel said, "did you go to the tavern?"

They were at the treeline. Before them, where the clearing began, was a barbed-wire fence. Beyond it was a kind of compound: a big red barn with a Live Free or Die mural painted on it, a semicircle of tents, three trailers and two jeeps, and what looked like a mix between a playground and an army obstacle course—monkey bars, truck tires lying on their sides in hopscotch intervals, a slide, and a series of shooting targets, shaped like humans, tacked to wooden planks backstopped with sandbags. Behind all that, overlooking it, was a large and dilapidated main house, with a widow's walk and crow's nest and wrap-around porch, gabled and listing and yet painted insanely yellow and bearing a bench swing, empty and rocking on the rotted-out deck as if someone had just been in it, or as if there were a breeze, but there was no breeze, of this Rachel was certain, because between the house and camp stood a flagpole where a Confederate flag hung limp as a sleeping insect.

BACK IN THE BRIDAL SUITE, Rachel turns the bolt with her key and chains the door. Jacob can always knock. What time is it? Ten a.m.? The room is like the inside of a shell: susurrus with the sound of waves. It's a narcotic. She can barely keep her eyes open. She climbs into the curled white chamber of the bed with her jeans and sweatshirt still on.

This time when they come to the creek in the forest, hundreds of small orange flowers speckle the bank. Don't step on them, Daniel says. They're endangered. She leans closer. The flowers look up at her. They are not flowers but little clay animal statues. She touches one: it's damp and soft and it takes a few steps. They're newts, actually, bright and orange and alive. Something's been lost. The forest riffles and thins. On the other side of the creek there is the barbed-wire fence and on the other side of the fence there is the empty graveyard where she knows that Samuel has just been doing his wedding dance around the bony finger he discovered in the dirt. She's sobbing the way she always does in dreams and never can on the other side of her life. Please, don't step on them, she says. Daniel is holding one of the newts in the palm of his hand. He stands below her, in the water, and only comes up to her knee. He is about four years old. Look, he says. Lizards.

Awake again and in the canted hall, jamming on her muddy shoes and trying to catch her breath.

Baruch told Daniel never to go in the forest but didn't tell him why. Has he told anyone that it's because there's a compound for backwoods Nazis next door? Didn't he own this island? Isn't that what he said when giving them the tour yesterday? Actually, she could not remember him saying he owned it, but he had implied it.

We are self-sustaining here...Another lie, or half-truth. She clenches herself around her anger, clings to it.

She had taken Samuel on a road trip in her MG. I didn't know you were rich, he said. Their first morning in the country they went hiking. The forest floor was damp and piney and the trail was covered in a beautiful carpet of orange newts. She grabbed his arm. She had never seen anything like it. No one had even suggested that this was something that might appear to you. It was like a surprise they conjured together, an impossible color blossoming out of dream. What are they? What are they? he kept shouting. She told him, and his nose scrunched around the word. *Newts?* He was sweet and excited. Don't touch them, she said but he'd already picked one up.

In the kitchen, Daniel was washing mint. "What are you doing down here?"

"Looking for wine," she said.

He unrolled two paper towels. He lay one down on the tile counter and emptied the mint from the colander onto it. Then he put the other paper towel on top and began to pat it dry with the tips of his fingers. The motion seemed fussy and particular and he did not look up.

"I know it's only eleven o'clock," Rachel said, "but I'm on vacation."

"Are you?" The air was fragrant with dented mint. He had not stopped pressing on it.

"I'm here to see the Lurio like everybody else."

"I don't drink anymore," Daniel said.

"Just one bottle," Rachel said. "Please."

A key hung from a nail by the walk-in pantry. He took it down, unlocked the door, and opened it into darkness.

At the base of the stairs Daniel rummaged in a wine crate.

"I thought this was a pantry," Rachel said.

He lifted a kerosene lantern from the crate and struck a match on the wall. The flame seemed to die in the globe before bubbling back to life. Rachel looked down: several gallons of kerosene rested against five boxes of matches.

"Is that safe?" she asked.

The flame guttered on the low wick and the shadows sighed toward them. Daniel held the lantern up by his face and squinted.

"Alex picks the wine because I don't drink anymore."

He didn't seem to want to step beyond the crates of kerosene. Rachel took the lantern. "Don't worry, I won't choose anything good."

"Alex only has good wine," Daniel said.

Whatever threshold this was, Daniel wouldn't cross it. He waited in the dark at the bottom of the stairs, while she headed in, looked left and right, and it was true, all the wine was good, and she was impressed that Daniel knew the difference, and then she reached the far wall, which was not actually a wall, but another door. "What's this?" she called.

"What's what?"

"In the back."

His voice echoed wetly, strayed and returned through the branching black chambers. "Oh," he said. "You must mean the vault."

Back in the kitchen Rachel watches Daniel cook.

The wine is open on the counter and she's three glasses in.

"This is good," she says.

"I told you."

Rachel loves to cook, she's good at it, and she watches Daniel with awe. His knife slides frictionless across the board like an otter slipping into a river. In its wake the air is splashed with shallots.

Again Rachel wants to ask what he's doing here, but she feels like he's already told her. There are so many futile forms of unnoticed excellence. She holds out the bottle.

"Why don't you drink?" she says.

"Why doesn't anyone drink?"

"Lack of aptitude?"

A minced shallot balances on the flat of his knife. He tips it into a bowl. "After boarding school, I worked in restaurants." He says it like an explanation, which it probably is.

"My best friend was a drug addict," Rachel says.

When it started, when only weeks after Rivkah first brought her brother Schmuley to NextSteps, and Rachel took him out and he said, *Please, please, I never want to be Schmuley again. Call me Samuel*, he had thrown himself at their affair with a wonder that for Rachel was a kind of arrival: she felt safe in his love, invulnerable, chiseled hard by his softness into a prism the world passed through, in shards of new color, onto the blank canvas of his life.

She took him to restaurants and movies, she played him hip hop, bought him tacos and tikka masala, watched him bite his first Big Mac, swore and wore tank tops, lay down on her back on their first night together, put his dick between her breasts and blew him.

He left his wife and child, he was hungry, he was a field ravaged by wind—everything bright and broken, alive as aftermath.

Then Rivkah died and his wife, with a generosity he hadn't predicted, offered him a divorce. He was free, he married Rachel, and then, though she had been the bird that bore him signs of the new world, he had to make the escape his own: after he proved his independence from the Haredim by marrying her, he had to prove his independence from her. He became rebellious and argumentative. He didn't like her taste in music or food, he wanted to live in the world but not a world that was discovered for him. She allowed this. She understood it. After all, he was like a teenager who would grow out of his angst and anyway, he was grieving for his sister. She practiced suffering and patience. But it wasn't what she had expected. She had hoped, maybe, to be reborn in his wonder, both vicariously and as its agent, but instead she felt like his mother. In the meantime he had almost no education beyond Jewish law. They got him a tutor, enrolled him in classes where he met friends, he came home drunk and angry, or drunk and happy, or drunk and horny. She was surprised to find that she accepted this too: it was a story about men that life had already prepared her for. But as she continued to accept his behavior he began to reject hers. Somehow he picked up an anti-hipster hipsterism—the castigation of anything pretentious, which in his mind was anything he didn't know about. And, with his upbringing, he didn't know about anything.

About six months into their marriage, he got home from class one night while she was preparing dinner. She had Nina Simone on the radio and had opened one of her favorite Italian Nebbiolos to sip as she cooked. She felt relaxed and sultry; she met him at the door, kissed him, took his shoes, handed him a glass. "Here," she said. "I got us something special for tonight." She began to tell him about it. In college Rachel had taken a wine-tasting class and in the fun and hapless year before graduate school she halfheartedly started training as a sommelier, and though she had found the rigorous professionalization of her pleasure less rewarding than she hoped, she still liked tasting and talking about wine, liked both sharing something she loved with him and, in sharing it, feeling her life shaken back into that threshold year when everything still seemed possible.

"Do you smell that?" she said. Nina chanted "Plain Gold Ring"; Rachel swayed as she talked. She touched his arm, she held her own glass up to his face. She had just turned thirty. Your life rushes on beyond you. There is no way to avoid regret. But the simple things, pleasure in the sensual moment, could often be enough. She talked about the scents of roses and tar. An Italian street in summer sun. She was aware of her loveliest self. "But then," she said and sucked in some wine, swirled it around and also let it redden her lips. "That taste—plums!"

He broke away from her and picked up his own glass. He smelled and frowned and didn't bother to drink. "You're such a snob," he said. "It's just grapes, Rachel. It's not a tar smell. It's grape juice."

She crumbled back to the stove, to the pasta sauce she was making.

"Wine all tastes the same," he said. "Or it tastes like Manischewitz."

This was his typical, increasingly snide wit. In the past she'd been sensitive. He was twenty-eight years old and had never looked at a map, didn't know history or much math, couldn't drive or navigate an airport or write English very well.

"Fuck you, Schmuley," she said.

She pours herself another glass.

"Do you like cooking here?"

"Living here keeps me sober."

"So you ascribe to Baruch's methods?"

"My grandparents were cold and where they weren't cold they were cruel and where they weren't cruel they were dead. No one is really alive here, but no one is cruel, either. I ascribe to that."

Ascribe. Is Daniel mocking her stilted diction? Her disbelief in her own belief?

He's arrayed his workstation on the counter with such order—a bowl of shallots, another of tomatoes from the garden, fresh basil, thyme, fish on ice, olive oil in a little glass bottle. Order, sensuality, fragrance of myrrh, the skid when the first shallots hit the pan, my hands like goats. She cannot see his mouth.

"Can I help you cook?"

He reaches under the counter and pulls out an extra cutting board. He hands her a knife, the bowl of cherry tomatoes. He cuts one to the size he desires. He faces her and smiles. "Roll up your sleeves."

JACOB WAS LATE TO THE TABLE and Baruch was waiting until he got there to make the toast.

"I'm sorry. I got lost," Jacob said.

"Fish tonight," said Boris. He was wearing the same jacket and pocket square.

"All you have to do is come down the stairs," Rachel said.

"Codfish," said Boris. "In a sauce."

Baruch lifted his glass. "In the next few days, people will begin arriving for the auction. I believe there will be an air of festivity, even of excess. This can be, as we have long hoped, a new beginning for us. We may become, if you don't mind an old man saying such a thing, like those fresh born into the Garden. L'chaim."

They drank.

"A new start," Mel said. "Wilder nature. Freedom and indulgence. Message received."

The room was silent. Freshly lit candles burned in a perfect row. Anna frowned and straightened her fork on the fresh linen. Outside through the French doors a violet dusk had fallen and thin twists of mist spooled over the low-tide islands like an image on a Japanese screen.

"And yet," said Baruch, "what is the purpose of suffering?"

"It doesn't have one," Sophie said. "Isn't that the point? My suffering isn't even mine."

"I'm thinking of the Lurio sketch that I was lucky enough to discover. It's a depiction of Job staring into the whirlwind. But I've often wondered, what do we learn from Job? Job, it seems to me, sets his own precedent, but what is the precedent Job sets?"

"That God is a sadist," Sophie said.

"Maybe," Baruch said. "And if so, I do not need to learn from God, because I do not want to learn to be a sadist. But can I learn how to suffer from Job? Job suffers and suffers and demands to know why. And God chastises him for this. He refuses to explain Himself, He rejects the premise that it's even conceivable for Job to understand anything He might explain. So from Job we learn to recognize our own incomprehension of His will. But if we cannot understand His will, that is, if we cannot understand why we suffer, can we understand our suffering?

"And if we can't understand His will as it relates to our suffering, if He rejects even our desire to understand what happens in our lives, is this a rejection of his covenant with us? The covenant with the Jews is less a contract than a human interpretation of causality—if I do this, the Lord does that. But His discourse with Job dismisses causality entirely. Understanding is beyond His nature, His nature is beyond His nature. Consider Adam and Eve's mistake—eating from the Tree of Knowledge. God does not simply surpass our understanding. His paradise is antithetical to it."

Joshua, angry, in class had shouted, "Are you saying the Shoah's meaningless? Are you saying that it doesn't mean anything?"

"Which makes us wonder," Baruch said, "what can we say about our suffering?"

"You've written books about your suffering," Rachel said.

"And what did that accomplish? I've tried to attest to my sorrow and by attesting to it to put it back into History, to give it meaning, but do I know what it meant? Of the essential functions of the universe, which of course I do not claim to even begin to apprehend, what can be transmitted? The Kabbalah would suggest that nothing can. Or everything, but what we recognize as having been transmitted is, by its very essence, what hasn't been transmitted. Or in the process of being exposed to our understanding has been leeched of its fundamental meaning."

"Sounds like quantum theory," Jacob said.

"How?" said Sophie.

"I'm not sure."

"Exactly," said Baruch.

And then, again, the sleepy silence of the previous night. The conversation retracted. Briefly, the terrible president washed through the conversation—it was impossible not to speak of him every time one spoke—and then, by mutual agreement, more pouring of wine, was banished.

But Baruch was still lively, he was on his feet, his napkin was still in his hand. At the doorway he pressed a small button on the wall.

"Tonight the cook must come and take a bow," he said, and then shuffled around the corner toward the kitchen and shouted, "Daniel, please, come take a bow."

Daniel stood before them with his heels touching and his hands stacked right knuckle in left palm and looked at his feet. To Jacob the pose seemed both affected and uncomfortable. Like Joshua suddenly pushing himself up from his seat, his face red and his eyes filling with tears.

"Bravo," said Sophie. Daniel looked up at her, as if he didn't expect anyone to speak, and nodded.

"Please sit with us, Daniel," Baruch was saying. "I'm done boring everybody for the night."

Daniel started to pull out a chair when there was a knock—or louder than a knock, it would have to be a smash almost for them to hear it, on the front door.

It had begun to rain and was nearly ten o' clock.

Baruch said, "Daniel, could you please see who that is?"

Daniel did. "Who could it be?" Mel said.

"The Moshiach," said Boris. "I hope we saved him some cod."

They heard the heavy door open, and waited, and heard it close.

Daniel returned. "No one," he said.

Jacob tapped the table, the chair leg, the table. He stopped. He clutched one hand with the other. He started tapping again. Rachel, on his right, looked over, caught his eye, frowned in something like a question. "This reminds me of an essay by Joseph Soloveitchik," he said.

"What does?" Sophie asked.

"The essay is called 'The Voice of My Beloved Knocks.' Soloveitchik compares the unanswered knock in the *Song of Songs* to our failure to recognize the appearance of a divine miracle."

"But we answered the door," Sophie said.

"That's true," said Jacob.

"We answered the door and there was no one there."

"You're right. It doesn't apply exactly."

"It's exactly the opposite."

The desire for silence, the unsaid, the unanswered. The knock the maiden in the *Song of Songs* forsakes. The command Jonah buries himself in sleep, in the ocean, in the whale to avoid. Jacob made Maddie a promise about the future and Maddie had said, "But what about the first baby?"

"Soloveitchik argues that Job does not try to understand. He accepts the suffering then accepts the miracle. He gets, you know, a whole new family."

"What a stupid idea," Sophie said.

"The suffering of Job is supposed to represent the Holocaust. The miracle is supposed to be Israel."

"Does that make it better?" Rachel said.

"At no point," Jacob said, tapping on the edge of the table, "was I saying this was a good essay."

"There are no miracles," said Boris. "I think that is the point of this story." And then the second knock came as loud as before.

"Daniel, please," said Baruch.

Again, Daniel returned. "No one."

"Are you sure?" Baruch said. "It is raining quite hard."

Jacob got up and went to the window glass. One veil for another, the rain had replaced the mist.

Rachel asked Baruch, "Do you have any neighbors on this island?"

"No."

"Really?" She said it too loud, almost performed, almost indignant. "I thought I saw…"

"None that would drop by," Baruch interrupted.

The room gathered silence. Everyone poured more wine. One of the candles went out. Smoke threaded upward from the table.

Daniel was still standing at the threshold.

"What are we waiting for?" Rachel asked.

Baruch placed his hands on the arms of his chair and stood slowly. His face was heavy, his cheeks drooped into jowls. "I believe," he said, "we are waiting for the third knock."

After the third knock, Daniel said, "I think I'd like someone else to answer the door."

There were no windows on the door in the low stone hallway. Jacob put his head to the wood and listened: only rain, swishing on distant wind, from the other side. "Hello," he called and waited and heard nothing.

He opened the door. A stooped old man stood clutching a small canvas suitcase to his chest. Water dripped from the brim of his woolen cap.

"Can't you see it's raining?" he said and thrust the wet suitcase into Jacob's hands. "Let me in. It's kalt as a witch's tit out here."

INSIDE, WITH THE DOOR CLOSED behind him and him now here with Jacob on the other side of the storm, he didn't seem so stooped. He was wearing a thin gray suit, a white shirt buttoned all the way up, and no tie. He took off his cap and wrung it out on the floor. His skull was bare but for strands of wet white hair, flattened against his scalp. Otherwise, he wasn't very wet. He blew in his hands, slapped the cap on his knee, and put it back on.

"Are you waiting for a tip or something?" he said.

"I don't work here," Jacob said.

"Oh, so you're one of the meshugeners? In which case, my apologies. Please take me to your rabbi."

His voice was high and accented, an odd New York hybrid, Brighton Beach with a querulous Yiddish lilt.

"Why did you knock three times?" Jacob said.

"Three times? Who knocks three times? Once is enough, if you're wanted." And he began walking down the hall, while Jacob followed again with a bag that was not his.

"Herr Doktor," the old man shouted as they entered the dining room. "Look who's here!"

Baruch was sitting again and drinking wine and he put his glass down and peered.

"Good evening," said Anna.

"Why did you knock three times?" asked Mel.

"What is this?" the old man said. "It's a door, not a wall. I knock, it opens. This is how it always goes. The real question is how you're treated on the other side."

He stopped, or paused in a posture of expectation: head cocked to the left and left eyebrow raised, his hands outstretched, palms up and open. But it was Baruch's house and if someone was going to offer him a place to sit, it would have to be Baruch and Baruch had still said nothing. The man took off his wet hat and performed a little bow.

"I'm sorry for interrupting your dinner, but as the Talmud says, you should always make room for a guest. You read the Talmud here with your doctor, yes? Of course you do. Without the Talmud, how else could you recover your wits? In this world, sanity is a relative quality. If someone is foolish enough to argue over whether a bean counts as bread, they must be worse off than you."

"We were just talking about that last night," said Mel.

"And look, not a one of you weeping! I don't care what they say about him in the papers, your rabbi's methods must work. Not that I would know firsthand. I am not a reader and I try not to ponder mysteries, but still I never forget a law and I'm pretty sure that you should treat even the lowest guest with distinction. It's not so much a question of hospitality as good sense. You don't know who they could be. So you treat a stranger better even than a friend. Isn't that right, rabbi? Then again, I am not a stranger, am I, Alexei? Or do you still not know me?"

Baruch's hands floundered on the arms of his chair. One pressed, the other fluttered. He seemed to be trying to stand but not remembering how.

"Eli?" he said.

"Ah-ha, not senile yet." The man laughed and opened his arms. "What, Herr Doktor, aren't you going to give me a hug?" And he pranced forward in wet shoes, squeaking across the wooden floor, where Baruch stood, finally, and met him with a flinch.

While the old man called Eli ate, Daniel lit new candles and brought out brandy.. The rain had stopped and the silver clinked on the bone china. The old man looked up and beamed about the room.

"This is a beautiful home, Alex."

Baruch nodded. "Thank you."

"God has graced you, yes? Wouldn't you say?"

"I have been very lucky."

"Lucky, sure. All of us who are not dust have some luck. But this is more than luck."

Baruch didn't respond. He was looking out the window, though with the candles relit the glass again was a mirror so he must have been staring at himself and Jacob wondered what he saw there. Everyone else was watching Eli eat. Like any great man, Baruch was accustomed to being the center of attention. He might not be as he was ten years ago in Berlin, at the height of his fame, but when he was on, like earlier at dinner, lecturing about Job, he was charismatic, funny, fast-talking, he still spoke with authority. And when he was down, as he had seemed last night, tired and bored, he was the center the room twirled to like a vortex in a tub. But now, hunched in his seat, he seemed to want to disappear.

Eli dabbed his lips with his napkin, speared a piece of pancetta, and brandished it to the candle flame. "What is this?" he said. "What is this little meat?"

"Pancetta," said Daniel. "It's a kind of bacon."

"A kind of bacon?"

"From Italy."

Eli lowered his fork. "You served me a bacon? I survived the pogroms and the clearing of the ghettos and the Einsatzgruppen and the wolves in the Ukrainian forest and the Ukrainians, as you'd now call them, in the Ukrainian forests, and the Red Army in their glee, all so you could sully my soul with an Italian bacon?"

Daniel's mouth became a hole the rest of his face started to fall through.

"I'm sorry," he whispered. "I didn't know."

"You didn't know? You didn't know you have to tell a Jew when you serve him pig? Even the Macedonians knew this. My grandfather, blessed be his name, cut out his own tongue with his mohel's knife rather than spoil his kosher at the mob's behest."

Sophie gasped.

"And me? A man of ninety years old. Or eighty-nine, actually, but what's one year to a little shit like you? A man of ninety years old, and I have never broken the kosher laws. Until now."

"That's enough, Eli," Baruch said.

Eli poked his fork at Daniel. "What, do you think I'm some kind of rube? I've been all over the world. Pancetta! I smelled it when I walked in the door!" And he popped the pork into his mouth.

Daniel fled, and Rachel followed him.

Baruch said, "You cannot behave that way in my house, Eli."

"Behave what way? I thought he was the cook."

"He's a patient and guest. As are all here."

Eli raised his glass. "I'm sorry, everyone. You have to understand, I'm an old man and an old man shouldn't make jokes. At my age, when I make a joke, no one can tell." He drank and put down his glass and looked back up, squinting. "Of course, Alex, it isn't right to scold me either."

"Why not?" Rachel said. She had returned, was standing in the doorway, and her face was flushed. "You upset him."

"Why not? Pancetta or no pancetta, I thought you were Jews here. It comes back to the Talmud. Don't you know the story of Doctor Pelimo and his guest?"

"It was Erev Yom Kippur, the evening before the Day of Atonement, and the rich man Pelimo was having a feast. All his guests had arrived and they were sitting around a table and there was no shortage of delights there. Fishes and fouls, soups, challah, maybe, I don't know.

I'm not sure where the story comes from, Babylon or Jerusalem, and anyway, I don't know what they ate in those places. But please, use your imagination and fill the table with whatever you like. The specifics aren't important. As it is said: if you stare too hard at the grass, you miss the lion. At any rate it's a nice feast and they are all assembled at the table. They sit, they say the blessing, they start to eat, and what should happen? A knock on the door."

He poured himself more brandy. He smiled at Jacob, then at Mel. "Just one knock, friends. That's all it took. Pelimo was a righteous man and proud of his righteousness, so he dispatched his servant to go answer.

"The servant gets to the door. He opens it. Whatever his difficulties, that at least he could manage. Whatever he'd been through in his life, he opens the door and outside there is a beggar. 'Let me have a piece of bread,' says the beggar, and the servant lets him have bread.

"'Let me come inside,' says the beggar. 'It's cold out here. On a holy night, why should some have shelter while I must shiver?' And the servant, he's a good Jew, he knows his master is a good Jew, he lets the beggar in.

"'Let me have a place at the table,' says the beggar, and though he is filthy and ragged and bad-smelling, Pelimo pulls out a chair and gives him a place at the table.

"The beggar sits, they resume their sumptuous feast, and the beggar begins to pick at his boils.

"'Stop picking your boils,' shouts Pelimo. 'Eat your soup and drink your wine and behave.'

"The beggar eats his soup and drinks his wine and then vomits all over the table.

"'Stop vomiting on my table, you wretch,' shouts Pelimo, and the beggar produces his filthy genitals and begins to pull out lice from the hair.

"'This is too disgusting for dinner,' says Pelimo, and the beggar dies right there in his seat.

"All over town people said, 'Pelimo killed a man at his own table,' and Pelimo, in his shame, abandoned his family and his servants and his home and threw himself into the latrine."

In the dumbstruck silence Jacob thought: I should have told that one in class.

"What was the point of that story?" Sophie asked finally.

"That's not in the Talmud," Mel said. "Is that in the Talmud? We didn't learn that one in Hebrew school."

"Nobody learns the Talmud in Hebrew school," Sophie said.

"The ultra-Orthodox do," Rachel said.

"Yes," Jacob said. "That story is in the Talmud."

Sophie turned to Baruch, to confirm perhaps, but Baruch—troubled, quizzical—was staring at his guest.

"My point," said Eli, "is that you shouldn't rebuke a guest. It's as good as killing him. On that note, how long has it been Alex?"

"You know exactly how long it's been."

"Spring 1945," said Eli. "Who would have thought we would both live so long?"

"I didn't think you did."

"I know," said Eli. "What a surprise. To me as well. I haven't forgotten."

"You knew each other in 1945?" Sophie said.

"Certainly we did. In 1943, in 1944. In '45. In the forests and the train depots, in the ghettos and ruined cities."

Sophie put her hand over Mel's. "So you could defend him to the press. You knew him. You could confirm his story."

"I've heard what they say. They say your rabbi is not who he claims. They say he was not there. It's hard to tell the world who you really are. I, for instance, never have. And no one else has either. I myself am not much of a reader, but I know I have never appeared in Alex's accounts. Which is fine. When something is shattered, no matter how hard you try you can never put back all the pieces. And if we gave voice to the dead, those of us who have known so many, we'd have no room for the living." He stopped, he placed his knife and fork on his empty plate and leaned back in his chair. "And yet, it turns out I am not dead. Some days, I feel almost alive. So maybe you're right, dear." He bowed his head at Sophie. "Perhaps it would be good to tell the world my story."

A moonless night, and again they've left without him. And again Rachel has decided to stay. Jacob tried to get her to join, he told her that this was something she needed to see, but could not tell her what this was. "I've never been so tired in my life," she said.

He was knocking on the doorjamb, a dresser, the windowsill. She watched him. "It will help you understand," he said. It was midnight. His knuckles on the wall—long, short-short.

"You've come to a sanitarium and become crazier," she said and turned off the lamp.

Now Jacob heads through the forest with his flashlight. It casts a wide beam in a pale and perfect circle and the world narrows to that circle, beyond the margins of the light the dark woods grow darker. He senses that he will only ever know or understand what is directly before him—scales of bark, the edge of a root bulging from the ground like a vein, humped moss, and beyond, in the wide Atlantic darkness, it is just void.

The trail turns down into the heavy tangle before the clearing; he is troubled by the old man's story. It was incomplete. He knows his Talmud and he knows that Baruch does too and what the old man left out is that the stranger who shows up to Pelimo's table in the night is not actually a beggar, is not actually poor or sick or there by chance, but is a demon in disguise, like the Adversary before Job, coming to test the house.

JONAH'S.

Air thick as pipesmoke. Sea wind through the broken windows. The blue spot. An angel standing in its glow says, a rabbi walks into a bar.

A diadem of barnacles sparkles across its forehead.

The angel bobs, its wings shiver and molt dust—the dust flashing, briefly incandescent, like embers, before passing out of the corona into darkness.

The tavern has altered since last night. Two more harpoons lean near the door where Jacob stands. At the far wall, below the windows, more buoys clutter the floor. A wooden ship's wheel with several broken spokes lies on the bar draped in dried seaweed. Something scurries among all this new garbage. It's as if the angels spend their days pillaging shipwrecks.

The angel says, A rabbi walks into a bar. He asks the bartender, What's kosher here? and the bartender says this is my mother's honey cake recipe.

As before, Mel and Sophie and Anna sit at a hightop not far from the tables where the other angels are propped. Baruch stands by the far wall, among the buoys, near the busted-out windows, stooped into shadow. He leans forward. "Yes," he says. "Good."

The angel says, When I was a little girl my mother gave me this book. She said this was my favorite.

"Continue," Baruch says.

The other angels shiver and bob. Their wings fracture into sound in a kind of reverb, both sharp and muffled, like the glass the groom smashes at a wedding. A strand of Maddie's hair had come undone and fallen over her left eye, across her cheek, her face jigsawed with delight. When Jacob brought his heel down on the pillowcase and felt the glass give, she jumped into his arms.

The room jitters. The angels flutter and clack their lips like beaks. Baruch takes a step forward.

The angel says, What's the best part of lean pastrami?

"Am I supposed to ask what?" says Mel.

"I don't think so," says Sophie.

The angel stares straight ahead, bows, and begins to shuffle to its seat. The motion unspools jerkily like old film jumping frames and as it approaches its table another shimmers into the arc of light and heads to the stage, they pass each other and freeze, driftwood again, before shivering on in opposite directions.

On this one's cheek: a rash of dark purple algae. Like a wet stone you could slip on.

The angel says, Three Jewish mothers are sitting in a café. They begin arguing over whose son loves his mother the most. The first one says, my son is a good boy. He calls me every Shabbos. The second one says, my son is a good boy. He calls me every night of the week. The third one.

Again Jacob left his phone in the room and again it pulses against his leg.

The angel says, What's with women these days?

The angel says, Before I got married I went to my rabbi. I said, Rabbi I have some questions about the wedding night.

Baruch deflates, he's sagging in the corner, he says, "That's enough for tonight. Mel, perhaps you should take your turn," and the angel returns to its seat and Mel stands, straightens his legs, and walks up to the stage, where his white sneakers glow pearlescent as something scavenged, still wet, from the sea bottom.

RACHEL, AWAKE, READS BARUCH.

When I was very young my father was the chief physician in a sanatorium on a mountain above the Aegean. Most of the patients were suffering or recovering from the fall of old Europe, the Great War, the appearance of trains, of photographs, of shell shock, of industry, of desire and syphilis, of magnetic interference, a creeping terror of automata, of, to be comprehensive, what my father called "the Wounds of the Age."

The sanatorium, which, as was the fashion, combined the attributes of a hospital, a health spa, and a luxury hotel, sat on a cleared plateau facing the sea. Behind it, the dry cliffs rose into blue mountains, and even in the height of summer its many terraces remained cool and shady well into morning. With my window open and the breeze coming the right way, as it did in the long season of those lost days, jasmine and hibiscus would scent the air, flowing in from the courtyard. On the southeastern side of the property, where the cliffs were not as steep, we had olive groves and citrus trees ranging down the limestone hills all the way to the town that flashed up white as a seashell.

She should have asked Daniel how he believed this, if he even did. How could anyone see it as authentic? But maybe this was the wrong question. What people wanted was the remarkable possibility, the child who survived without rage, sought no revenge, claimed no state as his own.

Rachel writes in her journal. *Dear Rivkah, I know you thought I was not real. But I would have been.*

We crave the remarkable, but the remarkable was Rivkah with her wig off. The bar, the jukebox, the bare arms in bad light.

Baruch: *In those days, even though we were waiting, we did not think of the future. We were waiting, but only for the end of the present.*

Outside, just beyond the glass, the tide's insistence. She feels the whole headland begin to sway.

Nothing mattered, I was a wicked scrabbling thing, the human world flamed out and fell like a leaf from the birch forest on the other side of the river in autumn—

She stands at the riverbank. On the other side, Sam, the huppah, and the river between them flashing, as if the sun just hit it, with the sudden light of an unveiled mirror.

MEL, ON STAGE, GRINS and says nothing. His suit shimmers like a microchip. He looks young, like he needs to go to the bathroom, his knees pinch together, his legs make a sheepish X. He is mute and eager and the angels lean toward him from their torsos; their carved wooden faces don't move. He pushes his hands into his pockets.

"Go ahead, honey," Sophie says from her seat.

The room is expectant, perched, precarious. The tavern slopes toward the cliff edge, the floor humped and tilted, leaning into the sea.

"I don't know where to start," Mel says.

"Start the same place you always do," says Sophie.

"I began with a song," Anna says.

The sea starts up again, waves out of nowhere, like traffic.

"My mother spent the war living in a cupboard," Mel says. "She was three when they began forcing people into ghettos, and my grandfather paid a local Polish woman to take her in and keep her hidden. The Polish woman was a widow and she had two other daughters of her own and she needed the extra money. The idea was that they would pretend she was a family member, a cousin or niece or whatever, whose parents had died. She didn't speak Polish very well, or what she did speak she spoke with a Yiddish accent, so they were supposed to just say she was a mute, a little slow. Anyway, how much do people expect an eight-year-old to talk?"

"Between the ages of five and eight, I didn't speak a word," Anna whispers to Boris.

Mel tells them about his first wife. How she used to refer to him as Polish. How she'd say, *Well you're Polish after all.* They'd be doing the things that young couples do. Studying each other's faces in bed. The physical investigations. "Very healthy," he adds, "from a professional standpoint. Very normal. Not that anything is or isn't normal," he adds. "Well, actually, some things probably aren't normal."

"Mel," Sophie says.

Really, what he meant is that they were happy. In bed. Nothing weird. Except. They'd be studying each other's faces afterward and she'd say, *Well of course your skin has purple undertones, you're Polish.* And he would get upset. Not the first time. The first time he explained. *I'm not Polish. I'm Jewish.* And his knees were stiff, that first time, just a little stiff, when he stood from the bed, or the next time, from the dinner table. *That's like me saying I'm Catholic, not Irish,* she said. *No,* he told her. He was always friendly, he was always kind, he didn't yell. He wanted to be liked. If you asked him, and he did, he asked himself, he'd say and did, he wanted his wife to like him. For many years this was the entire representation of his damage: in every situation he wanted to be liked. *No,* he said to her that first time, *It's not the same thing at all.*

He tried to explain Jewish life in Eastern Europe. For instance. Until the fall of the Soviet Union a Russian Jew was marked as a Jew, not a Russian, on their passport. It was a clear example, he thought. But general enough. It did not accuse. It did not, in its most specific details, demand that you ask what this enforced difference perpetuated or allowed. *That's Russia, not Poland,* she said. *There was no difference,* he said. Poland, Russia, Ukraine, under the Tzar, or the Hapsburgs, or the USSR. The Jews were separate. Polish wasn't their first language. Russian wasn't. *You people are very insular,* she'd said. *You keep to yourselves. You nourish your difference and then complain about it.* She was from a hardworking blue-collar family from New Jersey. They knew Jews the way they knew the Italians and Indians. He was groping for grievance, she said. He was nourishing a victimhood that was not his.

The conversation had not yet driven them out of bed or into clothes. He was under the covers, but she was lying on top of them with light from the streetlamp falling into their room so that she was lit, beautiful and aglow while he lay there in shadow, trying to explain himself to her halo.

The next time, he tried harder. The issue had acquired stakes they had not expected. It appeared in their lives like mold spooring in the walls. She felt betrayed. *Exactly*, he said. They were not prepared for it. ("How odd not to be prepared for history," he said now to the room, and the angels, earless, stared on). They weren't kids. After a reasonable courtship, after a few years of content marriage, you don't expect new issues. At least not ones that you generate yourselves, out of nothing. Or this is how it seemed to her, when he'd suddenly ruin a perfectly nice evening by getting upset and she'd just stare up at him, furious and flabbergasted, watching her life founder, she thought, on an issue so small, so semantic, that it couldn't possibly be serious. And yet she was unwilling to abandon it: she kept arguing with him, she kept calling him Polish, there were stakes for her too: he clung to some wound, she must have believed, that would fester in their marriage if she didn't stanch it now.

The last time she called him Polish it was half a joke and half a threat and so instead of arguing he told her about the Jews in Poland. They were at dinner at a restaurant on the Hudson and they were sitting by the window with views of the water. He set down his glass. The lights were dim enough for him to look out the window and instead of seeing his own face, he saw the evening they were supposed to have: a waterfall pouring into a wide river, its churning surface dazzled with stars. Then he told her about the founding of the

Polish ghettos in 1266 after the Fourth Lateran Council, the expulsions from towns, the laws forbidding Jews to live alongside Poles, a divide he reminded her that they, *the Poles,* made and enforced, the stripping of businesses and property, the escalating violence, the conspiracy theories and charges of blood libel, the pogroms after the Kracow fire, the Warsaw Pogrom, the Czetchowa Pogrom, the Siedelce Pogrom, the Lwow Pogrom, the Pinsk Pogrom, the Vilna Pogrom, the Przytyk Pogrom, and then, of course, the Holocaust and the extermination, the willful, complicit, gleeful, energetic extermination of the Polish Jews, which at first he didn't even talk about, he skipped, jumped right over to the Kielce Pogrom, in 1946, where Jews, returning to their hometown from the concentration camps, where Jews, he was shouting now, who *survived* the camps, returned home only to be massacred by Polish villagers, their former neighbors, who did not want to give their houses and property back.

The meal was over. He had started before their appetizer came and was still talking an hour later, monologuing through desert. Waiters came and went and finally, after the tears made mud of her makeup, stayed away. *Are you done?* she said. *Not yet,* he said. *I'm leaving,* she said and stood and he tried to do so too, to follow her out, or catch her, or apologize for shouting about Polish antisemitism all through their candlelit fifth anniversary dinner, but he couldn't stand.

"My mother spent the war living in a cupboard," he says again.

In the hospital, still unable to walk, he finally told his wife this: for a while, his grandfather would come by once a week. When he did, the Polish woman scooped his mother out of the cupboard and told her to act like all was well. Told her that if she spoke, if she said a single word to her papa they'd turn him in and put her in a soup. So she said nothing. Her father kneeled down and took her face in his hands. *Be good, sweetie*, he'd say, *be good to your new family. They are beautiful people*, he'd say and kiss her forehead and say, *Your mother misses you*, and he'd give her a toy or a treat, a piece of bread, or a honeycomb, and then he'd say, *Sweetie, can you speak to me? Sweetie, I love you, can you say you love your papa*? Eventually he'd give up. He always snuck out under the cover of darkness, he didn't have much time, and he'd kiss her forehead, bless her, pay the woman and leave with his sack of cloth samples—since he was pretending to be a Polish merchant displaced by the war—and head back.

And then one week he did not come. A few days later there was a knock. It was one of the woman's neighbors, with news. Apparently, Mel's mother heard from the cupboard, they had liquidated the ghetto without warning and all the Jews were killed or sent away. The Jew Rykiel, her father, though, had been caught on the road posing as a salesman and shot. He laughed. She heard him laugh. *Some people claim that the Rykiels had a daughter who did not go to the ghetto with them,* he said.

What kind of dogs would leave a daughter behind? the woman said.

The man made a noise like he was spitting. *You know how these Jews are,* he said.

After he left, the woman pulled Mel's mother out from the cupboard and beat her. *We'll be killed because of you*, she said, *I should turn you in right now*, she said, but of course if she did that she'd be shot too. After that, for the next two years, they let her out only once a day, at night, to go to the bathroom in a pail a few paces from the door to her cupboard. As soon as she was done they forced her to crawl back in, she couldn't walk, the cupboard was tiny and her feet were turned backward and as she crawled the starvation blisters all over her arms and knees burst over the floor and they beat her as she went, hitting her with sticks and ladles, while the daughters spit and the mother hissed over and over, *You should be grateful.*

Which his mother shouted at him once, and slapped his face, *You should be grateful* after he'd complained about the Superman toothbrush she'd bought him when what he really wanted, what he'd asked for, was a Superman action figure. *It's just a toothbrush*, he'd said to her. And she'd slapped him. *Just a toothbrush*? she said. *Just a toothbrush*? She slapped him again. *You should be grateful*, she said and as she did, as the last syllable stung the air she grabbed him, pulled him into her arms against her, and began to cry.

When the Russians came and broke into the house and raped the woman and raped her daughters, they did not find Mel's mother because she was hidden in the cupboard. They stayed for three days, five or six of them, she was not sure, drinking, taking turns raping the woman and her daughters every few hours. When she finally crawled out of the cupboard, dragging her useless legs and backward feet, the house was empty. The front door was open and she crawled to it and looked out and howled in pain at the first sun she'd seen in years, a winter light threaded with snow, falling over the ruined village.

When Mel was a boy, his father would put his mother into institutions for a few weeks a year where they gave her fresh air and gave her arts and crafts and gave her electro-convulsive therapy and when Mel asked why, asked where she was, his father said she was taking time to *rest*, that she needed *some quiet*, though when she'd come out, that's all there would be, a silent greeting outside the hospital walls where they waited, standing before the car, the gate closing behind her and her trying to smile, coming toward them and into the car and their home vacuumed of sound or upset, the windows closed, the shades drawn in an air of precarious silence, a slow motion world of order as thin and distorted as a bubble blown of soap.

Eventually, his father lost hope for a cure. That's what he said to

Mel, *There's no cure.* And from then on they made up a room in the attic—dark, the windows covered, just a bed and reading lamp. She loved it up there, with Mel sitting by her side every day, reading to her, talking to her, letting her talk to him, which, in those years in the attic, she actually liked to do.

The cupboard was, Mel's mother used to say, but she had trouble saying what. *The cupboard was*, she'd say, and then tell him how it smelled, which was like her and the soft rot of her rags and the meaty pus of her popped boils. She didn't want to talk about her parents, or even the Polish woman and her daughters, but lying in her sickroom in the attic with Mel sitting by her side, she wanted to explain to him about the cupboard. The cupboard was placed directly against the back wall of the house, pressed against the field that separated the town from the forest, and she could hear birds all day and sometimes animals snuffling around at night and she heard the knock on the door and the man tell the woman about her father and sometimes she tried to move, even though the woman told her if she made a single sound they would all be killed, her legs hurt so much, her butt hurt, her shoulders hurt, her neck hurt, she tried to move, but the cupboard was. In the years before that, when Mel was younger and she was in the institution, he'd visit her, and one time the nurse came in and said, *How are you feeling today?* and it was an impossible question in the same way and his mother answered, *Mel's here. He's my.*

Mel's father would drop him off outside the iron gates and he'd walk up the gravel lane lined by poplars leading to the institution, a dark granite estate with slate shingles and copper turrets. "Turrets," Mel says. "I didn't know the word. I thought they were called rooks because of a castle I'd read about in a book that was always referring to the rooks on the ramparts."

"What book?" says Anna. Mel thinks. "*Ivanhoe*," he says. "Or *Black Arrow*, maybe. One of those." "Those are hard books for a little boy," Anna says. "The Classic Comics aren't," Mel says and everyone smiles and the angels swivel between her and him, but at a second's delay, like they are watching tennis by trying to follow the pock of the racket, rather than the flight of the ball and are always a shot behind. "Actually, the Classic Comics were pretty tricky," Mel says.

One day walking up the lane from the road where his father dropped him off, walking between the rows of tended poplars, he says, he came to the institution and looked up and saw an old man in a sleeping gown and a fedora standing on the edge of one of the turrets. He had both his hands outstretched on either side to keep his balance and he looked like a gangster trying to surf. When Mel was inside he told the nurses that there was an old man balancing on the rook. *The roof? No*, he said, *the rook*. They didn't know what he meant. At first they laughed at him and made him try to say the word roof with an *f*. The nurses were also nuns, Mel explains, and couldn't help themselves from being a little pedantic and a little cruel. But he refused. He pointed up. *Not the roof*, he said, *the rook*. They didn't like being argued with and two of them walked away. *What's a rook, hon?* one of the others asked. But he couldn't explain. How do you describe a turret? What words for turret are there other than turret? *It's a kind of bird*, said one of the remaining nurses. *A kind of bird? What are you talking about?* the other nurse said. At no point did any of them bother to step outside and see for themselves. *I think he's going to jump*, Mel said. *Stop making things up or I'll tell Doctor Mettlekorn you're here*, said the first nurse.

Patients weren't allowed guests except on Sundays, but no one ever stopped him from entering the institution or visiting his mother. The front door with its iron ring pull was never locked. He'd take the ring in both hands, wrench the door open, and walk unaccosted down the linoleum halls to her room and she was always in it. There didn't seem to be any activities or exercises. There was no commotion or noise in the humid hall beyond the stick and echo of his own footsteps. The lighting was very low and all the other doors were closed. Only once in all his trips did a nun come in to check on her while he was there. *You're not allowed here*, she said. *But I don't suppose you're doing any harm, are you?* Mel didn't know. *You can stay,* she said. *But don't let Doctor Mettlekorn see you.*

If you listen hard enough you can understand what some birds are saying, his mother told him once. *For a long time,* she said, *for the long time during the cupboard I never saw a bird. I forgot what they looked like, but I heard them all day through the wall where my face was crunched, and I knew they flew. That was something I remembered: birds flew. What else flew? Wasps. Flies. Sometimes flies would get in the cupboard. But I knew how they sounded and it was very different from birds. Also, angels. Angels flew. I imagined that the birds were angels. They told me about my mother and sister. Sometimes they said they were alive and back in our house with our garden and were coming for me, but usually they said that they were all dead. I didn't want to hear them, but they wouldn't stop talking, and I was stuck all day long listening to the birds who I saw as very tall men with wings and boots up to their knees. Sometimes they rode horses and sometimes they were kind and other times angry.*

Mel looks at the angels. "Are you interested in this?" he asks, and they nod, all of them, or bow, really. They bend to a forty-five degree angle from their hips.

"When I was in training to become a therapist," Mel says, "I met a girl and we went on a few dates and one night I had a really strange dream about a phone that kept ringing and every time I answered it as soon as the person on the other end began speaking their voice got quieter and quieter like someone was turning down the volume on a radio and I couldn't hear what they were trying to tell me but I knew it was important and at that time because I was conditioned to assume that dreams were meaningful I started to tell my date about it, but she put her hand up and said, 'Nobody's interested in other people's dreams unless they're in them.' I thought you might finally be interested in this story," Mel says to the angels, "because it was a dream my mother had about you."

His mother knew almost nothing about the world, not the things that happened in it or the words for those things, until she was put in a displaced person's camp. Here there were parents with dead children and children with dead siblings and often when these people met a child, an orphan like Mel's mother, they told them everything they thought they'd ever need to know about the world in one heartfelt rush because they figured they'd all be dead again soon.

They told her about the camps and Zionism and the boats to Palestine and how to make honey and about sex and love and rape, put words, many words to what she had heard the Russians do to the Polish woman and her daughters. But they never asked her anything, nobody asked anybody anything, but Mel's mother liked to ask Mel about his friends and the games they played—she liked knowing that he had friends and that he played games with them outside in the sun and so he told her all about hide-and-seek and kick-the-can and stick-ball and frog-catching and all the things he did with his friends except he didn't do those things because he was always upstairs in the room with her.

Time wasn't real in the attic with the big maple tree outside the one small window and the light in summer blooming through its thick leaves in a green dapple. His mother rarely noticed that he couldn't be with friends because he was with her, she didn't recognize the passage of time when she was in her states, and when she did, in the rare occasions when she'd say, *Shouldn't you be with your friends?* he'd walk alone into town where he'd pick up a candy for her, usually a peppermint candy because her stomach wasn't good and she loved treats, and come back after a while and say, *We went to the creek and saw three fish,* or, *We hid in the bushes and threw water balloons at squirrels,* and finally, *Look, Mother, I brought you a* present and she would cry and cry and kiss his face and rub his hair and say, *Oh, you take care of me, you always visit me, you never forget, and you bring me treats and in the cupboard I never got to keep my treats.*

Once, as he was leaving the institution, a nurse came up to him with a clipboard and said, *you have to fill out this form or we can't release your mother.* He was maybe eight and couldn't understand the form. *My dad should do it,* he said, but his dad never came in the institution and the nurse knew that and said *no, it has to be now, all you have to do is fill it out and sign it or we can't let her go. Can you call my dad?* he asked and she shook her head and said, *hurry fill it out before Doctor Mettlekorn becomes angry.*

The last time he visited his mother at the institution, three buses were parked in the lane just beyond the portico. They were taking the patients on some kind of field trip. The doors opened and in a rush the patients poured into the lane. Or actually, Mel says, it was more like a wave—some were rushing forward while others were barely moving, which made sense since some were manic, assumably, and others nearly catatonic, and it continued like this, the patients surging forward and then halting behind a sleepwalker or heavily tranquilized dreamer, before pushing past them again. There were three buses and there were three nurses to put the patients on the buses and each patient held in their hands a big blue piece of construction paper with a number written on it in black marker. The numbers, Mel quickly learned from a desperate nurse, designated the patients' general disease as they were then understood, schizophrenics, neurotics, psychotics, depressives, social deviants, etc.—each was categorized according to a number and it was important that certain numbers traveled together, while others must absolutely be kept apart, though the specific method to this system he couldn't tell except it was imperative that they not deviate from the order Doctor Mettlekorn had decided upon which was that Groups Two, Three, and Six were supposed to go in Bus One; Groups One, Five, and Eight in Bus Two; and Four, Seven, and Nine in Bus Three. It would have made more sense, though been less precise, to just divide them into three groups, though this might not have worked either since the nurses were running around herding patients and arguing over which bus was Bus One and which was Bus Three, because although all three of them were immediately and wordlessly able to agree on Bus Two every time, One and Three were dependent on whether you started counting at the bus farthest from the door, as Nurse One did, or nearest as Nurse Three did, while Nurse Two just stared sort of dumbly and let the other two, surrounded by increasingly agitated patients, argue. Then it began to rain. Not drizzle, Mel says. Rain. Pour. Some of the patients were frantic and some of the patients were, as he'd said, pretty much asleep, but once it began to rain, they all became jubilant. Laughing and running in circles and holding their numbers over their heads. Almost immediately, the construction paper started falling apart in people's hands and staining their fingers and clothes and the numbers ran into black smears. Though he was just a little boy, he tried to help the nurses. He took patients' hands and led them to the buses, he ran around looking at their numbers or trying to figure out what number they might once have held. At one point he found his mother, but he just pushed her toward a nurse. He didn't want to see what number she carried even though it wouldn't have mattered because he didn't know what the smeared and disappearing numbers stood for. *Doctor Mettlekorn is going to be so mad,* one of the nurses said to him. Her hands and face and habit were stained with blue dye that joined with the rain pooling from her cap and streaked down her face like the blue tears characters wept in comic books.

"Is that when you decided to become an intergenerational sexologist?" Anna asks.

"Yes," says Mel.

RACHEL SLEEPS AND THE HOUSE sleeps around her. All over the estate windows are wide and the wind sweeps off the sea and flows in, opens and closes doors, pauses, drops, and rises again in the sighing corridors of swollen wood. If she were awake she'd hear the hallway compress and expand, the groaning accordion of its frame gusted into sound. But right now Rachel is alone and the only one asleep and she is dreaming for the house.

A child steps out of Samuel's apartment in Park Slope and crosses the street. She cannot tell if it is Samuel's boy, so she follows him, as Samuel begged her never to do, and he goes up a set of carpeted stairs, inside now, and opens the door to a bedroom where a woman with hair matted to her head like the place in the grass where deer slept is trying to read a stack of *Reader's Digest.* Embossed on the thick wallpaper is a pattern of different seasonal squashes. The room is humid, the walls smell damp. Outside, through the window, huge blue pelicans begin dropping out of the sky and landing in the river. *My legs won't straighten*, the woman says to her boy, and the door closes in a fresh gust of owled wind.

Rachel wakes and Jacob is not there. She is awake and the wind is asleep. Like a dreaming body sinking into a mattress, the house settles into the weight of silence. Moonlight washes the room. Everything glows. She sits up in bed and looks. In the absence of any other light, the distinction between shadow and illumination is sharper than usual. This is a gift, waking into this moment, but what is she supposed to do with it? Artists used chiaroscuro to create perspective, to fake the world's three dimensions and make their subject appear real and solid. But here the effect fails. The lunar room feels anything but real. Solid, sure. Solid and glued together like a doll's house, but fragile, shimmering like ice, about to shatter.

She holds up her hand. It's strange, a lovely adornment, a shape water has frozen into, the bones and ridges in the skin, glowing, hollow—she can see the moon pulsing through the skin between her thumb and forefinger.

After Sam died, she covered the mirrors for seven days. Even though they were divorced they were still living together and everything around her reflected her grief, but nothing reflected her. She vanished from the apartment. She was nothing but pain. A groping, sweating, everpresence of pain. At the time she thought she understood, viscerally, the Jewish custom of covering the mirrors. She had no body except this loss, no form but this decay. Now her hand is another kind of mirror. She had been wrong. When she threw the towels over the glass, this is what she was hiding.

Jacob did not sleep. He found the little room again. The radio was on, glowing, green, like the light off a river. *Welcome patriots,* a voice said. *I know you're on the road and heading south.* Jacob turned it down. He got up and walked the halls, came to the bottom of a staircase. At the end of the hall a set of unlatched glass doors opened and closed in the breeze.

If his father had been here, had lived long enough, had lived as long as Jacob had expected him to live, what might he have said to the angels?

The last time he saw his father they sat in the hospital cafeteria after hours. The lights were off, but the exit signs and LED security trim, all the pale markers of emergency, throbbed over them. Jacob had thought, I'll apologize. But his father was staring at the damp linoleum. He rested his right hand on top of his left and squeezed as if he were consoling himself, and when Jacob reached out to touch him, he startled and looked around, in the wrong direction, and there was no way in.

The beloved knocks, but we turn our faces to the wall.

At the end of the landing he went out through the glass doors onto a little stone balcony. Over the ocean, the horizon was lopsided: there was no moon and the stars all seemed to have slid away to the southeast, though he wasn't actually sure which way he was looking. Unlit, the sea and sky inked together in a watery pitch, except far to his right where the stars were a dazzled scramble, like a crystal glass dropped and broken.

In the morning, Rachel again got coffee and blueberries from the buffet in the sunny dining room. A little deeper into the house, she heard the clatter of dishes: Daniel must be in the kitchen, washing up. The same place she left him last night, crying. She had wanted to ask why, but she didn't want to find out. Or, no she wanted to find out, but didn't want to have to respond.

She ate the berries, refilled her mug, and went out onto the lawn. This morning she had unpacked her sketchbook and pencil. The day was absolutely different from the one before—it felt different, it looked different—but she couldn't tell how.

She balanced her mug on the edge of a marble balustrade and opened her book. Like yesterday, the sky was cloudless and vivid, empty all the way to the point where it met the ocean, which was also empty, but not like yesterday. It roiled with tumult, a storm she could sense but not see.

She looked harder: the water was darker than before, it seemed wintery, water of a different season reflecting a different, troubled sky.

The alteration wasn't just color. It was compositional. She tried again. She couldn't capture the difference she knew was there. Yesterday the wide Atlantic distance had felt open, beautiful, full of freedom. The view welcomed her. She felt herself pouring out into it all. Today the horizon was an endpoint, fixed, foreshortened, closer than before, storming forward. She closed the book and turned away from the water and passed again around the house, by the huppah, also empty, before heading up the path through the open meadow again.

This time, she found Eli sitting at the base of the bronze rabbi, eating an apple. A tennis racket lay in the grass by his feet.

"I was going to play tennis," he said. "But no one was awake."

All the doors on the hall near their room had been open and the buffet picked over.

"Everyone's awake," Rachel said.

"I was going to play tennis but then I realized I'm ninety years old."

"Eighty-nine, I thought."

"At a certain age you realize you have to stop doing things that used to be easy. And then, after a few more years, you wonder how you ever started."

"What age is that?"

"Sixteen."

Rachel had hoped to be alone. With the sculptures and then, afterward, with the view from the top of the hill. The valley's claustrophobia would open to a wide horizon. This forced perspective might not induce sanity, but it might be a kind of therapy. Instead: a weird old man with an apple and a tennis racket. And he seemed to be making jokes. She laughed. Out of reflex. Politeness.

"Sweetie, I'm serious," he said. "I can't even imagine the things I did when I was sixteen."

He took a bite from his apple. He looked tiny, sitting there beneath the bronze rabbi. His little eyes in his little head were focused on her sketchbook.

"You came to draw the statues."

She started to hide the sketchbook behind her back, before stopping herself. "I don't know."

"When you look at these, what do you see?"

"I'm not looking," she said. "I'm talking to you."

"So look. Let me tell you, you can divide the world between those who look and those who don't."

Her therapist had said, *Take stock, check in, see how you're feeling.* Right now: blazing resentment. He had interrupted her solitude and then wanted to tell her how to use it. Another old man expounding on how the world was divided? She wasn't interested.

"I don't think anyone would play tennis with you," she said.

He must have borrowed clothes from Baruch, or else his clothes were from before his old age, or else he had stolen them. He was wearing shorts and a polo shirt. Both were baggy on him. His tube socks came up to his knees. His knees were bright and round as onions. "You can't be an artist without looking," he said. "I don't know much, but I know that."

"I'm not an artist," she said.

"But you want to be?"

She shook her head.

"Then why draw?"

Here's something grief had taught her: There are many different ways to be angry.

"Last night at dinner," she said, "that wasn't a joke gone wrong, was it? You're just very rude, aren't you?"

"It's a problem of timing. My generation, where I'm from, we didn't learn niceties."

"Some did."

"They died.

"Was that the difference?"

"What do I know? Ask Alex if you want a formula. I might not have learned which sleeve to wipe my nose with, but here's what I do know—as soon as something becomes a rule, I don't believe in it."

The problem with her job was that she couldn't put down the phone. As long as the caller rambled, she had to listen. Almost everything felt this way. Once when arguing with Sam she'd said, *What is it you want? What do you think it means to be happy?* He had said, *To be able to walk away*, and then done it.

So she said goodbye and began to head back up the hill.

Jacob found a deer path down to the sandless shore. At their base the cliffs were wreckage, this beach, this whole island a slow accident of jagged boulders and small dead pines ripped down by the waves. Closer to the water, the ancient, rusted hull of a boat was abandoned in the sea grass. He breathed in. He tasted salt and seaweed, crab shells cracked and picked bare by birds amid stagnant pools, the slime of dead things made fresh. This much was certain: The flood was coming and no one could say we were not warned.

Birds appeared on the water. A group of them, both huge and stunted-looking, with squat bodies and low wedge-shaped heads, like some kind of floating tool. They were looking at him, they appeared of this landscape, strange, wind-blunted, moaning. Maybe they were ducks but they were not like any ducks Jacob had ever seen and he turned his back on them. He did not want to be moaned at by some bad dream of ducks.

He followed the broken shore: empty shells, hundreds of snails cracking underfoot, wild lilies leaning toward him, tall and alien as angels. Wind gathered on the water, the waves were not choppy but they seemed to be coming faster, rushing forward, as if a boat had gone by.

When Jacob opened the door to the old man last night, there was only the rain washing through the portico. No car, no sound of a car, no departing halo in the valley.

Now on the shore he came to a granite boulder as big as a boat. Baruch had said the cliffs were schist, the shore stones were whatever shore stones were; Jacob didn't know many rocks but knew granite and there was no other granite in sight. Certainly nothing that could produce a boulder as huge and strange as this. It must have been dragged and left there by a departing glacier. He stepped closer; it was moaning. He stopped. The sound continued. Maybe there were more of those weird ducks behind it? He walked quietly, he looked: sitting on the wet pebbles with his back to the boulder and eating raw eggs with his hands was Boris.

The old man called her back.

"I'm sorry if I've offended you," he said. "I don't mean to be impolite."

The sun was finally overhead, and in the time between her turning away and turning back, the light had changed and the landscape, now golden, glowed as if seen through honey.

"On the other hand, I don't mean to be polite either," Eli said.

He was still sitting there, propped against the bronze rabbi, and she wondered if he could get up on his own. *On the other hand...* He sounded ridiculous, a lilting, high-pitched, Yiddish burlesque. A sinister Topal. Here was the thing about Jewish jokes: how did you know when they were jokes?

"Alex thought I died in 1945," he said. "But not only did I live, I immigrated to Palestine, if you can believe it. I was going to be a Zionist, but it didn't take. It turns out that being a Zionist is just as pointless as being a communist, which is what I thought I was before I was a Zionist. That's a story for another time. I can tell just by looking at you that you're not interested."

"You can't tell anything just by looking at me," Rachel said.

"Oy. Sweetie. It's an expression. I didn't mean anything by it. Worse, it doesn't mean anything. Which is my point. Many years after I went to Palestine, once Alex was already famous, I saw him give a lecture at Hebrew University. It was the first time I'd seen him since that afternoon in 1945, when he thought I died. He was speaking, if I remember, about language and about how essentially impossible it is for language to convey meaning. The audience nodded. They took notes. Some of them sighed. I'm serious. For them, this was profound. The room smelled like hibiscus. Do you know what hibiscus smells like?"

When Rivkah was trying to get clean, Rachel had bought her every kind of herbal tea she could think of. They had sat together, at her kitchen table, tasting and discarding all of them. *This one?* Rivkah had walked the box of hibiscus tea over to the trash. *This one not even scotch could save.*

"It doesn't smell like anything," Rachel said.

"It smells like that room at Hebrew University in 1974. There is a divide, Alex claimed, an ultimate, essential, catastrophic divide between words—Hebrew words I mean, the new language of Israel conjured out of the old language of the Bible—and what they are trying to convey. Not with everything, not with, say, this tennis racket. A tennis racket is a tennis racket. There's nothing to convey there. Basically, it's a neologism. The worst, most degraded part of language. Tennis racket, fuel injector, Pontiac Trans Am. Stuff. Meaningless."

What was she doing here, listening to Eli rambling amid the bronze insanity, eating an apple in small and terrible bites? In grad school she had a therapist who told her every desire was dialectical. *I can say that to you*, her therapist had announced, *because you're a grad student and you'll know what that word means.* He had winked. *It makes treating you so much more fun.* It had been their last session. Most things were confusing, desire apparently was dialectical, but occasionally the universe still produced clear laws: avoid a therapist who winks.

Eli was still talking. "Most words, this is what Alex was saying, are too fraught with meaning to convey truth. Does that make sense? There are too many layers. Words are boxes. Crammed full with shit, everything they've ever had to represent. You'd have to see it all at once. All of history would have to erupt in every expression of every word—I think this is what Alex was saying—for a word to ever even come close to approaching truth."

"Like God," Rachel said.

"Yes! Like God. Everpresent in history and evermeaningful. Or, on the other hand, not like God at all, since, if you asked me, He is completely absent. Absent from history and human action. He hides from us, He forgets us, He sleeps while we suffer. Totally without meaning, God. What do you think?"

"I don't have any feelings about God."

"Who cares? Who has feelings about God? Morons. The question is, does God have feelings about you?"

"No," Rachel said.

"It's like when I mentioned hibiscus. For me it's a room in 1974, but for you it's something else. That much is clear."

"Save me the theory," she said. "Postmodern semiotic disjunction was tired even in 1974."

"I'm an old man. Almost a hundred. I get things wrong, maybe? I fail to identify boundaries. I conflate. Sue me! Alex was talking about mysticism. Or mysticism and psychological healing. If we cannot transmit the truth, how is transcendence possible? If it's impossible to say what has hurt you, how can you heal? Because even if there was a divide, he was not saying there was an absence. There is a difference between an absence and a divide. Ultimately, you cannot secularize language, even Hebrew, even after Babel. You cannot make the words of the bible *Pontiac Trans Am* and *tennis racket*. You cannot remove meaning, if it's there that is, even if you cannot express it either. We are constantly at odds with our own experience. So how do we express what is inexpressible? And, and this is the exciting bit—what happens when we do? A transformation of the communal self, Alex called it. A forced reckoning with truth in history. Revelation, basically. Language, made whole by whole expression, will rupture *meaning*, that is to say *wholeness,* back into History. Or so Alex claimed. To me, it seems unlikely. It requires that at the heart of experience, language, creation, whatever you want to call it, again words are inadequate—there is meaning."

"And there isn't?"

Eli wandered between the statues. He looked up at them and bent to inspect their bases. He was smiling and spry, nimble in wet shorts, and the wind was picking up.

"These are disgusting," he said. "They disgust me. Rabbis with beards? Yentas? Yeshiva boys and young ladies wandering home from the baths?"

"They're a testament to the lost, I guess."

"What isn't? Did you see Alex's face last night? It was the first time he'd seen me since 1945. At his lecture, of course, I was invisible. I was one of many. And anyway, he thought I was dead and people do not see the dead. Do you remember when I told you there are two types of people?"

"It was five minutes ago."

"Those who look and those who don't. But you can divide those who look into two types as well. Those who see and those who don't. And of those who see there are also two types. Those who see the dead and those who don't. So really there are six types of people, each more rare than the next. Alex looks and Alex sees, but until last night I do not think Alex saw the dead. It's why he's managed to be such a success. To be sane and coherent. To actually talk to people who don't know he's lying. Most of us are different. Of those of us who look and see and saw what we saw, most of us see the dead. Which is why we're vegetables. Mumbling. Facing backward, always facing backward, like people in a storm, afraid to get wind in their eyes."

In her early days on the phone in the empty office, she wondered: why are these people calling me? What was the impulse to actually dial the number and have no real question? Were these people dialing numbers they found on bathroom walls, on leaflets, in phone booths back when there were phone booths? Someone would call and she'd lift the phone to their madness or theories or unassailable loneliness.

She looked at Eli. Chuckling and babbling. Chewing slowly. What was he trying to tell her about himself?

"The question is," he said, "how much should the dead legislate to the living? What hold should they have over us?"

Even in the valley the wind was up. Like yesterday, a flock of tiny birds burst out of the forest, flew past them, wheeled in a tight oval like a toy on a string, and zipped back in.

"Do you know the story of the Corpse Bride?" Eli said.

She had it wrong. The whole time. He was not talking about himself at all. She whispered. "How did you get here last night?"

"I took the train. And then I flew the rest of the way. Or I went to sleep in Brooklyn and woke up here. Or I lay down under a willow tree on the Danube and stood up on the doorstep in the rain like a stork. What difference does it make? Trust me. I'm a hundred years old and the present is always more sudden than you'd think.

"In the story, a groom on his wedding day is walking in the fields with his friends before the ceremony and he comes across the skeletal finger of a dead bride killed in a Cossack pogrom sticking up out of the earth. It's no surprise. I've walked in those fields and they are all seeded with the bones of dead Jews. Anywhere the ground was soft enough to dig—dead Jews. Which is why if I went back, which I wouldn't, I would never eat vegetables in Ukraine. I'm surprised their radishes, may they rot, don't sprout with tefillin. But still, the groom. As a joke, or maybe not as a joke, he puts the ring intended for his living bride over the dead finger. He is careless. He is selfish and young and he should have known better."

"Why are you telling me this?"

He tossed the apple core over his shoulder. "Did you see that? That's what I want to give you."

"An apple core?"

"Freedom. Not many who lived as I lived can toss the core away. Most deaths by cyanide come from refugees eating apple seeds that they are too compulsive to discard. I'm serious. Grannies collapsing into their soup with seeds in their dentures. Happens all the time." He stood, he had left the tennis racket somewhere, his hands were empty. "The dead are starving and we are the apples they eat. They will never throw us away. Our obligation sticks in their teeth."

In the basement Rachel always answered the phone when it rang. Before that, though, she sat outside in a café, in bright sunshine under a flowering tree, watching her phone vibrate on the table.

"Watch Alex," Eli said. "See if he doesn't eat the core."

Boris was not moaning, but cooing. He sat with his back against the boulder, facing the cliffs. Jacob kneeled next to him: sand and pine needles and bits of leaves stuck to his cheeks and chin. When he saw Jacob he stopped cooing.

"I was hungry," Boris said.

"Did you get lost?"

He shook his head.

"Can you stand?" Jacob said.

"I got here, didn't I?"

How? Jacob could not imagine him making his way down the deer path. He held out his hand and helped him up.

"Let's get back to the house," he said. "What do you think?"

They walked slowly together along the beach, Boris leaning on Jacob's arm. The shore opened to the cove beneath the house, with its shipwreck and flowers and mysterious birds.

"Eiders!" Boris said and clapped.

"That's what eiders look like?"

Boris winked. "Eider that or something else." He began to giggle.

"Tell that one to the angels," Jacob said.

"They'd just fuck it up. And anyway," Boris said, "they should be in the arctic by now."

"The arctic?"

"That's where they spend most of the year. They just come down here for a few months. To hatch."

Three steps later, Jacob realized: he was talking about the ducks.

The tide was coming in and between the water and the cliff, there was not much shore to walk on. "I was just thinking about your poem 'Caraway.' The one about the Baltic," Jacob said.

"Why?"

"It's beautiful."

"If it is, it is."

"*All day long the Baltic kneads/ like my mother's floured fingers/ the new black bread of the shore,*" Jacob recited. He looked over at the waves bunching toward them and then thinning away. "I can see what you meant."

Boris squinted at the sea. "Probably not."

A set of concrete steps led up from the shore to a trail above. When they reached it, Jacob saw that it was the trail that went to Jonah's, a trail that didn't end, as he had believed, at the tavern, but continued beyond it, where they were now, before winding farther into the forest.

"Why did you stop writing?" It was not Jacob's question to ask, but from one who gave up his vocation to another, he wanted to know.

"I died," Boris said. "And the dead must not write poetry."

She turned to go, he called her back. He wanted to tell her one more thing.

"After Alex's lecture there was a reception and his acolytes were discussing his theories. Just as I have been. *There's a divide between words and truth*, they repeated. *An ultimate catastrophic divide*. A woman approached me. At this time I was still young or, no, it was 1974 and I wasn't young anymore but I still cared when a woman approached me. She said, *Do you agree*? We were standing at a little table, just the two of us because I had been standing alone, eating dates and olives, while outside, through blue-tinted bulletproof glass, date palms, maybe the palms that had produced these very dates, swayed in the wind and I looked through the blurry blue glass—the glass intended to keep us safe from machine gun fire—from date to date palm, and though I couldn't see the wind I saw the tree bending in it and she was smiling at me and her hair actually was moving a little, also like the tree, in the breeze from the air conditioner and I was very cold, suddenly, and we were speaking in Hebrew, which is a language I've never liked and I said, *I've forgotten, what was your question?* and she said, *Can we never use language to express the truth? Do you think there really is a divide, an essential divide, between language and history?* Outside through the blue bulletproof glass Jerusalem was blue and the sun was blue and the date palm was bending under a cold blue wind that wasn't actually cold, not even close, but beneath the vent there in 1974 with her I couldn't imagine it as anything but freezing. *No,* I said. *It's not a divide, it's an abyss.*"

"Sewers are very cold," Boris said.

He was in the clawfoot tub Jacob had helped him into. The room filled with steam around them and Jacob opened a window to light that seemed to pour into the steam like cream purling into soup. Then the steam was gone and the light remained carrying the water's motion with it, rocking on the ceiling in phantom ripples, whether the reflection of the bath or the sea Jacob couldn't tell. Down the long hall a door blew open and then slammed.

Boris held up his hands, pruned by the hot bath. "Beneath Vilna all the children turned green."

Jacob found a washcloth and wet it in the sink. "Can I help you wash?"

"I can wash."

"I meant your face," Jacob said. "Since there isn't a mirror by the tub."

When he was young Jacob had imagined this would be one of the wordless ways he would make amends, by caring for his father in his old age. But instead they sat in the hospital cafeteria after hours and his father, out of his silence, said finally in a response to a statement Jacob had made days earlier, "So you are going to change your name?" and Jacob nodded and his father said, "To what?" and Jacob decided right then for sure and said, "Jacob." His father did not ask why, but by then his face was a bagful of rats squirming with different pains, and they had to wait together until the night's drugs kicked in and he became overstill and overslow, open-mouthed, inattentive and slack, and Jacob recognizing him again, found himself lucid and angry, still undisguised, and too late for a blessing he would not earn.

"Did you hear me about the green children?" Boris said.

"I did. Sorry. I was waiting for you to say more."

"Look at me," Boris said, peering down at the loose sail of his body. "I'm floating away."

Rachel approached the house. She'd left Eli hopping among the statues, demented. Now the sanitarium—she would not pretend it was anything else—squatting dumbly above the glittering scales of the open sea. On its turrets, a crow, or maybe not a crow, some kind of big black judgmental bird, roosted. Rachel thought: rook. But wasn't that just a kind of European crow? It must have been a raven. Anyway, it was gone and her perspective had changed: from the bottom of the hill the top of the roof was invisible. She wrote a note about Lurio once: *He moves your eye to what you don't want to see.* Now she was looking at a jeep with a Confederate flag decal parked under the portico. The jeep empty, the door to the house wide open.

Last night she had read the final paragraph of Baruch's memoir. *For many years after the catastrophe, even when I was what the world called safe, when I'd hear a knock on the door I'd want to hide. This, I've found, does not abate. But if you are lucky, as I have been, if you find your way back into life, as I have, there is always a knock on the door. So what can one do if one does not want always to hide, but leave the door open?*

Jacob helped Boris dress. "Suspenders or belt?"

"Half the time, I can't undo the belt. The other half I can't close it."

"Suspenders it is."

In his clothes, with the morning washed away, Boris again seemed stacked inscrutably back into himself, irritable and mysterious. His hands were steady: with a tortoiseshell comb, he folded his oiled blue hair over his scalp like a crow's wing.

Downstairs somebody was pounding on the door.

Rachel was alone in the lobby with a man wearing combat boots, a Confederate flag T-shirt, and what she thought, but could not quite be sure, was a Prussian-era pointed Pickelhaube helmet. She waited behind him. He did not see her. He stood with his hands on his hips, which were wide and almost matronly in his quick-drying khaki cargo pants. He didn't seem willing to step into the bright room before him—he wouldn't even look that way. He began to shout, "Barak, get down here. It's happened again."

The house echoed; a curtain, somewhere, luffed, and then: silence. He shouted again and glared at the desk, as if beneath the unlit banker's lamp there might be a service bell he could bang. Rachel, still behind him, to say something, said, "Excuse me?"

He turned; one hand jerked to steady his helmet.

Rachel said, "Can I help you?" She was trying not to look at the helmet.

He jutted a finger at the unmanned desk. "Do you work here?"

"I don't think they use that desk," Rachel said. "This is a private residence."

"I know very well what this is."

Rachel would actually like to have heard, at that particular moment only, what this awful man had to say, but before he could add anything there was Daniel, creeping down the stairs with Baruch just behind him, immaculate in a white linen suit and a poppy-colored shirt.

"Shale!" he said. "My neighbor, welcome." His accent, usually an unplaceable urbane European smorgasbord, became distinctly German, he pronounced the "w" as a "v" which he didn't usually do, and

Rachel wondered if it was intentional, if, with his Mark Twain-as-vampire performance, he was trolling his *neighbor*, as he called him and then, of course, the rest came together: the decaled jeep and insane getup, the crazy compound on the other side of the island.

Shale, almost shy, grunted *hello*. Then they were all together at the stair's landing and Baruch ushered them into the main room. They clumped in and squinted in the sunlight. The sea flared in the polished helmet.

"It's happened again," said Shale.

Baruch was all question. Raised eyebrows, open hands. "At my age," he muttered, "you can say that about most things."

Shale explained, "The chickens."

"The chickens?"

"Assaulted."

The room continued to fill. Boris and Jacob and Eli right behind them.

"Where did you come from?" Eli said and Jacob, thinking for some reason that he was being addressed said, "I just followed Boris." Mel and Sophie bounced through the French doors in tennis whites. Shale backed against the green chair and looked around with fear at, it was safe to imagine, the most Jews he'd ever seen, though this was not, Rachel thought, for most people, a terrifying situation.

"When you claim that your chickens were assaulted," Baruch said, "I do not know what you mean."

"It's the same as last week. Their coops were broken into."

"A fox, certainly?"

"There were tracks, Barak. Human."

Baruch gestured down at his crisp pleats, his white suit, his unblemished two-tone shoes. "Certainly you are not suggesting that I stole your chickens?"

"It was the eggs that were stolen."

"Eggs? Just eggs?"

"They were Bantam Specials."

Baruch put his hand to his mouth. "Oh, I didn't realize. That is a special egg. A very fine egg. One of the best eggs. Sort of bluish in the shell, yes? Quite orange inside, if I'm correct."

"That's how they look naturally. Orangey. Orangey is the natural look of an egg when they're not being pumped full of chemicals by the federal inspectors."

"Alex has stolen some chickens in his day," said Eli.

"You believe it's the inspectors who inject the chemicals?" Rachel asked.

Eli slipped between Boris and Jacob and slunk up next to Baruch, and Baruch took a step away from him toward Shale, who shuffled back into the armchair. "Why wouldn't they?" Eli whispered.

"Certainly, it's the companies who inject their eggs?" Rachel didn't know how she got talking to Eli again. She could see a fleck of apple, chewed and then drooled, on his chin. He had pranced among the statues and said, "Do you know the story of the Corpse Bride?"

The geezer looked at her and knew her dreams. It wasn't that she was making an impression on the world, it was that she was transparent and, even worse, powerless in her transparency: her body was the glass Renaissance painters candled images through so that men like Eli, with cracked nails and cadaver hands, could pick up the quill of her life and trace.

Rivkah had pulled off her headscarf, she had rolled up her sleeves and said, *I want to be seen*, and Rachel had thought yes, yes, yes. To be seen. To see another see you. But that wasn't what this was. This was exposure, as pitiless as the gaze in that Rilke poem, that cosmic gaze, *for here there is no place that does not see you. You must change your life.* Which was what she was trying to do, here, now, among these people, and instead of changing anything, of acting, of reaching out and finally making a gesture that might alleviate some hurt, Baer's or her own or even Daniel's, whatever it was, she was talking and talking, she was arguing with Eli about nothing. She should have stuffed her fist into her mouth and not spoken until the world, laying its wonder in her cupped palm like an egg she did not need to steal, spoke back.

And anyway, amid her new unnoticed silence, Eli was a lively twinkle of delight and was taking the conversation to Shale. "What's the difference who injects the eggs? There's no authority you can trust. It's every man for himself. Tell me I'm wrong?"

"It was the same with the canning of herring," said Shale.

"That's right," said Eli. "It was the same with the canning of heron."

After his neighbor was gone, Baruch stood in the drawing room surrounded by the others.

"I don't understand what he was accusing us of?" said Anna.

"Stealing eggs," Baruch said. "He claims that someone has been breaking into his stupid fucking chicken coops."

The mud caked on Boris's cuffs and shoes. His sticky face. Jacob turned and looked at him. Boris, smiling slightly, stooped and turning away to lean over an empty vase as if there were flowers in it that he could smell.

"Of course this is how it starts," Eli said. "With accusations."

Baruch's annoyance like a buzzing phone. Small again, round-shouldered—he took off his glasses and pinched the purple marks the pads left on his nose. "Nothing is starting, Eli."

"Stolen eggs? Cheating him on a business deal? Soon he'll be accusing you of poisoning his wells..."

Before he left, Shale shouted that he was gypped. That Baruch had cheated him and Baruch scoffed and said something about a podcast and then there was Eli, skittering between them out of the house and under the portico saying, "You mean you were *Jewed*" before Shale drove off, slow and careful of the jeep's undercarriage, up the dirt road and back into the forest.

"You are in business with that man?" said Sophie.

"No," said Alex Baruch.

"It sounded like you are," Mel said.

"Our relationship is not financial," Baruch said. "I do not pay him, he does not pay me. I found the Lurio in his shitty house sitting between the lobster traps but behind the buoys, framed on the wall next to the posters of naked shiksas on motorbikes. So clearly it was valuable to him. He struck a hard bargain, as a man would who dangles his art between the nudey posters. Eventually, I bought the Lurio from him for five hundred dollars and the promise that I would give him access to my windmill power so he can heat his idiotic camp and produce his radio podcasts. That is a deal, not business."

"This feels like a semantic difference," Sophie said. "I don't like semantic differences."

Mel touched Jacob's arm. "I think he can just say podcasts?"

"I believe the word everybody is looking for is *collaborate*," said Eli.

When the room hushed, there was only the sea through the open doors.

"Did you see his truck?" Mel said

"It's nothing compared to his compound," Rachel said.

"His what?" Jacob said.

"He has a whole compound in a clearing on the other side of the forest."

"You mean there are more men like that on this island?" Sophie said.

Baruch swiveled back toward them like someone had just shouted his name, and he was upright again, pulled taut, he looked directly at Sophie. "There are more men like that everywhere."

RACHEL FOUND DANIEL IN THE KITCHEN. He wasn't doing anything. The kitchen was already clean, he had already cleaned it, but in its cleanliness it expressed, she felt, a hidden disorder.

"Have you noticed," she said, "that some rooms feel crazier than others."

"My grandparents raised me. It was my job to light the samovar every morning even though they never drank tea."

"I don't think that's what I meant."

"Every room I've ever been in feels crazy."

When she entered he had been facing the door with both hands open at his sides like the kid in hide and seek who can't find a spot.

"What are you doing here?" he said.

"Looking for wine."

"It's nine thirty in the morning."

"Looking for you, then."

He brushed his hair out of his face and then shook his head and his hair fell over his eye again. *He likes me*, she thought. Everywhere, the scent of lemon soap, the feeling that what you see is not what was here.

"You're not really married," he said. "Are you?"

"Do you want to know?"

"That's never mattered," he said. "My entire life all people want to do is tell me things I don't want to hear."

There was no space between them. They were both at the counter beneath the drying herbs and the copper pots hanging in the morning light. A tremble at the corner of his dark mouth.

"I don't want to tell you anything," she said.

He was a boy finished with his chores. He smelled like soap and grass. At first light he had cut the lawn between the patio and the cliff with a push mower. Now he was free.

"What do you want?" he said.

"To see the Lurio."

"What were we?" Eli said. "We were thieves."

This was not an answer to any question that anyone had asked. After Shale had left and Baruch had stomped off and Daniel had slithered out and Rachel had gone after him, Eli had spit in the gravel and turned and walked back into the house and the others, in a row, had followed him through the rooms crooked with wind and out the French doors onto the patio.

"Look at this view," he said. There was no view. The sea, the horizon, everything beyond the ivy-strangled balustrades and the hedge of rosebushes was gone. In its place, a solid white wall of fog. "That's what it was like after the war."

"Like what?" Jacob said. He didn't know what he was looking at. A moment ago they had been standing under the portico, squinting into sunshine.

"Like this. The dead space where a storm has been." He shook his head, twice, sharply, as if to clear his expression like an Etch-a-Sketch. "Or maybe that's not right. I'm old. I don't say what I mean. After the war ended the world was like the center of a storm, yes, I agree with myself, but it was a storm in outer space. Totally silent. A dark empty soundless plain of nothing, surrounded by the storm."

Jacob started tapping on the edge of an empty marble planter. He was looking where he was tapping and tapping louder, and he knew they were watching, all of the lunatics, but the panic continued to rise, he was nothing, he was a supplicant to the damaged dreams of others, he was ignorant and cruel, he deserved nothing and had been granted no special dispensation, and Eli was cackling and Mel was whispering and the sea was still absent, it had hidden like a man gathering himself into an attic, waiting in the darkness, leaving the ladder down.

“Look,” Rachel said, “you can see the wind.”

They huddled together in the open vault, a place too damp to keep a drawing like this for long, and she held it up, unrolled out of its cardboard tubing, to the flicker of Daniel’s lantern. She thought: if I trip, or if he leans in—flames.

She had not been this close to a Lurio sketch since her year in Madrid and had never touched one ungloved, as she was now. But this must have been how Baer had held it as a boy, and anyway, even if the intervening years had made it vulnerable, where was the law that the goal of love was to preserve? When she had asked Sam if he should keep speaking Yiddish, if she should learn it so they could speak it together, so she could one day speak to his son, he looked at her with a disgust that acknowledged one of the holes opening between them and said, *Why do you think I left?*

To preserve in memory, this was the terrain of mourning. Of sitting shiva and saying the Kaddish and lighting yahrzeit candles, of maintaining what was lost in ritual—but why did every present moment have to be an enactment of memory? The dead had no claim over the living. She should have shouted it into the old man’s face.

She tightened her grip on the page. It was stark and beautiful, it was everything she had taught herself to value and love, it was precious to her, but if it weren’t for Baer she would offer it now to the lantern. And even if she didn’t, it was inevitable. To destroy by touching—this was all she’d ever been able to do.

“We were thieves,” Eli said. Standing facing them all before the curtain of fog.

“It’s almost time for the baseball,” said Boris.

"We lived in the forests, we made raids in the night, we murdered when we had to."

"There's a double-header."

"In Katowice?" Sophie said. "That was the city of thieves he mentions in his memoir. Is that where you met him?"

"We lived in the forest and in abandoned train cars and in barns," Eli said.

"In a mill," Mel said.

"We lived anywhere there was something we could steal and yes, perhaps there was a mill. But it wasn't in in Katowice. It wasn't in Germany or Poland. It was on the banks of the Bug river just outside the Khmel'nik ghetto."

His lilt was musical, exaggerated with pleasure, he was almost singing. And almost dancing: he shifted from foot to foot like a child who needs to pee.

"Khmel'nik?" Sophie said. "Baruch wasn't in Ukraine."

"We were there almost the whole time. He also didn't write about his golden fingers. He kept us alive with those hands and those wide eyes, that sweet child's mouth. He was the smallest among us. We could set him on the road. He could approach refugees fleeing from the ghetto."

"You stole from Jews?"

"Who else was there?"

She said it again: "You stole from Jews."

"Jews." The word was phlegm to him. "What is a Jew?"

Baruch had written: *Imagine a continuum: Torah, that is to say the idea of Torah, that is to say the idea of God, that is to say the idea of a world redeemed—and then the Catastrophe. The moment when Torah vanishes in a cloud of smoke. In Jewish tradition this has always been the way questions are asked: first we remember the past, and then we wonder about the present. So let us remember, but now that we have remembered what cannot be forgotten, let us also not forget the future, which we cannot remember. That is: a cloud never clears entirely, but when it thins, when we can see through it, is anything left on the other side?*

"Jews," Eli said again. "What was a Jew but a person who is judged by his devotion to the Law? But what Law? And what devotion? Judged by what court? And to what end?"

Anna was covering her face and crying. "What are we going to do?"

"Watch the baseball," Boris said and took her hand.

Rachel held the sketch up to the light.

In Lurio's final rendering of Job, the painting composed entirely after the war and included in his Tanakh, there is just the devastation of God's trials compressed out of sequence and overlapping geometrically in the background: men in fur coats bearing sabers and looking more like Cossacks than Chaldeans riding away from razed houses and smoking pyres and the bodies of camels, their stomachs opened in vivid slashes, askew and sprawling behind him, his own body bloated with disease, gazing out of a Cubist collage of horrors from which God's presence is entirely absent.

On the other hand, in this sketched study, Job stares up into the sky, with his right arm extended, palm out, as if shielding his face from the sun. But it is not the sun; there is almost no sense of shadow, and Lurio has marked the upper margins of the paper with *JOB 38*—the chapter where God chastises him from the whirlwind. The reference is unnecessary; the image bends under wind: Job's hair and beard, the hood of his cloak, even the skin around his eyes pull away, pour almost, toward the left foreground of the paper, pushed back from the unseen place where the Lord, assailing Job with the truth of creation, must be. Even Job's position, way to the left, near that corner, suggests a person struggling against the force that fills the rest of the space, which—beyond a lightly charcoaled farmhouse, more blur than line, and a willow tree smoking away on the wind—is empty.

Rachel stared. Baer had said Lurio was happy with the study, that before the war he was planning on painting from it, but she couldn't imagine how. It was nothing like his final painted clutter of atrocities. And yet in this absence she sensed a tension, because it was an absence representing wild abundance. It was all possibility, a negative space standing in for the violence to come, ripe, expectant as a stage, an emptiness where the Lord must be.

"I thought it was night but really it was morning," Eli said.

They clustered in the game room. First pitch was at one, so it was important to make sure that they had figured out the TV by ten. There were two remotes, plus the antennas needed adjusting and the trick was, according to Boris: sometimes you pointed it at the window and sometimes you pointed it away from the window.

"Like a prophet," Jacob said.

"What?" Sophie sounded angry.

"You know," Jacob said. "Sometimes you look to the sky for the message and sometimes you bury your head in your hands and hide."

A sudden marvel: a room full of silent Jews.

"It was a joke," Jacob said.

"In the painting, he's looking straight ahead," Rachel said. "He's looking at us. There is no God. There is no one responsible for all this devastation. There is nothing except us and him and the lonely chaos of the world in between. But here, he's looking up." She let her finger dent the space just ahead of his eyes. "God might be cruel and invisible," she said, "but God is still listening."

"So this shows that Lurio's perspective changed," Daniel said. He was not sneering. He was looking at her hands. He was making sure he understood.

"That's right."

"So it's important?"

"It's important."

"But it's sad?"

To ask that and not be sure. The rabbi had shuffled around her apartment, eating cookies and inspecting her preparations. She had asked a question. She had made angry phone calls. She stood in the mirrorless rooms and screamed into Sam's ballcap. Eventually the time came to pull down the coverings, but she didn't.

Daniel, now, beside her. His heels together and one arm crossed in front of his chest. The other still held the lantern in which the fine lovely features of his face flickered with a pain he wasn't feeling, a memory that wasn't his, Sam coming in late and drunk and crying, and how was it that nothing progressed? That when she finally ripped down the towels, it was as if her whole life were mirrors, every moment, warped and doubling away, an old man dancing among graves, Sam turning and running from her as she reached out to him and, clutching his hand, found Daniel's now in hers, in an empty basement where the phone never stopped ringing.

"It was a joke," Jacob said again.

"About prophets?" Sophie said.

"Don't ruin the baseball," Boris said. The TV was on, the channel set. First pitch was hours away.

"What was the joke?" Anna asked.

"This place," said Mel, "is really ruining jokes for me."

"We were three days ahead of the Russians," said Eli. "And walking west. It was black. The bombed-out forest and the burned towns and the muddy fields where the ice had melted and the clouds overhead as black as a river bottom. I didn't realize that it was morning. And then I saw a light."

Sam left a note, pitiful as anything else he wrote in English, and if that had been it, if that had been *the only hard evidence*, said the Haredi rabbi like some TV detective, Hercule Poirot if Hercule Poirot wouldn't make eye contact or touch her hand and turned his back on the grieving, *he could discount it*. But first Sam called everyone he knew and nobody answered and he left messages. So, because his death was clearly a suicide that could not be mumbled into an accident, his family did not sit shiva.

Rachel did. Her apartment was his last home, and if there was a ceremony for remembering him, for elevating his soul, she wanted to honor it. But she didn't know how; she had never observed shiva before. She called her parents and asked them and they had no idea and were oddly, as they were with all of her interactions with Judaism in general, embarrassed. They were the kind of Jews who disdained the tribalism of refugees, which is to say, they called the doctor not the rabbi, but would still only call a Jewish doctor. Finally, Rachel reached out to Baer, and he said he would come over and help, but then phoned her later that morning and asked if she wanted to meet at the café.

He was there, early as always, reading a newspaper. She kissed him and went up to the counter to buy him some food. After it had come and he'd eaten, he looked up, almost startled. He reached out and put one hand over hers.

"What do you want to do for your husband?"

"Sit shiva, bury him in a Jewish cemetery. Mourn him."

"He's a suicide?"

She nodded.

He pulled his hand back. "You can't."

"That's bullshit."-

He dropped his spoon into his bowl and rummaged, distracted and angry, like he'd lost something, in the newspaper. "I never sat shiva for any of my family."

She began to cry. The paper he was reading was two weeks old.

There was no one to show her pain to.

"On the other hand," Baer said, "it's important to grieve."

He called around and found a reform rabbi, the son of one of the other cafeteria-goers, who would help her prepare the shiva and would intercede for her with a Jewish cemetery.

She met the rabbi in her apartment, she offered him what food she had available: Oreos and bourbon. "Growing up," he said, "we were only allowed to eat the other ones, what are they called, the ones that were not as good? The ones that Oreos copied?"

"Hydrox."

He clapped his hands, he smiled under his red beard, he looked delighted. "Hydrox!"

She took Daniel's hand and put it to her mouth.

She didn't know how to ask the rabbi the question she wanted to ask. She said, "Because Sam was Haredi. And because he left. Does this count?"

"You mean," the rabbi said, "will it work?"

She tried to smile. He was wearing an orange polo shirt. A reform rabbi in a polo shirt overseeing Sam's funeral rites. Sam had been horrified by her accounts of her bat mitzvah and Cantor Ken picking away at the acoustic.

The rabbi chose another cookie. "It depends on who you ask," he said and held up the Oreo. "Sometimes newer is better."

The volume on the TV was down, but it was an old TV with big speakers and the room jittered with static.

"We were approaching a house," Eli said. "And there was a light on. I thought it was night, the middle of the night, but really it was morning. You don't understand. To live as we had, for years as we had, and not know when it was? Impossible. And yet I thought it was night, the middle of the night, or even earlier. But it was morning."

"I don't understand why he's saying this," Anna said.

"Quiet. I'm trying to tell you who your rabbi is. We were maybe three days ahead of the Russians. We could hear their tanks. But not everyone had fled. I knew this immediately. I could smell the smoke of woodstoves and up ahead there was a light. I couldn't tell at first, but it must have been coming from inside a house at the end of the road that was really the beginning of the village, or the outskirts, depending on where you were, on the road like us, or in the heart of the village, as a few people still were for some reason."

He put his hand on Jacob's shoulder.

"I'm not a meshugener. I'm not like this one, I don't need to knock on my head to know what's in it, and I'm not too senile either, even though I'm nearly a hundred. So I know this isn't how you explain anything to anybody, but what I'm trying to express is that, in that moment, I was confused—my perspective, as you might say, was altered. At first, I thought it was night and then I saw the light and the first door of the first house with its window lit up against the dark and knew my mistake—I knew it was morning, I knew *when* I was, but then at that moment approaching that door in the blue dark with the light on and the smell of woodsmoke and the smell of rotten radishes in the fields or of rotten bodies, I can never absolutely tell one from the other, though the radishes would have been old and rotten because new ones had certainly not yet had time to grow and, old or not, no one in those years was leaving food uneaten, but with all that, and just for a second, as I groped to know that it was morning and not night, I forgot where I was and thought we were outside the ghetto, Khmel'nik, on a warm night, and I thought we were not approaching the house and the ghetto but walking away from it, as we had, down the road where we met the family who were, like us, also fleeing the city, but without their papers giving them permission, if they ever made it to Kyiv, to cross the Dnieper, that black dog's dick of a river, though they didn't know that yet."

"Bodies," said Baruch, appearing in the room, "smell nothing like radishes, Eli."

Eli waved. The TV coughed into fog. Boris hustled to it. Jacob thought: there are good questions and there are bad questions. A philosopher should know the difference.

"But then I remembered where we were," Eli said. "And when we were. And why we were there. The house glowed like that last house at the edge of the ghetto. But this time we were walking the other way. We were seeking entrance and lodging after a long time in the forest. In the mud fields around us lumps of ice glowed like potatoes bobbing in soup, though I had not had potatoes in soup for years. The moment felt—how should I say it? How would you say it, Alex?—sacred, maybe? Ordained? From the forest we had watched them march their Jews into fields just like these, or exactly like these since all the fields of Europe were the same fields of flax or hay or rape stomped through with the same boots and now the war was over and we could come out of the pines. It was morning, not night, and lights were coming on in the village as they had in the ghetto. Yes, sacred. Yes, ordained. Yes, righteous. After all, it's a Law that you should be hospitable to guests."

The static, the sound of voices suddenly outside, in the hallway. The sea.

"Then we approached the front door," Eli said.

"Suicide," the rabbi said, "is not very Jewish."

(She covers her mouth with Daniel's hand. He still holds the lantern between them like she's something he wants to discover.)

The goal of the prayers, the rabbi had said, was to elevate the soul of the departed. But where were the procedures for the mourner? Sam was gone, he was a microspasm of heat puffed into nothingness or less, nothing at all, but in his absence she was thickly embodied, she collapsed into herself, her head and arms and legs were bludgeons she dragged through a world she wished she could smash, her chin was lead, her falling cheeks trawled her eyelids over her eyes, sometimes she could not open them at all, even her hair felt wet and heavy, her neck ached with its weight, while at her center a well opened up, caving in under all this sudden density. And sinking.

Because they were divorced, she was not allowed to keep his body in her home. There would be no one to guard it during the formal mourning period. She was not even supposed to be in the room with him, though she had been the one to identify him at the morgue. Even if he had known how, he would not have bothered to change any of his emergency contact information. And now he was alone.

(The body grows deeper and deeper. Like water forging a gorge).

Sam didn't say anything as he left the apartment that morning. The night before, she'd waited up for him, like his mother or his wife, and had been in the chair reading when he came home late, stooped, with his chin down and his shoulders folded. He looked slapped and chastised, as he did when he prayed. She knew the posture. He'd been with his girlfriend and they'd been fighting.

(The weight of her grief, her body's gradual collapse. Time becomes depth, not sequence. In the basement, with her lips against Daniel's, inhaling his shudder. A plumdark sinking).

Rachel crossed the apartment and stood close to him. "You stink," she said. He was always shy and he tried to back away, but the door was there. She wanted to see him; he still looked like the man she'd watched him become. He was wearing the baseball cap she bought him and the jeans she bought him and the stupid green Abercrombie knit shirt he had seen on a manikin once and loved and she'd bought it too because she realized that for him its preppy shittiness signaled the assimilated invisibility he craved and while secretly she did not want to transform him, or not into that, not into whatever he wanted to be—she liked to see how certainly he mistook simple generosity for a gift that only she could give.

He put his keys away and faced her. Looped in his collar were the sunglasses she'd bought him as a Hannukah present.

"Does she like the way you dress?" Rachel said. He quivered, his eyes were red, he'd been crying. "You were supposed to visit your son," Rachel said. "Or was that just your excuse? Since I'm the only person in the world who cares if you see him."

(The kitchen sink drips in the pipes above them. She cradles the back of Daniel's head as she kisses him and his black hair bleeds over her hand.)

"Suicide is a tough one," said the rabbi. "We're not like the Catholics," he said and chuckled. A chuckling rabbi in an orange polo shirt. "We acknowledge complexity. But scripturally, with suicide, there's not much to go on. Except Elijah."

In despair, the prophet Elijah had cried out from the wilderness for the Lord to take his life. But twice an angel had appeared to him in dream and comforted him. Made him arise and eat.

"To be honest, I always saw that as a metaphor for depression," said the rabbi. "You know. Get up, eat something. Live in the world."

She pushed Daniel away from her. His eyes were wide and black. "What am I doing?" she said.

Being led into the morgue she had asked, "Can I touch him?"

In the body's sinking there were no boundaries. What was an apartment without mirrors? After the angel saved Elijah the second time, the Lord passed by, preceded by catastrophic weather. *There was a wind—but God was not in the wind. There was an earthquake—but God was not in the earthquake. There was a fire—but God was not in the fire.* God was the catastrophe's wake, an aftermath of meaning. The medical examiner took the sheet between his thumb and forefinger.

Daniel was smiling. "I knew you weren't married."

She had wanted to confront Sam. He'd gone out and put on his favorite clothes, the clothes that made him feel independent and real—and come home crying. She did not blame him for their marriage or whatever it had come to. He was an infant in the world, she should have taken his hand and helped him cross the street of his new life, not demanded that he give her something and then let them both see how little he had to give. Compared to hers, his casual and constant cruelty was nothing. But that didn't mean she wasn't angry. He'd cheated on her and left her and divorced her for a Haredi girl named Ora, a girl he'd known all his life, or all of Ora's actually, because Ora was only twenty, and looking to leave, to go OTD as well, and Rachel realized, finally, that Sam resented her because when he saw her he saw a desired vision of himself in the future, a future he wouldn't reach, and right then, maybe that night, when he looked in the mirror he recognized the impossibility of his fantasy: stupid clothes aside, he would never be anything but diminished and empty, he would fall short of his dreams and she should have said, *We all feel that way sometimes*, she should have said, *I feel that way*, she should have said, *Trust me there are good and bad ways of looking, there are good and bad ways of seeing*, she should have touched his raw and lovely face, she should have slapped it as she did sometimes in bed and said, *You are real.* Instead she knocked off his hat and hissed, "Did you tell her that I bought you everything you're wearing?"

Finally, it was time, past time, to pull the covers off the mirrors. Like the medical examiner drawing back the sheet from Sam's face, she appeared again.

At the door, she asked the rabbi, "If suicide is such a sin, where was Sam's angel?"

"Did you ever think it was you?" he said.

"You stole from Jews," Sophie said to Baruch.

"What?"

"This man said you stole from Jews." She pointed at Eli, who was leaning over the pool table, racking the balls.

"This man," said Baruch. He raised an open hand, he waved, he was reaching for a word or pushing one away. "This man," he said again.

Eli, still futzing with the balls, didn't look up. "See, he doesn't deny it. Ask him if he denies it."

"This man is not even alive!" Baruch shouted, and sat down next to Boris on the couch before a blank TV.

The lantern on the ground puddled light at their feet. Daniel kissed her throat, he lifted her hair and put his lips on the bone behind her ear and his other hand, which she leaned into instinctively, on her inner thigh, what had she done, he'd come alive, "Stop," she said. "Stop."

She still had the Lurio, rolled in one hand. She could not put it down, she could not use that hand. A riptide of panic. "Stop," she said again.

He already had, he had immediately. The moving shadow opened and closed his face. "What?"

What was he, twenty-five? Younger than. And not crying. But. His lips also quivered.

His face like a clay vase missing a crescent shard, bewildered lilies sticking out.

"We need to put this picture back," she said.

"ANYBODY HOME?"

Two people, a man and a woman, about the same height and width and color—grayish—two older people, though not by the estate's standards, stood in the doorway to the game room. They were both wearing waders. They braced between them a big blue plastic bucket.

"We brought clams," the man said and gestured with his chin toward the bucket.

"Clams?" Sophie said.

Mel walked over to the bucket and looked in. "Clams," he said.

"We stopped on the way," the woman said. "On a cove and dug them."

"It was low tide," the man said.

"And muddy."

The room was quiet. They wore visors. The woman's hair overgrew her fluorescent visor like the forest retaking an abandoned swimming pool. So did his. Jacob stared. The man had a beard. That was the difference between them.

"Sorry for interrupting," the woman said. "We heard voices."

"Who are you?" Baruch said. He was standing now but had not come out from behind the couch.

"We heard voices so we thought, 'They must be this way.'"

"We followed the voices."

"Excuse me," Baruch said, "but who are you?"

"And then," said the man, "we thought, 'It's a TV.'"

"We heard the TV."

"We thought, 'Those are not voices, those are television.'"

"It's baseball," said Boris without turning around.

"But it wasn't television. It was you," the man said.

"Of course," the woman said, "one never knows the source of a voice unless they can see the mouth that makes it. Also we've been told our boy likes clams."

This time Sophie said, "Who are you?"

Baruch put his hand to his forehead. "Look what they've done to my floors."

"We are Daniel's parents," the man said, stepping forward from their mud.

At dinner that night they did not have clams.

"He made a seafood soup," Daniel's mother complained. "And he made it without clams."

"It's a stew," Daniel said.

"I thought that cioppino was a soup?" said Mel.

"This is a chowder, not a cioppino," Rachel said. And then, before Mel could object, "I helped make it."

"Cioppino," Daniel said, frowning into his bowl, "is also a stew."

His father: "But you can't make cioppino without clams."

"Clam chowder. Clam chowder. Who leaves out the clams in clam chowder?" From under the shade of her visor, his mother wiped a tear.

"It's a Portuguese chowder," Rachel said. "Not a clam chowder."

"But we stopped and dug them."

"And they're endangered."

"You stopped and dug endangered clams?" Rachel said.

"They might not be endangered," his father said.

"But they're rare."

"That's actually true," Baruch said.

"I haven't seen you in seven years," Daniel said. "Where have you been?"

Daniel's mother looked up and away from her bowl of stew. Her small eyes were as gray as clamshells. She leaned forward, squinting at the question. "You were with your grandparents."

"I know where I was," he said. "I was with your parents, and then I was in boarding school, and then I was in various kitchens across the mid-Atlantic, and then I was in rehab. Where were you?"

"You can't love others without first loving yourself, and we were learning to love ourselves," his mother said. "It was for your sake." She was florid and trembling. Her face clashed with her visor. She reached out across the table for Daniel's hand.

"My sake? You left me with those miserable dead people for my sake?"

Suddenly she was shouting. "Growing up wasn't so easy for me either. You should have had them for parents."

"I did."

All the dull faces gone aghast about the silent table. What was to be done? On the far wall, behind where Baruch slumped, was a painting Jacob hadn't noticed before of some kind of waterfowl and again Jacob considered the game from grad school, the Wisdom of Solomon. Solomon knew what it was to have a difficult father. Jacob remembered a legend about Solomon when he was a boy having a favorite gander whose goose-wife finally laid a bunch of eggs. Solomon delighted over the goslings, but one day when he was away from the coops, the gander pecked them all to death. A suspicious story, really. Nearly pointless. Did they have geese in the Kingdom of Israel? Who told this story? The Baal Shem Tov? To illustrate what? On second thought, maybe the legend was *about* the Baal Shem Tov. On the sideboard where the salvers usually rested was a basket of bread for dunking in the stew. Jacob had wanted a piece for the entire meal but there had never, he felt, been a good time to ask for it, and though this was still a bad time to bring up bread, it was a bad time to say anything, so he asked Eli to pass the basket. Here it was, the Wisdom of Solomon. Everybody began pouring wine and passing pepper, except for Eli, who left the bread where it was.

Instead he said, "Have you ever heard the story of the poor old man whose wife was a dybbuk? No? One morning, he wakes up and she's there. He knows she's dead. Everybody knows she's dead. She threw herself in the river. After all, they'd found her corpse. But concerning suicides the rules are clear and there was no one to guard her body and prevent evil spirits from entering. Still, one morning he awakes and there she is, in the kitchen as rosy-faced as ever. Rosier-faced, in fact, than ever, which isn't saying much, not about those people, starving as they were. It's not the point. Anyway, there she is, in the kitchen, cooking a chicken. The smell is wonderful. The house is fragrant with chicken and onion, the scent of its fat that he knows she won't waste, that he sees her gathering in bowls for dipping and frying. He's been so hungry for so long. Since the lean times before she died and since after, of course, since she threw herself away—since then this poor man has barely eaten. And here she is, his bride, alive again, in the morning, cooking. 'Where did you get that chicken?' he asks in wonder."

Eli picked up his spoon and used it to look through his bowl. He put it down and drank some wine and began to explore again in his stew. He looked up. "What?"

Rachel, furious. "That's it?"

"The crazy lady's not wrong," Eli said to Daniel. "In here some clams would have been nice."

Eventually Daniel's mother said to Baruch, "We wanted to thank you for looking after our son."

The candles were relit. Daniel had brought in brandy but the baseball was not over and the sound of the radio carried in from the empty living room and Baruch might have been listening to the game because he didn't answer.

"Why are you here?" Daniel said.

"Thank you for looking after our son, Mister Baruch," Daniel's mother said.

"They probably need money," Daniel said.

"Doctor Baruch," Anna said.

"Why did you show up now?" Daniel said. "You know there's an auction coming up? Who sent you?"

"Hospitality is a virtue," Eli said. "One should be courteous to guests. We discussed this last night and it seemed simple enough, but still, in application, it's tricky. Consider Lot and the angels. One evening Lot is just sort of sitting at the gates of Sodom. Why? Who knows? It makes me think he knows something's coming, but that's not the point. He's sitting there and the two angels show up. They are disguised as travelers, and he invites them into his home, insists that they don't want to pass the night in the street. Such foresight! That very night the rest of the city, all the men, young and old, congregate outside his house demanding to be given the two strangers so that they might rape them. Thinking quickly, I suppose, Lot instead offers up his virgin daughters to appease the mob, but the mob is not interested in his virgin daughters, the mob wants the travelers. Such a strange story. It leads to some questions, doesn't it?"

"And answers," Sophie said. "Lot is clearly a shit."

"I've never understood why anyone does anything in Genesis," Jacob said.

Daniel's mother was poking around in her soup. "Cod, cod, cod. Not a single clam."

"I have a mussel," Boris said. "Would you like a mussel?"

Daniel left the table.

Eli smiled at his empty chair. "My point is that there isn't a lot of obvious sodomy occurring in Sodom. Lot is not being raped. His sons-in-law are not being raped. So what's so special about these two?"

"It's a parable," Sophie. "The causality isn't supposed to be scrutinized."

Eli said, "The angels are there to destroy Sodom. The people of Sodom recognize them as enemies, or emissaries of an enemy. They are greeting them as you would an enemy."

"The story reinforces nomadic custom," Sophie muttered. "It's a story about hospitality. You said so yourself."

"Don't be stupid," Eli said. "It's a story about war."

WHEN SHE WAS NINE, Sophie tells the angels, her mother said to her, *It is always safer to suck it.*

Jonah's, midnight. Wind off the sea through the broken windows. A new lobster trap flipped upside down near the stage. Mussel shells scattered across the bartop like the angels have been feasting. Spot glimmer in their empty purple arterial swirl. Jacob doesn't know if it's the wine with dinner or the brandy after or the flutes of aquavit before but the floor feels perilous with its cliffward tilt. He leans against the bar with Baruch. The others, as always, at the hightops.

"Given the choice," Sophie says, "given the choice was how my mother put it, like sometimes you wouldn't be. Given the choice, she told me at nine, it is always safer to suck it."

The angels nod. With the motion their heads dip into the spotlight—salt-bright, barnacled, fake flare of recognition in their seaglass eyes—and then rise again into the tidal shadow of the leaning room.

"The prudery of Jews does not extend to refugees," Sophie said. "But our love of therapy does. Imagine all my therapists."

Mel starts to laugh.

Earlier an angel, onstage, had said, A mother gave her son two ties. A blue tie, said the angel, and a red tie. Which will you wear today? she asked him and he said, in the cupboard I never got to keep my treats.

Sophie says, "Every therapist would ask, what effect do you think this had on you? Which is why I like talking to you all," Sophie says, twisting away from Mel to face the angels. "Because you don't ask me anything."

In the light her hair looks blonde. She changed after dinner while Daniel raged about the upstairs halls and Rachel chased after him and his parents snored, facing each other in opposite armchairs in the main room, and now Sophie wears black wide-leg pants with a sharp crease and a white linen shirt, open at the neck, and stands silent, defiant as a saint, against the bare blue wall.

There is no cause and effect, Sophie thought, not really. There was the present, which—if you believed in time and causality, if you thought that the past was orchestrating to the present—was the effect. But as soon as it occurred, even as it was occurring, it was immediately just more cause. History was a möbius strip that produced itself out of itself. Sequence was only another form of reoccurrence. Some woman must have taken her mother aside in Bergen-Belsen or in the postwar streets of Berlin amid the gray ash sky and the vodka vomit in the gutter where they slept and told her, as she was telling Sophie, that if they gave you the choice, if they gave you a choice, the woman said to her mother huddled against the trunks of linden trees under the shadows of the Brandenburg Gate as Russian soldiers pissed on the statues of Prussian generals and then, pricks still out, turned toward the women, where Sophie has dreamt she stood with her own daughter, one she never had, and said, *If they give you a choice it is always safer to suck it.*

She was nine. They were sitting on the couch. They each balanced a cup of tea and a bone china saucer in their laps. On the coffee table before them were two swans carved from crystal. The swans' necks were flutes as clear as curved icicles, the intricate feathers in their wings transformed sunlight into rainbows on the wall. Every day her mother put on gloves and polished the swans with a special cloth. When Sophie's friends came over they were not allowed to watch

TV because to watch TV they would have to sit on the couch and between the couch and the TV there was the coffee table with the crystal swans. *When he is ready to express his sperm*, her mother told her, *most women will pull away a little.*

Her grandfather filling his pipe beneath the portrait of the Kaiser. *The Ostjuden live in the past,* he says to the family in the music room. *So they are treated the way Jews were treated in the past.* The tip of his match scratches on the box but does not catch.

It's an instinct, her mother told her. *It makes sense to pull away, but what you want to do is lean forward, let the organ go entirely down your throat, beyond your tongue, so that you can't taste it at all.* She touched the bottom of Sophie's throat, lightly, traced the hard U of the jugular notch, and then pressed. *Do you understand? Even in marriage this is a good technique. He will think you are excited. He will think that you are offering yourself to him and hungry for what he has to give, he will think you are trying to deepen your connection in that moment.*

"When really," Sophie, tells the angels, "you're doing the opposite, right?"

The angels have begun to rock forward, slightly, all of them, in unison.

She says, "I didn't need a doctor to tell me that my mother's sexual instruction framed sex as something from which you must absent yourself. As something from which your goal was to disappear."

She stops. She stares at the angels staring at her. "Absence is something you should understand," she says to the angels.

Slowly, together, their wooden heads recoil into shadow.

Unlike other refugees, her family lived in Hopewood, a little town outside of Albany, where there were no Jews, where no one had any thoughts about Jews, and where no one would look for Jews. They did not pass, they did not assimilate or go to church, they kept their eyes down in public, they were spendthrift and terrified of starvation, they filled the basement with so many canned goods that once when a man came to read the gas meter he joked, *You really are afraid of the bomb!*

"That's not right," Sophie says. "My mother was terrified and frugal. My father was bemused and profligate. My mother was always preparing for war. My father seemed not to remember it. My mother worked in a bank, as a teller."

Her father did not work. He came from a long line of Berlin bankers from before the Berlin bankers expelled Jews from the Berlin banks. As a boy he knew he would be a banker, he was prepared for it by his father and grandfather and his father's brother, as well, when the men gathered on Friday nights at his grandfather's house to talk business and politics and smoke cigars and drink cognac. Even though it was Friday, they did not light candles. On holidays they would, High Holidays and Hannukah, and then they would do it without much ceremony, his grandmother mumbling a quick prayer, long after sunset, before they sat down to their dinner. Most weeks, the men gathered in his grandfather's study, smoking the cigars he kept in a mahogany humidor in the bottom drawer of his precious Roentgen writing desk. There was a sofa in the study, but the men sat in chairs and smoked cigars and spoke of the bank and of banking and sometimes her grandfather recited from Goethe's *Hermann and Dorothea*, not often, but when he'd had a few extra cognacs—as a boy Sophie's father didn't notice these things, but this is Sophie's guess, why else would a Jewish banker recite Goethe, and why, if you were going to memorize Goethe, would you memorize *that* Goethe, lesser Goethe certainly, minor Goethe if there is minor Goethe for Germans or Jews who thought they were Germans, either way he must have been drawn to something in that not-great-Goethe, the tension, Sophie guessed, between bourgeois domesticity and rustic passion that when he had had a few drinks he could let himself feel as, if not a real (that is to say lived) possibility, at least an aesthetic experience —and they would all listen and nod along and consider how restrictive Hermann's father was, for not wanting Hermann to marry that poor refugee girl, or that's what Sophie's father imagined they were thinking because that's what he was thinking, *One day I will marry a poor refugee girl and I know Papa will let me.* And it was true, it was one of the ways the imagined life becomes real, one of the ways it feels that we will our childhood desires into a future we can never forgive ourselves for, because he did marry a refugee girl, though he was a refugee as well and his papa and mama and both his uncles, and grandfather and grandmother, said nothing, allowed it or didn't, blessed it or didn't, though the world unallowed nothing and blessed nothing, and if he secretly believed that, in fact, his father would have made an entirely different match for him, that possibility disappeared when they stepped off the train into the mud and his father was ushered to the left and he to the right, accidentally into his own shadow, alive still under the clouds of familiar ash.

Each week his grandfather gave him a Reichspfennig 5 coin. They were old, he told Sophie, from the twenties, and bronze, or bronze-looking, like a penny, he said, with two stalks of wheat on the back, also like a penny from back then, actually, he noted, and every week his grandfather presented him with the coin and said, *Now would you like to make your investment?* Though this was a game, it was a very German game which meant he didn't realize it was a game and he said, *Yes, Grandfather* and his grandfather would walk him over to his Roentgen writing desk, which he kept closed to display its fold-down front inlayed with designs—all in mother of pearl—of a court interior, pillars and statues and a floor laid out in checkered parquet and the grounds, assumably of that same estate or palace, a grove of willows overhanging a little pond, and an arbor in tortoiseshell, Edenic with lions and bulls and other beasts of field and forest lolling in harmony, and then he would say, *For your deposit would you like it to be a short-term account or a long-term account?*

Long-term, said Sophie's father.

And why is that?

Interest.

And what interest rate would you like? And Sophie's father would give the customary response and his grandfather would nod and say, *Very good* and turn the secret key beneath the desk and the front lid would roll back and the whole thing would unfold, by way of springs and levers and weights, into a palace scene, the same scene from the front but now in three dimensions, the many drawers and little cabinets becoming the pillars and walls and tapestries, and it was into one such drawer, a secret drawer hidden behind the open tail of an engraved peacock, that Sophie's father would place his penny. And every week when they opened the drawer to deposit the coin, the Reichspfennig 5 that was very much like a penny, there were always, instead of pennies, a little growing pile of silver 5 Reichsmark coins. *It looks like your account is doing very well*, his grandfather would say, peering down over his shoulder through his glasses.

Yes, Grandfather, he'd answer and then they'd close the desk and the men would sit down to talk.

When Sophie's mother came home from the bank, he would be waiting there in his armchair with a book or newspaper and his reading glasses down on his nose and he would say, *My cuckoo*—that was what he called his wife—*my cuckoo, how was your day at the bank?* And she'd take down her hair and make them each a martini and sit next to him and say, *The same.* And he'd frown since this was never the answer he expected and then, a moment later, smile, and it was the smile of a boy poised before a Roentgen writing desk, that is to say, said Sophie, it was the smile of a little child smiling at a shadow puppet before the bomb blows the wall away, and say, *What rates are they opening savings accounts for?*

She did not know what her father did during the day. He was always in his armchair by the time she came home, but he must have answered the door, because whenever door-to-door salesmen passed through town he bought whatever they had to sell. He could not work, she did not know why, and it was never discussed around her, but he could not work and he was always in his armchair by the time she came home. He didn't get up from the chair or meet the bus, but he was awake and smiling and not doing anything else, so he must have been waiting for someone and she was the one who came home every day to him in the chair, waiting, and usually surrounded by the neat unopened boxes of whatever had come in the mail.

"Did you ever have encyclopedias?" Sophie turns from the angels and asks Mel and Anna and Boris. "I did. Two sets. For thirteen days each."

There were also the samples: squares of colored cloth, fabric for dresses and drapes, pink rectangles of synthetic material masquerading as coat lining, tiny blue towels the size of her mother's thumb. And then all the little product models: the model chairs and model armoire and the model patio furniture and model grill, the model vacuum, the model pool of antifreeze blue in the model yard—a yard which, in reality, they didn't have. Out of whimsy or its total opposite, her father decorated their rooms with these models—the little toaster by the toaster, the stove by the stove, the tiny plastic vacuum perched on the shelf above the Electrolux—so that their lives were reflected in miniature, and every few months her mother, saying nothing, would gather them all and throw them away. Some things you couldn't send back—knives and a blender, Fuller brushes and two embroidered sets of kitchen napkins—and others you could, and their rooms became a sort of monument to the incomplete—partial sets of Great Books and illustrated Children's Classics, odd numbers of wine glasses and ice cream bowls as if they were refugees of a sudden massacre who fled their home with no warning and packed what they could grab—as if they came from a people who had escaped.

Her mother would come home after Sophie did and see what he'd bought and kiss his cheek and make her martini and say, *Thank you, sweetheart*, and pat his hand, and he would look up at her with hope though Sophie never knew for what, was never sure what he imagined this gift, this new one, finally doing for them, but he'd look up at her, his wife, and if she was not sitting beside him, he would reach out slowly with open hands like a dreaming child and would say when she sat, *Do you like it?* And she would say, *Yes, love it's very nice*, or *It's very beautiful*, or *It's very useful* and then finally she would say, *You know we can't keep it* and he would nod, yes, he knew, he would nod like of course they couldn't, like he was a banker looking up through the pleasant blue surprise of his pipe's first puff and, stabbing his match out in the bronze tray blackened by similar stabbings on his mahogany desk where he sat beneath the framed pictures of his grandfather and his father, he would lean across the quicksilver glimmer of their martinis and kiss her cheek—and this was another lesson of love that Sophie learned, how it was a gift offered against the gray dispossession of the present, intangible as smoke you tried to save by swallowing.

The swans were part of a set of other ornamental crystal animals. Two swans, two cats, two mice, two elephants. They came in a flat black wooden box with a silver clasp and green velvet interior, like the one a friend's mother used for the family silver. Sophie's mother had to drive five hours through the night to beg the salesman to take them back and give her a partial refund, minus the price of the swans and his commission on the set. That's what she told Sophie months later, when they were sitting on the couch with their tea. *My grandmother lived on the edge of a pond in Russia,* her mother told her. In the summer the pond and the ponds around her house, the ones in the forest and on the wastes, would fill with swans. *Is that why you kept them?* Sophie asked. *So you could remember your grandmother?*

Years later, during the first months of her residency, helping the wife of the chief resident prepare for a dinner party, Sophie, setting the table, said, *What else can I do?* And the chief resident's wife passed her a black flatware box of silver to polish. *That salesman didn't want to take any of them back,* her mother said. *But what would we do with a crystal elephant? That's what I asked him. You shouldn't take advantage of people, I said to him. He pretended to be angry when I said that, but he wasn't.* Her mother sipped her tea. Sophie, at the resident's house, had not opened the box. *I didn't think guests polished the silver,* she said. It was the beginning of a reputation she could not escape. *You have to ask the right questions,* her mother told her, *and sometimes you have to beg. You have to keep these swans clean,* her mother said, and the sun through the window rainbowed the crystal wings across the walls like the wings of angels, and her mother said, *Given the choice, it is always safer to suck it.*

Sophie stands in the blue spot glow. The room waits for her to continue. It must be near dawn. A loon cries on the open water.

So as not to fall, everybody clings to furniture. Baruch and Jacob lean against far sides of the bar. The others clutch hightops. The square windows in the corner tilt nearly into diamonds under the foundation's eastern sag and the moon, bisected through their dirty glass, glows like a lamp on in somebody's house spied from the outside, across the street. Jacob thinks: everything is about to fall into the fucking sea.

"The world is full of advice," Sophie says. "And for years I listened to it. I begged for it. Fifty steps to being happy? Ten tricks for a good sex life? I read all the articles and clicked the links. But it was like overhearing two different conversations at the same time. None of the remedies seemed related to the problem.

"It turns out I didn't need advice," Sophie says. "Advice was actually the problem. My mother had given me all the advice a person might need in their entire life by the time I was ten, which just made it clear to me that life was impossible."

Leaving Baer's, Jacob had stood in the street and thought much the same thing. The world was impossible, but it was also the only possibility. The night before, alone, watching the fire, he had listened to his sister talk. *You're giving up too easily*, she'd said. *Also, you have to let go of things,* she added and he hung up. In the street outside Baer's terrible apartment, a man on a bicycle rode by, ringing a bell. Jacob saw him often, this was his thing, riding by and ringing a cow bell with a black plastic handle. The first time it had seemed like a joke, one of those New York jokes, so idiosyncratic that though you realized you were witnessing a joke, you had no idea what made it funny. But he was serious, you could see that in his face and in the way he thrashed the bell through the summer dusk like a penitent's flail. For a while Jacob wondered what he was trying to communicate, but he began to think communication wasn't the point. Ringing the bell was a ceremony. If it was a warning, it was a ceremonial warning, a warning of something inevitable like death, which made it an act of mourning, the bell tolling rather than ringing. Jacob didn't want to be what his sister, what Maddie, accused him of being—that bike guy with a bell—just a static representation of damage that wasn't even his. He would take Alex Baruch's offer, he thought. He'd change things. He'd gotten a little excited. Then he'd heard the rest of Baer's story.

"Can you hear the ocean?" Sophie says. She must be talking to the angels. "Apparently," she says, "people find the ocean relaxing. Comforting. There is a theory that it mirrors the general sloshing inside the womb. But you wouldn't know about that, would you? To you, it just sounds like a fucking joke."

Earlier that night, the first angel on stage had not been able to begin. For a moment Jacob was certain it was staring at him, waiting for him to say something. He made eye contact, or he stared at the shard of muddy glass where an eye would be. The angel, finally, was speaking.

The angel said, What is the difference between deli?

"I thought I deserved some relaxation," Sophie says. "I blew up my life. After about a hundred years of school and residency I declined to practice medicine. I accumulated guilt. I did not light yahrzeit candles for my father or visit my mother. I did not achieve love or accomplish grandchildren. I abandoned the woman who loved me, but only, I felt, at an exceedingly shrill and needy volume. I suggested to her that she get a pet. Then I stole her rug. I couldn't sleep, I rarely digested food without diarrhea. Terrible queer failure that I was, I never orgasmed. Still, I was a doctor and I diagnosed myself: I required respite. Had I lived in my grandfather's world, I would have gone to a spa."

"You're at one now," shouts Mel.

"Finally," Sophie says, "I took myself to the sea."

It was winter, and she had just dumped her girlfriend of two years. She went to the Cape because she thought it would be deserted and bleak and melancholy, but mostly deserted, which is what she was looking for, silence, various shades of gray, and erosion, that is to say, loss on a grander scale than her own. Instead, it was full of poets.

How was she to know? She'd never been there, during all her time in med school and residency in Boston and now she was driving south with a single bag of clothes and a Persian rug buckled into her passenger seat.

When she hit the Sagamore Bridge she crossed it into exactly what she was looking for: empty towns, gray and shuttered against the wrong season, or if not shuttered, empty, forests of pitch pine and black oak along the highway. I'll drive to the end, she thought. In every way she felt like she was at land's end, world's end, she was at the edge of something unchecked. She reached Provincetown and parked. Things were open. Lights on in stores and galleries against the darkening sky. Was it a good idea to leave a nineteenth-century Persian rug in your car around here? She unhooked the rug, put it under her arm, and went looking for a drink.

Sophie says, "It should tell you everything you need to know about my distance from my sexuality, if that's what you would call it, my distance maybe from sex which was considerable, and from intimacy which was cosmic, that I had never heard of Provincetown.

"I went into the first bar I came across. It was a tavern with cedar shingles and peeling white shutters and a wooden sign hanging from its eaves with an appropriate name, something nautical and confusing like Sea Dog or Barnacle Beard. I figured it would be dark and empty and I'd have to keep an eye on my rug."

Instead, it was full of poets. They had pulled a bunch of tables together and the tables were covered with glasses. If they were men and had hair it was wild, if they were women it was short or it was pigtailed. They wore shawls and bulky sweaters or sport coats or flannel shirts or both. To a person their shoes were hiking boots. Sophie approached the bar, sat down, and put her rug on the stool next to her. The room quieted, they were watching. She ordered a whiskey, a good one, something expensive, and the poets cheered. They appreciated an order of whiskey, and no matter what bar they were in they were poets and so they appreciated a woman with money. She drank her drink and they drank theirs. They had already spent a month sleeping with each other. They were curious and bored.

One by one they approached and chatted and complimented her choice of whiskey. The men touched her arm, the women offered her cigarettes, none of them asked about her rug. Poets don't have patience for a long engagement and soon they had ushered her away from the bar to where they were sitting and with the generosity required of the lyric spirit, they let her buy a round for the table. Outside, through the leaded panes, winter darkness rolled out of the bay like a breeze. She watched it as they spoke, watched the street glow, then dim, then disappear, the glass blackstopped into her own blurry reflection.

The poets were talking. They were some kind of community. They said they had fellowships and residencies and Sophie, still in a tunnel, running forward but getting no closer to the crescent flame of day on the far side, had no idea what they meant when they said *residency,* felt only the pale spiral of her life after that night at the chief resident's house, saw the room around her grow dense and quiet as she watched her father eating in the window glass, saw him put down his fork and dab his lips with his napkin unfolded from his lap and say, *You know there are various types of interest.* She ordered more drinks for everyone. *Hyacinth*, someone said. *Betty's bare bottom*, the man across from her whispered, explaining something. *Betty's bare bottom*, he said again, revising himself, *as the rain came pouring down.* Her lover had said, *Are you listening? I talk and you never listen.* She was listening now. Comprehension assaulted her like a god descending: They were poets, so they were talking about the past. They were poets talking about the past, so they were talking about sex. *The wild gushing*, said another, *beneath the grandstands*. For them desire lived in first encounters, a touch, a nascent glance swollen with significance. Where, she wondered, did desire live in her? In med school, she peered down into a corpse opened onto the table like a well-packed suitcase. Exsanguinated, it was tidy, everything visible and fit neatly together, this former arrangement of all human possibility. But what was this vison of mortality teaching her that she didn't already know? *Honeysuckle, honeysuckle, honeysuckle,* said a poet making a toast to a flower or a euphemism. Her father had said to her, to her mother wearily flexed into her chair after a day at the bank, *You must understand the effects of a long-term investment* and she watched her mother seek out and discover, somehow always, her regions of tenderness. *He will think you are excited*, her mother said. *He will think that you are offering yourself to him and hungry*, she said, and this was all nostalgia was for Sophie, her father's blind and backward glance into the great ache of his unlived life, which she tried to explain a week later sitting in an understuffed leather chair looking anywhere but at the softening blandness of her newest therapist's face, down at her feet and the rug not much different than the one stolen from her in the bar in Provincetown, or up to the Lurio on the wall of Tamar at the Crossroads, and she told him, looking down or looking up but not at him until she had to, until his own gasp arrested her history and she had to listen and look up at him, her new therapist, because he was crying and whispering, as shocked as she was, *Yes, yes, yes, I know just what you mean.*

JACOB AWAKE, WRESTLED AWAKE, DOWNSTAIRS. *Let me go for dawn is breaking.* When was it? The moon was arced below the hedgeline; through the windows he could only see its glow pearled upward like a light from the sea. There were different chambers of morning here: when the birds began to wail, when the lobster boats rumbled out, and when the light appeared.

Let me go for dawn is breaking, said the angel in Genesis as he fought with the biblical Jacob. Considering this confrontation, the Talmud asked what had never seemed like the most important question: *How do we know when dawn breaks?* And provided an answer: *When you can tell your brother from a stranger.*

But there was a Hasidic parable that Jacob always preferred, not for its sentiment but for the way, read as Jacob read it, it revealed the confusion inherent in any family by reversing the Talmud's answer to: *When you know a stranger as your brother.*

Jacob's father, his mother, finally his sister, they were all strangers. Alone in his home with his shirt off and baseball on the silent television, Jacob's father would mumble, *There's no sin worse than cynicism.* But in the world, he was the scheister, the small-time bookie pulling tricks. *When we came to this country,* he said, *we didn't have two shekels to rub together.* He nodded at Jacob like this was something other than an idiom. They were eating ice cream and watching Little League. He spat in the dust, he waved to a neighbor. He said, *But we had one shekel and*—he whispered this to Jacob—*it was shiny. Hold up the coin,* he said, *and if it's shiny the rest of the world disappears. A rube looks at the coin and everyone is a rube. It's like that third baseman—Schwartz's kid,* he said, shaking his head at the hopelessness of the eight-year-old before them. *See his eyes? He's watching the bat, not the ball. His whole life he'll be like that.* Jacob, missing the point, wondered if his father knew what he would be like. *If you don't want to be a rube*, his father said, biting his ice cream as if it were an apple, *don't look at the coin.*

Joshua sat in his chair while Jacob leaned over him and cleaned his face with tissues and aquavit. The only light: the desk lamp. And not enough.

"Turn," Jacob said, turning Joshua's face with his hands into the weak splash of lamp light. The wet tissues melted against his brow. Quickly each time, it was Jacob's damp fingers on Josh's skin. Grit, gravel coming loose, scabs already forming, Josh cringing. "Stop," Jacob said and took his chin, tilted his head again.

Maddie hadn't spoken for the rest of dinner. At what point had Jacob stopped believing in his own life? He was like a patient who, feeling the wound, pries the suture's thread from the raw skin, and pulls. Jacob handed Joshua some tissues to press to the cut and went back to his desk.

"How did you get in?"

"I broke a window."

"You broke a window?"

Josh nodded. "Do you think I'll be expelled?"

"Probably."

"Really?"

"How the fuck should I know?" Jacob said.

For a few minutes he sat and watched Joshua cry. Again, he told himself: be a person. He poured more aquavit into his mug. What would a person do? Lift Jacob from the curb in Tel Aviv. An old man who said nothing. And took his hand.

"Joshua," Jacob said. "What's really going on?"

"I can't talk about it."

"A girl?"

Joshua twisted his own head, as Jacob had, as you would a dummy's, shaking *no.*

"A boy?"

"It's nothing like that."

"If you're worried about your grade," Jacob said.

"I'm so ashamed," Joshua said.

Jacob waited. He wanted to say, *There's nothing to be ashamed of.* But that probably wasn't true. Even this moment wasn't great.

"I didn't vote against him," Joshua said.

"You mean you didn't vote?"

"I didn't think it would matter."

"Why didn't you vote?"

"She stole the nomination."

"Oy, Josh," Jacob said. He drank. He refilled his mug. This was a teachable moment and he was looking for the right tone to take. "Dude." He meant to say it kindly, but he just sounded exhausted. This man was president, this Nazi whose father was a Nazi and surrounded himself with Nazis and revealed Nazis everywhere, hidden and pupal, whose words were mirrors reflecting the nation giggling at what they had thought was a joke but was just a shuddering neon vein of hysteria with no end, and it turned out Jacob didn't feel like teaching.

"Well, she won New York," Jacob said. "So I guess it didn't matter."

"I'm from Philly."

"One vote doesn't make a difference."

"That's not the point, is it?"

"No," Jacob said.

Joshua was waiting for him to say more. The walls coughed and quieted. The off-hours radiators turning down. "I thought you'd make me feel better."

"Why do you think that feeling better is the right way to feel?"

For the entire election, its slow shriek and six seasons, he had wanted to call his father and say, *Can you believe it?* Meanwhile, he did the things that everyone else did in the ways it seemed that everyone else was doing them: he watched TV, he read the newspaper, he panicked the internet, often all at once. But he didn't seem to be responding the way everyone else was. *This can't be happening*, he said to Maddie. *Be glad it's not Bush*, she said. *Or Cruz*. He needed to explain himself, but what did he need to explain? He was suspicious, angry, unsleeping. He padded the apartment in the night, he did not work, he did not research, he planned his class on Jewish Theology After the Holocaust. *You don't understand,* he said to Maddie, and Maddie agreed. *What do you want*? she said. He wanted to call his father and ask him what to do. He wanted to say, *You were right. You saw while we mocked and judged.* Though he hadn't been. The Nazi president didn't mean you couldn't trust the doorman, even if you couldn't trust the doorman. What Jacob really wanted was what everyone else had fled: to sit with his father in his childhood apartment staring at the TV while his father explained what they watched. His father, the bookie who knew the world was only a violent lure, found beauty in an elegant con. The president's bullshit would have disappointed him. *These rubes! The man doesn't even have a coin to show them.* They would have laughed together. They would have commiserated and raged. His father would say, *The man's a Nazi* and this time Jacob would answer, *You're right*. At the same time, Jacob was glad, if he was glad of anything, that his father, who had seen this in everything, didn't have to see this.

Joshua was still crying. "I'm despairing."

It was sweet the way he said it. The radiators were now entirely off. The time for not drinking any more aquavit had passed.

Jacob said to him, "I know how you feel."

"You didn't vote either?"

"Of course I voted," Jacob said. The Jewish idea was always that this had happened before. His father in the attic like *his* father in the attic. Jacob in the hall where the empty ladder hangs. Like the moment in the fairy tale where you needed to make the right choice. It was enough. He could come clean, explain, give comfort. "When I was your age I did something much worse."

And he told him what he had never told anyone. His screeds and sudden collapse in Tel Aviv, the way he changed his name when he returned and entered a new college under the new name—went on from there, graduate school, post doc, marriage, in the wake of his brief and wrongheaded righteousness had lived a life of curated uncertainty right up to this very moment, as this person he wasn't, but always had been. He put his hand on Joshua's shoulder, the water cooler in the faculty lounge across the hall gurgled, in the whole building only this light was on, the broken window had not yet been discovered. In welcoming him to a community of mistake, he was releasing him to try again.

Joshua did not respond as he expected. He jumped up, as he did sometimes in class. "You give us those essays telling us to be ashamed. For our assimilation? For our criticism of Israel? You say that we're the ones betraying the dead?"

"Those are not my essays."

"How can you tell us to feel bad?"

"You feel bad because you made a bad choice, Josh. Not a significant one, but a bad one. You should live with it."

Joshua had stopped crying, and now his face was lacerated with fury, like a room where the wallpaper is torn off to discover something obscene scribbled on the bare wall. "Who the fuck are you to tell us how to be?"

Jacob, who had never been angry, who shambled through the boulevards of his life dragging shame and fear and doubt, stood and began shouting. "You rube," he said. "Twenty-two years old and crying in your professor's office. Which makes sense, actually. You did what the Nazis wanted you to do. That makes you a collaborator. Do you understand that?"

The old man in Tel Aviv had taken Jacob's hand, raised him to his feet, and walked with him. In his apartment, saying nothing, asking nothing, he had made them each tea with mint and honey. He drank his, as most Israelis Jacob knew did, from a clear glass, but he served Jacob's in a porcelain teacup, faintly decorated in flowers of vanishing blue. The cup was chipped, faded, and once Jacob had finished his tea he saw inside it a thin circle where the cup was stained with the tideline of someone else's decades. The old man washed his own glass and then dried it and he put it on a bar cart where he kept other glasses, but no matching teacup and no saucer for the cup Jacob used. When Jacob handed it back to him, he took it with both hands and cradled it against his body before walking to the sink.

"I was trying to tell you something," Jacob said to Joshua. "I thought you'd understand."

Joshua stormed out, he made his complaint, and then he showed up again after Jacob's meeting with the dean. He already had the pills, but not the vodka.

"Fuck off, Joshua," Jacob said.

Let me go for dawn is breaking. Jacob had not been able to find his small weird room, and laid down on the couch in the lobby. In the night the sea had sighed on the French Doors, blowing them open, and the wind haunted the house: doors gasped and slammed all down the dark corridors.

The auction was tomorrow, was today. He had not made any kind of decision. He rose and passed onto the wet lawn: no birds, no boats, no light.

What was the joke Jacob told about prophets? Sometimes you look to the sky for signs, other times you bury your head and hide. Like Jonah going down into the hold to sleep as the storm groaned around the hull. Now for the first time since he'd come to Nod, Jacob turned his back on the sea and looked, really looked, at the windward side of Baruch's estate.

From here, at the northern exposure, the house stood in ruin. The nightblue lawn and shell paths, the terrace and planters weather-beaten and beautiful, the wild roses past bloom and stately in their windy decay, everything pale and luminous as hotel bar in Berlin where Jacob had first seen Baruch: that plastic room tinted with piano light and possibility, suspended in the last slow moment of Baruch's unreal grandeur. A black rash of mold spread along the house's upper walls, the northeast corner of the roof dipping toward the sea like a minuteman's tipped hat—the foundation, rotten as well, must be going.

It was all an illusion. The estate was enormous, rambling over ten thousand square feet at least, and Jacob had only seen about a dozen rooms, or fewer. He'd kept his eye on the bat and believed what he wanted to believe—that Nod's stature reaffirmed Baruch's own. But it was, like the man himself, a radiant sham, the shining shekel Baruch still held.

Jacob confronted Maddie finally, at the aquarium. She had been to a work function there and the aquarium had given them free passes for the evening hours and they had gone. The surprises of adult love. They couldn't quite believe it—that other adults came, or that they did—but here they were together, among fish, at the end of their marriage. They strolled on damp concrete in dim subterranean passages and pointed and drank wine from plastic glasses and tried to act like it was not unusual to find themselves here or that being here, ten o' clock on a Saturday at the aquarium, did not reveal some larger confusion. And yet the other visitors were mostly couples, a little younger than them, generally happy-seeming. Then again, Jacob and Maddie were maybe the only ones who were not high. Couples giggled at seahorses or stared in vacant awe at cuttlefish sweeping through the empty coral like some kind of lunar pods. A few seemed to be freaking out. "You are too sad," one guy kept saying to the giant

Pacific octopus, repeating it over and over before he began to cry—but to see the octopus, hanging from its rock like some overripe fruit, well he also appeared to be right.

For a while, they had a good time. Maddie was always enthusiastic. She leaned once against his arm, she pointed, his phone did not ring. They stood close to each other, they laughed at the same people and agreed on the same names for the turtles without recalling how they had once picked out baby names. Maybe interacting only in the moment—without history—was like intimacy, as long as intimacy didn't require understanding, which it didn't.

This was actually the subject of a recent fight where Jacob had refused to explain what happened at school or what exactly he'd said that had upset Joshua and that Joshua had told the dean. *You won't understand*, he'd said. *How can that be true?* she'd asked at first, and when he didn't answer, she said, finally, *I don't need to understand, I just need to know.* Since then, he had lost his job and Maddie became quiet, she met his self-deprecation and anger with silence or careful acknowledgement—and then his sister began calling. But tonight was fun and silly and she clung to his arm and he said, "I know about him."

They were in the North Atlantic room, at the tide pool exhibit, peering into what was basically a giant sandbox filled with water and rocks and various sea vegetables. You could use little shovels to reach in and explore. It was full of crabs.

"I wondered," she said. "I thought, *he must know*, but then I thought, *how can he know and not say anything*?"

"That's it?" Jacob had expected shock or apology or even anger.

"What else is there?"

Between them the laminated sign encouraged visitors to identify as many crab species as they could. There were hermit crabs and horseshoe crabs and jonah crabs and even the invasive green crabs.

"You're having an affair," he whispered. He had tried to scoop up a hermit crab and was still holding a pink plastic shovel filled with pebbles. "You're not even pretending to deny it."

"You said you knew. What's the good of denying it?"

"You're telling me you're fucking someone else by the crab tank!"

"You confronted me by the crab tank," Maddie said quietly. "God knows why."

Between your past and future there is your ridiculous present. Not everything was a mistake you had to make: he put the shovel down.

"Why didn't you tell me?" he said. "Why didn't you just leave?"

"Because I didn't want to leave you."

"But you do now?"

Jacob waited for her answer. Twice she opened her mouth and then closed it again, like the fish behind her, through the archways, circling the marine tank. "Why do they all swim in the same direction?" he heard someone ask.

"You know now," she said finally. "So now what I want doesn't matter."

Sometimes Jacob thinks, what does knowing mean? We know when morning begins, but not what to do with it. You could step into the ruined tavern and tell the cosmos what it did to your life, and it would answer with a joke. But Baruch was also wrong: what good did making an account do either? Jacob had said something similar in the aquarium. That knowing doesn't mean anything, that just because he knew didn't have to change anything—and she'd become angry.

"You'll whip us with this," she said and turned away from the tidepool. He followed her to the corner, where she stood under a mural of sea anemones painted as big as pumpkins. "This wasn't inevitable, Jakes. I wasn't always going to leave, do you get that?"

"And yet you are," he said.

Nearby a guy with one leg of his pants still rolled to accommodate bike spokes was yelling at a docent. "The penguins are asleep? What's the point of any of this without penguins?"

"It's night. They need to sleep," the docent said.

Maddie was staring at her feet. Her shoulders were turned inward like she was trying to fold herself up and her blouse billowed away from her body. Jacob's knuckles were going on the concrete wall just below the anemones. Everywhere signs by the tanks insisted DO NOT KNOCK ON GLASS and his urge to do it had tipped into nausea. His knocking on walls was always like knocking on a tank: against chaos and indifference you knock and the world, hearing its secret name sounded out in code, looks back. Maddie startled, she recoiled and caught herself, gathered her compassion and took his hand.

"This is what we call a self-fulfilling prophecy," she said.

Jacob understood what Maddie was saying. From the moment of his sister's first call he had felt the comfort of a terrible coherence. The affair confirmed all his fears: his successes were shams, his life was an illusion. Maddie, of course, wanted him to see the failure of their marriage as the failure of their marriage, that is to say not as a validation of his boyhood fears, but as their consequence—as if they weren't the same thing.

"Wake them up," the penguin guy was pleading to the docent now. His voice was filling with tears. "Please wake them up."

Jacob pointed. "It's not him, is it?"

Maddie smiled politely. Never in their relationship—other than fucking someone else, lighting candles and kneeling before someone else, while his sister watched and narrated—had she ever abandoned her decency. "Ask what you really want to ask."

They were suddenly alone. Their shoes stuck to the stippled concrete paths. The fans in this part of the aquarium didn't seem to be working and the air was dense with fish food and still water, like the time they had picnicked on a rocky beach at low tide on a hot day when the wind was down and seaweed rot and brine and flies bubbled from the tidal muck and they'd drunk a bottle of wine and fed sandwich scraps to gulls and made love, painfully, on the rocks as spiders skittered away from them. He took her hand. Against this reality, her hand in his, nothing had any weight. How was this something he had forgotten? But it was still there, and if there was one thing his life had prepared him for it was how emotion could be preserved in memory. He could atone. He could apologize and make promises. They could begin again, anew, if he just said the right thing, here in this last moment of their old lives, dimly registered by groupers drifting in blue incredulous boredom.

He said, "Why?" It was the wrong question, like a joke told by an angel, and he could see her disappointment. She had also felt the charge. It was a moment for a gesture, some plan for the future, or even just an acknowledgment of the present—if he'd knelt before her, or kissed her, or pushed her up against the wall—but he was looking back into the past. She lowered her eyes and met him there.

Daniel is kissing her again and she is kissing back and again they are in the kitchen.

"What are you doing down here?" he had said when he found her, early in the night while the others were at the bar and his parents were asleep. She was filling a bowl with espresso powder, she was drinking wine and drawing.

"I need to see the Lurio," she had said and put her palm on his cheek.

There was a term in curation that Simon used, almost incessantly, at the museum: *sight lines*. The way a space was arranged to greet, or control, or accommodate a visitor's gaze. From any fixed point, the sight lines could produce meaning, both from context and from anticipation: this is the heritage of what you are seeing now, this is what you will see. The lines from point-to-point invited visitors to join the past to the future in the darkening ink of their own sight. But Jacob, Baruch, Boris, Sam, Rivkah, Eli, the old creep—they had no future in their sight lines. They were a howl, a body hitting the water from a hundred and thirty feet. And her? The dead had no claim over the living. She could do what she was going to do.

Now, against the counter, Daniel smells like shampoo. His hand on her lower back doesn't feel dead. In his youth, she had imagined she would discover inexperience, but this only reveals hers. He is beautiful and sullen and worked in restaurants. That she finds him a little pitiful doesn't make him unfucked. He touches her face as he kisses her, he's gentle, nervous, excited, he takes his time. She's like one confronted by unexpected weather. The body in shock. She is astonished. She astonishes herself.

The sketch, in its tube, is on the counter.

She twists like a Lurio lover and clatters into the drying rack where the teacups and spoons from breakfast are arranged. "This isn't what I want," she says. "I don't want this."

The long chime from struck china hangs in the air like a siren. Sam calling her as she sat at the café. He'd gone out very early and come home very late, crying. Ora, his new girlfriend, had borrowed a car and they'd driven it all the way to a brew pub Rachel had taken him to on their Berkshires road trip. He'd wanted to show Ora something, impress her, but as they sat there puckering up at cider and whistling at prices and holding hands and giggling, a bird flew into the glass by their table and died. Ora drove home in silence. "Did you tell her I bought you everything you're wearing," Rachel said. The next day, as he slept, she went out for coffee.

"You're as bad as the rest of them," Daniel says.

"My husband is dead," she says.

He's on the stairs, it's the middle of the night, somewhere in this house his parents are dreaming about clams.

He turns and she reaches back out. "Don't tell," she says, and he doesn't ask her about what.

Earlier, before they were married, she told Sam she wanted to meet his son. "Don't be crazy," he said. He looked shocked, he was actually giggling. "Are you crazy? Don't be crazy."

"Crazy?" She repeated the word back to him. He had said it so rapidly it sounded like something else. He was still giggling. "I'm going to be your wife for the rest of our lives," she said.

One day, she followed him when he went to visit his boy. It was risky, she had to keep her distance; after that she chose days he didn't visit. There was a park they went to—his ex-wife, Shosha, and Benjamin, his son—and Rachel followed them there. Walking behind them, from the apartment where Sam used to live to the park, Rachel would say their names, *Shosha, Benjamin,* almost silently, to herself. When they reached the park, Benjamin would join some other kids on the playground and Shosha would sit on the benches with four other mothers, always the same ones, and watch them.

And on the other side of the chain link fence, Rachel watching too. Pressed up against it so that later she'd find its lines dented into her thighs. Drinking Dr. Pepper and saying, *This isn't creepy* to her herself, saying, *There's nothing wrong with looking.* It was the smallest possible thing. They were going to be a family, after all. She knew if she had friends they would tell her she was being crazy, they would tell her to stop. But stop doing what? She also knew that when you said that, *stop doing what*, you were doing something you needed to stop doing. But wasn't everything something you needed to stop? And wasn't that what everyone was always saying to her? Stop, stop, stop.

A few nights before she came up to Maine, Rachel headed to the cemetery and then remembered what had happened there. In the commotion she hadn't let herself check on Sam's grave, and now it was almost dusk and the river smelled like a sleeping animal. She turned instead toward the park where Sam's son played on summer afternoons.

When she arrived she thought it was too late, but a few Haredi kids were still there. The sounds of their games reached her, loud and indecipherable like voices carrying over water. The wind was down and the trees shading the painted benches where the mothers sat were barely moving and at first she couldn't tell the women apart in the green haze. And then, together, a few of the mothers stood and stepped into the light at the edge of the monkey bars.

Rachel recognized her immediately—his ex-wife, his first wife, to Rachel's eyes, his wife. She'd learned her motions by now, her comportment, her dreamy peace and presence. They had never spoken and there was no reason to think that they ever would. If the woman looked, she would not know Rachel, and why would she look, why would she take her eyes off her living boy, running now between the slide and the swings?

In the note he had left for Rachel to find, Sam had written, *I'm not who I thought I am*, and then corrected it to *I am not who I thought I'd be*. And then, still dissatisfied, either by the sentiment or the grammar, started to alter that to *I am not who I thought I*...but he could not find the right way to put himself into time, and had headed out and into the world to make his final correction: *I am not.*

Or so he had believed. But his son. He was already bigger than the last time she had watched him. Even though he looked like his mother—her full mouth, the dark line of her level brow—he seemed more his father. As if Sam were growing into him. His every gesture was an echo of Sam's, or not an echo, not a reflection or a forgery, but the thing itself, something real—Sam's. This was his son, the history and end point of his body, the beautiful living future the train couldn't cancel. There he was.

His mother called his name and asked him something in Yiddish. He turned to face her. She asked her question again. He was tall and solemn and lovely, Sam's boy. He was thoughtful. He was listening to his mother. He reached up and covered his mouth with his hand.

BY TEN O'CLOCK THE CARS were arriving and parking in the meadow at the base of the hill. Rachel was on the path beyond the huppah, with her sketchbook, hoping a different vantage would give her a fresh start on the horizon. The sky was still the problem. Where it met the ocean, a negative space she could not capture. What begins as absence, the need for fulfillment—this is supposed to become manifest as a *thing*. The immanence of desire and all that.

Lurio's question, or assertion by the end, was *What if there's nothing there on the other side of the whirlwind?* And her answer, after spending the night with his work, was that the sky was glass, on the other side of the self there was the self. Now she stared over the cliff edge: the roses, the waves, the horizon. She let her hand move and looked down. It wasn't what it had been yesterday and it wasn't what it was today, but she still couldn't say what was different.

During her fellowship at the Prado, a curator had told her: *Lurio always knew exactly what he was looking at.* She'd written that down. She'd quoted it to others and to herself to explain her own failures: Lurio always knew exactly what he was looking at. And she never did. She didn't really even know what it meant. The man who said it to her was an emeritus curator, and famous. He carried a Montblanc in his jacket and tapped it twice on the pad of paper she was taking notes in after his pronouncement and then walked away. She spent three months at the Prado and this was the only time he spoke to her, but he wore the whitest shirt she had ever seen. He flared down the corridors, bright as an idea. But maybe there was a problem with his English.

Sometime before first light Daniel had mown the rest of the lawn behind the estate. The tide was in and the wind was down and the morning smelled like sap and rain and the wet tear of mown grass. The freshness of aftermath. She closed her notebook. She was watching the commotion. Like a welcoming committee, Baruch and Eli and Boris had assembled under the portico. Their pants were all too high. Three old men with their slacks cinched above their navels. Mel and Jacob joined them. Again Mel wore bright white sneakers with his gray suit. No one seemed to be speaking, except Jacob, whose pants were a normal height. They ignored him. A red pickup truck with its lights on came down the gravel road and nudged into the meadow. The lights turned off, the engine quieted, and three Hasidic men disembarked. Rachel understood that the world was both boring and insane.

Seek out surprise, her therapist had said.

Like being a widow at thirty-two? Rachel had said. *That was a surprise.*

Her therapist shook her head and smiled at the same time. *I meant something more like dim sum.*

The guests gathered on the terrace and lawn and Daniel, who would not look at her, was very busy. He had unfolded things—tables, chairs, tablecloths—positioned a podium near the marble balustrade, and hustled now among his thousand appetizers—crab canapés, lobster salad, poached asparagus, and colorful dips framed by ambivalent flutes of damp celery. The cars that kept arriving parked in the field at the base of the hill, and Daniel ran back and forth, guiding the guests glumly toward the sea. Music from Boris on the violin. Five bottles of Sancerre were open all at once, the lavender lemonade was spiked, the punch, which Daniel had made but could not taste, was way too strong. His parents had already begun dancing, and when Simon showed up in his seersucker suit and an apricot ascot, Rachel was not surprised. Every American Jew in his heart wants to look like Warren Beatty.

All night she had wondered if he'd bother to come this far. Of course he would. He was the one who'd authenticated the sketch and he was probably going to try to get his claws into whoever bought it so he could display it at the Lurio exhibit. With him was an older woman, a trustee of the museum, who actually did look a little like Warren Beatty. Rachel poured another glass of punch.

"Of all the cough shops and sanitaria," she said, approaching, "you show up at mine."

Simon was flustered. He needed a hat. His pale scalp under his pale hair was already going a pale red. She should have told him she would be here.

"You should have told me you would be here!" he said.

"I didn't know," Rachel said. "Or I hadn't decided. I brought my MG."

"Your what?"

"What color is your MG?" the woman with Simon said. She wore cranberry slacks, a white and blue striped shirt rolled at the elbows, pearls. Rachel had seen her before, at functions, and for a moment she had a vision of a life she'd never have and didn't want to want—being utterly at ease with a crab canapé.

"Orange," Rachel said.

"What's orange?" Simon had not caught up.

"You could always paint it," the woman said.

"Paint what?" He wasn't getting it and Rachel felt like she had done something wrong, like she in fact shouldn't be here, inducing incomprehension, taking up space he hadn't invited her to take, eating fresh blackberries from a small bowl. She realized now what his failure to involve her in the Lurio curation had already revealed: he expected to find her in the basement. It wasn't her that he liked really, but the image of his own outstretched hand, leading her up the many steps, into the light.

Classic cars, however, were grounds for introduction and the trustee, Trudy Walton, introduced herself as Trudy Walton.

"Rachel is one of our educators," Simon said. "For the phone questions."

"I thought they all quit?"

Rachel curtsied. Then offered everyone a blackberry.

"Oh, look, there's Fedelman," Simon said.

Fedelman was America's leading authority on Lurio. He had been out of the country when the sketch was discovered; that's why Simon had been the one to authenticate it in the first place. Baruch ushered him onto the terrace and handed him a glass of punch. He was shorter than Rachel expected. He wore sunglasses. He discovered the lobster salad.

"That's Fedelman," Trudy said to Rachel, as if Rachel were a person who couldn't spot Fedelman. "He's here for the authentication."

"As a formality," Simon said.

"Of course," Rachel said

"Simon authenticated the sketch himself," said Trudy. "Did you know that?"

"I did my dissertation on Lurio. That's one of the reasons I wanted to work at the museum," Rachel said.

"Oh so you must have seen the sketch by now!" Trudy said.

Rachel said she hadn't. Perhaps, afterward, Simon would look back on this moment with clarity. Or a new perspective. But maybe not. A local news crew had arrived. They appeared the way local news crews did in Maine: like a high school football team on career day. They approached the terrace, they paused, looked around them, they were holding cables, a microphone and camera. What, Rachel wondered, had a communications degree from Machias prepared them for? Weather events, boat events, festivals involving muffins or fruit. So the setting seemed right, but—so many Jews! Briefly, she was frightened. They would make what happened next permanent. At the very least there would be the footage she must be careful not to appear in. She watched Simon see them. He turned his back on her, followed the camera's gaze toward Fedelman and Baruch, and set off toward the terrace.

Before the auction, as if things were running backward, people danced between the appetizers and the balcony. It was like a wedding. Anna danced with Baruch. Mel and Sophie, who had almost certainly taken a couples' class somewhere, attempted some kind of joyful swing to Boris's fiddling. Leaning alone against the far wall of the house, the Hasids smoked and tapped their feet. Shale was there in his cargo pants. His hair was combed. His helmet was missing. He was telling Eli about his podcast.

Rachel found Fedelman near the dips. He was friendly. He asked her about her work, about the Lurio show at the museum, to send him an essay if she ever wanted to. He gave her his email address and bobbed away to speak to a woman in a Hawaiian shirt, who was also his rabbi. *Oh, Sammy. If you could only see.* But what? The world was so beautiful. All these people gathered. Anna with her head on Baruch's shoulder, Mel talking to Boris as Boris played and Boris looking like he hadn't spent his morning in a chicken coop. But devotion was also a kind of beauty. And so was absence. The wind through the glasses like a spoon on a saucer. If she had stood in the dreaming fields trailing her beloved toward his nuptials, she did not do so anymore. The lilies were still blooming. Jacob was at her side with two glasses of punch.

"This is way too strong," he said.

She agreed and took the glass from him, touched his with it, drank. The wind was down and quiet. The sun was already a little low, just catching the top of the pines on the hill.

"I know we should have done more, but I don't know what we should have done," Jacob said.

"What did you want to do?"

"I suppose I'll take the job," he said. "We can raise money for Baer at the center."

He drank and looked out over the water.

In the car up she had thought, *Here is a friend.* He was a good person, kind to her uncle, friendly, funny and smart. But maybe he was like everyone else. Soiled by doubt. Shabby in his devotion. A little drunk all the time.

"You should really come to the tavern tonight," he said, and when she didn't respond and his glass was empty before him in his hand like a surprise, he said, "I'll be able to move out, anyway," and she assumed he was telling her something about his life that he thought she didn't know, when really, of course, at this moment it was the other way around and she wanted to tell him what she had done, but time running backward was still running and it was time for the auction to begin.

After everything, after the first speech, and then the second speech, she began to prepare herself for triumph. Take this in. All the small men in their earnest arrangement. Baruch at the podium. Fedelman and Simon behind him, wearing white gloves like a pair of footmen. "After catastrophe, there is catastrophe," Baruch said. "But if everything cannot be catastrophe, how may we discover its limit? I stood," he said, "in my neighbor's house, and he now stands in mine. Catastrophe to catastrophe, loss to loss, brokenness to brokenness." He paused. There was some kind of disturbance among the birds. And then he said, "But there is also restoration."

The water was indigo. There was no world but the horizon behind him. Fedelman, with Simon at his side, approached the podium.

In the story of the Corpse Bride, the mistake the bridegroom makes is pretending that the hand is alive. He is not aware of the consequences of imagination. But it must have happened a thousand times. The groom on his way through the fields after a spring rain where the storm has washed the mud away. And maybe he is aware? He knows what he's doing. A hand reaches from the field, and like a farmer tending to the future, he gets down on his knees and takes it.

On some nights before they divorced, Rachel would copy the Dutch Old Masters while Sam did his homework. A glass of red wine, a tray for ink, a candle. When she held the picture up for him to see, he said, "You can tell it's a knockoff."

"It's a copy," she said.

"This I can tell."

"It's how you practice," she said.

"Practice for what?"

Daniel presented the tube to Baruch and Baruch presented the tube to Simon who opened the tube for Fedelman who reached in and extracted the rolled sketch. In the night she had copied them side by side. She had made five versions, one after the other until the proportions were exact. Even at this distance, though, still rolled, the paper looked wrong. She had tea-stained it a week earlier, and yesterday she rubbed the espresso powder Daniel put in Boris's black bread into its corners. But it was too bright. Still, for a moment they would have to look. They unrolled it and Fedelman leaned in. Simon over his shoulder looking, stepping back, turning away.

Baruch putting one hand to his forehead, steadying the other on the podium.

The cameraman shuffling to get closer.

Fedelman laughing and taking off his gloves. "Absolutely not." Shifting to Simon. "Simon, what is this?"

And then Simon, who hadn't invited her up here, snatching the sketch and turning directly into the camera where if he saw himself, he didn't see much. His face was white, his expression had vanished, he was a white flap flapping whitely, like a flounder.

BOOK III: THE DOOR

I was born under the sign of Saturn, and my father, who knew what the slow rotation of that star meant, predicted that my life would be one of hesitation and delay. But History, for my father, was not a sequence or an escalation, it was simply a puzzle you might find scattered on the floor, in disarray but complete, destined to be recomposed, a Telos in which the present was determined by the shape of the piece he discovered in the past, and the future—as much as he considered it at all—was always the whole puzzle, complete, defined and unbroken, an exact expression of the original design, and as such he saw our world as infinitely readable, an image whose symbols, once decoded, revealed meaning—synchronous, beautiful, legible to the patient and the learned. And so, when he read those signs under which I was born, he was not seeing, I don't believe, the refugee's hesitation before the city gates, or the delay between opening one's mouth and being heard, between birth and a homeland, or between the soul's midnight question and the answer of its secret name.

—Alex Baruch, "Rupture and Repair: A Kabbalistic Reading of the Diasporic Self"

"There are two angels of the Sabbath," Boris says at Jonah's, "and they follow you home from synagogue. One is good and one is evil. That's what my father told me. Two angels follow you home from prayer."

> Earlier, at the estate in tumult: a gathering in the game room watching the local cable report about the auction: the reporter standing at the top of the hill where the long gravel drive begins. Behind her the valley collapses like a wave down to Nod, where

> they watch themselves watching themselves before the report is interrupted with BREAKING NEWS. A curtain of snow drops across the screen. "What's happened?" Anna says. And then the static lifts like

"The good angel and the bad angel," Boris says. "One to bless the home and the other to prosecute it. One to acknowledge good times and the other the bad. They each, plenty and ruin, security and distress, follow you home from shul on the Sabbath—"

"Like dogs," Eli barks from the back, drinking brandy at the bar with Baruch. "Like pigeons pecking at crumbs"

"—and you open the door and welcome them in," Boris says.

There is no microphone but he holds the mic stand, dragged out of the corner, for balance. By his left foot, the foot nearest the glassless windows, lies a skeleton of an eider duck. He shoves it away from him with his toe.

Under the spot: the skeleton bare and blue, picked clean as a shipwreck's sunbleached hull.

When the wind gusts, feathers flutter up and fall among the seats, some black and others white, falling through shadow and through spot, dark and iridescent, ash and snow

and the gravel dust of departing auction-goers
drifting behind the

reporter standing at the top of the road. The banner beneath her reads: *Famed Holocaust Pretender a Fraud Again*?

Boris, that old bear, touches his mouth with one big hand

and Eli drinks from Baruch's flask and crawls into a hightop chair and grabs the edge of the table and scrabbles forward to watch, grinning again as he was after the third knock when Jacob let him come hopping in out of the storm, grinning and still, not hopping or shouting now, his face drying like clay hardened in a furnace, staring at the stage where

the static lifts like a fog: BREAKING NEWS

the angels cannot manage even the beginnings of their jokes. *Where is my rug,* one shouts. Its voice is full of crabshells and feathers. The others lean and crash in their chairs, their wings snap like closets slamming closed. Two others take the stage at the same time. Little bones and scraps of meat scatter from their laps, dry blood brown as mud on their unopened mouths. They all talk at once.

Given the choice it is always better to.

This is the closet we kept my mother's honey cake in.

So on Yom Kippur a rabbi decides to play golf and when he makes a hole-in-one Abraham asks the Lord

"No," Baruch shouts. He bangs the bartop with the handle of his cane. "You have to listen," he says. "Try again," he says. He is standing next to Eli at the bar and they are stooped and short, their pants are too high, they stand shoulder to shoulder like saloon doors, swinging open under the press of the same hand.

Eli shakes his head and giggles. "I wonder why it's not working, Alexei?" he says. "Can't you see"

the TV has been on mute for hours, but they stare at it anyway, they watch the same figures squirm across the screen, "like grubs," Baruch says, the clip plays on a loop: people marching in Charlottesville. Pale, angry, squirming like grubs, marching, pale and angry, with terrible little mustaches, "like moles, actually," says Boris, and he's right. The tight faces and weak jaws, bared teeth chomping out of lipless mouths. The misplaced eyes, unspaced and rubbing up against their noses revolving into view, into the edge of the screen. "What is that they are holding," says Boris, "some kind of torch"

"Once the angels are inside," Boris tells the tavern, "you light the candles and sing the prayers and then, after you light the candles and sing the prayers, you welcome the angels, the angel of benediction and the angel of prosecution, and then after welcoming them, you usher them out."

"I know how they feel," says Eli.

"But before you usher them out, they inspect the home. If you have lit the candles and laid the table and said the prayers, you satisfy the good angel with the order of your Sabbath, and they both bless your house with similar comforts for the following week. But if your preparations have been inadequate, if the candles are not lit and the table not laid, if the kitchen has not been cleaned and the people are not dressed as well as they can be, then the prosecuting angel makes his accusation and you inherit similar disorder for the following week."

"What tables must they have found in 1938," Eli says, "to bestow such a future? Ask them that."

Anna kneels in front of the screen and puts her fingers on the lip of the man with the torch, marching on the same clip back, again and again in slow motion. "They are saying something," she whispers. "What are they saying?" Boris, the expert, finds the right remote

"And then," Boris says, "after we have greeted the angels, we ask them to leave."

Why? Boris asked his father. His father kept a shop in the village and often wore a beaver hat and a woolen waistcoat and he was not as devout as Boris's mother, the granddaughter of a rebbe, but he liked her devotion to the laws of her village, even if he himself kept tobacco in a silver case in the pocket of his tawny frock coat which smelled, when he gathered Boris to him, Boris's cheek to his belly, like clove and cardamom, and sometimes like the vanilla and poppyseed cakes he kept wrapped in paper in his jacket pocket, the delicacies of his own childhood, hundreds of miles away, in Subotica, that he liked to share with Boris who was otherwise *his mother's son from stem to stalk*, he claimed with no malice, with pleasure actually, because there was no one in this world he thought more wonderful than his wife, and when Boris asked his question, he patted Boris's stomach and said

Because it's bad manners to eat while others are not eating. Then Boris's sister asked, *But angels don't need to eat, do they?* Boris's sister who was only four, who was always only four, who, as far as Boris remembers, was born a baby, it's true, but a baby with a special precocity because he is certain, even now, that she was, in a matter of months, four years old, that although time was slow in those years, for Adela alone at first it galloped: she was born, in a few days she was four, and then, as if time's telescope has been turned around, it stopped, held her shrunken in its crystal eye and she remained four for as long as Boris could remember. *No, Adela, that's not right,* his father said. *You have it backward, dear. Angels are always hungry.*

Jonah's is full of bones and maritime salvage and angelic distress. A seal skin, feathers and fish heads scattered with sea glass and neon buoys. Like homicidal tourists, the angels shuffle and mumble amid clutter. *So a boy wants to marry, and he goes to the rabbi for advice*

Unmuted the chants, falling from the moving torch-line: *Jews will not replace us! Jews will not replace us!* For the first time in fifty years Anna begins to howl.

For the week between Sabbath and Sabbath, the two angels wandered the world, where Boris often saw them. In the morning, on the first tide of waking, when he looked out the window above his bed he would glimpse them strolling at the edge of the forest. Though they were always together, they were easy to tell apart because they each wore different hats. Like Boris's great-grandfather, the angel of benediction wore a tall black fur spodik hat, though it wasn't as clean as the rebbe's was, the fisher tail fur was matted, dull in some places, rubbed shiny in others, decorated with twigs from the forest, flecks of bark and dead pine needles, while the prosecuting angel wore a regular white yarmulke. There were other differences too. The good angel wore a green vest with brass buttons like the man on his father's English tobacco tin and the bad angel wore a butcher's smock stained with blood. The good angel took long steps, and the bad angel hopped. The angel of benediction was a blue cry, the prosecuting angel was the sound of the east wind through the birch leaves. In the spring, when the angels were hungry, they'd stick their heads into the beehives like bears. Sometimes at dusk they'd kneel and, bending directly from the waist, graze on flowers in his mother's garden.

Eventually he realized that as the Sabbath blesses each week, the week was in the days and the days of each week between the Sabbath and the Sabbath contained the angels of the Sabbath.

The honey was the good angel, the hive was the bad. After a storm, a rivulet of rainwater ran through the market street: the good angel. Old Man Mendel, Boris's neighbor, kept a dovecote behind his house, and sometimes Boris would see the bad angel sitting in there curled up in a ball atop the straw and shit with birds perched on his head and shoulders.

The cooing of the doves like water warbling through a sewer.

The sour place under the branches where the black walnuts bled.

The good angel, the bad.

After a while the angels noticed him watching them. In the past they'd carry on with whatever they were doing, smoking cigarettes or fishing with their hands in the creek or breaking chicken eggs into their open mouths, but now they'd stand and wait for him to finish his chores. They waved. There were secrets they wanted to show him:

a piece of stone the color of saffron for his father, for his mother a patch of wild rhubarb in the black soil of the forest creek. The days of summer were as flat as a glass table, and the angels of the Sabbath led him deeper into the forest where the trees were full of light. The angels were always foraging for insects, and they showed him which insects were the best to eat and they taught him how to sharpen an alder branch and dig at the base of new trees to find roots you could squeeze water from. They told him which farmers didn't check their chickens and which dogs were too old to bark. The sky when he'd come out of the forest was the color of wheat, like Adela's hair. *Mine was also blond as a boy*, his father said. *It'll change when she gets older.* When Boris was with the angels, Adela napped under the pear tree, and the good angel was wheat laying down after the deer have slept there. One day Boris's father came home with a little leather pouch—the bad angel—filled with a rich paste of black poppyseeds—the good angel—for his mother's hamantaschen cakes.

At night, the angels slept in a tunnel. They showed him how to follow the creek through the trees, to the other side where the forest ended and the fields at the edge of town began. Here between the forest and the fields the bank was damp and fragrant as used coffee grounds and the creek entered the halfmoon pipe of the sewer where the angels waited for morning. No one used this sewer any longer and the iron grate was too small for adults, but the angels could make themselves as small as Boris and Boris could slip between the bars.

"That was the summer," Boris says, "when I became serious about the violin."

Because he begged, his parents had found him a violin teacher. This was before Adela was born and his father traded Mendel a mahogany chest for his old violin. *You got swindled*, Boris's mother said. His father took her hand and danced her around the kitchen. *When was the last time that chest played us Mahler?* he crooned. Boris, five years old, scratched the bow over the untuned strings.

"It was the same summer I asked my parents if I could change my name to Boris," says Boris.

His teacher was old and smelled like licorice and he was always chewing something. He lived in town and made the walk out to their house every Wednesday, carrying his hat in both hands before him like a cake. With Boris's parents he was gruff and despairing. He had once played the violin in Leningrad. When Boris's mother asked him how Boris was doing, he looked at the floor, he wiped his brow with his sleeve and then wiped his damp sleeve with his dry one. *I've heard better-sounding pogroms*, he muttered. He pressed on his temples and closed his eyes. *He's no prodigy, but what can you do?* But in private he'd wink and ruffle Boris's hair and smile and say, *You're playing well, boy. That was very beautiful. I felt it in my heart.* Among Jews it was bad business for a violin teacher to be kind.

That last summer, Boris began to give recitals for his parents. They would carry chairs in from the dining room and sit in the kitchen with their backs to the window, and Boris, standing before the stove, would face them and play. During these recitals his father closed his eyes and smiled as if Boris were sharing some good news that he'd been waiting for, and as he smiled he began to rock back and forth, not in time to the music, but not outside of the music either, almost, Boris thought, like the branch of the birch tree just beyond the window, dipping in the breeze, nodding almost like the rebbe at prayer, and when Boris played his father was a swaying birch branch, while his mother was the opposite, his mother was a stone, rigid and still, she held but did not drink, did not even lift, a small glass of slivovitz that his father had brought back from his relatives, and stared hard at Boris, frozen, fixed, but not a statue, Boris says, because she looked expectant and surprised, leaning forward with her head beyond her knees, her neck as taut as the strings he played. And between them, dancing in the space of the violin's sound, Adela, four years old, would conduct with a twig from the pear tree she liked to nap under while Boris was with the angels.

One morning: flames in Mendel's dovecote.

Boris stands in Jonah's ruins. Shatter of sealight, Geary's beer bottles starting to roll, the tavern rocks.

"For my final recital," Boris says, "my parents sat with suitcases, open and half empty, between their knees. They had begun to pack," Boris says, "but did not finish. In the mornings they packed, in the afternoons they unpacked, in the evenings they began again. They opened and closed drawers, they gathered spoons and the Sabbath candlesticks and photographs and my grandfather's locket, they spoke to the neighbors and I practiced my violin.

"One night, I woke and they were in the backyard digging a hole near the edge of the forest. My father dug and my mother waited, I didn't recognize her at first, standing away from him, in shadow, as if they were there for different reasons, two people alone, but not far from each other in the dark. At her feet was a burlap sack. I sat up on my bed and put my chin on the sill and watched them. I was afraid the sack was full of kittens because Old Man Mendel said his cat, Esther, who never bothered the pigeons, was ready to give birth, and my father told me that in Subotica when cats gave birth you put the kittens in a sack and dropped the sack into the river and that's why the whole world wasn't cats, and Adela said, *But the whole world is cats*, and my father thought about that for a while and said, *Maybe you're right*, and I said, *If we have to put Mendel's cats in the river, can we put them in the tunnel instead?* and my father said, *What tunnel?*"

Boris before the angels lets go of the mic stand. The wind is blowing the wrong way and pine needles skitter from the door to the windows. The angels have begun to chew on one another's wooden shoulders.

"Finally," Boris says, "the moon rose over the forest, or some of it did, like a beluga's back cresting the surface of the Baltic, and I began to recognize my parents, and when my father was finished digging, my mother lifted the sack and lowered it into the hole and I could hear plates or spoons or china, though we didn't really have china, but it was something like that clinking and my father said, *Quiet*!, though he said it loudly and I knew then that there were no kittens in the sack and I went back to sleep, though I woke again a little later and they were still out there and I thought maybe I had dreamed the part about the hole because the hole was gone and the sack was still at my mother's feet and my father was digging again, this time a series of smaller holes, all over the garden, and I thought tomorrow he will plant the tomatoes he is keeping in that sack.

"The next afternoon, when I gave my last recital, I played Mahler. The suitcases were at their feet and Adela spun between us, barefoot and four years old, conducting for me. Her feet were as brown as tomatoes. She was four years old. For the first time in any of my recitals, my mother moved. She reached out and put one hand over my father's. Neither one of them looked at the other and I wanted to watch them both, to see what they were doing, to see my mother's thumb rub my father's knuckles, and I wish I had glanced over just one more time, but I needed to maintain my chin position and to ignore Adela and it was later in the day than usual, the sun was the lavender honey my mother drizzled over the hive's comb on summer mornings, and through the window I saw the angels in the garden, the angel of benediction and the angel of prosecution, waiting for me at the edge of the forest near the damp path down to the tunnel."

AFTERWARD, ELI. THE FRENZY of an insect revealed when the rock is lifted. Pushing himself off the bar, scrabbling into the mess of tables. But then, between things, he pauses. Between the high-tops where the angels sit and Boris on the blue-bleached stage. His face as serene as a ceramic plate.

Eli says. "Angels? Honey? The fiddle? What does any of that mean?"

"Violin," says Anna.

"What?"

"Boris plays the violin."

"They're the same fucking thing," says Sophie.

"The violin," Eli says. "Spoons and honeys," he says. "Sweets, the babbling brook, the sound of silver on china."

"That's enough, Eli," Baruch says.

"Is it? Is it? It's not enough, it's nothing. His sister dancing while he screeches on the fiddle? A dovecote, Alex? A fucking dovecote? I've read this man's poems, and I'm glad he quit. I've read this man's poems, and they're even worse."

"If they are, they are," Boris says.

"You can sit down, Boris," Baruch whispers.

Under the leaning windows: tumbleweeds of seaweed and feathers, splintered lobster traps, glowing buoys, bottles of beer. Streaks of gore stain the sills where the ducks have been dragged into the bar.

"Which pigeons did he eat?" Eli says. "Did he cook them or was it raining or was he afraid to make a fire? Tell me, Alex, do you remember those nights where any light was too much? Did he pluck it first or just bite into the breast like a beast? Ask him to open his mouth. Are his teeth still full of feathers? And the kittens in the bag—"

"There were no kittens in the bag," says Sophie.

"And the kittens in the bag," Eli says again, "did he eat them too or did the Germans hang them first? Do you remember the kittens, Alex?"

Baruch snatches his flask from the bar.

"Maybe he doesn't remember them." Eli turns to the angels. "That's possible. But it's something we saw from the edge of the forest. The Germans were making their way through the village. I don't think they had planned to stop. They had passed through before and there wasn't anything there, not much food or resistance. But this time they halted. A convoy of SS officers. One of them stepped down out of his truck and made a speech. I wonder if anyone even understood it. He said there was partisan activity nearby. If there was, we never saw it, if there was, you'd have thought, living in the woods as we were, we would have noticed. Unless they were referring to us? But we were just children, eating tubers. Still, they stopped. Still, they went from house to house. Do you want to tell your statues what they did there, Alex?"

"I've written about it," Baruch says. "That's a story the world knows."

I was myself a child when I watched the SS hanging children. I was myself a child, I know now, but I did not feel any sympathy of relation for the children I saw being hung. Those children were living inside, those children had mothers and beds, and blankets and bowls of soup sometimes. I heard them playing in the evenings and singing to their goats and at their lessons. What was I? I was alone, I was more forest than person, I spoke to the trees and hid in my cave and muttered at the stars and when they rounded the children up,

"But not about the kittens!" Eli, furious, bisected by electric light and tavern shadow. "The Germans went from house to house and any house without a man living in it was a house, according to the Germans, where the men were working with the partisans. So, to punish these missing men, these men who'd already been killed or drafted or starved or were away looking for work, they'd hang a child who was living there in his stead. Except of course, if there were no children either, or if, perhaps, the children were hiding. In which case they hung a family pet, like a cat. It was ridiculous, it was silly, I'd be lying if I said some of us didn't giggle. The soldiers built gallows and the children stood before the nooses on their own, but the kittens had to be held. Yes, we giggled. Imagine the SS in their gleaming boots and leather straps and oiled whips holding up kittens by the scruff of the neck and making speeches, addressing them as criminals. Of course we giggled, but soon we stopped, or I did. Why? I realized I had it backward. The SS weren't taking a kitten too seriously. They weren't treating a kitten like a person. I saw that as the hanging began. No, for them, hanging a kitten or a child before her wailing mother was exactly the same thing."

Birds on the water, Boris shuffling. The silence of the angels.

"Maybe Alex has forgotten. But I haven't. And I don't think he has either. I realized then there were no distinctions anymore. They had razed the earth and God had let them, He had turned his back and fallen asleep, He was not there and I never believed in Him in the first place but there was nothing, clearly nothing—history, meaning, reason, proportion, Torah, all those words and values and rules, the laws of rabbis and judges, of God and man, were forfeit and void. They were hanging children and kittens at the same time on the same gallows. The grass grew into the mud and the mud seeped into the earth and the earth crusted over nothing. Tell them, Alex, what is the difference between a piece of shit kitten and a four-year-old child clinging to her stuffed bear before the gallows?"

Baruch says nothing.

"Tell them the difference between a child and a kitten, between loss and longing, wickedness and opportunity. You're the great rabbi. What's the difference between Pelimo and his guest, between Jonah and his worm, Nineveh and Sodom and Jerusalem and Warsaw and Lvov and Khmel'nik. Nothing, gornisht. Am I right?"

"No, Eli," Baruch whispers.

Those children were living inside, those children had mothers and beds, and blankets and bowls of soup sometimes. I heard them playing in the evenings and singing to their goats and at their lessons

"A child and a kitten. Tell them." He shouts, he points at the angels. "A child fouling herself as she swings, dropping the stuffed bear her mother let her take, her dress sticking to her legs, her shit running into her shoes. You remember the shit in the shoes, don't you, Alex? You great fucking man, you remember the shit, you were upset about that, weren't you, Alex? Tell them why, tell them why the shit upset you. What is the difference between a dead child and a dead kitten?"

What was I?

I was alone, I was more forest than person, I spoke to the trees and hid in my cave and muttered at the stars and when they rounded the children up,

Baruch's brandy glass smashed against the floor.
"The child had shoes you could steal."

"A child had shoes you could steal. That's right. Like everything else. To wear or eat or to patch your own." Eli leans against the table, exhausted, quiet, thrumming with leftover energy like the fan on an oven after the oven has been turned off. "Remember us, watching. We said, *Those mothers should take the children's shoes before they go to the gallows*. We said that to each other. That's what one child said to another child while watching other children getting hung. *Their mothers should take their shoes*. We thought, what a waste! Of course we were glad they didn't. We'd seen enough hangings to know that the Germans insisted the bodies stay up. And that night one of us, if he was small enough, like Alex, a good enough thief, like Alex, could slip into town and—"

"Enough, Elijah."

What was I?

I was alone, I was more forest than person, I spoke to the trees and hid in my cave and muttered at the stars and when they rounded the children up, I wondered,

what they will do afterward, with their shoes?

"It's not enough! Honey, fiddles, carraway! What does any of that mean? Pigeons, a pear tree, poppyseed cakes? Is that what you saw, Alex? Of course your picture was a fake. Even if it was authentic, it was a fake. The shtetl, the yeshiva, the cantor singing to the faithful? Is that what you saw, Alex, or did you get shit on your hand when you stole a dead girl's shoe? Is that what you saw, or did you kill a soldier who was lost and asked you for water? Is that what you saw or—"

"No, Eli!" shouts Baruch. "I saw children hanging from trees and babies tossed on bayonets, I saw whole towns marched to the edge of the forest to dig their own graves, and I saw the dogs eating their bodies when the rain washed the mud away."

The tavern tilts and Anna cries out: Boris has fallen into the table and two of the windows shatter outward over the cliff edge and the angels all open their wings and when they do scraps of eider meat spatter the floor

> *There was a wind—but God was not in the wind. There was an earthquake—but God was not in the earthquake. There was a fire—but God was not in the fire*

In the new wind: a snowstorm of eider down

> *There is a moment*, Lurio wrote, *where what is real becomes what is visible.*

and Baruch, shaking and old, enraged and upright, brandishing his cane before him, shuffling toward Eli, shouting—

"And when it was over I saw my friends going from house to house"

"When it was over?"

"And kicking in the doors"

"What doors, Alex?"

"The doors of Jews"

"But no Jews there"

"And Germans"

"If they hadn't fled"

"Kicking in doors"

"Everything was allowed"

"Kicking in doors"

"All this in Berlin?"

"I wasn't in Berlin"

"You mean"

"I wasn't from Berlin"

"But your Herr Professor papa"

"Was a Thessalonkian stevedore"

"And you were not, have never been a German, you were"

"I was a shitty little Greek"

"Whimpering in Ladino when we found you"

"I was a thief and a pickpocket and a nothing and a whore, but"

"No doctor father, no daily rounds, no sanatorium"

"The sanatorium was real. It was on the mountain outside the city, facing the Aegean."

"A sanatorium in Greece! Don't be foolish. Who goes to a sanatorium at sea level?"

"Jews! European Jews. Ashkenazi come south."

"Even they wouldn't be so stupid, even they know the best place to die is at home"

"It was a hotel."

"At the hands of their neighbors"

"Not a sanatorium. A summer resort. Not a hospital. They'd come for weeks at a time to see what it looks like to live in society as a Jew."

"Society!"

"Salonika."

"A city of pickpockets and cutthroats and syphilitic fishmongers."

"A city of Jews," Baruch says.

BARUCH TELLS THE TAVERN: IT was supposed to be like Jerusalem without the journey, a city of Jews with better food. And industry, and theater, and rail lines to Vienna and Istanbul, to Bitola and the Balkans. Except that by the time he was born it was already over. Salonika, Selanik, Thessaloniki, port of exiles, once a Sephardic outpost of the Ottoman empire, had been reclaimed by the Greeks in 1912 and since then the policy of Hellenization had driven the Jews away, back into the world. Under the Greek nationalists, the Jews of Salonika had to close their shops on Sundays which meant they couldn't close them to honor their own Saturday Sabbaths, they had to learn Greek and speak Greek and use the Greek language and alphabet on the signs outside their shops or else pay a tax, the Ladino tax, and they began to leave, but not fast enough, the oldest Jewish story, "The only Jewish story," says Eli, and with the old story arose the old accusations—that they who had been living there for four hundred years were aliens, not Greeks whatever Greeks were, not citizens, not to be trusted, communist subversives, Bulgarian sympathizers, "Oh yes you can never make the rabbi shut up about Bulgaria," says Eli—and not welcome: in the Campbell riot, that is the pogrom of 1931, the year Baruch was born, his family was burnt out of its tenement house by a mob in the street. "And yet you stayed," Eli says. "The same thing every time," Eli says. "Who else makes the same mistake every time?"

"It was a sign," Baruch says. He was born into a world already in ash. He grew up in an apartment looking out onto ash, the blocks where the Jews had lived, the previous Jews of Salonika, of Spain and Portugal, Kabbalists and tradesmen, rabbis and great chefs, stevedores and gangsters—cinders and ash foretelling cinders and ash.

"Foretelling nothing," Eli says. "It wasn't a sign, it was a repetition and an escalation. If I punch you in the face and say I'm going to punch you in the face and then I punch you in the face and you say, after the fact, I knew he was going to punch me in the face—it doesn't make you a prophet."

"Cinders and ash," Baruch says again, says to the angels, "foretelling cinders and ash and Greek on every sign."

This was what he was born into: a world full of Jews mourning the loss of its Jews, elegy and change, the spice market and fish stands and the refugees fleeing east, the same direction the Greeks, cast from Turkey, had come from several decades earlier and he could feel it, he says, without knowing what he was feeling, the echo of the old expulsion booming down the boulevards of the town. "I was born into belatedness," Baruch says.

"Under the dog star," Eli says. "We know. Under the sign of Saturn, under Mercury in retrograde, under the waning moon and the dead olive grove, and the blighted palm trees, under Rachel's scurvy and the shadow of Jonah's hemorrhoids, we've all read your lies." The angels are nodding. "Your birth beneath constellations that aligned into nothing. Foretelling nothing, portending nothing, reflecting nothing, dead light from an empty sky. We've all read it and it means nothing. Babbles and shrieks."

"No," Baruch says, "it's true," he says. "And I saw my friends going from door to door."

Eli spits as if discarding something rotten. "Nothing's true."

The wind in the room angry and invisible as Lurio's God.

Baruch's father was a stevedore on the Old Ottoman dock. "And you?" Eli says.

Baruch turns. "You know."

Eli points at the angels. "Tell them."

Baruch was a thief because his uncle was a thief and his brothers were thieves, among other things, but not like him, they were bigger, thicker-fingered, dagger-bearing and resentful, born into the longshoreman's promise of port trade, but pushed out by the Greeks. When most of the others immigrated to Palestine, only his stubborn father remained in the trade, while the rest of the family, his uncle and cousins and brothers, stayed in Salonika and stayed on the docks, but as thieves, not stevedores, stolen goods the family profession by the time Baruch was born, a late child, into belatedness, on the wrong side of Palestine or Alexandria, a blessing on old parents, a beautiful surprise and a beautiful boy, and a pickpocket. Soon, he found the hotel. High on the hillside. With its oleander terraces. Its jasmine and terracotta-potted palms, the afternoons' cadence of slumber and shade and the town below flat against the Aegean like a flower pressed upon blue paper by the unbroken plane of summer light.

In season his cousin, Yacoel, was a kitchen porter there, where he had an arrangement with the chef: Baruch would steal fish from the mongers in the port and sell them to the hotel. Fish from the mongers, lemons and olives from the groves on the way up the mountain. He travelled with an older brother, Joshua, able to drive the donkey-led ice cart up the red hills while Baruch foraged for herbs and flowers: oregano and mint, whatever was in season. "Surely the chef had gardens of his own," Eli says. The herbs were for the guests. After selling the fish and the lemons and the olives, Baruch would sneak onto the grounds and walk across the terraces where the ladies sat with their tea. He offered them mint and flowers. Some of the flowers were rare others were common but not to the guests and Baruch, just a boy, already knew the ways to please his marks for whom everything here was exotic, ancient, and named with a lucidity that Jewish antiquity, with its iconless kings and nomadic ramblings, was not, and so he conjured Macedonian Wood Blossoms, Clytemnestra's Tongue, Alexander's Helmet. For every name, he invented a story as well: these, Pelagonia's Tears, grow only on the eastern slope of the mountain and collect rainwater for the hummingbirds to drink; these, Queen's Brocade, Thessalonike, wife of King Kassander of Macedon half-sister of Alexander, wore in her hair to remember her brother. Like the Sephardic Jews, the old Ashkenazi loved Alexander, that great leader who had let the Jews be, whose name Baruch had been given. And they loved Baruch's face. With its dimples and placid, compassionate eyes, earnest and unblinking as he unspun his stories in some dock-cobbled French. "They never saw the dagger in your other hand," Eli says. There was no dagger then, just mint, jasmine, roses that reached toward the sea. "Just an orphan in the road outside Khmel'nik. With the river gurgling like a slit throat." In the evenings he'd return to town and perform in the Salonikan theater. He was a little star. He was known for his sorrow. "Those eyes even the Germans loved," Eli says.

In the theater he played orphans. Styled crying in wide pantomime. "But when I was hungry, when the world was barbwire and then a sliver of air, I didn't cry. Not for years," Baruch says. "We never had any food once the Germans came. They lived off the land, which is to say they lived off us and we lived off almost nothing." They sent his old father and brothers to labor camps and everyone thought, this is bad, starvation was growing rampant, the men were away, weak and dying at labor, little Baruch wore his little star. One of his brothers was a communist and another was a Zionist.

"Like my uncles," Sophie says.

"Like everybody," Baruch says.

"So at least that part was true," Anna says.

"Yes, it was true," says Baruch. He's angry and indignant. He does not feel, Jacob thinks, as if he's ever lied. "My beautiful brothers. My beautiful foolish brothers. Communists! Zionists! Staying up late in the tabernas fighting. Moses, my communist brother, had a network that passed out leaflets. Do you know what they were about? Demanding better pay at the labor camps." Baruch has tears in his eyes. He shakes his head like a horse bothered for hours on end by a fly.

"This is my point," Eli says. "This is what I mean by nostalgia."

"Yes," Baruch says.

"They still didn't see."

"I know," Baruch says.

"They were looking backward."

"We were Jews," Baruch says. "And then when we had paid the ransom to have our men brought back, they put us all into Baron Hirsch."

"What?" says Mel.

"The ghetto," Jacob says.

"That's right," says Baruch. And for a moment Jacob doesn't listen.

This is the other side of his sin. With Baer he imagined he could understand; with Baruch it's even worse, he doesn't listen. He won't be witness to this, not again, he knows the Baron Hirsh ghetto and the deportation of Salonika's Jews because this is the story his father told him in New York on the way to the restaurant, and on the curb watching Little League, and in the empty apartment, his mother and sister already abroad, standing in Jacob's bedroom after Jacob had gone to bed to remind him what could happen. *I saw you playing with the Sheehan boy today. You are always following him around.* And from there suddenly, in the dark doorway pulled open to the rest of the dark rooms, *You have to be careful.* And Jacob screaming inwardly, *Of what?* knowing the answer was everything: the smiles of shopkeepers, the third baseman, the doorman, and subway cars, the census takers and the barbed wire of the Baron Hirsch and the roundup by dawn in covered trucks on the way to the station, the subway doors hissing open to angry fluorescence, scattering rats, a man playing a tambourine between cars, a cowbell tolled by a bike messenger in the street, Baer alone among kibble and cat piss, and the cramped cattle cars where parents held their dead babies while standing atop the crushed bodies of their own dead or dying parents, where women moaned for water and scrambled through shit for a gulp of air at the window that Baruch's brothers pushed him against, the narrow flash and shatter of the landscape breaking into his face, the window in this car, unlike the others where, because it was the first deportation out of Salonika and was decided on quickly and initiated in the dark, the barbwire hadn't yet been installed.

"They pushed me through," Baruch says. "They said we'll follow you. I knew they wouldn't fit. They pushed me through and three other kids as well. When I stopped rolling, the others were dead on the tracks. I was in an empty field, but I saw the forest. I ran away from the train and the train kept moving away from me. I was alive and running and the other two kids were dead on the tracks, split open like the fruit we served at the hotel, and my brothers and my father and mother and uncles and cousins were alive and on the train, where I left them, alive, on the train, where I left them, alive and heading north, toward Auschwitz, alive."

Earlier, marching between two rows of torches, a man wearing both a white polo shirt and a Confederate flag bandana, a man as incongruous and familiar as an uncle, kept shouting, "Auschwitz was a lie, Auschwitz was a lie."

Baruch, talking again, has the angels' attention. They have stopped grooming. Their mouths, filled with sea glass and bottle caps, splinter light. One of them peals like a foghorn and Baruch says again, "Auschwitz," says "alive." He kept running until he reached the forest line, where he collapsed in the silver border of birches surrounding the darker pines like rime ice. He could still hear the train or the blood in his ears pounding the same rhythm, not lengthening as it should into silence, and he stood again and headed deeper into the forest.

"Where you lived alone," Eli says, "on nuts and berries and little Jewish dreams."

Where he lived alone on nuts and berries and dreams of bream baked in parchment and thyme, of his older brothers floating in the Aegean, away from him, *You can't come here,* and his mother sipping wine before the Sabbath prayers and winking, *Don't tell,* and then hitching her skirt above her knees and wandering out into the shallows, and then deeper, before she began to swim. He moved east. He had no destination beyond the sunrise and he was not like others who survived, he did not hunker down. He kept moving, any place he stayed was a place he could die and he didn't want to die in any of these places so he lived in the forest or in henhouses, or under a bridge, or in a hollow he dug out of the riverbank. "All the hideaways my memoir described were real," he says. "Everything was real."

"Even your lies," Eli adds.

"Everything was true," Baruch says again, and Eli laughs and nods and says, "Everything was allowed."

Then Baruch met the others.

Who were thieves. And also children. Of whom he was the youngest. Living mostly alone. Sometimes in a mill, sometimes travelling with partisans. All of which he wrote about in his memoir, Jacob thinks. "But it wasn't in Katowice and it wasn't just for a few weeks. And you were not just our guest," Eli says.

"The war ended," Baruch says, "and we were like everyone else, refugees heading west."

"Two days ahead of the Russians," Eli says. "Or was it three?"

"You know it was three. Three days and three nights."

"I saw a light in a house," Eli says. "Do you remember? A house that used to belong to Michael, one of our band, do you remember, but now some German woman lived there. I saw that light and I was confused. I thought it was night, but really it was morning. We were walking through the bombed forest and the burned towns and the muddy fields. And then we saw a light, yes, the same light we'd seen before, you must remember, but I thought for a moment that we were not walking toward the house, but away from it, and the war was still on, and we were not in Poland but on the road outside Khmel'nik, fleeing east before they cleared the ghetto and you saved us all, you saved us, with your golden fingers, this certainly you must remember—"

THERE WERE FIVE OF THEM hiding in a mill beyond the ghetto. The Germans had taken the town during the summer, and now it was autumn and the mill was no longer safe. But where should they go? On each side of the mill: the ruined village and the ruined forest and the river they couldn't cross. From the west, rumors and the rumble of artillery and nothing, silence, from the east. One night, making his rounds on the road, Baruch met a Jewish family, two parents and four children, fleeing. It was dark, though there were candles and lamps lit in some of the windows and they came upon him sitting at the crossroads. He had dirt on his face, his shirt was torn, he was not wearing a jacket. They stopped, which they shouldn't have, they stopped and began to tell him things. They were still living but they had already acquired the refugees' desire to instruct the young, to preserve something in the next generation. They told him to be careful, they told him that the Jews were to be put into a ghetto and worse, those stories were also already making their way south, and east, the direction they were fleeing, east they told him, across the Dnieper River to Soviet territory. He offered to trade or sell them some lard. He didn't always offer lard, sometimes it was canned milk, or coffee, but it was usually lard and it didn't matter, he wouldn't ever leave with less than he had brought. They weren't interested. They had sold everything they owned and used the goods they purchased—cigarettes and cured pork, plus their one piece of jewelry, a family brooch—to bribe an official for papers to cross the river. They asked him if he had a coat. *I'll trade for anything*, Baruch said. He wasn't understanding, the father said. They were fleeing and he should too. *Find a way across the river*, they said. *A child like you*, they said and looked at their own children. Three boys and a daughter. Bundled with too many clothes, what they couldn't carry they wore. And then they gave him a piece of their bread, even though he could see they didn't have enough, and he took it and ate it immediately and they said, *Be safe*, and as they said that, as they said *Be safe*, an animal appeared in the road, a dog it looked like, "a black dog without a head," Baruch says, a dog without a head appeared from the forest, a black dog out of the black pines and began to run headless away from them down the road to the river. *Get out while you can*, the father said. He patted Baruch's arm. At least one of the children, maybe two, were older than Baruch, "but they just stood there," he says now, "like bushes piled in clothes, looking at their feet."

The dog was gone, beyond the curve in the road and the family followed it, heading east, away from the houses, candlelit as the ones Baruch would walk toward later, away down the road toward Kyiv and the river, hurrying away from Khmel'nik and what would happen there, and to them, toward the river that they wouldn't cross because by now Baruch, saving himself and his friends who were hiding at the crossroads, had their papers.

"ANYWAY," ELI SAYS, "as it turned out we didn't even cross the river."

"So we survived," Baruch says, "and the war ended and we were moving west. We were with a band of partisans three days ahead of the Soviet army, moving west through Poland, that was the plan, west through Poland, through the Warthegau, the *Reichsgau Wartheland,* even if it was all Germany now, home of the *Volksdeutsche*. Every day our numbers changed. At first there were only five of us, and by the end nearly thirty, travelling in little groups, racing the Russians, and when we reached the village. It was night."

"It was morning."

"It was still dark."

"There was a light on," Eli says, "in the house and we were walking toward it."

"I went out on patrol," Baruch says. "The war was over, but none of us had changed our habits and our habit was, when we left the forest to cross a road or field or raid a village, the commander of the partisans sent me, the youngest, or if not the youngest, the smallest, out on patrol because German snipers sometimes wouldn't shoot children, and I'd look around to see if the area was occupied or friendly or if there were snipers, as there sometimes were, sitting in the trees. So the commander of the partisans sent me out even if they didn't need to, even if there hadn't been snipers in the trees for months or more and the war was over and as long as we stayed ahead of the Russians we were fine, the war was over and we were the living."

And when he came back it was morning and most of the partisans were asleep, but his friends were not. "It was morning," Eli says, "and we were awake," they were awake and going door to door knocking, and then, when no one answered, kicking them in. "We knocked," Eli says. "That's what you do when you come to a door. We knocked. First soft, then hard. We entered. The question was, how were we treated on the other side?"

Most of the houses were abandoned, but abandoned hastily, within the last few days, and not yet ransacked. Michael had grown up in the village and told them about it, a village where many Jews used to live at the edge of the road at the edge of the forest. *My great-grandfather was the rabbi at the synagogue,* Michael said, *and when they burnt it my mother said, How will we recover from this? and my father said, Like we did the last time they burnt it, and he consoled us and was wrong, of course, because the next week the soldiers came and rounded everybody up, the young and the old, and marched them to the forest and made them begin to dig and*

"It was the same with my town," Eli says,

"at any rate when the death squad reached our village. We were not expecting them," Eli says.

"The first thing they did was demand more vodka or schnapps because this was the farthest east they had come and they were low on everything, including bullets, so they started with bayonets on babies, but not at first, at first everyone just stood there in the street and even though we'd heard of death squads by then, it didn't seem like anything was going to happen, they just rounded us up and stood with us, as silent as we were, in the street and asked for schnapps as if we were all going to join in a toast or some kind of ceremony, which we did, I suppose, because villagers were suddenly so generous with their stocks and liquor was brought out by the gallon and everyone gathered to watch, the whole town, all the villagers who were actually our neighbors because we were villagers too, if you think about it, but they were all there in the street like it was some kind of fair, entire families, laughing and pointing when the rabbi fell over and soldiers kicked his hat in the mud, watching still as the soldiers, finally drunk enough, started in on the babies with their bayonets. Someone had a secret store of sausage and they brought that out, some cured sausage and more drink and a few people even cheered when the soldiers caught the babies on bayonets, like it was a kind of sport, which maybe it was because the soldiers made the mothers toss their babies in the air so that they could catch them on their bayonets if the toss was accurate, though—and I personally did not need this assumption confirmed for me—many mothers, forced to lob their babies onto bayonets, will not do a good job of it, will not throw their baby directly at the point, or will not toss them high enough for the one catching to adjust in time, so although the villagers cheered when the soldiers caught the babies on their bayonets they didn't cheer much and this is what I was thinking about, Alex, when I raised my hand to knock, when we reached that door after you had rejoined us, somewhere between night and morning, the end of war and the end of my life, this is what I was remembering with my hand raised between the morning and the door, between the women holding their children on their shoulders so they could watch their neighbors throw their own babies onto bayonets and the woman in Michael's village who hadn't bothered to flee that warm house that wasn't hers."

"When I returned from patrol," Baruch says again, "my friends were going door to door."

"But one door opened without breaking it down," Eli says. "I knocked. And then when the door opened, I went inside. So did Michael and Aaron and Uri, and you did too, Alex."

"The war was over," Baruch says to the angels, and the angels open their mouths and recognition romps through Jacob, opening doors to rooms with mirrors like the angels have in their mouths, opening their mouths now with their rotten wooden lips and bottlecap tongues and the barnacle-crusted mirrors hanging at the back of their throats filmed with algae and mud and revealing only the smudge of light like the moon through an ancient pane of leaded glass. "The war was over," Baruch says again and Jacob recognizes the way the old man sees no one, the way he implores them to believe the same innocuous repeated statement, strings the dull thread of syllables into a loop rather than a sequence, like if he can just get it right, then the next sentence, the entire rest of his life, maybe, will follow. "We were three days ahead of the Russians," he says, "and my friends were going door to door."

Inside, there was a woman. Young.

"She was not young," Eli says, "we were young and we were not young."

At first they sought only to address her. After all this time, they didn't know what they wanted except to speak. She opened the door and stood there holding a rolling pin and they entered. As they did, she began walking backward through a hallway she must have come to know as her own, walking backward but looking at them, staring uncomprehending from the hallway, walking backward, silent, clean, warm, dressed, safe, German and anchored in the home of Jews who had dug their own graves at the edge of the forest and they approached her, these other Jews, muddy, it was spring and the field between the forest and the road, where the town Jews were buried, was mud and they crossed the floor in muddy boots into the kitchen where a warm bread smell was being born from the oven, and she should have offered them food or water or a bath, they were children after all and their mothers were dead, if she had offered them a bath or begged them not to hurt her or listened when they started asking for those things, food, water, clothes, bread, beer, blankets, a bath or beds to sleep in, but she shook her head at their German, she could not understand, she said, finally, her first words, she could not understand the rotten approximations of their Yiddish or their Romanian countryside German even if they were making themselves clear—food, water, beds, blankets, a bath—she could not understand, or wouldn't, "she wouldn't listen," Baruch says. She wouldn't listen or account for herself in that house, because she wasn't looking at their mouths, but at the mud, maybe she was looking down in fear, she must have been looking down in fear, but they were children and she was looking at the mud they had tracked onto the floor, "she was thinking," Eli says, "that we were muddy and she was clean and she was seeing us and she could not understand our muddy speech from our muddy tongues and seeing us she was seeing mud where she was clean, dirty Jews, how many times had we heard that, dirty Jews, muddy Jews in that clean house that wasn't hers, tracking mud, Jewish mud, mud from the graves of Jews, the mud of Jews made mud, through her house and we were mud and I thought, or maybe it was later, fine it was later, I admit it was later, years later, it was 1974 and I was in Israel on the abyss of history remembering the way she occupied that house, but later I thought about the Rabbi of Prague who made a man of mud to avenge the Prague pogrom, as we did, muddy children, there on our own reclaimed floor."

Baruch says, "In the first year after the war ended, I used to have this dream.

"My father is standing by the window in the apartment in Berlin," Baruch says, "smoking his pipe. It is after the war and I haven't seen him for years. I call out to him: *Papa, where have you been?* He turns from the window—my father, he's my father, and he turns from the window," Baruch says, "and his mustache is flaxen, his mustache is the color of flax like it was when I was a little boy and he's wearing spectacles, small, round golden spectacles, where the sun flashes and I cannot see his eyes and I cry again, *Papa, Papa where have you been?* Even though we're together in our apartment in Berlin I think that maybe he can't see me and I wave the way we waved to trains, the way I waved once from a train in Romania. I don't try to touch him because I'm afraid that if I do, if I cross the floor and try to touch him, he'll run away, or hide, or go back to wherever he's been. But he does see me. He sets his pipe down in the porcelain tray that he kept on his desk. It's shaped like an oyster's shell and coated in an iridescent paint so that it seems almost as if a pearl inside the oyster has grown and burst and spread like a liquid, a pearly liquid, across the inside of the shell and my father sets his pipe down," Baruch says, "in the shell from where we both watch its smoke curl upward in a stream. Finally, he looks up, away from the smoke. *You're a whore now*, my father says to me."

"What Berlin apartment?"

Eli on stage with Baruch, shouting

Through the listing open window: wind and the windmill, foghorns, thunder, distressed birds.

Sophie covers her face.

Angels clack and chatter like glass shattering.

"There was no Berlin apartment," Eli says, "there was no papa, no pipe, no pipe tray, no pipe smoke—"

"You're a whore now," Baruch says his father said in his dream. It was morning in the apartment but there wasn't much light. The war was over. They were clearing rubble in the street that he saw for the first time after the professor found him in the Displaced Persons camp. "On stage again," Baruch tells the angels, "I was on stage again in the DP camp, in their insane little theater doing insane little plays when the professor found me." Baruch was still a boy and still beautiful, cackling like a maniac in Yiddish theater that he didn't understand, cackling in Yiddish in parts that did not require cackling but the DP camp was like that and the plays were worse—frantic actors shouting their way through old Yiddish shows, screaming, lurid in whimsyless parody like the Corpse Bride demanding her wedding, laughing or weeping or breaking altogether, there was one actor who interrupted every show with sudden bursts of Hungarian song, while people watched and cheered and wept and muttered and picked lice from each other and fucked on hands and knees in the broad daylight. "A whole generation, most of Israel," Baruch says, "born out of that summer," with its wild intensities of insects and love, insects and life and memory deranging into dream.

the angels spread their wings like books blown open by wind

The professor found him on stage and took his hand. He took his hand "like I was a child." He took his hand as if he were a child and led him out of the camp, by the hand, "stole me," Baruch says, "like a watch, stole me as I had stolen papers, food, the partisan's silver cigarette case" and brought him onto a train, a train that was still running or rebuilt already and running again and brought him back to his apartment in Berlin where they were clearing rubble in the street. There was smoke in the air. The man was a philologist with golden spectacles. He promised Baruch a place in the university when the time came. He put his pipe down in the pipe tray and wiped his mouth.

"In my dream," Baruch says, "my father begins to cough. He has said what he said and then he begins to cough. Papa, close the window, I say. There is gas in the street, Papa."

Suddenly he is frightened again. Gas? he says and begins to cry and cough. Gas? There is? he says. He is crying. There is?

The professor put his pipe down in the pipe tray and wiped his mouth. *You know what you are now?* he said, and Baruch nodded, as silent as the woman had been with Eli and his friends screaming between her legs.

Take your turn, Eli howled.

"She was a Nazi," Eli told him.

A Nazi and a Nazi wife in a Jewish home waiting to keep house for her Nazi husband and her Nazi children, who they heard, toward the end, whimpering upstairs, and she wanted to scrub them, all these Jews, from the world, scrub their mud from their own floor, and they had an obligation Eli said, Michael said, Uri said, to sow the next generation of Jews starting here, right here, in this Nazi wife.

The kitchen: first the smell of bread being born from the oven, then blood and piss and sperm. The children upstairs crying. Eli's hand in her mouth, Michael holding her wrists down. *Are you a person*? Eli said. *Are you alive? Are you alive? If you are alive take your turn*

After Baruch fled, the partisans were still asleep, or playing cards or listening to the radio reports just louder than the echoes of the Red Army's tanks moving west.

Baruch stole the commander of the partisans' cigarette case and his bag of silver utensils that he had been collecting in their march and hid them in his friends' tent. He was already on the road when the partisans searched them and found the stolen silver.

The sun bled over the village like a cracked skull. Blue scars of smoke stitched the sky to the forest where the partisans camped.

He watched his friends being hauled to the town square for the firing squad.

From the hillside, the town was blurry, thinly sketched in charcoal. The faint rub of little fires, the willowy tangle of people gathered in the square. The quiet, and then the crowd, the blackening whirl where the eye focuses. It could be a market day, or festival, or Saturday afternoon as shul lets out, and the Jews dense and huddled darkly like smoke unleashed before they disappeared.

"Here's one you'll know," Eli says to the angels. "And don't worry, I'll tell you the end.

"So, the Baal Shem Tov, the great and blessed rabbi, hears a report that the Cossacks are coming. And what does he do? The same thing he always does. He goes into the forest, he finds his sacred meditating spot at the base of the biggest tree in the birch grove, he lights a fire and says a prayer—and the Lord hears his prayer and the crisis is averted.

"Time passes. The Baal Shem Tov joins his ancestors in Paradise, but the Jews are still Jews and the Cossacks are still Cossacks and when they come, the Besht's disciple, the Maggid of Mezeritch, does the same thing, more or less: he goes into the same forest and finds the same birch tree in the same birch grove and says, *Lord, I do not know how to light the fire, but I know the spot and I know the prayer*—and the Lord hears his prayer and the crisis is averted.

"More time passes. The Maggid is reunited with his lustrous fathers in Olam Habbah, but the Jews are still Jews and the Cossacks are still Cossacks and when the Cossacks ready themselves for their next pogrom the Maggid's successor, Rabbi Moshe Leib of Sassov, goes into the same forest and finds the same grove and says, *Lord, I do not know how to light the fire, and I do not know the prayer, but I know the spot*—and the Lord hears his prayer and the crisis is averted.

"Well, you know where this is going. Time passes for us all. Rabbi Moshe Leib of Sassov died. His sons died and their sons died, on and on across the generations, but the Jews, being Jews, were still Jews, and the Cossacks were still Cossacks and when it came time for the next rabbi to intercede with the Almighty on behalf of his people, he sat at his table in his own house in the depths of the night and cried out, *Oh, Lord, I do not know how to light the fire, and I do not know the prayer, or the tree or the grove or even the forest in which to find it, but I do know the story, Lord, which I will pass on to my own sons the way my father passed it on to me, so please let that be enough*—and it was. The Lord heard his prayer and the crisis was averted."

Eli looks down and quiets, like the angels, then

"So then, finally, there was us. We too were born hearing the stories of the dead, even in our wide exile, across all the towns and villages and cities of Europe, we heard the stories of the Lord's tender utterance that made the world new, of the patriarchs and the Temple and the Baal Shem Tov, and the Maggid, and Rabbi Moshe Leib of Sassov and what did we know? The world was still the world, a mother's love was still a mother's love, and as morning followed night the Jews were still Jews, every goy was a Cossack and the Cossacks were everywhere and when they came for us we did the same things that Jews had always done—this is how you know we're Jews, after all, and also how you know it's a joke—we ran to the forest and it was the same forest the Baal Shem Tov had run to, actually, and we kneeled in a birch grove, and in fact, it was the same birch grove the Besht had knelt in and we put our heads down at the base of a tree, Alex did and Michael did and Uri did and I did, I put my head at the base of the birch where the earth was thin and it might have been the same tree and we cried out to the Lord and all across Europe our people cried out and they cried in the voice of prayer and they called in the shape and flicker of fire and their voices rose in prayer and their bodies rose in ash and here's the punchline, now that we've reached it, here's the punchline, and listen because I know you struggle with these, but I want you to hear, for once, I want you to hear it and understand it and remember it, remember how the joke ends—we cried out from the forest and ditches and cattle cars and Lagers and we made our appeal from the weight of mud and the flake and nothing of cinders—and the Lord did not hear our prayer and the crisis was not averted."

Eli drinks, the tavern lists.

"If you're a character in a joke," Eli says, "then your life is a joke. Then your heart is a joke. Your dreams and doubts, your campaigns and aspirations, the safety you thought you built and the peril you avoided, the love you gave, the hurt you recovered from, your dead mother covering your eyes with her last touch at the edge of the river where the cherry trees grow so you won't see the bullets that kill you both, or your sister dancing between you and your parents as you play your little violin, your mother's hand settling over your father's, the glass of brandy your grandfather drank, the flower you wore in your hair, the raucous dreams your memory slides into as you wait in the cupboard, the night the two of you walked by the canal and heard the drunk gondolier sing lullabies to the pigeons and you knew that you would always love her. Grass stains on your linen pants. Pilsner poured from a fresh tap. Your baby's head held up to your nose and the empty silent space your husband's mouth makes in his face when you lift it from the street. Nothing but jokes. The street is a joke, the cherry trees are jokes, the mud and smoke, the rope arranged for a child's neck and the Torah's ark—all jokes. If you are a character in a joke you were always a joke. And nothing you dreamed or hoped or did or didn't do would ever matter.

"And that," Eli says, "includes that woman in her house in the spring of 1945 and any choice you think you made there. The light was on. We knocked or we didn't. The door opened or it didn't. She backed away down the hall or she was already on the road with the rest of the village. It doesn't matter. The woman you fucked or the women you thought you saved by killing your friends. The mercy you reclaimed, the forgiveness you summoned, your whole life of righteousness and forgiveness, smug or beautiful, meant nothing.

Nichts. Gornisht. Klum. That is what I've come here to say, Alex. I am your guest and I make this claim on your house: if you are a good man or wicked, if you are kind or cruel, comfortable or confused, proud or craven, exalted or found out, if your body aches or is free, if you remember your mother and father or if your life has been graced by oblivion. If you didn't fuck her because you thought it was wrong or you were too starving to have a prick, if your heart was full of mercy or vengeance, rage or timidity, it does not matter. Yizkor Elohim. I spit when I say it. We did what we did, but He didn't notice. Yizkor Elohim. We did what we did but He wasn't listening. Nothing changes. Look, they are marching again. They are calling for our blood, and the world is laughing. Yizkor Elohim. He does not remember or protect or exalt. He will not intercede, and He will not listen. He is asleep, His emissaries are rotten and sleeping, baffled and sleeping, deaf and dumb, incoherent and unconcerned, murderous and asleep."

RACHEL IN BED AWAKE. There was howling outside, on the water, wolves running on the dogpack wind. Too late to close the window, the curtains opened their mouths toward her. She was up and in the hall. She was carrying a sweater and her sketchbook. It was the middle of the night, or later than that, and she could feel that the house was empty.

By now Simon could be back in New York, if he took the fastest route and drove straight through. Or maybe he stopped somewhere on the coast at one of those places leaving fliers in the rest stops on the highway: a B&B in Camden or a yacht club in York. God knows he was dressed for it. This was probably what he'd always wanted. To vanish among WASPS and fresh seafood. She imagined him changing his Jewish last name in hotel registries, trailing his seersucker through the lobster pounds and fryshacks of Midcoast Maine, searching for sushi. And if there was no future for him, what about her? She had witnessed his humiliation. Even if he didn't know she was its author, to see it was enough. To know she had seen it. And if she got the real Lurio home to Baer? And he sold it, as he needed to? Certainly, Simon would have to be involved again somewhere along the way. Her days at the museum were over. Like Lurio's white space, the time between now and that moment was charged with inevitability.

Downstairs, in the drawing room, a desk lamp with a glass shade was lit by the French doors. Rachel rounded the corner quietly: Daniel was standing there with his back to her, watching his parents sleep. They were nestled upright on the mint loveseat together, his father's head on his mother's shoulder, both their mouths open in tender reflection in the door glass. She still wore her visor but his was upside down in her lap, neon and plastic and mostly imagined, like a child's toy.

Rachel, looking, liked what she saw. She opened her book and began to sketch:

Daniel, and his parents—vulnerable as children—sleeping beneath whatever he was feeling. His head tilted to the side, his neck long, bare, like something you should put your mouth on, or could, if you weren't drawing it. That had been her first mistake—to think she wanted to touch the thing itself.

And in the glass: a woman gathered out of the sea, her own reflection, holding her book, her pencil, him in her eyes.

He looked up and caught her there.

"Nazis are marching in the streets," he said. "And they are just sleeping."

Beneath his childish rage, his childish parents: soft, snoring, as fake as mascots. She could include it all, or anyway, as much as she wanted.

"You know you've ruined everything," he said. "Baruch. Any hope for this place."

Her hand was its own sail, and she kept drawing. The wolves on the water she now knew as loons. The world was full of recognition. When she had showed him her forgery, she had asked, *Will it work*? and he had just winced and said, *It's very good*. She held open her sketchbook, all her takes on the horizon. There were so many ways to correct error. Fire, erasure, sutures. The monk disguises his blot as a rose. To hide what was broken or to acknowledge it: another layer of paint or gold poured to seal the cracks. For all those years, if only she could have said what was wrong. But there is a difference between confusion and mistake.

The Lurio was coming with her. She felt her voice already beginning to form. This might be the wrong thing to do, but she meant to do it.

"Don't move," she said.

ONCE, JACOB AND MADDIE, CASTAWAYS in bed, a four-poster with white canopy curtains folded open and tied to the posts, billowy as sails. A spa in Vermont. Maddie's gift to them both. Floor-to-ceiling picture windows. The mountains pouring down into pastures.

"Sarah," Maddie says. "Rebekah. Rachel."

Ten in the morning and they are already back from a hike. Following trails leading into the woods beyond the spa's lawn. They hadn't consulted a map. The forest grew close and dense and they had pushed through a stand of juniper. On the other side, new weather: a shock of light, the smell of moss, a waterfall melting over a cliffside of blue rock. They stripped and swam in the glacial pools. Then the walk back. Every bird in the world was awake.

"Leah," Jacob says. "Sophie, Samantha."

"I like Samantha," Maddie says. "But maybe it seems…" Her head is on his chest. He can smell her hair, still warm from their hike. Sweat, sunscreen at the nape of her neck, the sweet oil of her skin.

Her mouth is half open and moving on his sternum—she's whispering to herself, which is something she does, some silent thinking, but this is the first time he notices it, a remaining trace of a lonely childhood, maybe, that, like everything else, he'll come to love.

"Yes?" he asks.

She laughs. "Sorry. I don't know. Maddie and Samantha. It's stuffy."

"You mean WASPy."

"WASPy? That's Gertrude, Abigail, Diane, Evelyn."

He finds the bedpost with the knuckles of his right hand. At first he's not even aware he's doing it. He kisses her head, he taps the post. This is what she'll never understand: it begins as devotion. But then—to do it once is to never be able to stop. Because now the pact is made and he knows how to protect her and it's such a small thing: tap, tap, tap. If he loves her, three taps. Who, knowing that, knowing that all he needs to give is his attention, could be so selfish as to stop?

"And if it's a boy?" Maddie asks.

"Reuben," he says. "Mordechai. Archibald."

"Seriously."

Earlier, her skin had tasted like their swim: a mineral whisper and the scent of moss, and he had believed that he could live wholly in his devotion. But now. If he could he'd give his child a name without history, untraceable and weightless, only his own. Like Kevin.

"I had always thought David," she says. "After my grandfather."

"No." He startles them both with the speed of the response. Jewish law prohibited naming a child after a living family member. It was one of those rules that every Jew followed, even the ones who didn't follow Jewish laws. (As with his tapping, so with this: why risk it?) Maybe, if he had told her then. He taps the post. *I love you.* Again, again. Years later, she would say to him, "This isn't love, it's fear," but what is love if not a kind of fear? He can already sense their departure: the town's rambling farmhouses and tidy colonials with window boxes, flowered trellises, hives at the edge of the pasture near the blue trees. Then, at its outskirts, all the farms of gray stone. Her silence expanding ahead of them, down the road.

He taps and misses. And misses. His heart gallops.

She notices, maybe she hears it, she sits up and looks at him. Certainly she is coming to all the wrong conclusions and he lets her.

Jacob on the cliff edge beyond the forest. Under a humid wind as fragrant and sickly as a poultice—salt, pine, rose petals. Above him the mold-damp shadow of Nod, leaning forward from its sagging foundation like an old man walking into the wind. He came to a door beneath some rotting eaves on the eastern exposure and finally it was a door he knew: the mud room he had wandered into that first night. Beyond it, in the chamber where he'd met Boris, he found Baruch sitting in the middle of the couch with his hands on his knees watching a television. He seemed tense, weary, clothed in some remote insult that Jacob didn't mean to interrupt. But he had. He was standing on the carpet with the door to the mudroom still open, drawing in the feverish breeze.

Baruch switched the channel from weather to weather. "In Maine this is all they show," he said.

"It's important if you have a boat, I guess."

"Maybe," Baruch said, "but they're never right."

"The Baron Hirsch was liquidated in 1943," Jacob said. "The Nazis occupied Khmel'nik in July 1941. You couldn't have been at both places."

Baruch switched the channel again. "Baron Hirsch. It's where I should have been in 1943," he said. "You must know how I feel."

Jacob didn't know how anyone felt, including himself. The self was like alchemy. Maybe it worked, but you had to believe in it. And not think of a rhinoceros. At the same time.

"I was impatient," Baruch said. "I was sick of being a stevedore's son. Of being a petty thief in a fish market. I had another brother. Not the communist, not the Zionist. He also worked in the hotel in the hills, and he knew a bellhop who seasoned north in the winter in Bucharest. Technically I wasn't old enough, but he got us jobs in Romania, and then when the Iron Guard revolted and it didn't seem safe, at a hotel in Odessa. We were just trying to earn enough money to get to Turkey. According to my brother, we had family in Istanbul. It doesn't matter. All those old Jews at the hotel in Thessaloniki made Europe sound so grand. I don't know what we were thinking other than that we were poor. We thought anything was better than where we were. We blamed our father for not going to Alexandria or Palestine. We were right, I suppose, but that doesn't make me feel any less ashamed. As it turned out we didn't make it to Odessa. We were captured. We were put on the back of a truck, and my brother pushed me out. I ran toward the forest. He was shot a few miles up the road, I think. The rest of my family, my parents, my two other brothers, my cousins were in Baron Hirsch until 1943, where I should have been, and then in Auschwitz as well where I also should have gone."

"You should have told the world the truth. You shouldn't have let them take your life from you."

"Living," Baruch said, "was just another way I betrayed my parents."

He stared hard at Jacob for a moment and then he patted the couch, as he might for a cat. Jacob sat beside him. He put his hand over Jacob's and sighed and his hand was calm and still as sleep. "Why are you crying?"

Jacob told him. Baruch nodded. He didn't appear surprised. He didn't say he had nothing to feel bad for.

"You're young," he said. "Or anyway, you're not old. You're alive. So what do you want now?"

"I want to be forgiven," Jacob said. "But I can't. Because my father is dead."

Baruch took his face in his hands and kissed his forehead. They were strangers. This was only the fourth time that they had ever been alone together. The heavens were cold, the gods were amnesiacs or statues of birds, there was no way to understand. The mysteries remained mysteries, but some of them were radiant and available. Jacob's father had not understood what Jacob was trying to tell him under the hazy green hospital lights. "Oh, come here, honey," Baruch said and then gathered Jacob into his arms where he was warm, still thick across the chest but bony and without muscle along the back and shoulders, he smelled of brandy and sandalwood aftershave lotion and the damp that lived in every room on this side of the house and Jacob knew this might be what it would have felt like to hold his own father if he had lived to be old or if Jacob had been able to come to him undisguised and embrace him, as he should have, before he died.

When they separated, Baruch did not pause. "I know what we will do," he said. He was excited, his eyes were bright and green. "I know just the thing," he said. "We'll say the Yizkor for your father."

And they did. *Yizkor Elohim, May the lord remember.* It was morning. The door was still open. Once they started saying it, the problem of doubt was gone. It was heard, it was unheard, it was an ordinary prayer, impossible, inadequate and almost enough. Their throats were clotted, neither one of them could sing. This is what it was good for. They finished the prayer.

Boris gamboling through the door. His hair was wild and blue. There was mud on his shoes. He still wore his pocket square. "What's going on?"

"We're forgiving David," Baruch said.

Jacob outside on the headland, calling Maddie. The cobalt sky bouldered with clouds. She was asleep but speaking, then awake, saying *What's wrong*, then awake and listening. He was trying to explain it all: what he had done in Israel, that his name wasn't really Jacob, that he had told Joshua. "Wait," she said, "what's your name?" She kept saying *wait*, she kept repeating the same questions, and then: "Wait," she said, "you told this kid?"

"Joshua."

"We've been together for a decade," she said. "More. We're fucking married," she said. She was groping for a way in. At another time this could be a point of sympathy: acknowledging that knowing what was obvious didn't get you any closer to understanding what was happening.

Now that he was able to speak, he couldn't stop speaking. He said it all again, it didn't make any sense at this speed, as a sequence of events where there was, at least in his life, no beginning. The signal had never been clearer. Baruch, then Boris, had taken him in their arms, he was on top of the hill and in the valley below him the statues he had seen from the car—rabbis and yeshiva boys, a priapic dybbuk—appeared small and dumb as toys.

"You've got to be fucking kidding me," Maddie said and hung up.

The speed of life here. Morning, midnight, and the days a bright and absent slash. Now dawn, the lobster boats were in the sound and the only birds were the gulls celebrating the trap's haul. Under the new sun the sea wrinkled like a blouse. His phone was ringing. Maddie's voice silver with tears.

"David," Maddie said. "David, David."

THAT MORNING THERE WAS NO BREAKFAST laid out at Nod and the guests helped themselves.

The wind died at dawn and though the doors to the sea were open, the house, usually rocking with water-light, was placid and drowsy. The curtains slept and the sand and dried grass clippings, dead ants and husks of rose hips and wild carrot flowers that washed in daily lay in an unswept tideline just across the threshold.

But the house was not quiet.

Baruch was on coffee duty, trying to recreate for everyone how they had made it in the woods during the war: a fistful of grounds tossed onto boiling water.

"This is a treat," he said. "Usually we used roots or ground-up alder leaves. Occasionally instant rations. Never actual grounds."

"It's terrible," Sophie said. "Isn't it?"

"Yes," Baruch said. "It's very bad."

He had coaxed her inside from where he found her, sitting dressed for tennis in one of the Adirondack chairs. From the drawing room, Rachel had watched her shouting at him, pounding her clavicle with her racket, then holding it to her chest like a baby, then dropping it, then covering her face, then taking his hand.

"Weren't you too young for coffee anyway?" Mel said and put on a pot.

"This," Baruch said, "is how you spot an American."

They scavenged what they could from the fridges: smoked salmon, scones, blueberries and melon. Boris shuffled in using Anna's sun hat as a basket from which appeared a dozen eggs, their shells were pigeon blue or a stony Atlantic gray, one a little larger than the others was a creamy jade. He cracked them into a pan, he was whistling as he scrambled them, the yolks opened and ruffled like bright orange flowers. Mel added smoked salmon, minced chives. "Boris, is that my hat?" Anna said.

No one asked where Daniel was. He hadn't been seen all day, and his parents left without saying goodbye. "Have to get back," his mother kept saying.

They stared at the group, blinking in their visors, smiling, suntanned, holding hands. "We really thought he would have liked those clams," she said.

And then they drove off in a little car shaped like a comma.

Throughout, Rachel watched from the kitchen, and then once the others had moved out to eat on the lawn, she gathered her blueberries and coffee, as well as some granola and yogurt and bacon, and followed behind them onto the patio. Sometime after dawn, after she was awake and showered and dressed, she had met Jacob outside her room. He was elated, his face was streaked with tears, he was pacing and silent. She was grateful that he didn't have anything to say, that he was a stranger still and she told him to go to bed. Now he was asleep, Daniel was missing, she was alone and quiet with her sketchbook, sitting under a lilac bush on the ghostly felt of its former blossoms.

She watched Baruch. The auction must have ruined him, but he drifted across the lawn like something caught on the breeze. He floated. He smiled. His hand was on Anna's shoulder. He directed Sophie and Mel in a chant where they droned the Hebrew alphabet. He put his palm on Mel's head, like a blessing. When he turned and crossed the patio and sat with Rachel under the lilac, he was still smiling.

"The whole world thinks it can spot a fake," he said. "But it's actually very difficult."

"Is it?"

"Maybe not in practice. But in theory. In practice everything is compromised and fugazi, broken and deranged. It doesn't take a tzadik to see that. But in theory? To call something fake, you have to be able to say what's real."

"I heard all this from your old friend," Rachel said. "Nothing in the world can represent the real. I thought we were beyond believing in the world or in the real or in nothing."

The more aggressive she became, the less angry he seemed. He was nodding and smiling, his eyes were full of tears.

"He's not my friend. He's not even alive. And that's not my point."

She waited. If there was one thing she knew, it was that he would tell her his point.

"I would recognize that sketch anywhere."

"Yesterday must have been pretty embarrassing for you, then."

"For many, perhaps. Some people are always embarrassed and some never are. My question is about you. Whoever you are, surely you are not just a thief?"

She wasn't going to grant the premise. She told him that. She wasn't going to grant the premise but, just adjacently of course, she had a cousin. And she told him Baer's story.

He was still. Throughout, as she spoke, he had been attentive, disconcertingly so, looking directly at her, making eye contact, and then finally turning away to stare over the water. Now, her story was finished and he hadn't moved. It was as if he were posing for her, and she could imagine him this way, how he'd look transformed by her sight, how—in the absence of clarity or honesty—she would discover the space where his intentions, his subterfuge or confession, didn't matter, and she would invent him: the patches of yellow and pink that would make his cheeks and brow, the bruised shades under his eyes and at his temples, cyan and scarlet mixed into lavender, thickening to clay. Everything fragmented by the lilac dapple: darker scales of leaves, branches waving like a skeletal hand. His face held a perfect geometry, but the world wrecked it.

Then he was speaking. "I'm sure Jacob will tell you the rest of the story. But here's what he doesn't know. By the time we reached the road that led to the river, there were local partisans waiting to ambush any who tried to cross the bridge. So the papers I had stolen for me and my friends were useless. And they would have been for anybody. That family would not have made it across either. Does that make anything any better?

"It was clear we couldn't cross the river and that we had to stay in German territory, but they would be cleansing the ghetto soon, everybody knew that. So what did I do? Among the papers there had been a sketch. I didn't know anything about it, but knew it was important enough that this family—who had left behind or sold almost everything they owned, they were carrying almost nothing good enough to steal—kept it with their most prized possessions. What else did I know? I had often watched, from my hiding place in the pines, a young SS officer who liked to sit near a spring in the forest and draw. So the next day, I approached him. It was madness, but what other choice did I have? I approached him in the forest. I took off my shirt and stepped out of the pines. Even then I understood performance and I wanted to appear to him like something he might value, a sprite or a faun, a thing of the forest, not the ghetto. I showed him the sketch. He could have just shot me and taken it, but this was art, I was bearing something beautiful and I assume this is where he imagined he would locate his humanity. He asked me if I could sing, he asked if he could sketch me. It doesn't matter. Then, after, I began to beg, but I made it sound like a trade. I asked him for our safe passage north."

She watched his face change, darker squares of blood in his cheeks, above his poppy-colored collar.

"So it is a sketch that saved my life once. I thought it might do so again."

From the tennis courts the irregular pop of the balls on broken clay. The seaborn sound bounced around them, warped and phantom, rebounding—miles off, and then near and loud as Rachel's heart. Distance bridged by wind. A grunt. Sophie's quick shout of triumph.

"Now I have nothing else to say to you or to explain or to ask," Baruch said, "except will you help me up? I'm not sure what I was thinking sitting on the ground. But life is like this, my dear. You are always arriving at the last thing you can do."

After he left, the horizon changed. There were so many ways to correct error, and sometimes all you had to do is wait. A bank of clouds that for the entire week she had not realized were clouds—had just thought was the sky, the end of the sky, its limit and edge—had lifted and from the cliff she was now looking across the water—across what was no longer the empty sea, but a channel—at the mainland, its shores and docks and ramshackle gray outbuildings and little boats and silly glitter of colorful moorings, glistening like neon beads in the town harbor. Here was the definition she had required. The border, the control of space her life begged for. She had not been as confounded as she thought. The horizon had not been the horizon. The endless sea ended. The world was there. She began to draw.

THAT AFTERNOON JACOB WOKE AND PACKED. He went from the landing to the stairs to the drawing room to the lawn. Something had broken in his sleep, a noise had shaken him awake and drawn him through the door to the headland where Mel was hanging his tennis whites on the line between the house and the huppah.

"The tavern fell into the sea," Mel said.

"The tavern fell into the sea?"

Mel beat his Umbro shorts with a broom. "Erosion."

"What do you mean, the tavern fell into the sea?"

Boris, gliding by, bearing remotes in both hands.

"Baseball time," Boris said.

First pitch at 4:07. Their last night. Even Rachel joined the gathering in the game room. "Yankees," Boris said. "And Red Sox." Sophie clapped and shouted "Go Sox" and did some kind of dance, punching the air and swiveling her hips.

"I just can't believe you," Mel said. "This is why women shouldn't watch sports."

"Is baseball really a sport?" Rachel said and everybody stared. Anna gave her, or the room, or the Red Sox, a thumbs down.

Boris, brandishing the remotes, stood before them and pointed.

Every channel was showing the same thing: a woman was dead in Charlottesville. The governor was on television, but the coverage kept cutting away from him to show the crowds. The tiki torches from the night before were gone, as were the polos and checkered oxfords, and the marching in circles and chanting in unison and the sense of suburban pantomime. Now: only the rage and disarray of a disaster—storm troopers in tactical gear, men carrying assault rifles and signs saying *The Goyim Know* and *Six Million Were Not Enough* and the networks trying to turn their leering into witness, even as they cut away finally, amid static and inadequate commentary, to members of a local synagogue staring dumbly into the cameras. They'd had to flee out the back door because gunmen were waiting in the street for their services to end. On another channel white teenagers beat a Black man with sticks in a parking garage. The President appeared on TV at his golf course in New Jersey, they muted him in the game room at Nod, they clicked away and they clicked back through the clutter of flags: Confederate and an Iron Cross and a Don't Tread on Me and a swastika and then, now that all the channels had the feed, again and again, at different speeds, looping like history, the grainy footage of the gray car making its human dent.

The door to the room slammed. Daniel behind them, his hands moving in insect havoc. He was saying something, he was pointing, he was a mirror of what he was looking at: in Charlottesville a man pointed into the camera and shouted, "The Jews will pay," a commentator on the ground said, "This is, in many ways, an economic reaction to globalism." Daniel was still speaking, it seemed he was talking to Baruch, but who could hear him? When the TV wasn't on mute it was at seventy-five decibels.

And then Daniel, collapsing back through the doorway, was gone again.

Jacob waited for Rachel to react. She stared into the empty space where he had been and then turned back to the television. Everyone else was attending to the essential: Sophie was comforting Anna, Mel was gripping his left leg, Baruch was helping Boris get the game on the radio. Jacob, who had once in high school shouted at his father, *Why do you do the same thing over and over?* and whose own life had made a joke of repetition, knew what he was seeing because he had seen it before: Joshua with blood in his hair coming to Jacob on the verge of mistake.

"We need to find Daniel," Jacob said to Rachel.

"We should split up," she said to Jacob, but Jacob said, "I'll get lost."

"What do you mean you'll get lost?"

"Haven't you noticed," he said.

"Noticed what? It will take forever to check everywhere," she said. But it didn't because the first place they checked was the kitchen, and after they checked the kitchen they checked the cellar. In the darkness at the bottom of the stairs she reached for the lantern, which was gone, as was the kerosene and a box of matches.

YOU ARRIVE AT YOUR LIFE, you recognize it, usually in retrospect, in its various genres: first as tragedy, then as farce. First as freshmen reading Marx, and then as seniors quoting Zizek. First as Walter Benjamin, then as Walter Benjamin. Loss, confusion. Hysteria, hilarity. First as suicide, then as fire.

She had followed Jacob. The opal porthole of his flashlight before them discovered the narrow trail between the fingerbones of low bare branches. She had said, "Where are we?" and he had said, "Near Jonah's" and she had not understood. "The tavern," he had said.

There was nothing but huddled trees, deformed and dwarfish, stunted under wind like Lurio's Job, and she, ready to be amazed or corrected or renewed by surprise, had said, "Where?"

"I think it fell into the sea," Jacob said and kept walking and later, still bearing that nonsense like an answer, they met Daniel at the path's other mouth, running toward them, away from the compound, which they could see silhouetted now with its barn and tents and its listing house with its Nazi grandma's stupid gabled porch all on fire.

Back at Nod, standing under the portico. The reflection of the flames spreading on the belly of the clouds.

It was Baruch who stopped her. She found herself again in his grasp. She'd been screaming at Daniel, a cringing chimneysweep smeared in soot. The wide white of his eyes.

"The trailers were gone," he said. "They were all in Charlottesville."

"Shale was there," Baruch said.

"It's August," Rachel shouted. "And you lit a fire in the forest. This whole island could burn down. There was a man inside."

"Am I the only one awake?"

"What?"

"Are you asleep?"

It was a question you would ask a sleeping person, a question people asked you in sleep.

Eli appeared under the portico, in a wheelchair. "First you knock, then you enter. They don't understand."

"I thought you left," Rachel said.

"Look at me."

"Why are you in a wheelchair?"

"I can't stand."

"Are you awake?" Daniel said again.

Baruch took Jacob's hand. "I've called the fire department, but they'll take a while."

The sound of sirens from the mainland carried over the water. A suture of black smoke across the sudden wound of the orange sky, bruising back into night.

Baruch leaned up against one of the pillars. "For a while I thought I would become a boat person and considered getting an island without a causeway. I suppose it's better that I didn't. Anyway, it's time for you both to go. Right now. Take my Subaru. Mel will return your sports car. Take Daniel."

"And the Lurio?" Jacob said.

He was the kind of boy who couldn't help but ask. He needed a blessing. That much was clear.

Baruch put his hand over Jacob's, then withdrew it as if in a change of mind or strategy. He straightened, he pursed his lips, he looked as she'd seen him first, an aristocrat, aloof as a cat.

"The Lurio was a fake, remember? I thought I recognized it when I saw it. But it must not have been what I thought."

"He used kerosene," Jacob said. "On everything. Unconnected structures. They will not think this is an accident."

"There's a line in the Gemara," Baruch said. "If you're a giant asshole, many people might burn your barn."

Again, Jacob asked him to come with him. "You'll be arrested," Jacob said.

"He needs to stay with me," Eli said. "I can't walk."

The truth was that most of Lurio's paintings in his Biblical sequence were considered failures at the time of their appearance. When they were revealed en masse he was already famous, a grand old man living in Canada, a survivor of the European cataclysm and people expected similar magnificence. But his Tanakh privileged the daily over the mystical and many of its images—domestic rather than awesome—seemed lonely, tired, disorientating or oriented squarely in sagging humanity. But this, Rachel believed, was his genius: in Abraham's potbelly and bad teeth a viewer saw the banal cruelty of her own father. And now, about to leave, she looked. She saw Eli stuffed into the wheelchair like Lurio's Abraham from his "The Binding of Isaac," where Lurio chose to depict the moment after the ecstasy, after the angel has come and Isaac had been freed, the wrecked fury waking in his eyes as he sees, finally, his father, Abraham, elderly and malevolent, insane with age, a hundred and ten maybe, sitting in a tiny heap on a log.

"If they blame me, they blame me," Baruch said. "But why would they blame me if I'm not really who I say I am?"

Rachel watched them give each other things. An old man sparing a son. You arrive at your life in its various genres: reoccurrence gives way to recursion, the gestures at forgiveness become blurred, small, disfigured by failing light. There is no vantage to see what's new because you think you are looking at the middle, from the middle, as it darkens. But Lurio had understood who was actually central in each story. And this is where his "Binding of Isaac" had focused, on this figure who Baruch now became: not the patriarch, or the saved son, or the angel appearing at Moriah. But the ram, emerging from the world's tangle and led to the altar. First as fire, then as sacrifice.

"Go," Baruch said, and they did.

THE CHILD MADDIE LOST would have been seven by now. The thought arrived unrequested, but fully formed, without the dimensions of surprise. Rachel drove and Daniel was sleeping in the back seat and Jacob, watching him, met Rachel's eyes in the rearview mirror, like parents discovering that overnight their child has become a teenager, tall and angry, whiny, wheedling, smelling of smoke. "Your wife is not leaving the apartment," his sister said in her message. "What's going on?"

Outside, the road's dark throat closing. Trunks of pines like the ribs of a whale. Then they breached into morning. Somewhere in southern Maine Jacob found NPR on the radio. The president was speaking, oily bubbles of speech popping from the irritated purse of his mouth. At some level divorced from his intentions or actions, Jacob had always assumed he'd be a father. He found himself preparing, imagining how, while sitting on the curb eating ice cream or watching Little League games, he would present the world differently than his father had, as beautiful and unburdened by history. It would be a lie he was telling, maybe, but how else could he let his child, who had not yet been born, who was never born, live his own life? And what would he tell his son about what was happening now? How would he show him, or convince him, quelling his own hands as they sought surfaces unblemished enough to knock on, that he was not afraid? "Turn that motherfucker off," Rachel said.

They parked somewhere and walked. The streets were hot and green and bad-smelling. A few blocks away Baer was waiting, Maddie was waiting. The Kabbalah school lay shuttered. In the park there were new flowers, all too big, born out of heat, half-rotten geraniums like balls of flame, scorched black-eyed Susans and sunflowers in rows, abrupt and towering as something awake, insane. Daniel, it seemed, was coming with them. They'd asked him where he wanted to go and he hadn't answered.

The man with the cowbell rode by on his bike. "Look," Jacob said to Rachel, but either she hadn't noticed or didn't care.

"I see that guy all the time," Daniel said.

Midday, the biker weaving between cars, ringing his bell. They stopped in a bodega and bought some sandwich meat for Baer. "I have theories about wind and electricity and birds," Maya had whispered on her message. She might be anywhere, watching. The burned convenience store was boarded up now but the warning tape in front was gone and the sense of emergency had passed. The cowbell, though, still tolled, a block over and getting louder, as the rider made his loop.

Baer didn't answer the door and Rachel used her key, and when they entered the apartment there was a visceral change in the texture of the air, like stepping into a greenhouse: damp, hot, rancid and vegetal. Rachel called his name and he didn't reply. In the kitchenette the counter was piled with small paper plates with little bits of food on them, cold cuts, a pickle, some canned tuna. Baer was on the floor in the next room, sitting against the bag of cat food with the big, orange, clearly dying cat in his lap.

"Look at him," he said. "He can't lift his head. I call and call," he said. "But you never come."

"Uncle," Rachel said.

"Is it too much to check on a cat? What else do you do?"

"Uncle," she said. "It's Rachel and Jacob."

Finally he saw them. "Oh, I thought it was the people from the vet. They say they won't make house visits."

"What's wrong?" Jacob asked.

"Look at him," he said again. "He can't walk."

"You should have called," Rachel said.

"Maine? I should have called Maine?"

"I would have come back. Or sent my parents over."

He waved. "Long distance."

So as not to look at anything else Jacob was looking at the cat. It lay on its belly in Baer's lap with its head cupped in his hands. Its mouth was open and its eyes were almost entirely closed. A paw dangled limply in front of it, as if it had reached for something and become exhausted.

"This is Daniel," Rachel said. "He's a friend from Maine."

"You made friends?"

The cat roused slightly and tried to look up, but Baer was petting it, and it couldn't hold its head up under his hand. The cat's chin drooped back into his other palm.

"He's sick. He won't eat. I tried everything."

That explained all the plates in the kitchen. Charting the course of Baer's panic. The desperation of trying to feed a pickle to a cat. "How long has it been?" Jacob asked.

"Four days?"

"Might just be the heat," Daniel said.

Jacob crossed the floor and sat beside Baer. There was dried shit in his lap and shit caked in the cat's fur and that was just at the edges Jacob could see—where the cat was pressed to Baer's body, he couldn't imagine, but he could smell. Under Baer's hand, the cat panted from his open mouth.

"You can bring him in?"

"Of course," Jacob said.

"There's some money in the drawer."

"We'll take care of it. But you know what they're going to do, right?"

"He doesn't even have a name," Baer said. "That was the deal we made."

He leaned over the cat and covered it with his chest. He petted the top of its head more rapidly, frantically. If the cat had been at all awake it would have protested.

"He's not usually like this. He's not a cuddler. If I'm in the chair, he wants the chair and if I'm lucky I get the corner. He's a glutton for anything I want."

The floor where they sat was covered with kibble. Baer grabbed some. "Look," he said. "Look, look." He started putting the kibble in his mouth. "Look, sweetie. I'm eating it."

Rachel was shouting, Baer was moving faster, eating more kibble, jerking the cat's head up so the cat could peer into his mouth and see the food there, but the cat's eyes were closed, and Baer howled "look, look, sweetie, I'm eating it" and reached for more. Jacob stopped him. Held out his own hand. "Spit it out," he said. Baer's eyes rolled like a spooked horse. He was crying, snot and kibble tangled in his beard, his dentures had come loose.

Life prepares us for itself. At its odd hours, apparitions gather offering their theories and sorrow. There is no one to forgive us. Our parents are dead. We carry their grief and fear until it becomes our own. We cannot understand it, it is the dark root of the world. But we have to meet it with something. Jacob was inadequate and ready. He felt no disgust. He held his palm up to Baer's dirty chin.

"Spit it out," he said.

After Baer had settled, Rachel unrolled the Lurio from the tube. Baer put both his hands over his eyes and then lowered them.

"That's it," he whispered. "I thought maybe I wouldn't recognize it. I was so little." He covered and uncovered his eyes again. "I thought I was imagining things."

He reached out to Rachel. "He just gave it to you?"

"Uncle," Rachel said. "How did you really lose it."

"We tried to cross the river, but my parents had lost our papers," Baer said. He seemed to be talking to the cat. "So we went back. On the way, the village patrol caught us. That's what they were called. Our doctor was there among them, and because our doctor was among them I wasn't afraid even though they were drunk and we knew they'd been killing the Jews they caught." He scratched the cat under its chin, he flattened its ears, with his other hand. "You know, I've never told anyone this," he said to the cat. "They asked if we had anything to trade and my parents said no, we had nothing, and I thought, I remember thinking this, *They are trying to protect my Lurio, they are doing this for me, but I am not a baby*. There was my doctor, with a rifle, smoking a cigarette, watching us with his usual expression, eyebrows raised as if he were looking over the edges of spectacles. I thought, *I am not a baby, I will save my family,* and I spoke up and told them I had a sketch by the famous artist, Alexander Lurio.

"My doctor was not an animal, he knew Lurio's work and knew he had stayed with us. They went through our bags but the sketch wasn't there. My mother was crying. Then they tore off our clothes looking for it, or anything else. Lurio had told me, 'You find yourself by copying others.' So every day for months I copied his sketch of Job until I thought I had gotten it just right, and I had tied my last version around my leg. It was the best thing I had ever made. 'Is this it?' my doctor said, and I nodded. He showed it to the others on patrol and they all began to laugh. I was too young, you see. I was actually only a little boy and it wasn't good enough."

Later, Daniel went to the bodega and brought back cleaning supplies and cleaned the kitchen. He had said nothing all day. He wiped down the counters and disinfected the fridge and mopped the linoleum. Then he left and returned with food which he began, carefully, as if dancing with a beginner who didn't know where to put their feet, to prepare. Jacob found the cat carrier in the closet.

"Shall I take him?" he said. "It's an act of mercy."

Baer repeated the word and shook his head. "Mercy?" he said again. He didn't seem any closer to knowing what Jacob meant.

From the kitchen: the sound of Daniel's knife on the board and then the smell of olives and lemons and chicken, couscous with parsley. The same fricassee he had made at Nod. "Mercy?" Baer said again, louder than before.

Daniel, silent, swift, almost smiling, was setting the table. A pale rectangle of sunlight appeared on the floor. "Eat something," Baer shouted at the cat. Lemon juice hissed when it hit the hot pan. Rachel pressed her lips to Baer's forehead and Jacob lifted the large orange cat from Baer's lap. Sleepily, sweetly, it reached out and clung to him, and Jacob lowered it for a moment and unhooked its claws from his shirt before he lifted it again.

ACKNOWLEDGMENTS

WRITING THIS BOOK REQUIRED ME to wander with some of the great and strange thinkers of the last century. It was a (painful) joy to spend time reading Gershom Scholem's correspondence with Walter Benjamin as well as Scholem's commentaries on the *Zohar* and glosses on the shattering of vessels and the possibilities for communal redemption in Lurianic Kabbalah—images and metaphors that ultimately structured this novel. While many thinkers and writers on Jewish theology, the *Tanakh*, and on Scholem and Benjamin's theories, philosophies, and views of history influenced this book, I owe special gratitude to Stéphane Mosès' *The Angel of History (*Barbara Harshav, trans.) whose readings of Scholem, Benjamin, Kafka, and Kabbalah were especially influential. I borrow, adapt—and misread—these writers with deep respect. I should also note that Eli's language draws significantly on Scholem's *Ten Unhistorical Aphorisms on Kabbalah*, and a reader will also see shimmers of Benjamin in the excerpt from Baruch's essay that precedes Book III. A novel can also be a kind of Midrash. As it is said.

In his class on Jewish Holocaust Theology, Jacob quotes from Joseph B. Soloveitchik›s essay, «*Kol Dodi Dofek*: The Voice of My Beloved Knocks" which was published in *Fate and Destiny: From Holocaust to the State of Israel*, edited by Walter Wurzburger. He also engages Eliezer Berkovits' *Faith After the Holocaust*.

To write fiction about the Shoah requires that the writer who was not there either appropriate or invent material. I have felt that testimony, even reconfigured and altered for fiction, honors the memory of those who experienced it better than subjecting the catastrophe to the limits of my experience. The depictions of the Shoah presented here have been altered to fit the novel, but I derived the atrocities—both their horror and idiosyncrasy—from the accounts of survivors; ultimately, I have chosen not to invent what shouldn't have been imagined.

I owe a great debt of gratitude to the Massachusetts Cultural Council, which provided me a Fiction Fellowship—just when I needed it—for the 2020 year, without which finishing this book would have been so much harder.

Similarly, I want to thank Eastern Frontier Educational Foundation's Artist Residency at Norton Island and the writers and artists I met there, the Damned Few. Special thanks to Stephen Dunn, whose bohemian vision made that island the refuge it is. May his memory be a blessing.

Mark Freeman shared his work on narrative and consciousness just as this book was coming together. I'm grateful for our subsequent conversations about stories, memory, and meaning making. I am similarly grateful to the work of Eva Hoffman. Her memoir as a second-generation survivor, *After Such Knowledge,* examines with nuance and moral force what this book attempts to dramatize.

I'm not a writer who shares work in progress, but the process of finishing what feels finished finishes with other people: Erika Goldman and my colleague and friend Shawn Maurer both read and offered their notes on various drafts. I am grateful for their insights and perspectives.

Sincere thanks to everyone at Dzanc Books, especially Chelsea Gibbons for her excellent and thoughtful copyedit and Michelle

Dotter for her patience, care, rigor, and insight. I am deeply grateful for her faith in this book as a reader, editor, and publisher.

Thanks also to—

The Green family of Harpswell, Maine who opened their home to a stranger, proving the Talmudic rule that Jacob fails to appreciate in these pages—we reach the dawn when we can recognize a stranger as family. My time working at the Green house was essential to the early framing of these chapters and—unemployed as I was at the time—this writing would have been impossible without their generosity.

Joanne Williams who so often over twenty plus years has offered me her fish hut in Harpswell—that is her support, hospitality and generosity, without which this book (these books!) would have been so much different and lesser than they are…and much less enjoyable to write.

Leah Hager Cohen—who read an early draft, discussed, and supported the project over the course of years and whose own presence—as a writer on the page and as a person in the world—remains inspiring to me. I am deeply grateful for her wisdom, example, conversation (about matters Jewish, literary, and human…as if those things can be separated), and friendship.

Zack Bean, friend and writer, who over the decades has (from border towns to axe-throwing arcades) helped me to remember—with his own seriousness and talent, good humor and perspective—that we do this for the love of it.

Krista Eastman, whose dedication both to the wild and beautiful sentence and to friendship has been a gift for nearly twenty years now.

My parents, Diane and Stephen, for their love, support, and wisdom.

And finally to Jessica, my best friend, best and first reader, inspiration in her strength and bravery, in her own art and wild intelligence. With gratitude for her belief in me and in the lives we've been trying to make, my beloved, whose knock I will always answer.